FATE OF THE SARACEN KNIGHT

BRADAMANTE AND RUGGIERO VOLUME II

LINDA C. McCABE

Destrier Books

Gualala, California

Fate of the Saracen Knight:

Bradamante and Ruggiero Series, Volume II

Destrier Books
P.O. Box 1791
Gualala, CA 95445
www.destrierbooks.com

Cover art design by Iain R. Morris

Author photo by Scott C. Nevin

This novel is a work of fiction adapting the legends of Charlemagne. Names, characters, places, and incidents are a product of the author's imagination or are used in a fictitious manner.

Fate of the Saracen Knight/Linda C. McCabe
ISBN 978-0-9836362-4-3

This is dedicated to the many storytellers who created the legends of Charlemagne, the scholars who study the impacts of those legends, and those who enjoy them.

Of loves and ladies, knights and arms, I sing,
of courtesies, and many a daring feat

- LUDOVICO ARIOSTO

Orlando furioso

Also by Linda C. McCabe:

Quest of the Warrior Maiden:
Bradamante & Ruggiero Series, Volume I

TABLE OF CONTENTS

PART ONE:

DISCORD AND DUELS

"**M**ay Mandricardo's manhood shrivel to match the size of his brain," said Marfisa.

Ruggiero shifted in his saddle. It was once again his turn in the warrior queen's game of curses. He had endured over one hundred such rounds since they left the village of Saint Antonin on horseback. No longer did he attempt cleverness and instead he uttered statements of what he wanted to see happen. "May I sheathe my dagger in Rodomont's blackened heart."

"May Mandricardo's manhood maintain the stiffness of boiled octopus," said Marfisa with a throaty laugh.

Ruggiero shook his head. He might be tired of the game, but her curses were flying faster than at the start. Marfisa had described a wide variety of ways she desired emasculating Mandricardo including chopping, burning, mangling, and feeding his body parts to farm animals. Ruggiero would have preferred paying closer attention to his riding than coming up with new curses for the two warriors they were following. Concentrating on the rhythmic pounding of hooves over the well-trod path of the old Roman road soothed his frazzled nerves. He hoped she would take a hint by the lull in the conversation.

The momentary quiet allowed him to appreciate the beauty of the rural countryside in Francia. They were riding on a minor road too small for the movement of large armies. Therefore this area had been untouched by the ravages of the war. Oak trees dotting the hillsides cast long shadows by the setting sun while tinges of yellow and peach lingered in the sky. The three riders they chased disappeared over the crest of a hill in the distance. Temporarily losing sight of their quarry was a consequence of riding in the rolling terrain west of the Massif Central mountains. Ruggiero wondered how well they would be able to see the riders once there was only moonlight guiding their way.

"Well? Have you nothing more?" demanded Marfisa.

Ruggiero groaned. Her game would end only when they caught up with their adversaries or arrived in Paris. "May Rodomont die falling off my loyal horse, Frontino."

"That was lame. Have you lost your anger against that vulgarian?"

"No. I want him dead, but I am ill-suited for cursing. I prefer action over words. How do you have an endless supply of curses?"

"I have been cursing men ever since I can remember. I knew enough as a slave girl to keep them to myself, but those dark thoughts kept me from going mad. The first curse I said aloud was as I plunged my knife into the heart of the drunken king who tried ravishing me."

"Why do you bear so much hatred toward men? Did someone succeed where that king failed?"

"No. Others have tried to take my maidenhead, but they now sing the songs of eunuchs — at least those who are still alive." Her smile twisted. "My first memory is when I was a little girl and I was passed from man to man in a caravan of bandits. They did nothing to damage my sale price, but they destroyed my innocence."

"I am sorry you were treated thus."

"Thank you," said Marfisa. "You are the first man to ever say such a thing to me. Men do not consider a slave girl's virtue as sacrosanct as a noble woman's."

"What does class have to do with it? No one should be forced to commit lewd acts," said Ruggiero.

"Are you mocking me?"

He was surprised at her reaction. "Why would I mock you?"

"I have never met a man who espoused such beliefs or who regarded me with respect. Most men scoff when they discover I am a woman-in-arms and realize too late that my skills are no jest."

"I do not think of women warriors as a joke," said Ruggiero. "Neither did our companions earlier."

"Why is that?"

"My mother was a respected warrior. She died giving birth to me, so I never knew her. As for our previous companions, they were grateful for your help. They also have a kinswoman whose military skills are renowned."

Marfisa's face lit up. "Another warrior maiden? What is her name?"

"Bradamante."

Ruggiero found it painful to say the Maid's name aloud. He did not want to talk about the woman he loved with Marfisa — or anyone else — until it was safe to do so. Their vows to each other were made in secret. Once the war was over, he and Bradamante could openly declare their love for each other and be married. Until then, discretion was required.

"Have you fought against her?" asked **Marfisa**.

"No and I hope I never will," said Ruggiero. "I have seen her in battle though, she is formidable."

"Afraid to fight her?" taunted Marfisa. "I would love to test my skills against any warrior held in great esteem. Especially a warrior maiden."

"I respect her. She is honorable, and for that reason, I wish her no harm," said Ruggiero. "I also consider you honorable. It would be tragic if you two fought. Whereas, Rodomont and **Mandricardo** are both without honor. They deserve to die at our hands, even if we all serve the same sovereign. My hatred of Rodomont goes beyond today's insult. He fought against Bradamante and could not win. So he killed her horse."

"He killed a horse in battle? You are right. He deserves to die."

"Rodomont has no respect for man nor beast. It is intolerable for him to ride my horse."

A wild thought crossed Ruggiero's mind. His guardian, Atallah, had tried repeatedly to distract him from his love for Bradamante. Might the sudden appearance of Queen Marfisa, a beautiful warrior maiden, be due to his guardian?

He called out in his mind, *"Atallah! Is this another trick of yours? After you swore the other day to no longer use magic against me or Bradamante?"*

Atallah's raspy voice responded inside Ruggiero's head. *"No, my dear child, I have kept my promise and did not cast any more spells on you. However, the stallion I gave you is enchanted and while you are at a gallop, it will allow you to send your thoughts to another. That is how we are speaking with one another. That is also how you and Marfisa have been talking with one another for hours. You were so caught up in the chase that you did not realize you were speaking to each other with your minds and not with your mouths."*

"So I can sends thoughts out to anyone?"

"You could, and she would be able to respond. You might not want to hear what she has to say."

"What do you mean?" wondered Ruggiero.

"You promised Bradamante that you would be baptized and speak with her father about marriage. Instead, you are on your way to rejoin Akramont's army. She will soon receive your letter explaining why you are

postponing your pledge. Do you really think you are ready for the recrimina-tions and pleadings of a woman in love?"

Ruggiero did not respond. The idea of hearing the voice of his be-loved chastise him and tearfully beg him to change his mind was more than he could bear. His attention was then called back by the shrill voice of his riding companion.

"Have you listened to a word I said?" called out Marfisa. "We should cease this reckless pursuit and make camp or find a place to spend the night. We shall duel with them in Paris. Our journey cannot be com-pleted in a single ride. Our horses need to rest."

"No. We cannot risk stopping," said Ruggiero. "Our horses might drop down dead or even turn to dust."

"Pardon?"

"Our horses have been at full gallop since this afternoon," said Rug-giero. "Neither their horses nor ours have slowed down, stopped to graze or even take a drink of water. They are not panting or foaming at the mouth and none have made water or dropped anything during our journey. There can only be one reason: magic. I warned against drinking from that fountain and yet all the horses drank their fill."

"If our horses die once they stop, would that end your quarrel with Rodomont?"

"Of course not. I am honor bound to fight him. Else I would be ac-cepting his insult to my integrity as a knight."

The light of the half-moon made their journey more treacherous than it had been during the day, but the three riders they chased had not stopped. Ruggiero vowed he would match them stride for stride. He did not trust either Rodomont or Mandricardo, and was unsure if he lost their trail if they would continue to Paris as they promised.

He was also concerned that either or both of those men might try and kill them if they slept. Resting near Marfisa and the appearance of impropriety was another worry. For Bradamante's sake, he did not want to do anything that might cause her heartache or doubt his fidelity. Un-doubtedly Bradamante would learn about Marfisa, her role in the rescue of Vivien and Maugis, and that he left for Paris with her. It was likely Marfisa's beauty would be mentioned at the same time, although in Rug-giero's eyes no woman could outshine Bradamante.

As they passed over a crest in the road, the three riders were once again in view. Ruggiero chuckled as he realized that he had nothing to fear from either Rodomont or Mandricardo that night. The two men were locked in a struggle trying to outdistance each other and overtake the rider who led this expedition to Paris.

Both men wanted desperately to claim Doralice of Granada as their own.

CHAPTER TWO

*B*astards. *They are both bastards,* thought Doralice. *I wish they would both die and rot in Hell.*

Doralice had surrendered trying to control her horse. She had wrapped the reins around her arms and held on for dear life, while willing herself to not fall off the saddle. An evil force had possessed her palfrey and caused it to gallop northward. Soon after the wild ride began, she had bunched her skirts beneath her to soften the repeated bouncing on the saddle. She was sore from riding and wanted nothing more than to crawl into a warm bed and fall into a deep slumber. That is after she slaked her incredible thirst and ate a meal. However, she did not dare end this ride nor slow down the pace because she knew it could mean her death.

No need for her to look behind; she could hear the thundering hoofbeats of the horses ridden by Mandricardo and Rodomont. Neither man could be trusted in keeping his word to postpone their duel until the war was resolved. Both men had claims over her and the only thing stopping them from killing the other was this unrelenting ride.

Her life and her future depended upon how her father reacted to the news that she was no longer a virgin and had married someone other than the man he chose. She might well be racing toward her own death at the hands of her beloved father.

Please Allah, guide this horse to Paris, prayed Doralice. *Everything will be sorted out there. Paris, I need to get to Paris.*

❊

CHAPTER THREE

Renaud stepped out of the peasant's house and smiled at the bright summer sky. The crisp morning air held the promise of a beautiful day. The new information he gleaned from the peasant reinforced his confident feeling this was going to be the day they found Orlando and then, his beloved Angelica. Of course, he had convinced himself of that certainty every morning for the last week and each day had been a disappointment. They were on Orlando's trail, but they continued to be a day or two days' journey behind him.

"Did you learn anything from her?" asked his brother, Guichard.

Renaud mounted his horse. "Two days ago, she saw a knight dressed in black sleeping under one of her trees. She was wary of him. Said he looked 'wild.' She was happy when he left without approaching her or her son."

"So we have no direction to follow," said Guichard, as his horse settled into an easy stride alongside Renaud's. Their squire, Emile, rode the spotted mare behind them.

"He has been working his way southeast, and I see no reason to deviate from that course."

Guichard gave an impatient sigh. "Do you know what day this is?"

"Thursday?"

"More than just Thursday. Do you not realize the significance of today?"

"I have not the patience for riddles," said Renaud. "Pray tell me what sets this day apart from the rest."

"Today marks a fortnight from when we started our mission to find Orlando. Tomorrow we begin our journey back to Paris."

"But we are close to finding him," argued Renaud. "We cannot return without him."

"We have been close to finding him for over a week now, and yet he still remains elusive. Must I remind you of the promise you made to Charlemagne? You vowed to look for Orlando for only a fortnight and return if you could not find him. We must begin our journey back tomorrow whether or not we find him today. You cannot delay returning.

After all, you are not just another soldier to the Emperor; you are one of his twelve paladins."

Renaud fumed. Charlemagne insisted on Guichard joining him. His younger brother was there acting as his conscience and enforcing the agreement with the Emperor. Guichard was worse than a nagging wife.

As they rounded a bend following the Aveyron River, the village of Saint Antonin came into view. The valley was nestled among sheer cliffs of gray and white rock. The settlement dated back to the time of the Romans, but had grown in size over the last few decades after their grandfather, *Pepin le Bref,* founded a monastery on the site to commemorate Saint Antonin. The Christian martyr's remains were miraculously ferried up the river in a boat guided by angels.

Nearing the western edge of town, a dozen men gathered. Drawing close, Renaud realized it was for the gruesome task of digging graves. Stacks of bodies in shrouds awaited burial. His pulse quickened at the sight. Perhaps Orlando had gone into another murderous rage. If so, then they were close to finding his kinsman and hopefully the woman who held sway over his heart. Renaud bowed his head and gave a sign of the cross before advancing to a man dressed in a monastery robe supervising the gravediggers.

"What happened here?"

The monk looked up at Renaud. His eyes took in the golden helmet bearing the head of a lion as its crest and then to Renaud's shield with a silver lion on a field of red.

"Count Renaud," said the man. "The Devil was at work here yesterday. A massacre took place north of town."

"Was this the work of a single man? Perhaps a knight dressed all in black?"

"A single man cause this kind of carnage?" the monk said as he gestured toward the corpses. "No, this was the work of the four horsemen of the Apocalypse."

"Four men were responsible?" asked Guichard.

"Yes," said the monk. "They rode on horseback and slaughtered these men. A few people escaped and sought sanctuary in our monastery. Later, those butchers mocked our village by feasting in our town square, while blood still dripped from their armor. They attracted more demons who dueled with the revelers over their ill-gotten treasures. That fighting destroyed several market stalls."

"Can you describe those men?" pressed Guichard.

"The shutters on the monastery were closed to avoid evil spirits from entering hallowed ground. However, one of the villagers told me that he saw a young blond soldier almost get killed moments before a skinny man waved his hands and uttered a curse. A black storm cloud appeared out of nowhere and attacked a woman's horse." The monk made a sign to ward off the evil eye.

"Which way did these men go when they left?"

"Half of the demons headed north on the old road heading to Paris. The rest took their wagonload of riches and headed westward on the road to Bruniquel."

Renaud turned to view the road on the other side of the Aveyron River about half a mile away. A dozen soldiers surrounded a wagon heading eastbound in the direction he thought Orlando had gone. The wind picked up and flags bearing the standard of a white falcon on a field of blue fluttered in the breeze. Renaud's blood chilled at the sight of the House of Maganza.

The monk noticed where Renaud's attention had shifted. "Count Ansel was fortunate to be in the rear of the procession. He fled and survived the attack, but he is in mourning over the loss of his son, Bertolai, and a cadre of his most trusted soldiers. That wagon bears the corpse of his son who will be buried at Altaripa. Count Ansel believes he was betrayed and vows to seek vengeance on those responsible for this tragedy."

Renaud had no desire to utter empty condolences to the House of Maganza. His only regret was not being in Saint Antonin a day earlier so he could have joined in on the attack of his family's longstanding enemies. He knew better than to publicly admit such ill feeling for the dead, especially in front of a member of a religious order, so instead he bowed his head hoping that he appeared respectful.

His mind turned to the problem of his planned journey for the day. Due to the rocky gorges of the Aveyron River, there was no other way to go southeast except travel on the same road and direction of Count Ansel's men. The caravan would slow their progress and once they drew near the Maganzas there was sure to be bloodshed.

Bad blood between their houses had existed for generations. If there was to be a battle that day, the odds were against them. Count Ansel's party outnumbered Renaud's by at least four to one. Renaud did not want to waste time attacking his family's enemies, but instead wanted to figure out a way to use the same road without being seen.

The sound of a horseman galloping down the road behind them made Renaud turn around. He squinted as he tried determining if the man was friend or foe. Renaud clutched the handle of his sword. The horseman stopped in front of them and Renaud was relieved to see the man not bearing armor or weapons.

"Count Renaud of Montauban?"

"That is I."

"At last. I have an urgent message for you."

"Thank you," said Renaud as he received a leather tube.

The messenger gave a curt nod and proceeded to ride off in the same direction as Count Ansel. Motioning to Guichard, they left the monks to their unpleasant task and crossed the bridge. Once they were safely out of earshot, Renaud drew out parchment sealed with the mark of his uncle Bueve.

"What is it?" asked Guichard.

Renaud broke the seal and read the message.

From Aldigier caretaker of Agrismont to Count Renaud of Montauban

My brothers Vivien and Maugis are hostages of Lanfusa. She refused my repeated offers for ransom. Instead she agreed to hand my brothers over to Bertolai in exchange for more wealth than I could amass in three lifetimes. I beg of you to rescue them from certain death at the hands of the evil Maganzas. The transfer is to happen on Wednesday the tenth of this month at midday in the village of Saint Antonin. May this message be delivered to you in time.

"This message was delivered a day late," said Renaud. "If there was sorcery here yesterday, it was from Maugis. The blond soldier was likely our brother, Alard. If Count Ansel knows our family seized the ransom, it would be even more dangerous to head eastward. Our search for Orlando is over. Instead, we are heading for Montauban."

CHAPTER FOUR

Amir Akramont wiped the sweat from his brow with the trailing end of his turban. The midday sun was beating down without a cloud in the sky to provide relief from the scorching heat. He readjusted the fabric covering his head, making sure his iron helmet was not visible. Hiding underneath a white cotton tunic, he wore a shirt of mail.

His gaze went upward once more to the stone walls surrounding Paris. Walls his engineers determined were thirty feet tall. At another time of day, in another season of the year, he might have been standing in the shadows of the wall, but on this day he had no such reprieve from the hot summer sun.

Dipping his ladle into a wide necked dolium holding fresh drawn water, he poured it into a soldier's flask. The soldier grunted as he retrieved his replenished vessel without looking Akramont in the face. A servant was considered beneath a soldier and not warranting any comment or even acknowledgment.

Akramont performed this humble task hundreds of times earlier that day to similar non-responses. None of the men suspected that the commander of the Muslim army would be performing such a menial chore. He employed this subterfuge not as a method of spying on his men, but as a way to get close to the walls and examine the gates for any weaknesses. He was determined to find a vulnerable spot in the fortifications and exploit it.

"Hurry up and stop staring off into space," barked a soldier as he elbowed his way to the front of the line. "Parched men are waiting for water. Here, let me do it myself."

The broad shouldered man grabbed the handle of the ladle and tried wrenching it free from Akramont's grasp.

Akramont seized the man's wrist and hissed. "Let go of it."

The ladle moved back and forth as the two men struggled over its control. Akramont scowled as he committed the soldier's looks to memory. He had a pointed face with a patchy beard, red-rimmed eyes, and an overabundance of yellowed teeth that overlapped one another.

Akramont was reminded of a rodent and the man's s foul breath reinforced this comparison.

Sabri stepped forward and touched the man on a shoulder. "Stop this now, or you will face the lash."

"And who might you be old man?"

"I am Sabri, the governor of Algocco and a wazir to Amir Akramont," he said in a low voice. "You have caused unrest in the ranks with your insubordination. This is your last chance to avoid punishment for I will talk with your commander, Amir Marsilio. How you react now will determine my recommendation to him. Please tell me your name."

The man released his grip on the ladle and tossed his head. "I am Amir Marsilio's nephew, Feraguto. My uncle would not have me whipped."

Sabri kept his voice low. The other soldiers had grown silent, but from the frustrated looks on their faces they were unable to hear the dressing down of their brash leader. "Feraguto, I heard of your exploits at Charlemagne's Pentecost tournament last year. Of how you refused to accept defeat and turned what was a test of prowess into a duel to the death, killing your opponent, Argalia, as well as his sister Angelica's four bodyguards."

Feraguto gave a lopsided smile. "Her guards were monsters and they deserved to die. My only regret is that Angelica escaped. I wanted to plow her ripe body until she screamed out my name."

Akramont glanced up at the Frankish soldiers guarding the towers. They had taken an interest at what was transpiring near the base of their wall. Several archers had their bows drawn in case this was all a diversionary tactic to distract them while a surprise attack was launched.

"Rumor has it that you killed Argalia by using your blade in an area considered forbidden to attack," said Sabri.

Feraguto chuckled. "He wore enchanted armor. His groin was the only unprotected spot."

"So the rumors *are* true," said Sabri. "While I admire your tenacity, I abhor your methods and for violating the terms of engagement. It is dishonorable. I shall have a long talk with my friend, Amir Marsilio, about you. It will be his choice whether to make an exception on your behalf, or use you to set an example for the others. You will now go to the back of the line, and wait until everyone else has received his water. Then, if there is any left, your flask shall be filled."

Feraguto face became even uglier as it twisted with anger and loathing. He turned and stalked his way to the end of the queue.

Akramont suppressed a smile as he filled the flask for the next soldier. Disguising himself as a servant had not only allowed him near the city walls, but to observe his forces. These supply line trips provided him with more insight into the morale of his troops than a month full of reports from his wazirs.

The idea for this disguise came to him during the burial of his cousin, Daniso, who had perished along with thousands of soldiers in the ill-fated first assault on the city's walls. After throwing a handful of dirt onto Daniso's grave, Akramont had looked up at one of the towers surrounding Paris. He had stared at the structure as if it was a mortal enemy who caused the death of his kinsman. Akramont vowed to get close to those accursed walls and discover a place vulnerable to attack. He commissioned his mapmakers to draw detailed maps of each gate, which he poured over with a fervor bordering on fanaticism. Though he had surveyed the walls every day, he had been unable to identify even one loose brick or crumbling mortar. He blamed Gradasso's successful attack on Paris the year before as the cause for the fortifications being newly reinforced.

Sabri walked beside Akramont as he pushed the wheeled cart carrying the dolium toward the encampment. The elderly governor was a soothing influence on him and provided a sense of continuity as his late father had depended upon Sabri's sage advice.

"My patience is wearing thin," said Akramont. "Waiting for the people of Paris to starve and Charlemagne to surrender is taking too long."

Sabri nodded. "Our men are bored and restless. They came here for war and are unaccustomed to standing guard with no end in sight. They are turning on themselves. Last night I broke up two fights in the food line. These warriors need to do more than blockade city gates."

"Agreed. Tonight, we shall plan our next assault using the replacement siege towers and catapults. I have not decided which gates to bombard yet."

Akramont's attention was diverted as he saw in the distance a woman on horseback entering the gate to his camp. "Who could that be?"

CHAPTER FIVE

Doralice clung to her horse's neck while riding all through the night without stopping. She had closed her eyes when she could no longer see straight. Exhaustion and hunger had caused her vision to become unfocused. That scared her more than the continual threat of dying by falling off her steed. It was when her horse's steady gallop changed into a canter that she forced her head up and looked around. The harsh sunlight caused her to squint as she appraised a large encampment surrounded by tall wooden fencing. Flags bearing yellow and blue quartering fluttered in the wind. She was unable to recognize the small symbols on the flags as they danced before her eyes. Two mounted sentries greeted her as she neared the gate of the camp.

"Is this Paris?" she rasped.

"It is. What brings you here my lady?" asked one of the guards.

"Stordilano, the governor of Granada, is my father. Please take me to him."

One of the men called out a command and the gate opened. As her horse walked into the camp she felt hundreds of eyes upon her. A soldier led her horse forward through the myriad of tents, each one bearing a different multicolored flag proclaiming the identity of its inhabitants. The sight of a red and green flag with a pomegranate in its center brought tears to her eyes.

An old man emerged from the tent. "Doralice? Is that my Doralice?"

"Yes, Father."

Doralice recognized her father's voice, but not the man who stood before her. His hair had changed from gray to white since she last saw him. He dropped to his knees and began praying. The commotion brought forth Fidelia from inside the tent. Doralice was relieved to learn her beloved governess was still alive.

The elderly woman's face lit up with joy. "Our lady has returned!"

The soldier held up his arms to assist Doralice dismounting her horse.

"My lady, my lady," said Fidelia as she unwound the reins from around Doralice's arms.

Doralice fell into the soldier's arms.

"She is hurt, my lord," said Fidelia. "She needs to be taken to the women's tent. There I can bathe her and tend to her wounds."

The soldier carried Doralice. Being held was comforting as was his masculine scent. She closed her eyes as sleep began to overwhelm her.

"I never gave up hope that Allah would return you to me," said her father. "You are safe now my child."

Her dreamlike trance ended as her feet touched the ground and Fidelia put a supporting arm underneath her. The soldier smiled before she turned to enter the women's tent. Her father held open the flap, tears in his eyes.

"Before you go inside, I must know," said her father, "did Mandricardo harm you?"

Doralice did not have the strength to answer his question. "Later, first I must rest."

CHAPTER SIX

Akramont was astounded as Mandricardo and Rodomont rode into view. The two warriors were quickly admitted inside the gates of the Muslim army's camp and an audible cheer rose up to greet them. Akramont abandoned the cart he had been pushing and ran to the entrance with Sabri at his heels.

Once inside, he made his way through the crowd in time to see Rodomont dismount a warhorse adorned with a tattered and torn surcoat. The strips of fabric hanging from the side of the destrier were blackened with grime. He wobbled as his feet touched the ground.

Rodomont grabbed the neck of the squire holding the horse's reins. "Guard that horse with your life. Do not allow anyone to take him. Do you understand?"

The squire's eyes bulged as he tried nodding.

"If you fail, I shall make you swallow your own entrails."

As Akramont drew near Rodomont, he discovered the man's foul mood was matched by his foul stench. The mixture of body odor and bodily waste was overwhelming. Rodomont's skin had taken on an unhealthy pallor of greenish-brown, the same shade as his dragon hide armor. He looked as if he had not rested for weeks and was teetering on madness.

Akramont removed his turban and helmet. "Praise Allah," he said loud enough to be heard over the noise of the crowd, "for bringing back two of my best commanders."

Mandricardo dismounted and handed the reins of his horse to a waiting squire without comment. Though exhausted, he appeared smug compared to Rodomont.

"Come to my tent," said Akramont. "There you shall be fed and you will tell me of your adventures."

Both warriors walked with pronounced bowleggedness and followed Akramont. Once inside the royal tent, Akramont offered cushions to the two men and ordered his seneschal to ready food and drink for his honored guests.

"I would prefer standing," said Rodomont, as he grabbed a goblet of water from the seneschal. He drank so fast that drops spilled down his front. "A messenger called us back to your war. We rode all day and night to be here. Had it not been for the promise I made to Doralice, I would be the only one standing before you now."

Mandricardo also remained standing and snorted at Rodomont. He picked up the goblet offered to him and savored the water as if it was the elixir of life. After draining the last drop he turned to Akramont and said, "He and I have an unsettled dispute regarding Doralice that we deferred. Our truce will not last long. You shall soon be without him."

Akramont's sense of elation at seeing these two men evaporated. Neither one deigned to call the other by name, as if that common courtesy was too great to bestow upon their opponent. He glanced at his two closest advisors, Sabri and Marsilio. They appeared as unsettled as he was by this display.

"Where is Doralice now?" asked Akramont.

"She arrived in the camp before we did," said Rodomont. "I assume she was taken to her father."

"Ah, she must have been the woman I saw entering the camp. I understand the love of a woman can drive men to madness. Since there is bad blood between you, I insist that you avoid each other. Neither one of you will be allowed near Doralice until after we defeat Charlemagne. I need both of you, and I cannot allow a disruption to my mission." Akramont looked Rodomont directly in the eye. "We have not put forth another sustained attack since that fateful night when you left our service. With both of you here now, we can proceed in our final push for victory."

Sounds of cheering soldiers erupted again outside the tent.

"What now?" asked Akramont.

"They are probably happy to see the children who followed us," said Mandricardo.

"Children? What children?"

"That boy knight Ruggiero, and a girl," said Mandricardo, before taking another long drink.

"Ruggiero?" Akramont rushed from the tent, elated at the news.

He bounced on his toes to see over the heads of men who were cheering as Ruggiero's black horse walked slowly down the pathway between the tents. Akramont beamed at the sight.

The tide turned against his forces ever since Ruggiero left the field. Akramont openly blamed Brunello for Ruggiero's disappearance, but secretly knew it was due to the sorcerer Atallah's actions. With the restoration of this prophesied youth in his ranks, Akramont had a renewed sense of optimism for victory against Charlemagne.

"You have returned," said Akramont as Ruggiero dismounted. He embraced his favorite knight. "Never leave my side again."

The crowd parted again and another rider emerged, a woman wearing mail armor with long black hair and a haughty look on her face. She bore a shield decorated with a golden phoenix on a field of green.

Akramont's jaw dropped. "Are you Queen Marfisa?"

"My reputation precedes me," she said with a smile. "You must be Amir Akramont."

"Praise Allah for sending such warriors my way." Holding out his hand, he helped Marfisa dismount. "Come to my tent for food and drink."

As they neared his tent, yelling came from within. Upon entering, he discovered Rodomont and Mandricardo being restrained by Marsilio and Sabri.

"Doralice is mine," yelled Rodomont.

"She loves me and does not want to be touched by your filthy hands," taunted Mandricardo.

"Stop! I command you," bellowed Akramont.

Both commanders were struggling to free themselves. Akramont was grateful they were weakened by their long ride; otherwise his two elderly advisors would never have been able to hold them.

Ruggiero entered the tent and yelled at Rodomont. "Surrender my horse!"

"Surrender my standard," said Mandricardo as he snarled at Ruggiero.

"This bastard insulted me," said Marfisa as she pounded Mandricardo's chest with her fists. "He shall die for that."

"Guards!" called Akramont. "Guards!"

Eight men entered the tent. "Restrain Queen Marfisa, Rodomont, and Mandricardo," ordered Akramont.

The guards locked arms with the three warriors.

"Sabri, take Mandricardo to your tent. Ensure that he is fed and rested. He is to be held under guard until further notice. Marsilio, you will do the same with Rodomont, but make sure he is bathed. Once they are secured and asleep, return to my tent as I need your counsel."

Mandricardo and Rodomont were escorted out of the tent, Sabri and Marsilio followed.

"Release Queen Marfisa and then wait outside," said Akramont to the guards. He poured water in goblets and offered them to Ruggiero and Marfisa. "Come, you will have food and drink, and I will find a tent for you. I want to hear of all your adventures since I last saw you in Toulouse, and how you came upon your illustrious companion. Do not bother me about your disputes with Rodomont and Mandricardo. Those can wait."

CHAPTER SEVEN

Bradamante was sick with worry about Ruggiero. She sat on her bed alongside her trusted handmaiden, Hippalca, who drew out a letter from the folds of her dress.

"Ruggiero gave me this and bade me give it to you in private."
Bradamante seized the parchment.

From the knight Ruggiero to the lady Bradamante

My beloved Bradamante

It is with a heavy heart that I write this letter. I know not how this will find its way to you but I have faith God will provide a trusted messenger. Today after our cruel separation a messenger from Amir Akramont found me. His campaign is in desperate straights and has given urgent orders for me to report to Paris. I have sworn fealty to him and my honor as a knight rests on that vow. If I were to refuse to return to his side in his hour of need it will be looked upon as the mark of a disloyal coward. The plans we made earlier today were done in ignorance of the current state of the war. I cannot marry you at this juncture in time for it would be seen as an attempt to circumvent my sacred oath to my sovereign. As if my vow to serve Akramont was proffered only to secure knighthood without any sense of loyalty and that I abandoned him when defeat appeared imminent. Your reputation would be equally subject to ridicule for you would be considered an unwitting partner in deception and dishonor. I cannot allow our love and our marriage to be looked at in such a disrespectful manner. Therefore I must delay my pledge of marriage to you. Akramont is depending upon his knights to liberate him. Once that is accomplished and after I have secured the severance of the bonds of service to him I shall spend the rest of my life serving you and our love. I ask that you grant me a month to accomplish this task. Then I pledge to you my loyalty and devotion as your husband for the rest of my days.

Your servant in love

Ruggiero

Tears fell onto the parchment smearing the ink as Melissa's words from Merlin's cave rang in Bradamante's ears.

"Should Ruggiero remain a Saracen, he shall bring about the defeat of Charlemagne and the fall of the Frankish Empire."

There was still a small thread of hope from which to cling.

"Tell me Hippalca, was he baptized?"

"No, milady. As I first came upon him, Ruggiero was leaning against a fountain in the courtyard. He was resting in the shadows of the abbey."

Bradamante threw her arms around Hippalca. "I have failed everyone."

The walls in her chamber seemed to be closing in as Hippalca held her.

"It will be my fault," Bradamante said. "Charlemagne will be defeated, my family shall all be put to death, and Christendom will fall. All because of my accursed pride and lust for vengeance."

"There, there, milady." Hippalca patted her on the back. "You are overwrought by a letter, nothing more."

Bradamante pulled away from Hippalca, wiped the tears from her cheeks and walked over to the open window. The wooden frame holding the stretched linen fenestral windows leaned against the wall. She stared at a tall oak tree on a distant hill as two birds flitted from branch to branch.

"I am upset because I failed in my duty. My quest was to secure Ruggiero's baptism as a Christian and ensure our marriage. Instead, he is on his way to Paris to rejoin the Muslim army and we shall all suffer."

"I do not understand milady," said Hippalca. "Ruggiero is a great warrior, but why are you certain all those terrible things will happen because of him?"

"An enchantress named Melissa predicted the future. I met her in a cave near Foix when I went to rescue him. She told me Ruggiero and I were destined to love one another, but she warned me that he had two divergent fates. If one did not come to pass, the other one would."

"What were the prophecies?" Hippalca had a plain, earnest face. She had been Bradamante's only confidant growing up. Bradamante never dared divulge insecurities to her family, and could not share with them the workings of her heart. Hippalca was the only one she trusted, and who could help her devise a plan to make things right.

"The first prophecy was that Ruggiero would be baptized a Christian, marry me and I would bear his son who would later sire a line of heroes," said Bradamante with a wistful smile. She withheld the rest of Melissa's prediction that the Maganzas would murder Ruggiero before the birth of their son. That portion of the prophecy was too painful to contemplate, and Bradamante could not see any point of saying it aloud if this tragic fate was no longer possible.

"And the second prophecy?" asked Hippalca.

"Ruggiero would remain a Muslim and bring about the defeat of Charlemagne." Fresh tears fell down Bradamante's cheeks. "If Akramont's forces win, then the Frankish Empire will be like Hispania and under Muslim control. It is likely my entire family will be killed since my mother is Charlemagne's sister. Even if my life wAS somehow spared, I could not marry Ruggiero if his actions led to the death of my family."

Bradamante stood and began pacing around the small chamber. "Had I been at Ruggiero's side when the messenger delivered Akramont's summons, I would have persuaded him that I was his destiny and he would not have returned to the war. He would have listened to me for we are as one heart. I would have taken him inside the abbey to be baptized and today he would be pleading for my father's permission to marry me."

Bradamante gave one last look at Ruggiero's letter, rolled it, before hiding it under a loose floorboard. This was not something she wanted any of her family to stumble upon, but she could not bear the thought of destroying the only memento she had of his love. After hiding it, a new thought came to her. "Had I stayed with Ruggiero, I would have been there as he rescued Richardet."

"What do you mean?" asked Hippalca.

"Forget whatever story you heard. Richardet was about to be executed for the crime of fornication when Ruggiero saved his life."

A blush quickly formed on Hippalca's cheeks.

"During the time when my mother was worried sick about Richardet's disappearance, and while Alard performed searches throughout the countryside, my twin brother was warming the bed of a noblewoman."

"Was she married?"

"No, but before he came into her life she had been a maiden." Anger once again rose inside Bradamante. "Her father was off at war, so they did not have his blessing or permission to marry. Instead they followed their passions, and when word reached her father, he ordered Richardet's death." She shook her head. "My brother is not worthy of your admiration or affection."

Hippalca nodded and cast her face downward. "He must have loved her."

"I believe he did," said Bradamante.

"What happened to the lady?" asked Hippalca. "Was she sent to a convent?"

"No, Muslims do not believe in convents or monasteries."

Hippalca's mouth fell open.

"Yes, his lover was a Muslim, she was also my friend," said Bradamante. "I worry how her father will punish her."

"Do you think he will have her killed?"

Bradamante shuddered. She did not want to consider Fiordespina's death, but could not deny the possibility.

The door opened and Clarice walked in holding her baby. "What is this? Bradamante, your eyes are red and swollen. Could it be that the great warrior maiden has been crying?"

Hippalca stood and bowed toward the lady of the house.

"Leave us." Clarice commanded.

The handmaiden left the room. Clarice sat on the small wooden chair in the corner, began rearranging the top of her dress and suckled her son. There was a small moment of solitude as she focused on her baby. Bradamante took one step in the direction of the door causing Clarice to scowl.

"You came home the other night with three horses and I find you here despondent over the loss of a fourth horse. What were you thinking when you sent a girl to travel with an expensive destrier? If you needed someone to transport that horse somewhere, why did you not ask your brother Alard?"

Bradamante looked out the window. There was no point in responding, especially when her sister-in-law was only in the beginning stages of what promised to be a long tirade.

"Honestly, I do not understand why my husband crows about your judgment," said Clarice. "I have yet to see anything worthy of praise. If you cared about men as much as you care about beasts, perhaps your father would not have such difficulty in finding suitors for you."

Three riders appeared in the distance. Bradamante squinted, but could not make out their standards.

"You should be married by now and with your own child," said Clarice. "Your father made a grievous error when he allowed you to become a soldier. No man wants a wife with cropped hair and broad shoulders. It would be like bedding another man."

Bradamante resisted the urge to argue. Clarice was insufferable, but she was still the lady of the manor and protocol required deference be accorded her. A glare bounced off the helmet of one of the riders.

"Could it be?" asked Bradamante, her eyes fixed on the men.

"Of course. Why else would your father have not found a husband for you yet?" said Clarice. "To deny that your unnatural actions have caused men to find you unattractive, despite your high station in life, is to deny reality. Turn and face me. Turn and face the life you should be living."

Bradamante turned and smiled at Clarice. "Renaud and Guichard have returned."

CHAPTER EIGHT

Fiordespina had difficulty breathing as she stared at the towers of Paris looming in the distance. Beneath the massive walls was a large encampment housing the Muslim army. Wooden fencing surrounded the camp and multicolored flags fluttering in the breeze decorated the top of tents. The sight filled her with dread for she would soon be facing her father. There would be no joyous greeting as she was being brought to him as a disgraced and fallen woman.

The horse drawn cart seemed to be crawling forward prolonging the agony with each clop of the horse's hooves on the road. She fought the urge to jump out and run. Where would she go? How would she fend for herself? She could hunt, but only with a hunting party. It would be madness to attempt escape. Besides, it was far too late for any such desperate attempt at avoiding her fate. Had she wanted to run, she should have made her attempt at nighttime during her journey northward. Her punishment was imminent and inescapable.

Neron, the stern chief attendant, stopped his horse and waited for the cart to pull alongside him. "Adjust your veil."

That command broke more than a weeklong silence. Neron insisted no words be spoken so Fiordespina could better reflect upon her sins, and worry about her punishment. Fiordespina's hatred of him intensified when two days into their journey, Neron caught Placia, one of her elderly servants, whispering to her in their tent at night. The following morning, he dressed down the old woman in front of the entire traveling party, struck her across the face, and knocked out a tooth. From that point on, only Neron dared break the oppressive silence.

Fiordespina obeyed his order taking the length of black fabric over her head to cover her face. Neron spoke with the guards at the gate, and they were granted entry into the Muslim encampment. She flinched as the sounds of the camp assaulted her ears. Men were laughing and shouting, jesting with one another. Placing her head on Placia's shoulder, she closed her eyes for a last few moments of peace before being presented to her father.

The wagon stopped and Placia nudged Fiordespina. She lifted her head to see Neron's outstretched hand offering to help her out of the cart. His hand was as cold as death and matched the look in his eyes. She realized then that he also risked losing his head.

Two guards stood outside her father's tent, barring the entrance.

"I am Neron. Amir Marsilio is expecting me."

The guards stepped aside. Neron lifted the flap and made a motion for Fiordespina to enter. Her father was inside, along with his wife and young daughter.

"Remove your veil," said Neron.

As Fiordespina uncovered herself, her step-mother Rosenda's normally beautiful face transformed into one suitable for an avenging fury. "Why is she here?"

"I sent for her," said Marsilio. "Beyond that, it is none of your concern. Leave us."

With that, Rosenda scowled and covered the eyes of her young daughter as they left the tent.

Fiordespina knelt in front of her father with her forehead placed on his prayer rug.

"Neron," began Marsilio, "I gave you strict orders to safeguard my daughter's virtue. Explain your failure."

"I was duped, my liege," said Neron. "Our hunting party came upon a wounded knight. Your daughter, against my express warning, insisted on feeding the fallen soldier. Later she brought him back to the villa to tend his wounds. There it was revealed that the soldier was actually a woman."

"You saw proof of this?"

"No, but Placia witnessed the soldier undress and told me she was a woman. I also knew from the soldier's tongue and customs that she was a Christian. Fiordespina tried passing her off as a Muslim soldier, but I had no doubt she had to be Duke Aymon's famed daughter, Bradamante."

"What does this have to do with my daughter taking a male lover?" asked Marsilio.

"Bradamante had suffered a grievous head wound. I was surprised when she left only a few days later. Your daughter led me to believe her guest would be staying longer to recover. Fiordespina saw to Bradamante's departure, while I was pre-occupied with other matters. I berated myself for not having instructed all the guardsmen against letting her leave for she would have made an important hostage."

Marsilio poured a glass of water for himself, and drank as Neron continued his story.

"The next day, a soldier arrived at the villa wearing an embroidered surcoat, the same one Fiordespina had made. The soldier was riding on a horse given to Bradamante. In every detail the rider appeared to be Bradamante. Fiordespina was overjoyed at the return of her friend. I felt relief at having another opportunity to take a valuable hostage and I vowed she would never escape the villa again."

"You admit that you did not verify that my daughter's guest was a woman?"

"I failed you on that account, my lord. Bradamante left and her twin brother returned in her stead. I did not pay as close attention as I should have in this matter and did not assign a female attendant to assist with the dressing of her guest. Fiordespina and her friend became inseparable. They spent all hours of the day and night together. Only when you wrote back saying Bradamante was leading the defense of Marseille, did I discover the truth and find your daughter in bed with a man. Later after torturing him, I learned his identity."

"Stand and look at me."

Fiordespina stood and raised her head.

"Did you take a man to your bed?"

"Yes, Father."

"It is within my rights to have you put to death," said Marsilio with a pained look on his face. His eyes softened as he wiped a tear away from her cheek. "You are beautiful. You remind me of your mother when I first met her. You were to become Amir Akramont's third wife. You will see how young and handsome he is and realize what is now denied you due to your selfish and sinful actions."

He poured a goblet of water and offered it to her. "You were being protected in Cordes. After the conquest of the Franks you would have been brought forth and married to Akramont as part of the victory celebration. Instead of being married to one of the most powerful rulers in the world, you disobeyed your father and debased yourself by playing the harlot with a Christian. I will have great difficulty finding a man who would agree to marry you now. You have proven yourself unworthy of my love, just as Rosenda always said."

Fiordespina's hand trembled as she raised the goblet to her lips. She had feared he would order her death, but instead he showed her mercy. Perhaps her punishment would be the loss of his love. That thought punctured her heart. She remembered her talk with Bradamante about marriages being arranged for political alliances. She had worried about her father marrying her off to an elderly man, whose touch she would revile. Her father had been working to marry her off to the leader of the Muslim forces, a young man who is said to be handsome and devout. How could she have ever doubted her father's love?

And yet, she followed her heart and loved a man. A man of her own choosing. A man who loved her in return. Her only regret was that her love did not last.

Her thoughts were disturbed as the sound of snoring came from a darkened corner of the tent. It was then Fiordespina realized someone else was there. A sleeping man with a bare chest was lying on his back covered only with a sheet. A leather suit hung nearby emitting a foul stench.

CHAPTER NINE

A istulf stood on a rocky hillside above the crashing surf. His life was much like a piece of driftwood being tossed about the churning waters. Although he was the heir to the throne in the kingdom of Essex, the last two years he seemed to be captive to the whims of Fate.

He left Francia over a year before on a journey to the Far East to return the coveted destrier Bayard to his kinsman Renaud. While there, Aistulf was abducted and seduced by the sorceress Alcina. Once she tired of him as her lover, she transformed him into a myrtle tree as a silent souvenir of her sexual conquest.

Aistulf smiled as he reached up and stroked the golden feathers on the neck of the hippogriff. "Thank you, Kamal. You recognized when Ruggiero tied you to a tree on Alcina's island that it was not a normal tree. Had it not been for your talons attacking my enchanted form, I might still be rooted in one spot."

The creature's eyebrows twitched back and forth giving him a quiz-zical look.

"Because you attacked my trunk, I was able to warn Ruggiero about Alcina and her evil ways. Had he tethered you to a real tree, you might still be held inside her stables."

A strange clicking sound came from Kamal's throat and his feathers appeared ruffled.

"She was horrible, but that is in our past," soothed Aistulf.

The hippogriff's attention shifted to a rabbit hopping along the bluff top. Aistulf released the reins and watched Kamal become airborne be-fore swooping down upon the small animal. A normal eagle would have torn the rabbit apart with its talons, but the hippogriff's head was large enough to swallow its prey whole.

Aistulf was still amazed such magical creatures existed because hip-pogriffs were born of the unlikely mating of a griffin with its mortal enemy, the horse. Kamal looked like a gigantic eagle in the front, but with hind legs of a horse. He was yellow throughout with his beak, talons and wings appearing to be made of gold. Aistulf was suited for such a magnificent creature because his armor was gold plated, adorned with pearls, and bore an emblem of a leopard.

However, having Kamal as company for the last few days had been an adjustment. He had ridden the hippogriff while on Alcina's island as Ruggiero had been gracious enough to let him have a go with the flying animal. Controlling and guiding the creature had been easy when the flight was only around a small island. But, no matter what Aistulf tried, the hippogriff refused to fly northward.

Instead, they had made their way to the Atlantic coast and spent two nights sheltering in a small abandoned hut. Aistulf was feeling restless and wanted to leave. As a paladin of Charlemagne, he felt obligated to return to military service.

Aistulf mounted the hippogriff. "There is a war raging and my liege depends on me."

Kamal flapped his wings and they took to the skies in a southeasterly direction.

Aistulf pulled the reins in the other direction. "No, we are going northeast."

A fierce northerly wind blew them in the direction the hippogriff had chosen. He looked at the trees below, the branches remained still. The wind blew only on them.

"What is going on?" Aistulf called out. "Who is behind this?"

He then heard the last words of the enchantress, Logistilla, said to him. *"You are meant for great things, Aistulf. Do not hurry back to be a mere soldier of war; you must use your tools and gifts, and set off for the skies."*

"Logistilla?" he asked. "Are you directing me after your death?"

As soon as he said that aloud, he knew she could not be the one responsible. Logistilla had been the positive energy that opposed Alcina. No, this was someone else's work. Someone else did not want him returning to the war, but who and why?

"I used your gifts of the magic horn and the book of enchantments to break the wizard Atallah's spells," shouted Aistulf. "Now I have Ruggiero's hippogriff and have taken to the skies. What more do you want from me?"

Silence greeted him. Pulling on the reins harder, the hippogriff turned around and they faced the ocean once again. Aistulf fought the frustration rising within him. As a large wave crashed on a boulder, he was reminded of the coastline in Essex. *How long has it been since I last saw my father?*

That question made Aistulf yearn to see him. An image of his father on his deathbed floated before his eyes, causing him to wonder if his father was alive or dead. If his father died, word would be sent to Aistulf, but how would such a message find him? Or might the seneschal simply seize the throne for himself? Then again, a kingdom without an heir would be vulnerable to attack from neighboring kingdoms. Had any rivals invaded and conquered Essex? What had transpired there during his long absence?

He swallowed hard. The uncertainty was maddening. If I lost my lands and title, would I remain one of Charlemagne's twelve peers? Or would I be lowered to a mere knight?

"Fine," Aistulf announced into the wind. "I shall not return to Charlemagne's war, but instead I will journey to Essex and visit my family."

A fierce gust of wind turned the hippogriff around so they were once again headed southeast.

"I am not allowed to return to Charlemagne, nor am I allowed to return to my father," said Aistulf through gritted teeth. "What would you have me do?"

A dove flew past and Aistulf watched as it soared through the air. The white bird circled over a small pond, followed a stream and landed on the topmost branch of a tree where a dozen or so sparrows were gathered.

"A spy in the sky? Is that what I am to be?"

The wind gave a gentle push allowing Kamal to glide with ease.

"Why south? What is in the south that you want me to see?" called Aistulf. "There is Hispania and...North Africa."

Then he understood. Rather than concentrating on the vulnerability of his father's kingdom from invasions, his mission was to discover the vulnerabilities of the lands of Charlemagne's enemies.

CHAPTER TEN

Clarice jumped up in reaction to the news of her husband's return. She clutched her infant son who had been nursing and clumsily placed him in the crib before rushing to the open window. "Renaud is here?"

She craned her neck out and after a few moments, gave a little shriek and rushed to her trunk. Rummaging through her dresses, Clarice pulled out a red gown.

"The wretched war must be over." Clarice removed her hat. "Help me dress."

Bradamante's heart swelled at the thought of the war being over. Ruggiero would soon come to be with her in Montauban.

Her mind became consumed with thoughts of how to approach her father about Ruggiero while she absentmindedly assisted removing one dress from Clarice and helping her into another. After tightening the laces on the back, Bradamante understood the sudden change of outfit. The red satin gown flattered Clarice's ample bosom.

"I will leave you to finish your preparations," said Bradamante.

"No, stay with me." Clarice clutched Bradamante's hand. "I need your help."

There was a note of desperation in her voice. Clarice frowned when she saw stems rather than fresh flowers in a vase. Richardet had absentmindedly ripped apart several flowers earlier when Bradamante railed at him about his sexual relationship with Fiordespina. Clarice gave a squeal of delight as she swooped up stray rose petals on the floor. She rolled the petals between her thumb and forefingers until she expressed a few drops of red liquid and smoothed the fluid onto her cheeks and lips.

"Is it too much?"

Clarice normally had an air of confidence about her. She had green eyes, long black tresses and a fair complexion. The red of her gown would have washed out her face without the careful touches of color to her lips and cheeks. She should have no worries about her attractiveness, but the unannounced visit from her husband transformed her into a bundle of nerves. With persistent rumors of Renaud's infidelities, Clarice undoubtedly wanted to appear as attractive as possible to assure her marital security.

"The roses enhance a healthy glow about you, that is all," Bradamante reassured her. "You are as beautiful as ever."

Satisfied, Clarice grabbed a towel and tried rubbing the purple stains off her fingers. She was combing her hair when a horn sounded, signifying the return of the master. At the sound of the blast, Clarice dropped her comb. Her hands trembled as she put on her hat, picked up her sleeping son and walked out of the chamber.

Hippalca appeared at the top of the stairs, out of breath. "My lady," she puffed. "Lord Renaud has returned."

"Thank you," Clarice said as she took a few deep breaths. She hesitated at the top of the circular staircase then turned to Bradamante. "Please carry my son."

This surprised Bradamante. Clarice carried her son up and down the stairs numerous times each day never trusting him with anyone else. Clarice was also unaccustomed to asking anyone for favors, instead as the lady of the castle, she issued commands. This request came out of either concern she might trip on the stairway and hurt her child, or out of a need to look beauteous as she descended. Maybe, a little of both.

Bradamante took the sleeping child and held him to her chest. She did not expect him to be quite so heavy. The boy snuggled against her shoulder, but did not wake. It was then she caught a whiff of lavender in his hair. He had been bathed downstairs before Clarice brought him to their chamber. Bradamante closed her eyes and remembered the image of her future child's face in the pool of water in Merlin's cave. Her arms ached at the sight and wanted to hold a child who had not been born, and now she held an actual baby. Tears stung her eyes as she kissed the top of his head. Her destiny was to bear Ruggiero's child. Hopefully it would not be long before she was reunited with her beloved and they could begin planning their lives together.

She walked in a deliberate manner down the spiral staircase, relishing the warmth of this small child next to her chest. Previously, she felt awkward around babies and would sooner shovel out horse stalls than venture near an infant. Now she found herself pausing on the stairway to revel in the sensation of feeling a baby's heartbeat.

Muffled noises could be heard from the courtyard without distinct words. Bradamante heard her mother's shrill excited voice, followed by her father's soothing baritone. Then came a mixture of loud voices and laughter from her brothers and cousins. Before stepping outside, she savored her last moments holding baby Aymon and imagining he was the son she would bear for Ruggiero. She emerged in time to see Bernard rush into Renaud's outstretched arms.

"Father!"

"Let me see how you have grown." Renaud stood back and appraised his son. "How old are you now?"

"Four!" squealed Bernard.

"Of course you are," Renaud said as he tossed the little blond boy into the air causing him to shriek with delight.

Clarice stepped forward and Renaud set down their son. He favored her with a smile resembling more of a kindly uncle greeting a distant member of the family than the look of a hungry lover overjoyed by a reunion.

"My beautiful wife." Renaud gave her a chaste kiss on the lips. "Guichard said you bore me another son."

She smiled and waved her hand in Bradamante's direction.

Renaud's happy demeanor changed abruptly. "Sister, what happened to your hair?"

Richardet laughed. "Bradamante claimed she roasted in the hot sun under her iron helmet and had to cut off her locks."

Her brothers Guichard, Alard, and Renaud joined in the laughter while there was a stony silence from her mother and Clarice.

"If Richardet wore a dress, I would have a hard time telling which twin was which," said Renaud. This brought about another round of laughter and a pointed smile from Richardet to Bradamante.

Once the laughter subsided, Renaud's face sobered. "Why are you here and not in Marseille guarding the coastline?"

Bradamante felt her cheeks burn under Clarice's glare. Renaud's attention had shifted from his dutiful wife to his sister's new masculine appearance. She ruined this moment because she had not worn an ugly matron's hat to cover her cropped hair.

Their father stepped forward and asked, "Is the war over?"

Renaud shook his head. "No, there is still a siege on the city of Paris."

Bradamante's heart sank. Ruggiero would not be coming to Montauban soon; instead he was heading for the war. He might still be the cause of Charlemagne's defeat and her family's demise.

"Why are you here then?" asked Duke Aymon. "Beatrice, please see that meals are readied for our returning sons."

Beatrice nodded and kissed each son on the cheek. "Welcome home Renaud, Guichard. I look forward to hearing your adventures."

Aymon watched his gray-haired wife bustle in the direction of the kitchens. "She is never happier than when issuing commands to the servants."

Clarice took the baby and handed him to Renaud. "Here is your new son. I named him Aymon, after your father."

The baby woke and gurgled a smile at his father. Renaud beamed. "My blue eyes and your black hair. Such a handsome boy. Heavy, too." He planted a kiss on Clarice's cheek.

"Come, let us go inside," said Aymon. "You can have something to drink while waiting for your food." He gestured toward a young man holding Bayard's reins. "And who is this young man?"

"This is my new squire, Emile, son of Guy, Duke of Burgundy."

Bradamante felt another pang of guilt. She and Guy had commanded the forces in Marseille, but she left after giving him an excuse about an urgent family matter. It would have been impossible to tell Guy the truth. Worries sprung up in Bradamante's mind about how this young man would relate his time spent in Montauban to his father. Might Emile say something that would prove her excuse to leave Marseille to be a lie? Then again, if Ruggiero brought about the downfall of Charlemagne, concerns about her reputation would be rendered moot.

While the party moved into the great hall, Clarice commanded Richardet to retrieve clothes for his returning brothers. Renaud and Guichard slipped into a side chamber while Emile helped them out of their armor and into comfortable tunics. After rejoining his family, Renaud sat next to his brothers at the long banquet table rather than at the head table. Renaud became the lord of the manor after their father was named the Duke of Dordogne, but the new castle for Aymon and Beatrice was not finished. Until its completion, the duke and duchess remained in Montauban and still occupied the best bedchamber and places of honor at the U shaped table.

"Have a bath drawn for me," Renaud said to Hippalca. "I am certain my wife would prefer a clean husband enter her bed tonight."

Clarice smiled at him from the high table. It was evident she approved of him bathing and his suggestive tone.

"But first, fetch me some cider," said Renaud. "After I have quenched my thirst, I shall be able to properly enjoy a bold red wine."

Clarice wrinkled her nose. White wines were considered to be fashionable for nobility and reds were for commoners. Bradamante knew Renaud's request was based on his personal preference, but this was still seen as debasing himself in his wife's opinion. Clarice and Beatrice cared more about maintaining the appearance of expectations of nobility than did the rest of the family.

The place settings had not been cleared from the earlier meal when Richardet had been reveling about his recent adventures with his kinsmen Maugis and Vivien. The men returned to their places and called for more wine. Soon platters of roasted lamb along with boiled carrots and turnips were set before the new arrivals.

"So why are you here and not in Paris?" asked Richardet.

"Charlemagne sent us to seek out our kinsman Orlando and bring him back to the war." Renaud took a long drink from his goblet.

"I thought he returned to service when you did, right before the battle of Toulouse," said Richardet. "That's what Guichard's letter told us."

Guichard nodded. "I wrote on the day after the battle while we were still nearby and a messenger could get it delivered here without difficulty. Renaud was sent to Britannia to muster reinforcements to fight the Saracen horde. Orlando turned up missing the following morning."

"Why did he leave?" asked Richardet. "Was it because of..."

Renaud gave an almost imperceptible shake of his head. Richardet glanced at Clarice who had stopped fussing over her baby and staring intently in their direction.

"Who can say for certain why he left?" said Guichard. "Charlemagne sent us on our mission after an attack on Saracen troops a day's ride outside Paris. Those reinforcements were slaughtered by a lone knight."

Alard whistled. "There are not too many warriors who could manage such a feat."

"Exactly," said Guichard. "That is why Orlando was suspected. Renaud had just brought nine thousand new troops for the defense of Paris and helped repel the invaders during an intense battle. The next morning, the emperor sent us to find our kinsman."

"We followed his trail and came close to finding him, but were always a day or so behind," said Renaud. "This morning we came upon monks readying numerous graves north of the village of Saint Antonin. I thought Orlando had struck again, until I heard there were four warriors involved in the massacre. None of them matched his description. I was puzzled about who was involved in the massacre until a messenger found me and delivered a letter from Aldigier. He asked for help in rescuing his brothers, Vivien and Maugis."

"Half-brothers," sniffed Beatrice. "They are only half-brothers, since Aldigier is a bastard."

Clarice nodded in agreement.

"Yes," said Renaud, "but Aldigier is still my full cousin, regardless of his mother. Alard, tell me what happened yesterday in Saint Antonin."

A smile played around Richardet's lips.

Alard shook his head. "I was not there. Ask Richardet. It was he, Aldigier, and two Saracens who rescued our kinsmen."

"Our youngest brother was on a rescue mission?" asked Renaud, stroking his mustache as he looked at Richardet. "Perhaps you are ready for knighthood after all. Tell me what happened, where is Aldigier, and about the Saracens in your party." He turned to Maugis and Vivien. "But first, I want to know how you two became hostages of Lanfusa."

Vivien, the older and more muscular of the two brothers, made a motion that he would tell the story. He ran a hand through his long brown hair and took a swig of wine. "It was during the battle of Narbonne when the infidels first washed upon our fair shores. I saw Maugis unhorsed and almost trampled to death by Rodomont's steed. I went to my brother's side, and discovered he had been knocked out. I was overpowered and Feraguto took us both hostage. He recognized we were from the House of Lyon and could fetch a fair ransom. His foul mother Lanfusa was put in charge of keeping us prisoner and securing payment for our release."

Bradamante remembered that battle well. She had been re-assigned from Marseille to help defend another stretch of coastline from the North African army's incursion. She fought Rodomont for the first time and — out of desperation because he could not best her in a fair fight —

he killed her horse. Trapped under the weight of its body, she was not found until the next morning when the dead were being readied for burial. The one saving grace was the depression on the ground preventing her from being crushed to death or having broken any bones.

"Why did you not use your magic to free yourself?" asked Guichard before taking another bite of lamb.

Maugis gave a thin-lipped smile. "They knew my reputation as a sorcerer and bound my hands behind my back. I remained that way the entire time we were held. I cannot cast spells without the use of my hands."

Beatrice scowled and left the room without saying a word. Bradamante knew her mother equated magic with consorting with the devil. Beatrice had often exclaimed that Maugis should be disavowed from the family due to his sorcery. She became livid when her brother Charlemagne honored Maugis by elevating him to the title of paladin, one of twelve peers. That meant her favorite son was considered equal to a wizard.

Aymon walked over to Maugis and said in an undertone, "Pardon my wife. She does not understand the ways of men or the needs of war. I shall remind her about the expectations of hospitality. Until the morrow." With that he followed his wife upstairs.

Renaud, Maugis, and Vivien shared a laugh while Clarice frowned at them from a distance. She sat near Beatrice and Aymon at the head of the table, since she bore the title of new lady of the manor. Bradamante knew Clarice wished her husband had joined her in that place of honor rather than sit with his kinsmen at the lower tables. Clarice appeared distinctly uncomfortable being at the high table alone, with only the baby in her arms.

"So little brother, tell me of your part in this adventure," said Renaud.

"I visited Aldigier the other night, and met a virtuous Saracen knight on my journey," said Richardet as he pushed his empty plate away. "After our supper, Aldigier relayed the news of his brothers being traded to the Maganzas the next day. We devised a plan to rescue Vivien and Maugis."

"The monk said there were four horsemen of the Apocalypse," said Renaud. "Who else was in your party?"

"We met a warrior on the road who challenged us at first," said Richardet. "Then Ruggiero, the noble Saracen, spoke of our need for haste since we were on a rescue mission to save two men from slavery or certain death. His speech converted the warrior from a challenger to an ally in our quest."

"An amazing ally," smiled Vivien. "She won my heart. A stunning mix of bravery and beauty."

Renaud looked at Bradamante. "You were there as well?"

Bradamante shook her head, unable to speak. She had not heard of Marfisa's beauty before. The realization Ruggiero had left on a journey with a beautiful warrior maiden was disturbing.

"No, my savior was Queen Marfisa," said Vivien.

Renaud choked on his wine. "Queen Marfisa is in Francia?"

"You know of her?" asked Vivien.

"Know of her? I fought against her and then later, alongside her in the war in Cathay. She is a fierce warrior and unlike anyone else. Most trained warriors have a rhythm in their swordplay. She is as unpredictable as wildfire, whereas my fair sister's style is cold and disciplined. I hesitate to pass judgment as to whose skills are greater, Bradamante's or Marfisa's."

"Or who is more beautiful," agreed Vivien. "I found a silken gown in the wagonload of riches and bade her to put it on. Her raven black hair and fair skin looked wondrous in purple. And the dress showed off her womanly curves." His hands traced an hourglass in the air. "She is a fiery vixen. I would love to see her passion in bed."

Bradamante caught Vivien's eye and his smile faltered. She had long held affection for her older cousin since he had supported her military training and prowess. He also flattered her, which she now saw in a different light. Vivien was no different than most men. His charm was all in an effort to bed women for the sport of it, without concern for women's reputations or future.

"Alas, I shall never know for certain," he shrugged. "The only man she showed interest in was Ruggiero and they left to join the Saracen army in Paris."

Bradamante's spirits sank. Her beloved was in the company of a beautiful woman who was an accomplished warrior, shared his faith, and showed romantic interest in him. Might Ruggiero's eye wander from one warrior maiden to another? There would be no complications keeping them apart.

Renaud paled. "This is terrible news. I do not want Marfisa as an enemy again. Tomorrow we are all leaving for Paris." He motioned to Hippalca who stood near the walls. "Have the kitchens prepare food for travel for eight people to carry on horseback. We cannot be slowed down with a wagon. And what happened to Aldigier? I still have not heard why he is not here."

"After our rescue we had a feast in the center of Saint Antonin. Mandricardo and Rodomont came upon us, leading to many arguments and duels," said Maugis. "Aldigier was wounded. We left him in Bruniquel under the care of a surgeon."

Bradamante scanned the table and realized Renaud's count of soldiers leaving the next morning included herself. For the first time in her life, she was heartsick at the thought of returning to war. She doubted she could even lift her sword let alone swing it.

Bernard had been sitting peacefully next to his father, but his face was beet red. He clenched his fists, stormed over and punched Vivien in the stomach. "Take it back! There is no woman warrior better or prettier than my auntie."

"I surrender," laughed Vivien with his hands raised in mock protest. "Your loyalty to a kinswoman is a virtue, and you are correct. I should not tease our own fair warrior maiden." He winked at Bradamante.

Clarice made her way to the table while holding her baby on one hip. She twisted the ear of Bernard. "You will respect your elders, not attack them. Even if they insult those you love. Do you understand?"

"Yes, Mother. I am sorry, Uncle Vivien," said Bernard, his face twisting with pain.

Clarice released her hold on him. "Say your good nights, it is time for you to go to bed."

"Must I? I want to stay up with Father."

"What is the fifth commandment?" asked Clarice.

"To honor my father and mother," Bernard intoned.

"Yes, and you shall see your father in the morning," said Clarice. "Come Bradamante, I need your help arranging our chamber."

Clarice then leaned down and whispered in Renaud's ear and nibbled on his earlobe. A smile crossed his face as he pressed his wife's body against his. It was a smile that did not match his eyes.

"Try not to stay up all night with your kinsmen," said Clarice. "You have a long journey tomorrow and will need a good night's rest."

Bradamante followed her upstairs and wondered if Clarice's worries about Renaud's wandering affections were justified. Whether or not she cared to know the details, Bradamante would soon learn about the state of their marriage as she would be spending the night in the same bedchamber with her brother and his wife.

CHAPTER ELEVEN

The sun had already set and while the oppressive heat of the day had subsided, Akramont still found the air in his tent stifling. Had it not been for needing the counsel of his closest advisors, he would be strolling along the banks of the Seine River.

Patience was a virtue and Akramont found himself wanting to bolt like a runner in a footrace. He gave a grateful sigh as Sabri and Marsilio returned.

"Are your honored guests resting comfortably and under armed guard?" asked Akramont.

"Yes, my lord. Mandricardo is fast asleep," said Sabri.

"Rodomont is as well." Marsilio frowned. "Where are Ruggiero and Marfisa?"

"They are sleeping in Gradasso's tent." Akramont handed his advisors goblets filled with fresh drawn water. "Did either man pose any difficulties?"

Sabri shook his head. "Mandricardo ate his fill before promptly falling asleep."

Marsilio ran a finger around the rim of his goblet. "I would like to request another tent be found to house Rodomont."

Akramont raised an eyebrow. "Why?"

"My daughter, Fiordespina, arrived in the camp. She is a delicate young woman and could pose as an irresistible temptation for a man such as Rodomont, especially since he is forbidden to see Doralice."

Akramont steepled his fingers as he considered other commanders he could trust to house such a powerful and reckless man.

"There is another problem with Rodomont," continued Marsilio. "It is his armor. He insisted it be brought inside my tent, however its stench is overpowering."

Sabri nodded. "His armor and sword are heirlooms from his notorious ancestor Nimrod. He was the man arrogant enough to build the Tower of Babel with the intention of climbing into heaven to challenge Allah himself. I remember that armor being used by Rodomont's father and grandfather. It can only be cleansed by fire." He took a sip from his goblet. "Have a soldier use a long pole to hold the dragon's hide above a fire not used for cooking. Once the flames touch the skin it will be consumed until all the dirt and sweat is purged. Take care that no one breathes those fumes."

Marsilio chuckled. "I do not doubt that Rodomont's sweat is poisonous. Perhaps I should order a fire built so that the winds carry the acrid smoke inside the walls of Paris."

"Speaking of walls," said Akramont, "it is time we mount another offensive. Now that Rodomont, Mandricardo, and Ruggiero returned, I see no reason to wait any longer."

He rolled out the map upon the table and began placing wooden soldiers on it surrounding the various gates.

"Might I suggest that before we make our next assault, we motivate the troops?" said Sabri.

"How so?" asked Akramont.

"The men in camp today were happy at the return of Mandricardo and Rodomont, but they do not know Queen Marfisa. She conquered six kingdoms and is a powerful new ally. I suggest we allow these warriors another day to rest and then we gather the forces in the old Roman arena to hold Saturday afternoon prayers, followed by a celebration in honor of these commanders."

"We should honor Ruggiero as well," said Akramont.

"I recommend that you officially recognize Gradasso and Sacripant as well," said Marsilio. "Their pride would suffer if they stood by watching others being honored, and they were not, especially since Sacripant brought us five thousand soldiers all the way from Circassia."

"Agreed," said Akramont. "We shall call the army to the arena, lead the afternoon prayers, and provide a banquet. We shall honor Ruggiero, Marfisa, Rodomont, Mandricardo, Gradasso, and Sacripant. Then after the sun sets, we shall attack Paris." He placed more wooden soldiers on the map.

CHAPTER TWELVE

Renaud reflected on what needed to be done that night. He needed to bathe, manage his beautiful nagging wife, and prepare to leave for Paris on the morrow. While the household appeared unchanged in his prolonged absence, his family had changed. His oldest son spoke only a few words when he left, and now sounded like a little adult. Clarice had given birth to a new son. Alard and Guichard had chiseled cheekbones and full mustaches, whilst Richardet had grown taller but retained his boyish good looks with sparse facial hair. Bradamante was now a great beauty, but he found her cropped hair hard to accept. He wondered if this was a ploy by her to avoid being married off.

"How is my bath coming?" asked Renaud.

"It is ready, milord," said Hippalca as she carried two empty buckets from the small antechamber and headed for the kitchens.

Renaud took another sip of wine and regarded his cousin, Maugis. His long black hair looked greasier than ever and he emanated a rank smell.

"After I am finished, it will be Guichard's turn," said Renaud. "Then Emile, Vivien, and Maugis. A month long captivity with Lanfusa would cause anyone to reek."

Maugis walked over to Renaud's side, leaned down and said in an undertone. "How was your trip to Cathay? Did Angelica welcome you with open arms and open legs?"

Renaud grabbed his cousin by the throat, slamming him on the table. Lamb bones went flying, goblets knocked over. Red wine stained Maugis' white tunic.

"Of course. You enchanted that ship! You are the only one to ever use magic against me." Renaud's grip intensified causing Maugis' eyes to bulge as his hands flailed helplessly. "Why did you interfere with my duel with Gradasso?"

"Let him go," said Guichard trying to pull Renaud off their kinsman. "Lest you kill him before he can answer you."

Renaud pressed his left arm down onto Maugis' chest pinning him against the table and released the grip on his throat. "This is a private matter between us. Guichard, take the others and leave. I swear I will not kill him, but we will have words no one else should hear."

Guichard reluctantly led Vivien, Alard, Richardet, and Emile into the courtyard. He cast Renaud a warning glance as he closed the door, leaving the two kinsmen alone in the dining hall.

"Why did you interfere with my duel with Gradasso?" repeated Renaud.

"I - I," stammered Maugis as he struggled for breath. "Angelica ordered me."

"She was in Cathay at the time. Were you there as well?"

He nodded. "As her prisoner."

"Tell your story from the beginning and do not lie to me, or I shall ensure you have no descendants," said Renaud as his left elbow dug into Maugis' chest and his right hand pointed a dagger at the man's loins.

Maugis whimpered, "Show some mercy, Renaud."

Renaud moved the dagger deeper and felt fabric tear. The blade rested against bare skin. "Your acts damaged my reputation. People accuse me of cowardice for using trickery to avoid a fight with Gradasso. They also say I abandoned my duty to my emperor. Now you will tell me what you know and what you did."

Maugis swallowed hard, beads of sweat on his face. "She took me prisoner that first night at Charlemagne's tournament. I left the banquet distressed because I did not trust Angelica or her brother Argalia. I went to my room and divined the truth by using a pan of water and scrying. Her father, King Galafron of Cathay, sent his children to defeat Charlemagne and his knights. Angelica was the bait and Argalia the trap. Argalia wore enchanted armor and bore a golden lance that would unhorse anyone even if it only glanced an opponent's shield."

Renaud remembered the events of the following day. There had been over thirty knights who vied for Angelica, but only two jousts occurred. The first jouster had been Aistulf. He was thrown to the ground in his first pass and taken away as Angelica's prisoner. No one was surprised by that turn of events. Aistulf was widely regarded as the weakest of the twelve paladins. The second joust was against the fierce warrior Feraguto. Renaud had been surprised to see him fall, but not surprised when Feraguto refused to accept defeat. The ensuing duel and death of

Argalia led to the chaos of dozens of knights chasing after Angelica and all trying to claim her.

"The plot was to kill Charlemagne, take his knights prisoner, and bring them back to Cathay to serve King Galafron," said Maugis. "I could not let that happen. I cast a sleeping spell over Angelica, her brother, and her four giants. As I stood over Angelica with my sword in hand, I became entranced by her beauty. I knelt down to satisfy my lust, but she woke as soon as I touched her. Somehow my magic had not worked on her. She screamed, breaking my spell on the others, and I was bound by her giants. Angelica found the magic book in my satchel and used it to conjure demons who transported me back to the castle prison in Cathay."

"Then what happened?" Renaud rotated the dagger, causing Maugis to wince.

"After Angelica returned to Cathay, she spoke of nothing else but her desire for you. She forced me to discover your whereabouts by magic and I saw the planned duel the next morning with Gradasso. She ordered me to create a magical ship and transport you to her side. I did not think you would mind being brought to a beautiful woman wanting to be bedded."

"Now, you must do my bidding, or I swear to make good on my promise to castrate you."

Maugis gulped. "I will do whatever you wish."

Renaud released his cousin. "Tell me where Angelica is."

"Let us go to the bath," said Maugis as he backed his way toward the small antechamber.

Three lamps lit the room containing a wooden bathtub filled with warm water. Maugis moved his hands in a circular motion over the top of the water as he began going into a trance. Renaud could not see anything but the reflection of the flames dancing on the water. Maugis stared and tapped his fingers a few times on the surface.

"What do you see?" asked Renaud.

"Angelica has married and is traveling eastward, back to Cathay."

A look of resignation passed over Renaud's face. "Orlando?"

"No. She married a handsome young man, definitely not Orlando."

"Where is Orlando?" asked Renaud.

Maugis studied the water. He touched it a few more times and his brow furrowed. "I cannot see where he is."

"Is he alive?" asked Renaud.

"He must be for I do not see his death." Maugis shook his head and turned away from the bath. "I have never seen waters like this. They are murky. He lives, but he is not well. Not well at all."

This news disturbed Renaud. *Might Orlando have gone mad? If so, what would he find if he caught up with his cousin?* He remembered something his brother mentioned the first day on their journey to find Orlando.

"Guichard suggested I may have come across one of Merlin's fountains during my travels. This was due to my sudden changes of heart regarding Angelica. After you were taken prisoner by her, Feraguto killed Argalia. Angelica fled for her life and she was pursued by almost every knight at that ill-fated tournament. Bayard helped me outdistance my rivals. At one point, I had to rest. I quenched my thirst at a fountain in Arden Woods and when I awoke, Angelica sat by my side begging to be my lover."

"What happened next?" asked Maugis, nervously licking his lips.

"I spurned her," said Renaud shaking his head. "I woke to find that I despised her. I found her repulsive."

"Do you still hate her?" asked Maugis.

"No," scoffed Renaud. "I burn for her, just like I did the first time I saw her face. Just like every other man did when she interrupted the banquet and walked into that hall."

"When did your change of heart take place?"

"After returning to Francia, I found myself again in Arden Woods. Only this time, I drank water from a stream and she drank of the golden fountain."

Maugis nodded. "Guichard is probably right. I believe you and Angelica drank of opposing magical waters."

Renaud laughed. "Had I only drank of the stream that first time and not of the accursed fountain, I would have taken her maidenhead in those woods. She would be mine now and not someone else's wife." He shook his head. "Angelica has possessed my thoughts ever since the day I drank from the stream, and that magic colors everything I do. I need to forget about her. She is poisoned fruit from an evil tree. You must remove her from my heart. I do not want to go unto my own wife, and feel as if I am being unfaithful to Angelica."

Maugis nodded. "I can do that for you, but first you must get in the bath."

CHAPTER THIRTEEN

Bradamante was willing herself to fall asleep. She pictured herself floating on a cloud as she drifted over nothingness. No problems, no worries. Just sleep.

Her sleeping nephew, Bernard, rolled over and kicked Bradamante, shattering her attempt at slumber. The small trundle bed was lumpy and uncomfortable, but she had few options available to her. She could not sleep in Clarice's bed because Renaud was home. The room her other brothers shared would be cramped with the addition of Vivien and Maugis. Her parents' chamber had their servants sleeping nearby to provide assistance should anything be needed. Her only other option would be sleeping in the main dining hall with the rest of the servants, or in the stables with the horses.

Neither Beatrice nor Clarice would allow such humiliation to be visited upon a member of the noble family. Not even for a single night.

Bradamante lay in the spare bed, dreading the imminent arrival of her brother. She wanted to fall asleep and stay asleep throughout the night. She did not want to hear anything between Clarice and Renaud. The difficulty would be in trying to overcome her battle instincts. The snap of a twig could mean the approach of an enemy or a large animal. Either one could mean death if a soldier did not wake in time to defend himself.

Clarice began humming as she finished nursing her baby and laid him down in the crib. The curtains were pulled shut around the large bed as it faced the trundle bed near the wall. A small oil lamp on a nearby trunk gave a warm glow about the room as Clarice's shadow danced upon the scarlet bed curtains. Bradamante began imagining Clarice and Renaud's silhouettes entwined. She rolled over and shut her eyes in the hope of banishing the image from her mind.

The door opened with the barest of sounds and Renaud walked softly across the room. He pulled off his boots and undressed without saying a word. He blew out the lamp and rustled the covers as he climbed into bed.

"You do not know how much I missed you," said Renaud, his voice low and sensuous. "Or being next to your beautiful body in bed." The sounds of kissing and the removal of more clothing made Bradamante cringe.

"Husband, we cannot," whispered Clarice. "The Church forbids us to know each other while I am nursing."

"Is that why you are so bountiful? But why are you nursing? Commoners nurse. Why did you not find a wet nurse as before?"

Clarice gave a little moan of pleasure before answering him. "I found no woman in the village who I cared for. They were coarse and ill-bred. With you gone and no promised time of return...I chose to suckle our child."

"Your body has never been more desirable."

"Husband, it is also a Friday."

"Clarice," said Renaud, his voice was soft and his words punctuated with sounds of kissing, "that is a foolish law written by bachelor priests ignorant of paradise in a marital bed as well as the burning hell a husband feels when separated from his wife. Do not worry about the sin of coupling on a Friday, for though the hour is late I believe it is still Thursday. However, any sin would belong to me and one I would gladly do penance for. Your sin would be in denying me my conjugal rights. It would be impossible for me to be this close to you and your womanly form and deny myself until Monday."

"You said something like that the last time we were together. Anyone who consults a calendar and remembers the events of Charlemagne's accursed Pentacost tournament will know Aymon was conceived when the Church expressly forbade it."

"Full term children are born every day of the calendar year, even nine months after Advent and Lent. The Church baptizes all."

"It was because of *her*."

The kissing stopped. Bradamante knew Clarice would not refuse her husband's entreaties, but she would first make him account for his actions.

"What?" asked Renaud, his voice rising.

"You burned for her just like every other man when she walked in the hall that fateful night. Later you came to our bed and used me to satisfy your lust. The next morning you disgraced our marriage by entering your name in her evil contest. I saw your anger when Feraguto killed her brother before you had your chance to joust. To joust and earn the right to deflower her. What did you want? To divorce me and marry her? Or just humiliate me by using her until you became bored and then allow her to be shared among Charlemagne's peers?"

Angelica, thought Bradamante. *Neither one dared utter her name.*

Clarice continued. Her voice was firm and clear. "You were like a dog chasing after a bitch in heat. The last I saw you was the night I conceived Aymon. The next thing I knew, Charlemagne ordered you to lead troops south of the Pyrenees and defend Amir Marsilio from the scourge of Gradasso. Later, I heard tales of your adventures in the Far East. What were you doing there? I also heard rumors of you dueling with your cousin Orlando over that harlot. Are those all lies? Tell me where I stand with you. Do you still want me as your wife?"

There was a palpable silence before Renaud gave a heavy sigh. "You ask a lot of questions and you have a right to know the truth. Yes, I was in the Far East, but I was taken there against my will. Maugis was imprisoned by her and compelled to do her bidding. His sorcery brought me there. Yes, Orlando and I fought over her. Sorcery had polluted my heart, but Maugis lifted that spell. You may verify this truth with him in the morning if you like. He will tell you his part in that sordid affair, how I was bewitched and how he brought me to Cathay as well as cleansing me tonight of her evil influence. I come to our bed as a husband who loves no other woman but his wife."

"Did you lie with her?" Clarice asked, her voice wavering.

"Never. Do not concern yourself with thoughts about her ever again."

"You swear?"

"I swear on the bones of my ancestors, I did not lie with her and you are the only woman who controls my heart."

Clarice began crying and Renaud comforted her in his arms.

"Why did you not write to me?" Clarice asked through sobs. "You could have sent me a letter after the battle of Toulouse. You were nearby and yet did not spare the time it would take to scratch out a few lines of *Dear wife, I am still alive.* I had to hear that happy news in a letter Guichard wrote to your father."

"There is no excuse other than spells which held my heart and mind under its sway."

"And why dear husband, did you not follow me up here after supper? Instead you made merry with your kinsmen for hours before finally deigning to spend time with me."

"It is true that upon my return I tarried with my kinsmen. Guichard and I have been on a mission for Emperor Charles for the last fortnight without a decent meal during that time. In talking with my kinsmen, the truth about the sorcery upon me was revealed. I would not be the same man, if Maugis had not released me from such torment. As soon as the spell was lifted, I came straight to you. I swear, there is nothing that will tear me from your side until morning."

Bradamante cringed as she heard the sounds of kissing.

"I missed you terribly, husband," said Clarice, her voice husky. "Do not ever stay away from me that long again."

There was more rustling behind the curtains, and then giggling.

"If lying with you this night is a sin, I would willingly spend a year in Purgatory as penance," said Renaud.

Tears flowed down Bradamante's cheeks as she heard moans and grunting. She touched the eagle pendant hanging around her neck and said a silent prayer for Ruggiero. Her mind then traveled back to the afternoon she spent in Ruggiero's arms and her hand traced the swell of her bosom remembering his loving touch as the rhythmic sound of Renaud and Clarice's reunion ended with groans of pleasure.

CHAPTER FOURTEEN

D oralice woke with a painful thirst. Her mouth felt as dry as a wheat field after a long drought. She did not recognize where she was. The inside of a tent, but where and why? She was lying on her stomach, dressed only in the barest of shifts with bandages on her arms and legs. As she tried sitting up, the pain in her body overwhelmed her, causing her to howl in agony.

"My lady," said a familiar voice. "Let me help you."

Doralice was relieved to see her beloved attendant Fidelia appear by her side.

"You have many wounds, but I think you might be able to rest on your hip without it hurting too much."

Fidelia gently lifted Doralice and helped balance her on her left hip. Doralice leaned against the elderly woman whose presence exuded warmth and compassion.

"Water," she rasped.

Fidelia lifted a goblet to Doralice's lips. The first few drops were difficult to swallow with a swollen tongue and cracked lips. After a few mouthfuls, she calmly drank without fear of choking. She drained the goblet, but still felt parched and motioned for more. Fidelia's eyes glistened as she handed Doralice the refilled drinking vessel.

Once she satisfied her thirst, Doralice felt pangs of hunger. She could not remember the last time she ate. She could not remember much of anything.

"Where am I?"

"You are safe, my dear," said Fidelia. "You slept in your father's tent in Paris for nearly an entire day. I bathed you and tended the wounds on your arms and legs in the women's tent. Afterward you were brought here to rest and be with your father."

The wild ride from the south of Francia to Paris roared back to her mind as well as her unresolved anger toward Mandricardo and Rodomont.

"Food, please," she begged.

"Roana, fetch some stew," said Fidelia.

Doralice was happy to hear that her other attendant, a young woman with dark skin, had also found her way to Paris.

"I am sorry that I left you and Roana behind," said Doralice. Her throat tightened as she remembered the sight of her two attendants clinging to one other as Mandricardo carried her away on horseback.

"There is no reason for you to feel remorse," said Fidelia. "A madman abducted you. You tried pleading our case, but he willfully disregarded your thoughts about our welfare. Thankfully, Devant returned and helped us rejoin your father's service."

"Devant? Where is he?" Doralice tried to look for the diminutive man, but she turned her head too fast and pain tore through her backside.

Fidelia rested one hand on Doralice's shoulder and applied gentle pressure to calm her down. "He is with your father in Amir Akramont's tent. They will be back here soon. You need to save your strength."

Doralice nodded, but still felt guilt for having abandoned her two constant companions in a foreign land. She closed her eyes and remembered the corpses of men who had once been her armed escorts, and died due to Mandricardo's wrath. At least Fidelia and Roana had their choice of weapons to protect themselves with as well as numerous horses to choose from to continue their journey to Paris.

Blinding light flooded into the tent as the flap was raised to allow Roana inside. The young woman carried a steaming bowl of stew and flatbread. Doralice tore off pieces of bread, dipped them into the lamb stew, and stuffed her face as if she was a starving animal thrown a scrap of food. She devoured the meal without tasting, for all she knew it could have been rancid. It was warm and she was famished. Only after she sopped up the last drops from the bottom of the wooden bowl did she recognize her unladylike table manners.

"Thank you Roana, for bringing me this meal," said Doralice. "I am sorry for such a display, I do not know what came over me."

Fidelia shook her head. "My dear, I have tended you since the day you were born. I nursed all your wounds throughout your childhood. Never have you been so hungry before. A lady should not explain herself to anyone, especially her servants. However, it is gracious of you to worry about our feelings and that is one of the many reasons we love you so."

Roana nodded in agreement, but had a faraway look in her eyes without even a trace of a smile on her face.

"What is wrong with her?" asked Doralice. "She has not said a word to me."

Fidelia nodded. "She has not spoken since..."

"The day I abandoned you?" offered Doralice.

"No. The day she was attacked by a Frankish farmer. He was angry about the loss of several goats by our soldiers and he..." Fidelia paused as she gave a tearful glance toward Roana, "...stole her innocence."

Fresh guilt washed over Doralice. She should never have left her two attendants alone without protectors. She had spent so much time thinking about that fateful day when Mandricardo entered her life, how she might have acted differently, but she could think of no other scenario where she, Fidelia, and Roana remained alive.

"I am sorry," said Doralice as she grasped Roana's hand.

Roana nodded as tears fell down her cheeks.

"Devant returned to our camp with Rodomont," said Fidelia. "Your betrothed took a fresh horse and set off immediately to rescue you, while Devant collapsed in exhaustion. The farmer came by later that night while we were making our supper. I could not rouse Devant, so I came to Roana's aid."

"Did you kill her attacker?"

"I had no choice," said Fidelia. "Just as you had no choice."

Doralice's throat tightened. Fidelia did not understand what happened between her and Mandricardo. He gave her a choice. Agree to become his queen and submit to his advances or risk being branded a harlot for having been alone with a man. There was also nothing that would have stopped him from ravishing her. Her fate was sealed the night she welcomed him to her bed. She would soon discover how her father would react to her decision to become Mandricardo's wife.

"That madman will never harm you again," said Fidelia. "You are safe here."

Doralice could not let her servant continue to believe a falsehood. "Mandricardo is my husband."

Fidelia's jaw dropped. "You married him?"

"I may also be carrying his child."

"No, you are not," said Fidelia. "As I cleaned your wounds, I also cleaned blood from between your legs. Your long ride was harmful in many ways."

Doralice closed her eyes. A new world of possibilities opened for her. She could marry Rodomont now that there was no worry of her bearing another man's child. But did she want him as her husband?

"Fidelia, promise me that you will not speak of this to my father."

The old woman wrung her hands. "I serve your father. I cannot keep secrets from him."

"I beg of you. That knowledge is power. It may determine my fate, and I do not wish it used against me. I want to wield it as my own weapon."

Fidelia gave her a sad look. "I cannot make that promise to you. Your father already knows."

CHAPTER FIFTEEN

Bradamante paced outside of the chamber she shared with Renaud and Clarice. She needed to speak with her brother. Alone. She tried catching his attention during the morning meal, but there was too much commotion. Renaud had been bouncing his son Bernard on his knee between giving orders to the servants regarding provisions for the long journey to Paris.

Renaud expected Bradamante to join his expedition; she felt it would be best to tell him in private why she would not. Her emotions about Ruggiero leaving the area without being baptized were still raw. Richardet knew in vague terms that she and Ruggiero were acquaintances, but hopefully he did not suspect anything more. Should she give her excuses for not going back to war in front of Richardet, as well as her other brothers and cousins, she was afraid they might band together and mock her. Ordinarily she could withstand good-natured teasing, but this morning she was fighting back tears at the thought of Melissa's prediction that her kinsmen were heading off to their deaths. Keeping her voice steady and absent of fearful stray notes could only be accomplished with Renaud in private, so she waited outside in the hallway, her arms aching from holding his heavy armor.

Renaud and Clarice were engaged in saying their goodbyes to each other in the solitude of their chamber. With each giggle and moan heard through the door, Bradamante's irritation increased. Unlike the previous night, there could be no dispute about the day being a Friday. According to church law, intimacy was forbidden between husbands and wives on Fast Days. Yet, from the sounds emanating from the chamber there was no denying Renaud disregarded that particular religious dictate.

Bradamante leaned against the wall and stared at the beams in the ceiling. She was hoping their interlude would soon be over. The sounds served as a painful reminder of how close she had come in allowing her passion for Ruggiero to overwhelm her sense of propriety. Now she wondered if that might have been her only chance to be physical with a man she loved and desired. Within weeks, she and all her family might be facing execution for being related to Charlemagne. If that was to be her fate, at least she would face her final judgment as a virgin.

Sounds of rustling clothes came from within the chamber. Soon the door opened and Renaud leaned out into the hallway, wearing only his breeches.

"Emile!" he shouted. "Come and..." He paused after seeing Bradamante holding his armor. "Never mind Emile!" A lopsided grin broke out over his face. "Did you wish to play squire for me, sister?"

"Yes, there is something I must speak with you about."

Renaud held the door open for her. Clarice was standing before the mirror and brushing her hair, she looked surprised to see Bradamante.

He turned to his wife. "Clarice, if you would please, give us the room. It seems my sister wants a few moments alone with me as well."

Clarice readjusted the drawstrings in the bodice of her dress. "Come back to me soon." She kissed him on the cheek, slid a finger down his bare chest, turned and walked out of the room.

Bradamante retrieved Renaud's quilted gambeson from the top of his trunk. She held it as he slipped it on, then tied it closed for him.

"Guichard was right," Renaud mused while looking Bradamante over from head to toe. "You grew into a great beauty in my prolonged absence. It is past time for you to be married. Once this war is over, I shall dedicate myself to finding a proper husband for you since our father failed to do so."

A few months earlier, Bradamante would have welcomed such an offer, but now the thought weighed heavily on her heart. She helped him don his shirt of mail.

"Of course, he should be worthy of you." He moved the armor to rest properly on his shoulders. "A man whose strength of arms would not be inferior to yours. At least match your skills, otherwise his pride would be wounded and this would cause discord in your marriage."

Renaud slipped on his boots before Bradamante attached the greaves to his leggings. He looked off in the distance as he went through a mental roster of potential suitors; his index finger made check marks in the air as he shook his head a few times. "No, not him or him. Who else would be suitable?" he mumbled to himself, his eyebrows furrowed.

She attached his belt around his waist before handing Renaud his dagger and sword.

"Now it is time to get you dressed," he said. "I am surprised you are not already in your armor. Is your gambeson here?"

"I am not going with you," she said.

"What? You are not going. Why?"

This was the part she had dreaded. She had to be as honest with him as she could. There could be no more delay in telling him an uncomfortable truth. "Something terrible happened in Marseille and I lost my nerve in battle. I fear I would be more harm than good for the war effort at this time."

"Tell me what happened." Concern was etched on his face.

Bradamante sat on top of Renaud's trunk. "We ended the siege in Marseille. After one brutal night, our enemies were driven from our shores and they abandoned their efforts to claim that port city." She picked at a stain on the skirt of her dress. "Guy and I approved the mission. Count Geoffroi had volunteered to use a rowboat at night and destroy their fleet by fire. The ships were close together and the flames jumped from prow to prow." She closed her eyes and the images from the horrific night flooded back to her. "In my sleep, I still hear the screams of men as they burned. The next morning, the harbor was filled with charred remains and the swollen corpses of those who had drowned trying to escape the fire."

Renaud sat down next to her and put an arm around her shoulders. "Burned flesh is a terrible smell, one that will stay with you for a long time. However, if that effort drove our enemies away, it was worth it."

She rested her head on his shoulder. "I know, but the cruelty of how they died haunts me. I approved that mission, so their blood is on my hands."

"Geffroi is a brave, honorable man. He should be rewarded for the victory. I will tell Charlemagne of it when I see him again."

She swallowed hard. "Geffroi *was* an honorable man. He died that night as well. His burned body washed up on the shore with arrows in his neck and arms wrapped around his shield. His death is another heavy burden."

He stroked her hair. "Is that why you returned to Montauban?"

Bradamante's throat tightened. She had given several stories as to why she needed to leave Marseille. They were not outright lies, but none told the truth. She could not say an enchantress sent her on a second mission to rescue Ruggiero from being held prisoner by the wizard, Atallah. Instead, she told her co-commander, Duke Guy of Burgundy, that an old woman bore news about her family. It was almost the truth. That is if one considered Ruggiero, the man she intended on marrying, as being a family member.

"I left Marseille because of a warning from an old woman." Bradamante shivered. "She claimed to be a seer and warned me a family member was in danger."

"A seer? I thought you did not believe in such things."

"It is true, I distrust magic," she said. "I was skeptical. The first time she came to me, I did not believe her. I asked her many questions, and she did not know the answers. She returned after the siege on Marseille was lifted. She had the answers to my questions, and an even more dire warning."

Renaud sat back and looked at her in the face. "What kind of questions did she answer?"

She closed her eyes. "Those of a personal nature. Answers she could only derive by being a clairvoyant. I accepted she had a talent for seeing things that are hidden. That is why I left the next morning in the hopes of saving a loved one's life."

"Do you think it was Vivien and Maugis she saw?"

"Perhaps," she shrugged, "but perhaps she meant Richardet."

"Richardet?"

"Yes, his life was saved a day before he helped rescue our cousins."

"Did you rescue him?"

"Alas, I did not." She stood and leaned against a wall. "Richardet's life was saved by the courageous Muslim warrior Ruggiero, the same man who helped save our cousins. I was not at their rescue because I thought I was needed in Montauban, instead I should have been in the village of Saint Antonin. The irony is I sent Hippalca there on an errand that very morning, when I should have gone myself. Had I been there, I would have been the one to duel with Rodomont and Mandricardo, rather than our kinsmen having that honor.

"Yes, and you would have met and fought with Queen Marfisa. That is a duel I would love to see."

A knot grew in her stomach at the mention of Marfisa's name. "She helped liberate our kinsmen. I see no reason why we would have dueled." Bradamante gave a heavy sigh. "The morning is slipping away, you should leave to make the most of the daylight hours."

"Are you certain you will not join us?" asked Renaud. "Perhaps this talk of dueling has helped you rediscover your nerve for battle."

Bradamante shook her head. "I would defend my loved ones like a mother lion protects her cubs, but I lack the heart to make war. Not today. It is deadly for one to hesitate in war as it will mean your death or the deaths of those around you."

"If you change your mind, you shall always be welcome by my side."

She gave him a wistful smile. "Please, find an excuse to give my brothers and cousins. I will not see you off in the courtyard as I do not wish my melancholy disposition to cloud your departure and spoil the journey."

"If you will not be a part of my expedition, I must ask you to provide us with something to help our cause."

"What do you need?" she asked.

"As much as I would like to take the wagonload of goods from the Maganzas, it would be impractical at this point in the war to bring a wagon with us," he said. "Instead, we will use several pack horses to carry our provisions. Alard mentioned you returned to Montauban with several horses."

"I did. Have Emile ready the dappled gray gelding for your journey. The horse's name is Nikephoros which means to bear victory."

Renaud kissed the top of her head. "Thank you, dear sister. May our victory celebration come swiftly and with it, news of a husband for you."

Bradamante walked to the open window frame and stared at the neighboring hillside. She heard the clatter of Renaud's boots as he walked down the hallway. The warriors would soon be on their way and she would remain behind with her parents and Clarice. The idea of being hundreds of miles away from the battlefront and unable to influence the course of the war was torturous. However, the idea of witnessing the Frankish army being defeated by Ruggiero was as intolerable as the thought of her harming Ruggiero. The chance she might kill him during the chaos of a battle made her unwilling to lift her sword. It was best that she remain in Montauban.

Renaud had been right about Bradamante's distrust of fortune telling and magic. She held out hope that Melissa's clairvoyant powers were not always correct. Perhaps there was still a chance Ruggiero might convert to Christianity and marry her. Only time would tell.

As she stood looking out the window, the urge to see her brothers before they left became irresistible. Bradamante left the chamber and walked down the spiral staircase. Rather than entering the courtyard where the party was gathering, she instead climbed another set of stairs inside a tower. There she stood near an arrow slit where she could hear the milling voices. Peering out of the gap in the stonework she saw the horses being brought forth from the stables. Three were being used as pack animals while the other seven were saddled for the journey.

Renaud said his formal goodbyes to his parents before turning his attention to his sons. He threw Bernard into the air, making the boy laugh. Then he kissed the top of Aymon's head before giving Clarice a lingering kiss.

"Father, why do you not use a wagon to carry your food?" asked Bernard.

"Taking a wagon would slow us down. Horses can step over logs or go around mud, and they never break a wheel." He tousled his son's hair before mounting his horse Bayard.

"Where is Bradamante?" asked Vivien as he looked about the courtyard.

"She agreed to safeguard my castle while I am away."

"What? She is not coming?" said Richardet.

"She helped lift the siege on Marseille," said Renaud as he placed his golden helmet on his head. "Now is the time for the glory of lifting the siege on Paris to be shared among the men folk of this family."

"Why is she not seeing us off?" asked Richardet.

"Staying behind is not something she is accustomed to and it did not sit well with her. I am certain she will come to accept the hardship as you and Alard did before. It is simply her turn to guard my home."

A few hearty guffaws caused a blade of discontent to twist in her heart. The sounds from her kinsmen demonstrated they relished the idea of her being compelled to serve in a menial fashion. Renaud would never ask her to perform such a task when she was a far more skilled warrior and strategist than their brothers. She had to swallow her pride and be content with the reality that Renaud had covered for her absence without divulging any embarrassing details from their earlier conversation.

During periods of time when Renaud was not in Montauban, the security of his castle rested with his trusted seneschal and guards. Having a warrior family member present merely added to the image that the House of Lyon was secure.

Duke Aymon stepped forward and spoke to Guichard. "I wanted to thank you for all of the letters you sent. You are far better at corresponding with your family than Renaud." His lips twitched in a smile as he glanced at both Renaud and Clarice. "I shall be leaving on Monday to return to oversee my castle's construction. I ask you to continue sending updates to me whenever it is safe to send a messenger."

"Of course, Father," said Guichard.

Renaud seemed impervious to his father's teasing and the mocking of Clarice's criticisms that the duke must have heard on many occasions. Instead, Renaud turned his attention to directing his party. "I want Richardet, Emil, and Alard to take the reins and guide the pack horses with our food."

"Brother, could you please stop calling me by that childhood name? Call me Richard from now on. I am a man."

Renaud smirked. "Have you killed anyone yet?"

"Uhhhh," stammered Richardet.

Renaud turned to Vivien and Maugis. "Tell me the truth, did he kill anyone during your rescue?"

Vivien shook his head. "No. Had it not been for Ruggiero and Marfisa coming to save them, both Richardet and Aldigier would be dead."

"Well then," said Renaud as his horse began walking, "once you kill a man in battle, I will consider you to be a man. Until such time, you will still be my little brother, Richardet."

CHAPTER SIXTEEN

R uggiero stood in Amir Akramont's tent wearing the white linen tunic and breeches given to him by Atallah. The amir had insisted Ruggiero come attired in his best clothing and not armor.

Marfisa refused to follow the same request. Dressed in full armor, she stood with her arms crossed and scowled at the amir holding a purple dress.

"This was found in your horse's saddlebags, so it must be yours," said Akramont.

Marfisa turned her head away. "It was given to me as a reward for my acts of valor."

"Does it fit?"

"Yes, but I do not wish to wear it."

Akramont gave her a warm smile. "Today I will be introducing you and Ruggiero to the entire Muslim army. Well, except for those soldiers who will be serving on guard duty. My desire is for you to make as strong an impression as possible and help inspire the men on our final push for victory."

"I have worn armor since the first day I took up arms and seized a kingdom," she said. "Being out of armor makes me feel vulnerable, as if I was naked. How can I inspire respect from your men if I am dressed like a mere woman rather than a fierce warrior?"

"Purple is the color of royalty and you are a queen. The men will see your beauty and they will want to bed you."

She flinched as if a fly buzzed near her.

"After hearing you conquered six kingdoms, the men will then want to wed you."

Marfisa cast him a patronizing look. "I conquered seven kingdoms, not six and I will never marry. I will never submit myself unto a man."

"That is your choice, but there will be many a man who will aspire to having a wife who could provide them with multiple kingdoms upon taking marriage vows."

She laughed. "Yes, I conquered seven kingdoms, but I never remained in any of them for long. I am restless and traveled on my own over the last year. I would most likely have to re-conquer every one of them to reclaim my right to rule."

"Details," said Akramont with a wave of his hand. "Let the men believe what they want. They will then compete against each other to catch your eye. They might dream of having a warrior wife who could help them conquer neighboring lands." He again held out the dress to her.

"Will Rodomont and Mandricardo be wearing armor?" she asked.

"No. All the honored guests will be wearing finery."

She rolled her eyes then snatched the gown from him. "This will be the last time I wear anything besides armor before the victory celebration."

"My wives will help you change," said Akramont as he directed her behind a curtain.

Convincing Marfisa to put aside her warlike ways had not been an easy task. The sounds of fussing by the amir's wives were soon followed by sounds of exasperation from the warrior queen. Ruggiero and Akramont exchanged smiles and both took care not to laugh. Had any sound of amusement escaped their lips, Ruggiero suspected Marfisa would become enraged, storm out of the tent, and refuse to participate in the day's activities.

Akramont invited him to sit. "Please bring us some tea," the amir said to an attendant. He gave Ruggiero an appraising look. "You have been transformed in only two months from an eager novice to a poised and confident warrior. I long to know what brought about this dramatic change in you. You arrived here exhausted and could not keep your eyes open. Now that you are rested, I wish to hear of your adventures." He sat down and a look of concern crossed his face. "Are you sore from the torturous ride here?"

Ruggiero nodded. "I am, but less than I expected. The hot bath and massage yesterday helped remove the aches and pains from my limbs. I wish to express my gratitude for arranging those for me."

"Think nothing of it."

The attendant returned carrying a tray with cups and a tall serving pot. After being served a cup, Ruggiero closed his eyes to savor the taste of mint. "This reminds me of the tea Atallah made for me."

Akramont raised an eyebrow. "Where is Atallah? Please tell me he abandoned his attempts to prevent you from being in my war."

"He vowed never to interfere in my life again," said Ruggiero. "I know not where he is, but I am certain I shall see him again."

Akramont took a long drink, and then sat back. "Our stores of tea are running low, but today is a celebration and therefore is worthy of such a treat." He placed his cup down on a table and steepled his fingers. "Atallah is not here to interrupt us, so tell me how it was growing up on Mount Carena with only a wizard for company. Did you feel lonely?"

"Yes, but I did not realize it at the time. Atallah kept me busy from dawn to dusk. I hunted and wrestled with wild animals. We practiced swordplay and the art of the joust. He also taught me to read and speak several languages."

The sound of Marfisa cursing loudly in a foreign tongue was followed by soothing words from Akramont's wives.

"I learned several languages, but *that* was not one of them," said Ruggiero.

Akramont snorted. "Thankfully, I am also unfamiliar with that tongue."

"I learned Arabic from the *Quran,* Greek from *The Iliad,* Latin from *The Aeneid*, and also learned to speak Frankish and Urdu." Ruggiero took another sip of tea. "My life changed the day you held a tournament on the plateau beneath our castle. All the images of knights in battle I imagined for years sprang to life before my eyes. Had Atallah not allowed me to leave the castle, I would have thrown myself from the ramparts. I trained my entire life for that day. Thankfully I met Brunello. He gave me his horse, armor, and a sword to use. I had all I needed to enter the contest and prove my worth."

"I saw you from a distance bearing Brunello's shield and wondered how his skills improved so dramatically," Akramont chuckled. "I should have realized it could not have been him." He closed his eyes as a grimace came over his face. "That was before I learned of a death in my tournament."

Ruggiero swallowed hard at the reminder of his shame.

"Bardulasto was a fierce warrior," said the amir. "I was devastated by his death. He would have been a strong commander in this campaign. However, once I heard the entire story about how he attacked you, shattering the rules of the tournament, I understood why you killed him. He acted without honor and because of that, his death was not a tragedy." He traced the rim of his cup with a finger as his lips twitched into a smile. "That was the day I named you my tournament champion, I made you a knight, and you swore fealty to me."

Ruggiero nodded and returned the smile, but inwardly he thought of his promise to Bradamante to honorably sever his bonds of allegiance to the amir. He did not know how he would accomplish such a feat, however any future with his beloved depended on being freed from Akramont's service.

"Tell me what happened after the battle of Toulouse," said the amir. "That is when you became lost to me."

Ruggiero thought back to that fateful night and sorted through the various events, knowing he could not discuss everything with Akramont. Certain details, such as killing Muslim soldiers to protect Bradamante, would be impossible for the amir to understand or forgive. He took a deep breath. "After the battle ended, I realized Atallah was no longer by my side. I worried he might have been killed or injured. I began searching for him."

"Did you find Atallah?"

"No," said Ruggiero shaking his head. His mind wandered to the duel he discovered between Bradamante and Rodomont. Initially, he became furious when Rodomont refused to allow another soldier to leave and follow his sovereign after the battle was over for the day. This simple matter of courtesy caused Ruggiero to take over the fight for Bradamante. He had no idea that the soldier he relieved was a beautiful woman and destined to become the love of his life. Had he not interceded on her behalf, she might have perished at the hands of that filthy bastard.

"Why did you not come to the royal tent that night when you did not find Atallah?" asked Akramont.

"I kept searching amongst the thousands of dead bodies. The fog rolled in and I became lost. I somehow came across Mandricardo and Gradasso."

Akramont nodded. "Gradasso told me how he met you and that you were searching for someone."

"The next day Brunello found us. We were on our way to rejoin your caravan when we came upon a man whose wife had been abducted."

"Is that when Atallah took you and Gradasso prisoner?"

Ruggiero nodded. "Yes. Atallah seized a woman the previous day. He left my side during the battle of Toulouse to create an enchanted castle. He thought I was not ready for war and wanted to protect me once again. The difference was he no longer kept me in solitude as I spent my childhood. Instead, he abducted others to provide me company."

Akramont stroked his beard to cover a growing smile. "Gradasso told me of glorious feasts, as well as a bevy of beautiful women who bestowed favors upon knights who distinguished themselves in the joust."

"Many enjoyed the comforts Atallah provided," said Ruggiero as he shifted in his chair. "I wanted nothing more than to be free and live the life I was destined for."

Akramont's brow furrowed. "So you did not enjoy the company of the women?"

"I ignored them," said Ruggiero. "Atallah hoped they would distract me from my imprisonment." He could not admit the women were meant to serve as a distraction from Bradamante. He was proud he resisted the temptations of the beautiful women Atallah provided. He had been faithful to Bradamante's love. Only after his memory was stolen from him by the evil sorceress Alcina, did he succumb to his base impulses. Ruggiero's cheeks began to burn as he remembered being in Alcina's bed.

"Did you enjoy the company of the men?" asked Akramont.

"I ignored them as well. I refused to participate in mindless games or feasting."

"Gradasso said that it was a Christian warrior who tricked Atallah in a duel and brought about everyone's release."

"Yes," said Ruggiero. He found it interesting Gradasso did not mention it was Bradamante who freed them. Perhaps Gradasso did not want to admit that a woman warrior succeeded where he had failed.

The flap to the tent was lifted and a girl in a white cotton dress entered, a blue headscarf covered her black curly hair. Ruggiero recognized her as Akramont's sister. A wide smile crossed Akramont's face as he stood.

"We shall talk more about this later," said the amir as he walked over to embrace her.

She was a mere wisp of a girl whose body had not yet developed womanly curves. Hala had been the first girl Ruggiero ever saw. After the tournament on Mount Carena, Akramont knighted him and Hala handed Ruggiero a jeweled dagger as the prize.

He remembered wanting to gaze at the soft contours of her face and feeling bereft as she was whisked away leaving him surrounded by hardened warriors who slapped his back and told him stories from wars past. The next morning the army left to begin the invasion of Francia.

During the journey on the Mediterranean, Ruggiero dared to dream of a marriage with Hala, which would make him a part of the young amir's family. He shook his head at the memory. He had been naïve and did not realize marriages in noble families were arranged to leverage political advantage. What advantage would there be in Hala marrying a young knight without any lands or title? The amir could certainly find better prospects for her.

His former dream of a marriage with Hala was a distant memory and before he met Bradamante, the woman who now captivated his heart to the exclusion of all others. He faced obstacles in marrying Bradamante, but he would somehow discover a way for her father to agree to the marriage.

Hala's eyes met Ruggiero's briefly before she blushed and bowed her head. Ruggiero still thought she was pretty, but he now realized she was more a girl than a woman. She also appeared to be stunted from the long shadows cast by her powerful brother.

Ruggiero had been lost in thought when he realized Akramont was waiting for his response to a question. He bowed his head, "*As-salaam-alaikum,* Hala."

She looked up at her brother.

"You may return his *salaam,*" said Akramont.

"*Wa-alaikum-salaam,* Ruggiero," said Hala, her cheeks aflame.

A rustling sound of the tent's inner curtain announced Queen Marfisa's return as she emerged dressed in the full-length purple silk gown. Her womanly figure was highlighted by the golden threads in the bodice, her long hair plaited into a braid coiled on her head. She appeared discomfited wearing a dress, but she held her chin high daring anyone to challenge her right to such finery.

He thought back to when he saw Bradamante wearing a silken gown. She was beautiful and appeared, unlike Marfisa, as much at ease wearing a dress as in battle gear. Ruggiero surmised the difference was because

Bradamante had been raised in a noble family and wore gowns when not engaged in war. Marfisa had grown up as a slave. Perhaps she felt self-conscious wearing clothes designed for nobility.

"Queen Marfisa, may I present my sister, Hala," said Akramont. "Hala, this is Queen Marfisa. She is as fierce as the famous Berber Queen Kahina who defended her lands and people against the conquering Muslim army."

Hala's eyes went wide as she bowed her head in a respectful manner. Marfisa gave her a smile as she looked the girl over from head to toe. Her face hardened as she turned her attention to Akramont.

"You brought a child to war."

"I brought my family with me," he said. "I cannot assure their protection when I am hundreds of miles away."

"Has she been taught how to wield a knife and protect herself?"

"Of course not. She has guards for that."

Marfisa scowled at him. "I shall move to her tent tonight and be in charge of her personal guard when I am not otherwise engaged in battle. I will not allow any harm to befall her."

"As you wish," said Akramont. "I will have you know she has many soldiers assigned to her protection."

"Are they all eunuchs?" she asked. "If not, you might need someone to protect her from her own guards."

Akramont took a deep breath. "They are men who have served in my palace for years. I trust them, but I will not turn down your gracious offer to stay within her tent."

The curtain rustled again as Akramont's wives joined them. Ruggiero had not seen the two women since Toulouse and forgot how beautiful they were. They were tall, willowy and wore complementary silk dresses representing the colors on Akramont's standard. One dress was gold with a deep blue sash and matching headscarf; the other dress was deep blue with a gold sash and headscarf.

Ruggiero realized he could not remember which woman was which. He remembered they had similar names, neither could he recall, and similar likenesses. He thought they looked like sisters, although they were not. Try as he might, he could not remember their names nor tell them apart.

"It is time for you, dear husband, to be properly dressed," said the woman in the golden dress.

The woman in blue retrieved a gambeson and held it out for Akramont to wear over his white cotton tunic. The thick quilted shirt used for protection while wearing heavy armor came down past his waist and not the same one Akramont had worn before. This gambeson was covered with embroidery with multiple colored threads. Ruggiero stepped closer to examine the intricate designs decorating the fabric. Quranic verses along with names of prophets, Caliphs, and four angels were stitched in a flowing pattern. The effect was stunning and transformed the piece of utilitarian clothing into a work of art.

"I have never seen a garment such as this," said Ruggiero as he walked around the amir, admiring the shirt from all angles.

Akramont beamed. "This is a talismanic shirt, designed to protect the wearer from harm. I saw Marsilio wearing one and decided I needed one myself. He swears it has kept him safe for decades and may have saved his life on more than one occasion. I asked Alia and Anika to create one for me." He kissed the right hand of both his wives. "I believe their effort surpasses Marsilio's."

His wives smiled at the compliment.

Akramont had a satisfied look upon his face. His long black hair was freshly oiled. He took two pieces of linen and wound them into a turban so that his head had a golden cover surrounded by a circle of blue. He looked at Ruggiero. "Where is your head covering? You wore one in Toulouse."

Ruggiero felt heat rise in his cheeks. "Rodomont stole my horse Frontino. My belongings are in Frontino's saddle bags."

Akramont looked puzzled. "But you arrived on a black destrier, and the clothes you are wearing were found in those saddle bags."

"Both horses are mine. I demand Frontino be returned to me. Rodomont abuses animals. It is an insult for him to ride my horse."

"Enough," said Akramont with a pained expression on his face. "For now, you may use one of mine." He handed Ruggiero a plain white cotton turban. Akramont then pulled out a golden silk headscarf and offered it to Marfisa.

A look of revulsion crossed her face. "I will not wear that. I would appear like one of your wives."

"We can discuss that possibility later," he said with a smile, "but you must cover your head."

FATE OF THE SARACEN KNIGHT 73

Marfisa gave him a sharp look. "There is only one covering I will wear upon my head and that is my helmet. You demanded I not wear armor, but instead wear a dress. I agreed to that, but I insist on wearing my helmet. I shall resemble the warrior goddess Athena." She defiantly donned her helmet.

Akramont sighed and held out his arms to his wives. "It is time for us to join the festivities at the arena.

CHAPTER SEVENTEEN

Bradamante sought refuge in the stables. Here she could spend time with her horses, a brief respite from worrying about Ruggiero bringing about the defeat of the Frankish Empire and the executions of her entire family. If it was God's plan, she must accept it.

As she brushed the coat of her snow-white mare Eos, she noticed a few drops of dried blood. The brown spots were a visible reminder of her vengeance against Pinabel and gave her an unsettled feeling of guilt that could only be removed by Charlemagne. She held out hope that if she had the chance to detail Pinabel's crimes, that the emperor would absolve her actions. If not, her immortal soul would be damned to Hell.

"I thought I might find you here," said a familiar voice.

Bradamante turned to see her father smiling at her.

"Your mother was fretting that you snuck out and followed your brothers on their way to war."

Bradamante returned to brushing Eos. "Of course not. Renaud and I spoke, and I was to remain here."

He stepped inside the stall and offered an apple to the mare. "Your mother mentioned a promise you made about spending the day weaving with her."

Bradamante sighed. "I forgot."

"I understand," Duke Aymon said, "but your mother believes she can make you forsake the warrior in you."

"It will not work."

"I understand," he said. "However, you should spend time at the loom with her. Help us keep her spirits from turning dark."

She nodded. "I must first see to the needs of my other horse, then I shall fulfill my promise to her."

"We have stable hands," said Aymon.

"They could feed Eos, but they should not approach Rabican."

Her father raised an eyebrow and followed her as she entered the end stall holding a pitch-black stallion with a fierce demeanor. He pawed the ground and snorted as she drew near.

Aymon remained behind the stable door watching Bradamante. She stood there calmly and waited for the horse to grow accustomed to her presence.

"I know, I know," she said in a soothing voice, "you do not like having been kept in a stall for days. You wish to run in the hills."

The horse gave a sharp nod of his head.

"We shall ride soon," she promised as she stepped forward and began brushing his coat. The stallion closed his eyes and extended his neck in response.

"Ah, you like that do you? I shall have to pay more attention to you."

Rabican nickered as she combed his mane. Bradamante noticed there was a strange scent about him, instead of smelling like dust and sweet grass like Eos did, Rabican smelled more like a smoldering fire. She wondered exactly how swift this magical horse was.

After brushing him, Bradamante left the stall and joined her father waiting for her in the tack room.

"Does that belong to Aistulf?" he asked pointing to an ornate golden saddle encrusted with pearls.

"Who else would have a saddle like that?" she said half-joking. "I saw him the other day in the Gresigne Forest, before I came upon Alard. Aistulf talked of embarking on a journey and could not take a second mount with him. He bade me to look after Rabican as he had once cared for Renaud's horse Bayard."

"Why did he not take his expensive saddle with him?"

Bradamante thought of the magical beast Aistulf had used. The wings on the front of the flying creature posed a difficulty for normal saddles. Knowing her family's distrust of magic, she did not want to divulge anything about the hippogriff, nor about Rabican's true nature. "He found it ill-fitting on the other steed."

The answer seemed to satisfy her father. "The last time you were home, I told you I would be leaving to oversee the construction of the castle on the banks of the Dordogne River."

"I remember."

"Then the next day, you left and Richardet disappeared. Your mother became distraught and made it impossible for me to take my leave."

"Will you be going now?"

"Monday at daybreak," he said, reaching out to lift her chin. "I have no worries about the security of this castle with you here. My only concern is how you will fare."

"I do not understand."

He smirked. "Without me or your brothers, there will be no family here to deflect the attentions of your mother and Clarice."

CHAPTER EIGHTEEN

Doralice was surprised when Roana brought out the silk dress with a crimson bodice, green sleeves and a green skirt. Those bright colors were on the flag of Granada.

"It is time for you to be dressed," said Fidelia.

"Why must I wear this today?"

Fidelia and Roana shared a look. "Your father will answer your question when he returns."

She raised her arms and allowed the dress to be lowered over her body. The sleeves covered all of the bandages on her arms, and the skirts covered the dressings on her legs. "Tell me. What are my father's plans for me today?"

"I cannot," said Fidelia, as she adjusted the lacing of Doralice's dress in the back. "That is for him to say."

Doralice worried about what the day held for her with the wearing of finery and having her hair styled in elaborate braids. Fidelia would not say another word, and Roana remained mute.

Her father returned to the tent and was wearing a red silk tunic and green silk breeches. The best clothes he had brought with him. Doralice stood to greet him and forced herself to smile for her father. Her neck, back and legs ached, but she ignored the pain for her father's sake.

Stordilano stood before her with tears in his eyes. "My beautiful daughter. Merciful Allah brought you back to me." His hands trembled as he brought her right hand to his lips.

As she kept her head held high, Doralice remembered seeing her father the day she arrived in Paris. In her dreams he had transformed into a ghost, but now she understood. His hair had gone from gray to white and deep lines were etched on his face. It was as if he had aged ten years in a few months. She did not think it was due to the war, but from his worrying about her safety.

He cleared his throat and smiled at her. "Devante told me how Mandricardo murdered all your armed escorts. Fidelia told me he abducted you while blood still dripped from his armor." He paused, seeming to struggle for words. "Both Mandricardo and Rodomont are in the camp.

They arrived shortly after you did. They are under armed guard, but they both claim you as their wife and want to fight to the death over you. I need to know, did Mandricardo ravish you?"

She lowered her head. "There were no witnesses, so it does not matter the circumstances. My actions since that fateful day were done so I could survive and return to you. Had I displeased him, I would be dead. Mandricardo took me as his wife. The marriage has been consummated."

"How did you manage to come to Paris?"

"One of Amir Akramont's messengers found us in a village and ordered both men back to the war. I made them swear to put aside their duel until after they returned here. I was afraid for your safety." She raised her head and looked her father in the eye. "They are both cruel, selfish men. Please, do not force me to be with either of them. I would rather stay by your side, be your loving daughter, and take care of you in your old age."

"If your brothers had not died, I would grant your wish," said Stordilano. "However, I must consider what will happen to you upon my death. You need a man to provide for you and that means a husband."

"Do not make me marry Rodomont," she begged.

"I know he is a cruel and violent man. He is also vengeful. Should I break my word to him, he will attack Grenada and murder our people. I must think of my people, as well as my daughter."

Doralice squared her shoulders. "Mandricardo will not give me up without a fight."

"Perhaps both men will suffer mortal wounds during their duel to the death," he said with a whisper of a smile.

"When will that be?" she asked.

"Amir Akramont ordered all duels be deferred until after we conquer Paris and the Franks. There will be a celebration today in honor of Rodomont and Mandricardo returning. Gradasso and Sacripant will be honored as well. There are two others the amir is including in the celebration. I forget their names. Mere children." He waved his hand dismissively, and then walked around Doralice inspecting her dress. "You are beautiful. Everything I could ever hope for in a daughter." He held his arm out. "It is time for you to be seen."

CHAPTER NINETEEN

Ruggiero found it odd walking through the deserted Muslim camp. It was as if the empty tents swaying in the breeze housed ghosts rather than soldiers. He was anxious to see the famed Parisian wall, but would have to wait until he left the confines of the camp since the billowing tops of the tents and its wooden perimeter obscured the city's fortifications.

Six soldiers walked ahead and six walked behind their procession. Akramont strolled arm-and-arm with his two wives, followed by Hala and Marfisa, with Ruggiero as the last dignitary. The two soldiers leading their assemblage each carried Akramont's standard. The brightly colored flags with blue and gold quarters fluttered in the breeze.

Hala's black curls bounced as she skipped. "I love my family's standard with its design of three spindles and a distaff," she said to Marfisa. "The distaff is the pole holding fibers before they are spun into thread. Both my brother and I are following our family's heritage. He is a leader in battle, and I am an expert weaver. Those flags are my handiwork."

Marfisa gave a polite nod. "I chose a golden phoenix on a field of green for my personal standard."

"Ooooh, that sounds impressive. I look forward to seeing your design," said Hala.

"Well, it is only on my shield," said Marfisa, sounding a little embarrassed. "I never took the time for a banner to be made."

"I could make one for you," chirped Hala. "I have nothing else to do all day in my tent, but sit at my loom."

Marfisa scowled at the amir. Ruggiero could tell that the warrior queen was unhappy about a young girl spending her days sequestered in a tent.

"It is nice being out in the fresh air and sunshine," Hala said as she spun around. "You look really young to be a queen. You must be younger than my brother. Tell me, where is your kingdom? How old were you when you became a queen? Did you marry a king or did you inherit your kingdom after your father died?"

Ruggiero struggled with his composure, trying hard not to laugh at the startled look on Marfisa's face. Neither Mandricardo nor Rodomont had issued such verbal challenges to the warrior queen, nor had it been done in such a rapid succession.

"Slow down, little one," said Marfisa. "I cannot remember all of your questions when you barrage me in such a manner."

Hala tipped her head back and laughed. It sounded like the peal of a bell. "Are you moving to my tent tonight? I hope so. We can become close friends and share secrets."

Marfisa took a deep breath. "How old are you Hala?"

"I turned fourteen last month."

"The very age when I became a queen. I never married, nor did I inherit anything. I seized the kingdom by force."

Hala stopped walking. Ruggiero almost tripped over her. She stood stock-still and stared at Marfisa. "What happened?"

Marfisa yanked on Hala's arm to start her walking again, "I was sold into slavery as a young girl. One day as I was readying a bath for my king, he tried taking my virtue."

Hala's jaw dropped. "No!"

"I was prepared. I always wore a knife under my skirts," said Marfisa. "I had stolen the knife years before from a drunken warrior who had fallen asleep at banquet. That lecherous king was the first man to taste my wrath. After killing him, I donned his armor and proclaimed myself queen."

Hala cast a worried glance at her brother. "But what about the king's family? His guards? Surely they protested his killing."

"They did. Using the king's sword I killed many of the guards before they surrendered to me. After spending my life as a slave, I had nothing to lose," she said as she stuck out her chin. "I shall find a dagger for you to wear always and I will train you to protect yourself."

Hala gave her a broad smile. "My brother was right when he compared you to the legendary Queen Kahina."

Ruggiero gave a low chuckle. Akramont's sister would never be the same after spending time with Marfisa. The transformation from a polite young lady to a budding warrior made him wonder when it was that his mother would have first trained in combat. Unfortunately, he knew nothing about his mother's childhood as Atallah never spoke of it.

Ruggiero began daydreaming that his mother, Galiziella, started her martial training at the tender age of three as Bradamante had. He smiled as he imagined his beloved as a little girl with a fierce look on her face while wielding a wooden practice sword and shield.

All thoughts of his mother and Bradamante left his mind as they left the Muslim camp. In the distance stood the city of Paris. Ruggiero gaped at the height and the magnitude of the walls. The stone was a dull tan and he could see three massive gates, each was guarded on either side by round turrets. Numerous arrow slits were scattered throughout the walls and turrets. The fortifications curved toward the river with more gates beyond his line of sight. His mouth went dry as he considered the massive amount of land within its confines and how many souls were inside those walls. Their numbers were likely in the tens of thousands. *How many were starving?* he wondered. *How many were doomed to die in this war?*

Marfisa pointed at the nearest port. "That will be my Salarian Gate!"

Hala looked confused. "What does that mean?"

Akramont smiled at Marfisa. "That is the spirit I want displayed when I introduce you." He turned to Hala. "The Visigoths sacked the city of Rome by breaching the Salarian Gate. *Inshallah,* we shall enter Paris and introduce its residents to the glory of Islam."

They turned onto a different dirt road that headed eastward. A stone structure caught Ruggiero's attention and he realized it was the old Roman arena. From a distance the rounded structure looked impressive and stood about twenty feet tall. However, upon coming closer Ruggiero realized that it was in ruins. The walls had uneven stonework. Layers of limestone had been removed while some stubborn bricks remained attached mid-air.

"This is all that remains of what was likely an impressive Roman monument," said Akramont. "At least there are still adequate benches for the men inside."

"What happened here?" asked Ruggiero. "Was this because of a war?"

"In a manner of speaking," replied the amir. "After the fall of the Roman Empire, the infidels cannibalized this arena. They used it as a stone quarry to build the city's walls rather than cut new stone."

Ruggiero felt his stomach turn. He thought it wrong to deny future generations the ability to experience architecture built well enough to last for centuries. He felt a legacy had been stolen.

"This will serve our purpose," said Akramont, "but it is a shambles of what it once was."

"Does Bizerta have an arena?" asked Marfisa.

"Not anymore," said Akramont. "Centuries ago there was an uprising against the Romans in the Maghreb. After the rebellion was crushed, Bizerta was punished and Rome dismantled their beautiful monuments and used the stone to build elsewhere. There is nothing Roman left in Bizerta."

Ruggiero sensed a note of bitterness in Akramont's voice. He wondered if the amir would have preferred his capital to be filled with buildings from the famed civilization known for their feats of engineering and beautiful architecture.

As they approached the large entryway, the procession halted and the sound of clapping could be heard coming from within the arena. Akramont motioned for the group to remain where they were and he walked into the tunnel.

He soon returned. "Amir Marsilio graciously started the festivities. His son and nephew are entertaining the men with a song they wrote about this war."

Try as he might, Ruggiero could not hear any words above the clapping. He hoped the song would be sung another time.

Akramont cast a defiant look at the wall surrounding Paris. "Should the cowardly Franks think we are distracted and emerge from behind those walls, our guards will sound the horns and alert us. Then we will engage with them again on the field of glory."

"If that happens, I will be unarmed!" said Marfisa, her face contorted with rage.

Akramont looked as if he wanted to pat her on the head. "All the armor of the honored warriors, including my own, is being held in a wagon outside this arena. Should the need arise, it will be brought to you without delay. Now, my wives and sister will enter with me into the arena. I will introduce all of the honored warriors, saving your introductions for last. Then I will lead the afternoon prayers, followed by the feast."

A soldier from inside the tunnel motioned to Akramont. "Amir Marsilio is ready for you."

The banner men led the procession down the sloped incline to the front of the tunnel. Akramont and his wives were followed by Hala, Marfisa, and Ruggiero. As they neared the opening, Ruggiero could hear Amir Marsilio's voice clearly for the first time.

"Our commander, a man who is descended from Alexander the Great and the son of the late Amir Troiano, the noble blood of conquerors runs in his veins. Akramont called for this campaign for glory. *Inshallah*, we will succeed where preceding generations failed and will extend the reach of Islam throughout Europe as it has throughout Asia and the Maghreb. I give you the great Akramont, Amir of the Maghreb."

Several horns were blown, followed by the sound of clapping. Cheers erupted as the banner men walked into the arena carrying Akramont's flags fluttering in the air. The amir beamed as he strode into the center followed by his wives, his sister, and two soldiers. The crowd responded by roaring their approval. Ruggiero could not help but wonder whether the cheers and clapping was directed more for Akramont or for his beautiful wives.

Two guards stood at the front of the tunnel with their arms by their sides. As Ruggiero walked closer to get a better view, they changed their position to standing with their legs apart and spears pointed at him.

Ruggiero raised his hands in a sign of non-confrontation. "I will not go out until he calls me. I just want to see the festivities better."

One guard cracked a smile. He resumed his previous position with his legs together and his arms at his side. The other soldier followed suit.

The center of the arena was filled with sand where gladiators once fought and was surrounded by stone benches rising in a semi-circle. There was also a stage where dramas had been performed, above the center pit. Ruggiero was surprised that Akramont had not used the stage, but considered the amir may have wanted to avoid the possible conflict of all the "honored guests" elbowing one other while seeking prime positions onstage. He also could not assess the safety of the stage from his vantage point.

Akramont embraced Marsilio, who was also wearing a talismanic shirt. Marsilio's was embroidered with only red and black thread, while Akramont's had at least six different colors. The two men held each other briefly before Akramont broke away to address the crowd.

"I wish to extend my deepest gratitude to Amir Marsilio for not only beginning today's festivities, but for joining this campaign against the Franks. His forces from Al-Andalus helped start this war. I have no greater ally than Marsilio. I knew when I set out on this expedition that we required his full support and expert advice. Marsilio has been a rival to the neighboring king of the Franks for nearly thirty years. There is no one who with more experience fighting Charlemagne and surviving than Amir Marsilio and that is why he is one of my most trusted wazirs." Akramont then gestured toward the ugly Feraguto who stood in front of a large drum and a handsome young man holding a pear shaped stringed instrument. "*Inshallah*, our victory will inspire new verses for his son Matalista's song that will be sung by future generations!"

Matalista's long black hair was held back by a tether, his head covered by a yellow cap that matched his tunic. He gave the amir a gracious bow. Feraguto bore a look of expectation on his face that he would be the next recipient of the amir's praise.

Akramont smiled and nodded as the aged Sabri, wearing a full-length white tunic and matching turban, made his way to the center of the arena and stood next to Marsilio. "My other closest advisor is Governor Sabri. I grew up knowing that my father considered him to be a wise counselor, and he has continued the tradition of providing me with his sage advice. He has survived countless battles over his many decades of life and recognizes when an army should retreat to fight another day."

Akramont then waved at one of his wives. "To demonstrate my appreciation for all that Sabri has done for my family, I married his beautiful daughter, Alia."

She smiled and bowed to both her husband and then her father.

"My other beautiful wife, Anika, is Alia's cousin and a daughter of the late Governor Garamanta," said Akramont. "I married her in another demonstration of my deepest gratitude, for her father was gifted in the art of divination."

A hush fell upon the crowd.

"Garamanta attended the war council when this campaign was first discussed. He divined that our victory over Charlemagne was dependent upon our bringing a special warrior into our ranks. That our victory would be impossible without him. I am proud to say that after considerable effort, we located this prophesied warrior and he is once again by my side. *Inshallah*, victory will be ours." Akramont smiled as he turned toward the tunnel and locked eyes with Ruggiero.

A chill ran down Ruggiero's spine. Atallah had mentioned prophesies surrounding him, but he had never said specifics other than Ruggiero should forget about Bradamante lest he die a premature death like his father had.

Marfisa raised her eyebrows as she stared at Ruggiero. "Is he talking about you?"

Ruggiero shrugged. "How should I know? I think fortune telling is based on superstition and should not be trusted."

Marfisa gave him a knowing smile, while Hala gaped at him from a distance.

"Speaking of victory, I wished to announce good news. Both my wives are carrying my future heirs who were conceived on the field of victory after the battle of Toulouse."

The women gave demur smiles while the men in the stands stomped their feet in approval and clapped. Hala jumped up and down with excitement. Sabri looked uncomfortable.

Marfisa scowled. "This is wrong. He should not be flaunting his wives."

"Today would have been complete had Governor Garamanta been here to share in this good fortune. Unfortunately, he passed away and was unable to marry my sister, Hala, who is almost of marriageable age." Akramont gestured for his sister to come forward. Thunderous applause greeted her as she bowed her head to Amir Akramont, her cheeks were once again all aflame.

"He planned on marrying her off to an old man?" Marfisa clenched her fists. "He better not try that again."

Akramont swept one arm in the direction of an empty U-shaped box of seats. Two soldiers guided the three women to the top box as they sat down next to each other on a stone bench. In a nearby box, Ruggiero noticed a woman seated with a girl on her lap and a gap between her and a lovely young woman wearing a yellow dress with matching headscarf. Marsilio's gaze was upon these same women. Ruggiero surmised that the young lady might be Marsilio's daughter Fiordespina. He felt as if a hand was squeezing his heart when he looked at her sad face. She likely believed that her lover Richardet died a horrible death by fire. Somehow Ruggiero needed to fulfill his promise to Richardet and inform

Fiordespina that he was still alive. He did not know how he could get near her to convey such news, nor did he think it wise to try and pass the information in a written message. Such missives could be misdirected and even if she did receive it, he was unsure if she had been taught to read.

Akramont clapped his hands once to bring attention back to himself. "Today I shall introduce other leaders who have joined this campaign and whose leadership will ensure our ultimate victory. The renowned Gradasso, king of the vast kingdom of Sericana, has joined my inner circle of advisors."

Gradasso emerged from a different tunnel. He wore a red tunic with a yellow embroidered dragon that reached down to his knees and a golden turban. His face was covered with scars and it bore a smile that did not reach his eyes.

"Gradasso's forces overwhelmed Charlemagne's last year in Paris," said Akramont. "The Frankish emperor is cowardly due to that embarrassment and this time stays behind his walls rather than engage with us openly on the field of glory. With Gradasso's advice, *inshallah,* our army will overwhelm and defeat the Franks."

The crowd roared its approval.

"Why is Gradasso here?" asked Marfisa.

"He is obsessed with two things," said Ruggiero. "He wants Renaud's horse Bayard and Orlando's sword Durindana. That is why he invaded Francia last year and has not returned home."

She nodded. "I know both Orlando and Renaud from the war in Cathay. I can attest that Renaud's horse is a fine animal and Orlando's famed sword is worth coveting."

"Gradasso and Mandricardo started fighting the first day I met them over Durindana. They would have fought to the death over a blade neither one possessed."

Marfisa rolled her eyes. "Idiots."

Akramont walked Gradasso over to stand near Sabri. He then motioned for a burly man wearing a long red tunic with a design of a black boar to enter the arena. "We are fortunate that King Sacripant of Circassia has joined our campaign bringing with him five thousand troops."

"What?" shrieked Marfisa. The two guards restrained her from rushing onto the field. Marfisa growled as she watched the bald man with a matted beard walk over to the amir.

"How do you know him?" asked Ruggiero.

"I first fought for him, and then against him while in Cathay," said Marfisa. "Our duel was interrupted when a vile little thief stole his horse and my sword." She snarled as Sacripant puffed out his chest. "Once our victory is assured, both Sacripant and Mandricardo will die for insulting my honor."

"Not only did King Sacripant bring us much needed reinforcements," announced Akramont, "he generously gave advice on how to win prolonged sieges."

Sacripant was led to stand near Gradasso. Akramont smiled as Rodomont strode out into the center of the arena wearing a knee-length green tunic and holding a flagpole with his banner bearing the face of a beautiful woman.

"Ugh," said Marfisa. "What did he use to dye that fabric? It looks like bug gut green. He is repulsive."

One of the guards snorted as he tried holding back a laugh.

"Rodomont was the first man in my war council who agreed to this campaign," said Akramont. "He could not wait until all the forces were ready. So his army became our advance forces. No one has been a more stalwart ally or fierce soldier than Rodomont."

Ruggiero snarled as the arrogant commander soaked in praise from the amir.

"Only one man survived the fiendish traps set by the Franks during that fateful night last month when the walls of Paris were temporarily breached," said Akramont. "Rodomont forced his way into the heart of Paris and singlehandedly destroyed hundreds of homes. If the Franks know the name of one Muslim soldier, they know and fear Rodomont."

Rodomont waved his banner as cheers from the crowd rang forth.

"He left this campaign when he heard his beloved was in danger. The famed beauty, Doralice of Granada, is now with us safe and unharmed," Akramont said as he gestured in the direction of a box where Doralice sat behind her father. Her face was expressionless as she stared at Rodomont waving a silken likeness of her. "I am proud to say that Rodomont returned to fight this war!"

Rodomont appeared pleased as he was led to stand near Sacripant.

"We have another leader who traveled a long distance to join our cause," said Akramont. "He first joined us after the victory in Toulouse."

Mandricardo stepped out into the sunshine, wearing a knee-length gray tunic, a smile plastered on his face.

"I give you Mandricardo, Khan of Tartary!" announced Akramont.

Ruggiero watched Doralice. Her face remained stone-like as Mandricardo smiled and waved in her direction. Then a commotion shifted Ruggiero's attention. There was a flurry of activity among the assembled dignitaries as Sacripant pushed his way forward.

"Murderer! You shall die for killing my brother Olibandro!" said Sacripant as his hands encircled Mandricardo's throat.

CHAPTER TWENTY

Akramont erupted with fury. "Guards! Separate these men."
Soldiers pried Sacripant's hands from Mandricardo's throat.
The Khan of Tartary massaged his neck, took a few deep
breaths, and then after he regained his bearings, a haughty look came
over him. Mandricardo brushed his tunic as if the attack had been an
unpleasant piece of dirt. There was another flurry of movement as Rodomont lunged at Mandricardo, but was quickly restrained by numerous
guards. Mandricardo sneered.

The bleachers were abuzz with thousands of agitated voices. Akramont knew he had to seize control of the situation before the army lost
all respect for his command.

"Take them away," he said, waving a hand at the three who had
caused him so much difficulty. "Throw them into the cages beneath this
arena where the Romans once held animals."

"I am sorry, my lord," said a guard, "but the area under the stage has
been filled with dirt."

"What is wrong with these infidels? Do they not know how to treat
Roman monuments?" Akramont shook his head in anger and lowered
his voice. "Fine. Take them outside, place them in shackles, and then
bring them to my tent. Have Ruggiero and Marfisa brought there as well.
Do not hesitate to shackle them if they show any signs of violence. I will
tolerate no further outbursts."

Akramont walked over to the calm Marsilio and spoke into his ear.
"It seems I must interrupt my plans to settle scores between squabbling
children. I must impose upon you to lead the men in prayer in my stead.
Then give them their feast. I may be forced to relent and allow one duel
before the sun sets, so do not allow the men to leave after they eat."

"It shall be done," said Marsilio.

Akramont turned to the crowd, many were no longer paying any attention to the center of the arena. The men were arguing amongst
themselves. He raised his arms and the noise lessened. *"Allahu Akbar!"*
he said in a booming voice.

The crowd responded, *"Allahu Akbar!"*

He smiled as he lowered his arms. "As you witnessed, this event did not proceed as expected." Laughter greeted him. Akramont sobered and the laughter ended. "I had no prior knowledge of the history between Sacripant and Mandricardo. Neither of them was aware that they had both joined my campaign until a few moments ago. They are being taken aside and I shall entreat them to channel their anger into our war effort. If they refuse to place the noble goals of this war above their feuds, there might be a duel for you to witness today." Murmurs of excitement rippled through the crowd. "For now, Amir Marsilio will lead you in prayer and you will have your banquet. However, you are not to leave this arena until I return and dismiss the assembly."

He strode out the tunnel as the sounds from the crowd grew into a cacophony. The anger Akramont had held in check in front of the crowd was now a simmering rage.

Sabri caught up with Akramont as they neared the gate to the camp. The elderly governor almost tripped on the hem of his tunic.

Akramont held an arm out. "Steady there, my friend."

They stopped walking while Sabri struggled to catch his breath. "Do you wish to listen to my advice any more?"

"Of course. This was not your fault," said Akramont. "The blame rests with that ugly brute. How dare he embarrass me in such a manner." He spoke in a hushed tone so that his personal guards would not be privy to their conversation. "I hate Sacripant. I have hated him since the day he arrived and repeatedly insulted me. If he did not command five thousand soldiers, I would flog him for his disrespectful behavior and for today's spectacle. I need all of these warriors in the coming battle, but I cannot allow this bad blood between so many commanders to continue. It might poison my campaign."

Sabri nodded. "It would be better to allow for a controlled spill of blood rather than allow it to become a bloodbath."

Akramont leaned in and whispered in his elderly advisor's ear. "If I could dictate the outcome, I would rather Mandricardo die. He is the main source of conflict in this camp. Almost all the quarrels are with him."

"He brought no men with him, only discord," said Sabri.

"If only Sacripant would go away while leaving me his army..." chuckled Akramont.

"That would be a beneficial outcome. You mentioned there might be one duel today, what about the other disputes? When will they be settled?"

Akramont looked skyward and shook his head. "They would all kill each other if given the chance. I must somehow get them to defer their fights until after the war is over, but still allow one duel to go forward."

"Might I suggest having them agree to choose which dispute is settled by having lots drawn?" asked Sabri.

"That could work," said Akramont.

Sabri began scouring the ground for small rocks. "I will label these with the opposing combatants initials as we listen to their pleas."

Akramont helped him find ten similar sized rocks. "I hope this will be enough."

Sabri gave a low chuckle as he shook his head.

"Now, let us proceed to my tent," said Akramont. "I will perform my afternoon prayer. I must do that before hearing any petitions."

"As it should be," said Sabri. "Will you be leading those men in prayer as well?"

"We shall see if any of them even ask," said Akramont.

As they resumed walking, Akramont found he had regained his balance and purpose. He had come to understand why his father had trusted Sabri so implicitly over the years. His sense of reason helped neutralize the venomous atmosphere threatening to upend his war effort. Sabri had seen many prideful men over his lifetime and understood the dangers of allowing tempers to go unchecked.

Akramont entered his tent and spoke to his chamberlain. "Bring forth two pitchers of water for me as well as a small pot of paint and a brush."

The man bowed and left on the errand. There was a sound of clanking as Sacripant shifted from resting on his knees to sitting on the ground.

"How long must I wear these?" asked Sacripant.

Akramont closed his eyes and put a finger to his lips. "Shhh."

Mandricardo and Rodomont also wore iron shackles and were kneeling on the ground a few feet away from each other and from Sacripant. Guards stood watch between each man ready to restrain them if necessary. Ruggiero and Queen Marfisa sat quietly in chairs across the room from the three men in chains.

The chamberlain returned with the requested items setting them down on a nearby table. Akramont gave one pitcher of water to Sabri along with a bowl. The two men slipped off their sandals and began their cleansing ritual.

"*Bismillah,*" said Akramont. As he washed the dirt off his hands, he imagined he was washing away the hatred borne inside the hearts of the men who ruined his gathering. Splashing the cool water on his face, a sense of calm came over him. By the time he finished washing his feet, he was in the proper contemplative mood for prayer. After drying his feet, he looked up and saw Ruggiero staring at him. The young man wanted to speak, but waited for permission.

"Was there something you wished to say Ruggiero?"

"Yes, my lord," said Ruggiero. "Marfisa and I would like to join you and Governor Sabri in prayer. May we also have water?"

Akramont motioned to his chamberlain to fulfill that request. He shared a look with Sabri. Ruggiero had passed the test that the three commanders had not. There was no doubt in his mind that Ruggiero was a devout Muslim, whereas the other three were not. Rodomont never prayed. In fact, he demonstrated hostility toward worshippers, including the desecration of a church during his one-man rampage of Paris. The memory of that horrific event soured Akramont's stomach for he worried that Allah might punish his campaign because of Rodomont's acts of sacrilege. Sacripant was no better with his wanton consumption of wine and abuse of Frankish women he had taken as plunder. Mandricardo, in contrast, been seen praying, but only when there was an audience. Akramont had doubts about Mandricardo's piety, but he gave him credit for not flouting disrespect of Islam or its followers.

While Ruggiero and Marfisa performed *wudu*, the chamberlain arranged three prayer rugs on the floor. Marfisa finished her ritual washing and raised an eyebrow after seeing there were only three rugs.

"Queen Marfisa," said Akramont. "You may conduct your prayers behind the curtain where you changed earlier."

"Why must I go to another part of your tent to worship?"

He cocked his head toward the three men in shackles. "I was thinking of your modesty. I do not mind having these men stare at my backside while I kneel, but I did not think it would be proper for them to view you in the same manner."

There was a softening in her face as she nodded and walked behind the curtain. Akramont chose the middle prayer rug while Sabri and Ruggiero were on either side of him. The three men spoke in unison as they performed their *rakats*. The act of communing with the Divine helped ease Akramont's spirits. As his forehead touched the prayer rug, he realized that both his anger and his headache were gone and replaced with serenity. Upon finishing his prayer, he motioned for his chamberlain to roll up the rugs.

Sabri struggled getting up. Time took its toll on the old man as he continued the slow transition to standing. He walked over to the table and sat down spreading out the rocks collected earlier.

Marfisa rejoined them with a look of expectation on her face. Akramont remained standing, but insisted Ruggiero and Marfisa be seated.

He was now ready to address the three men in chains. Taking a deep breath, Akramont allowed the glory of Allah to fill him once again with strength of purpose. "Your actions today exemplifies why I insisted on your wearing finery and not armor. I knew better than allowing any of you to bear weapons around each other. Your pride is as large as the entire caliphate." He then locked eyes with Sacripant. "You undermined my authority by your childish display in front of the entire army. It shall take a Herculean effort to reestablish my pre-eminence after this. I shall not tolerate any further disruptions. Are we clear on this?"

Sacripant yawned.

Akramont turned his attentions to the Khan of Tartary. "Mandricardo, you stand accused of killing Sacripant's brother, Olibandro. What say you of this charge?"

"It is true," he said with nonchalance. "I invaded Circassia while Sacripant was in Cathay, unsuccessfully wooing the princess Angelica. Olibandro was left in charge of his kingdom. I saw something worth having and took advantage of an opportunity." He bore a satisfied smile on his face and cast a sideways glance at the snarling Rodomont.

Sacripant grunted. "He admits the crime of murdering my brother. You cannot deny my right to seek vengeance."

"You have the right to avenge your brother's death, but I must insist that the duel be deferred until after the war is over," said Akramont.

"Need I remind you of my reasons for being in Francia?" said Sacripant. "I care not one whit about your war. I told you the first day I joined your camp that it was a convenient place for me and my army to await word on Angelica's location. Rumor has it that she traveled west to Francia with Orlando. My secondary reason for coming here was to avenge my brother's death by the hands of this miscreant."

Mandricardo laughed. "Angelica would have to lose her senses to ever consent to marrying the likes of you. That would be both her sense of sight and her sense of smell."

Sacripant lurched forward, but was restrained by guards whose arms encircled him.

"You are wasting your time chasing a blonde with a heart made of ice," said Mandricardo. "Whereas, I am satisfied having a brunette with a cunny on fire."

"Dead! You are a dead man!" yelled Rodomont as he strained against guards holding him back. "You shall die for raping my Doralice."

"I did not rape her. She offered no resistance to me, nor did she lie there like a dead fish. She is a passionate lover who wraps her legs around my waist and rocks her hips urging me to fill her with my manhood."

Rodomont gave a guttural sound as his face turned purple.

"Enough!" said Akramont. "I recognize your dispute cannot be easily settled." Mandricardo's deliberate taunting angered him. He spoke to Sabri, "Record Sacripant versus Mandricardo and Rodomont versus Mandricardo."

Sabri began painting the names for those disputes on two separate rocks.

Taking a deep breath, Akramont turned his attentions to Marfisa. "Now fair lady, tell me of your challenge with Mandricardo."

"He saw me wearing this dress and assumed I was an ordinary woman, unable to defend my own honor. Mandricardo wanted to distract Rodomont from Doralice and offered me up as a substitute bride." She growled. "As unthinkable as it is for me to consider submitting myself to any man, those two would rank among the last men on earth I would ever marry." Her nostrils flared. "Mandricardo jousted with several of my companions and then he fought me over his claim that I could be treated as a slave to be bought and sold. Our duel was interrupted before I was able to send him to Hell for insulting me."

Akramont nodded. From the short time he had known this warrior queen he understood this insult was something she would never forgive nor forget. "Do you also have a dispute with Rodomont?"

"No. While I find him repulsive, he has done nothing against me. However, I have an unsettled dispute with Sacripant. His insult was lesser in severity than Mandricardo's. I served as a commander in his army in Cathay until he insulted me. I cannot allow insults to my honor or my integrity go unpunished."

Akramont began to feel his headache return. "Sabri, record those disputes as well. Now Ruggiero, tell me of your claims against Mandricardo and Rodomont."

"Rodomont stole my horse," said Ruggiero. "There is an old proverb which says that a horse is attached to its master's honor. I cannot allow Frontino to be abused by a man without honor."

"We have replacement horses here," said Akramont. "Many of our men died in a recent battle, so we have their mounts. This dispute can be settled without losing either one of you."

Rodomont sneered. "Even if you gave me another horse, that would not undo the insolence shown to me by this boy. If Marfisa is allowed to fight with two men who insulted her honor, I must be allowed to do the same. He does not even credit me for defending the honor of a woman who was deflowered by a selfish and vainglorious man."

Akramont nodded to Sabri to write their names down as well.

"My dispute with Mandricardo also centers on honor," said Ruggiero. "We both bear the standard of a silver eagle on a field of blue. It was borne by my noble ancestor Hector of Troy. Mandricardo does not claim him as his ancestor, but instead —"

"I bear the armor once worn by Hector of Troy," interrupted Mandricardo. "I won that eagle by force of arms and I will not allow anyone else to use it."

"He is demanding that I deny my heritage and allow his dishonorable character to besmirch my ancestor's honorable name by using his standard and armor."

Akramont pinched the bridge of his nose. "How many disputes is that?"

"Six, my lord," said Sabri.

"I cannot allow all of these duels to proceed," said Akramont. "If I did, there is a good chance once all was said and done that Marfisa would be the only one left alive."

Akramont was pleased to see flashes of anger in the three shackled men's eyes. He had found a way to get to the heart of their pride by elevating a woman's skills over theirs.

"I will allow one duel to go forward today. It will be chosen by a drawing. The others will be deferred until after the war is finished. Since honor is the underlying cause of all of these disputes, you will all swear to me *on your honor* that you will respect this agreement. If you do not, you will leave this camp immediately."

Ruggiero rose, "I swear on the honor of my noble ancestor Hector of Troy."

"I swear on the honor of all women," said Marfisa.

There was a pronounced silence as the remaining combatants cast wary looks at one another.

"I swear on Doralice's honor," said Mandricardo.

"*I* swear on Doralice's honor," growled Rodomont.

"I swear on the honor of my dead brother, Olibandro," said Sacripant.

Sabri took the six stones and placed them in a leather bag.

Akramont shook the bag, withdrew one stone and announced, "The duel will be between Rodomont and Mandricardo."

CHAPTER TWENTY-ONE

Ruggiero sat next to Marfisa in one of the reserved boxes in the old Roman arena. The box resembled a large brick horseshoe with a stone bench in the middle. The inside of the arena was less impressive than it appeared when he stood in a tunnel. Marble had been removed in many places, allowing weeds to grow among the gaps in the stonework. Orange and green-colored moss covered some of the stones while a few rogue trees had sprouted high up on the walls.

The men in the stands did not seem to care about the state of the arena; they clapped in time with the music. Matalista played a song on his lute while Feraguto banged out a rhythm on his drum.

Hala bore a large smile on her face as she walked toward them with two plates heaping with breads, cheeses, berries, and roasted drumsticks. "I saved some for you."

"That was kind of you," said Marfisa as she accepted a plate.

"I wanted to make sure my friends were taken care of," she said as she tucked a few stray curls of black hair under her golden headscarf.

"Thank you," said Ruggiero. His mouth watered as he surveyed the food. He bit into a drumstick and discovered it had a richer taste than he had expected. "What is this?"

"Duck. A farmer nearby raises them," said Hala. "However, there was only enough to go around for the dignitaries. I had to intervene before Feraguto and Gradasso ate them all."

Marfisa took a bite from her drumstick, closed her eyes, and had a blissful look on her face as she chewed. She opened her eyes and smiled at Hala. "I have never tasted anything like this. Thank you."

Hala grinned. "You are my friends. I want to help you in any way I can." She sat down on the end of the bench next to Marfisa. "Tell me what happened in my brother's tent. Is there going to be a duel?"

Ruggiero leaned forward and spoke in a low voice. "Between Rodomont, Mandricardo, Sacripant, Marfisa, and myself, there are six different disputes."

Hala's jaw dropped.

"Amir Akramont decided there would be only one duel before the war ended," he said.

"And?" asked Hala. "Who is going to fight?"

"Rodomont and Mandricardo," said Ruggiero.

"Good," said Hala with a harsh note in her voice. "I hope they kill each other."

Marfisa raised her eyebrows. "Why do you hate them so? Did they do anything to you?"

Ruggiero wondered the same thing. He stared at Hala, waiting for her reply. He clenched his fists at the thought of either of those brutal men harming such a sweet young girl.

"No. I only know them in passing," said Hala, "but I know they are bad men. Besides, both of you have quarrels with them. If they both died, my worries for your safety around them would go away."

"You are the first person to express any worry on my behalf. I am touched," said Marfisa.

"I am glad you do not know them," said Ruggiero, "for they *are* bad men."

Hala gave him a smile, blushed, and bowed her head. Ruggiero thought if he changed the subject, perhaps she would forget any embarrassment she felt around him.

"Hala," he said. "There are some women here whom I do not recognize. Perhaps you know them?"

"I do," she said, recovering her poise. "In the neighboring box, the woman holding a young girl on her lap is Rosenda, the wife of Amir Marsilio. I forget her daughter's name, but the young woman sitting next to her wearing yellow is her step-daughter, Fiordespina, she is Matalista's sister."

"Have you met her?" asked Ruggiero.

"No. She arrived a few days ago and is being kept inside her father's tent." She lowered her voice, "Rosenda is not happy Fiordespina is here. She tried having her moved to my tent, but Amir Marsilio refused. There is some scandal, but I do not know the details."

Ruggiero kept his face impassive.

"In the next box is a young woman wearing a green-and-red dress. She is Doralice of Granada."

"I pity her," said Marfisa. "She is being fought over by Rodomont and Mandricardo. I cannot imagine being married to either one of those beasts."

A worried look crossed Hala's face. "Nor could I."

The drumming grew louder and faster along with the clapping of the crowd. A sense of anticipation was building as the men stomped their feet with the beat of the drums. The attendees stood and roared their approval as Akramont emerged into the waning sunlight.

Outstretching his arms as if embracing the crowd, the amir bore a large smile on his face as he. "*Allahu Akbar!*"

"*Allahu Akbar!*" the crowd repeated in unison.

He gestured for everyone to be seated. Akramont repeated the gesture until the sound in the arena was lowered to a quiet buzz.

"This has been a long day for everyone," said the amir. "I trust you enjoyed your banquet?"

Cheers erupted.

"And the entertainment by Matalista and Feraguto?"

More cheers.

Akramont nodded. "There will be a duel for you to watch. A match to the death."

The crowd roared.

The amir smiled before raising a finger to his lips as a hush settled over the arena. "I will announce the duel, but first I must finish the introductions I started earlier."

The crowd groaned. The men did not care anymore about introductions. They wanted their blood sport.

Akramont had a smile on his lips as he made a motion with his hands to lower the sound again. "This must be done first, so that all the honored guests be recognized for their true worth by the full army."

The groans changed to grumbling. Ruggiero hoped Akramont would hurry up lest he lose the attention of the audience.

"Earlier I mentioned how the late Governor Garamanta was skilled in Divination. He predicted our victory over the Franks, but only if we had a certain warrior within our ranks. I sent expeditions scouring the mountains in my country to find the castle holding this young man, but they failed. It was only after an envoy returned from the East with a magical ring could we overcome the enchantments keeping him hidden in the mists."

Ruggiero felt a chill in his veins. All his doubts were removed. The amir was speaking about him.

Akramont raised an arm in Ruggiero's direction. "Please stand and be recognized. This is the prophesied warrior, Ruggiero. He was with our forces in our historic victory in Toulouse. Afterward, a wizard took him away, but that threat has passed. Ruggiero returned to us and will be instrumental in our victory against the Franks!"

Ruggiero's face burned as he nodded at the polite applause of the crowd. He sat back down and avoided looking at both Marfisa and Hala.

As the sound of the crowd dissipated, Akramont continued. "The last honored guest is a famous warrior you may have heard about, but wondered if she was merely legend or if she truly existed. I am referring to a woman who conquered seven separate kingdoms."

Whispers grew between the men trying to guess who Akramont was speaking about. The men started to crane their necks to get a better view at the woman sitting next to Ruggiero.

"From the East comes a warrior of unparalleled skill, unbridled fury, and natural beauty. I bring you the infamous Queen Marfisa."

Marfisa stood with the barest of smiles on her face as she basked in the cheers of adulation. Hoots and hollers were heard from men nearby, but she would not look in their direction. Akramont had sown the seeds of desire in the army regarding her renown, but did not mention her resolve to remain unmarried.

"Now, we will have our duel," announced Akramont. "The men who will be fighting to the death are Rodomont and Mandricardo. They are fighting over the honor of the fair Doralice of Granada."

Doralice was breathing heavily and looked as if she was about to be sick. Her father placed an arm on her back causing her to wince.

"Who do you think she is rooting for?" asked Hala.

"Neither," said Marfisa.

The two shared a laugh.

The crowd cheered as Mandricardo walked into the arena wearing the antique brass armor that had once belonged to Hector of Troy. Ruggiero snarled as he watched his noble ancestor's armor being worn by a scoundrel waving as he strode about the arena.

Rodomont emerged from another tunnel wearing green dragon-hide armor covering him from the top of his head down to his metal boots. Only his face and neck were exposed.

From a third tunnel came Gradasso and Sacripant still wearing their finery. Guards followed the two kings and handed them the swords to be used in the duel. Sacripant handed an overly large antique iron sword to Rodomont.

Gradasso stared at the blade in his hand, but did not give it to Mandricardo.

Two horses were led into the arena. Ruggiero became enraged when he saw his stolen horse being brought to Rodomont. It was outrageous for Frontino to be used in this duel. Biting his tongue, Ruggiero struggled to keep the solemn oath he made to the amir.

Sacripant bore a strange look on his face as he walked toward Frontino. He circled the golden horse bearing a white mane and tale before placing a hand on the horse's right flank. His face turned red and he yelled at Rodomont, "This is Frontalatte! How did you come upon my stolen horse, Frontalatte?"

"What?" said Rodomont.

"This is my horse. It was stolen from me in Cathay!"

Gradasso raised the sword above his head. "Durindana rightfully belongs to me! I will never surrender this blade to anyone."

CHAPTER TWENTY-TWO

R uggiero was in Amir Akramont's tent for the third time that day. He knelt on the ground with a guard on either side of him. The other "favored warriors" also knelt and were surrounded by burly soldiers in a semi-circle while Akramont paced. Marsilio and Sabri stood in the background.

The tension in the air grew as Akramont paced. His color was a sickly yellow under the glow of oil lamps. New creases appeared on his young face as if he aged ten years in a single day.

"Earlier there were six disagreements between five warriors," Akramont began. "Now we have eight between six warriors. Or, are there any more?"

Ruggiero began running the tally through his head and came up with the same number.

"I cannot have my finest warriors killing each other! I wanted *one* duel," he gestured with his index finger in the air. "Just one duel, and I could not get even that accomplished. Tonight we were to attack the walls of Paris as a united army with a single purpose. That was my intent. It will not happen, why? Because of your childish, selfish actions! I had to dismiss the warriors and return them to their routine guard duties rather than begin a full out assault."

Akramont's hands shook with rage. "It is like a Greek tragedy where the gods require a blood sacrifice before ships can set sail. I will not allow your petty differences to continue disrupting my war. I want you spilling Frankish blood, not each others'."

"Doralice's honor is not a petty difference," snarled Rodomont.

"Do not speak unless I call on you," barked Akramont. "That goes for the lot of you." He wiped his brow and took several deep breaths before continuing. "Gradasso, I recognize you spent years of your life and a fortune on a quest for Durindana. You did not come here because of my war effort, but let me remind you of one thing. Renaud and his horse Bayard are within the walls of Paris. So while you are in my camp, you will remain under my command."

Gradasso's eyes burned like embers as he stared at the coveted sword lying on a table across the room. Rodomont's sword was next to it.

"I understand and respect your claim for ownership of Durindana." Akramont turned his attention to Mandricardo. "I also remember your vow to reunite that famous sword with Hector of Troy's armor. You fulfilled that vow. Now you can bind another sword to your side."

"Over my dead body," said Mandricardo.

"That can be arranged," snapped Akramont. "For the time being, neither of you will have Durindana. It will be guarded and no one will use it. If I have to station fifty armed guards to protect one sword, I will. Do you understand me?"

Mandricardo and Gradasso looked at Akramont with resentment.

"Governor Sabri, please take the source of such discord and find a secure place for it until the war is over," said Akramont.

Sabri walked over to the table, retrieved the sword and left the tent without a word. Mandricardo and Gradasso both ground their teeth.

"In the meantime, I will have the finest sword in our stockpile from our fallen soldiers brought forth for you to use," said Akramont as he waved a hand dismissively at Mandricardo. He took a deep breath and turned to Sacripant. "Now. Tell me why you believe that horse was once yours."

Sacripant gave him a cold smile. "I saw Frontalatte being born. I would recognize him anywhere, but to assure myself — I checked his right flank. He bears the mark of all my horses." He raised his right hand and pointed to a signet ring.

Ruggiero squinted to see the marking on the ring and his heart sank.

"Frontalatte was stolen from me during the war in Cathay," said Sacripant. "He is the finest steed I have ever owned and I want him returned to me."

"Tell me the details surrounding the theft of your horse," said Akramont.

"I was dueling with Marfisa. We were on foot and a dark little man jumped on my horse before snatching the sword right out of her hand."

Akramont raised his eyebrows and looked at Marfisa. "Is this true?"

"It is," she snarled. "I chased that dwarf for days, trying to recover my sword. That is why my dispute with Sacripant is unsettled. Due to the actions of a conniving little thief."

Ruggiero lowered his head in shame.

"Now," said Akramont standing in front of him. "Can you tell me how Frontino came to be your horse?"

"The day of your tournament on Mount Carena," said Ruggiero. "I needed a horse and a sword to enter the contest. Governor Brunello presented them to me as gifts." He took a deep breath before turning to Marfisa. "Pray tell me what your stolen sword looks like."

"The insignia on the pommel matches my helmet and shield," she said. "There is a golden phoenix on its hilt."

Ruggiero gave a sigh of relief. "The hilt of my sword has a ruby on it." He turned to Akramont. "I believe King Sacripant's story. Frontino bears a mark on his right flank matching his ring."

Akramont snapped his fingers at his seneschal. "Fetch Brunello. Bind him and be sure to bring the sword he adores."

The man nodded and left on his task.

A tense silence hung in the air as Akramont attempted to pour himself a goblet of water. His hands shook as he held the pitcher and spilled water onto the tabletop. Without pausing to wipe up the spill, he took a deep breath and downed the entire contents in one smooth motion.

The tent flap opened and the seneschal led Brunello inside. The dwarf's arms were bound behind his back and he was forced to kneel before the amir.

Akramont turned to Sacripant. "Is this the man who stole your horse?"

"He is."

"Brunello, you stand accused of stealing King Sacripant's horse back in Cathay," said Akramont. "What say you to this charge?"

Brunello affected a humble smile. "I was doing your bidding my lord. You asked me to travel to Cathay and steal a ring from Princess Angelica. I had to sneak my way into a castle under siege. After I slipped the ring off her finger, I had to escape from the castle. Once outside, I discovered my horse was gone. How else could I return to you, but by stealing someone else's horse?" His smile faltered. "As soon as I saw a fine horse without a rider, I jumped on his back and returned to you without delay. I knew the fate of this war effort depended upon my returning to you as swiftly as possible."

Akramont ran a hand over his face and nodded. "I see your need for a horse, and I am grateful you returned to Bizerta as fast you did. I demonstrated my gratitude by bestowing the title Governor of Tingitana to you. Stealing a horse is normally a crime punishable by death, but in this case it was done to further our noble cause. Therefore, I rule the horse be returned to King Sacripant, after any personal belongings in the saddlebags are returned to Ruggiero. All disputes regarding this horse are now settled."

Rodomont spoke up, "Except for that insolent young — "

Akramont lifted a hand to silence him. "I spoke my last word on the subject. Any insults to pride will be dealt with on your own, but *after* my victory. Not before."

The amir closed his eyes, took a deep breath and returned his attention to Brunello. "There is another matter. That of a stolen sword."

Brunello fidgeted.

"Queen Marfisa accused you of stealing a sword out of her hand. She described the pommel as having a golden phoenix matching her helmet." Akramont gestured to his seneschal to hand him Brunello's sword. He examined the weapon and looked at the helmet on Marfisa's head. "They match. How do you answer her accusation?"

Brunello looked at his feet. "A similar pleading my lord. I could not sneak into Angelica's castle while carrying a large sword. I left it behind. I hid it, but not well enough because it was gone when I went to retrieve it." He shrugged his shoulders. "I was traveling through several armies' worth of soldiers and would be going through vast territories. After claiming a horse, I needed more than a dagger to defend myself for my long journey back to the Maghreb. I saw a distracted warrior and I seized what I needed."

"You admit to stealing her sword?" asked Akramont.

"Yes."

Marfisa growled at Brunello. "This vulgarian laughed at me."

Akramont silenced her with another motion of his hand. He set the stolen sword down on the table next to Durindana and Rodomont's sword. "Brunello, you admit you stole the horse you gave to Ruggiero. You also gave him a sword. Was that stolen as well?"

A small smile played on Brunello's lips. "Yes, my lord, it was."

"Do you know who you stole it from?"

Brunello grinned. "Orlando."

There was a collective gasp in the room.

"Orlando?" said Akramont, his mouth agape.

"How did you do that?" asked Gradasso.

Akramont glared at the king. "This is my interrogation." His face was stony as he turned back to Brunello. "How did you steal a sword from Orlando?"

The dwarf had an air of smugness about him. "Orlando was fighting another warrior and using his favored sword Durindana. I had long heard tales of this famous Frankish warrior and slowed down when I recognized his standard. I wanted to see for myself if he was worthy of the praise heaped on him. I saw a jeweled pommel of another sword attached to Orlando's saddlebags. I thought if he could have two swords, why not me? So I rode up next to him, detached the scabbard, and galloped away."

Brunello bore an expectant look on his face as if he thought Akramont would find his tale praiseworthy for his stealth and guile against an enemy.

"Why did you not keep Balisarda for yourself and give the other stolen blade to Ruggiero?" asked Akramont.

"Balisarda is too heavy for me to swing," said Brunello. "It hurt my back and arms when I used it."

Marfisa stepped forward and grabbed Brunello by his neck. "I warned you back in Cathay what I would do if I ever caught up with you."

Armed guards tried restraining her, but she began fighting. The helmet flew off her head and into a guard's face. She elbowed one guard squarely in his midsection and kneed another in his groin. The three soldiers were on the ground, writhing in pain as more guards advanced.

"Stop!" yelled Akramont. He raised a hand and the remaining guards took a step back and waited.

Marfisa's ornate braid had fallen apart, her hair stuck out at odd angles. She stood in an aggressive pose, her teeth bared, and a wild look in her eyes. "I will abide by the vow I made to you. I will postpone my quarrels with Mandricardo and Sacripant, but I cannot allow this vile creature to continue breathing. Allow me to seek my revenge with him or I will join Charlemagne's side tonight. Ask Sacripant about my changing sides in battle after having suffered insults to my honor."

Sacripant nodded. "She had been a staunch ally of mine, before, well...I forget why she turned on me."

Akramont's gaze went from Marfisa to Brunello and back again. There was a look of resignation on his face. "I will not allow his blood to be spilled in this tent or in this camp."

"Fair enough," she said as she reclaimed her sword. "I will take him outside the camp and take care to not stain the ground with his blood."

Marfisa dragged the whimpering Brunello out of the tent by the rope that bound him.

CHAPTER TWENTY-THREE

D oralice sat by herself on a cushion inside Amir Marsilio's tent while a few feet away from her, a group of noble women sat in a tight circle. She recognized Amir Akramont's wives from their introduction in the arena. They were speaking with a woman stroking the hair of a young girl curled in her lap. She assumed the woman was the wife of Amir Marsilio. The women nodded as she entered the tent, but did not invite her to join in their circle.

She wondered how long it would be before her father returned for her. Doralice began chewing her nails, a nervous habit she had given up years before. A cough made her look up.

"Do you remember me?" asked a young woman standing in the shadows. "We used to play together as children during royal banquets."

Doralice stared at a face that was both strange and familiar at the same time. After a few moments, she recalled events from years before. "You are Amir Marsilio's daughter. Fior...Fior..."

"Fiordespina," she finished, and sat down next to her.

"Of course. How could I forget?" Doralice felt a pang of guilt for not recognizing a childhood companion or remembering her name.

"Mandricardo and Rodomont were going to fight to the death over you," said Fiordespina. "What do you think will happen now?"

"I do not know."

"If you could choose between the two, who would it be?"

It was as if a snake coiled around her heart and began to squeeze. "Choose? Between those two?" Her breaths became shallow. She glanced over at the wives of Akramont and Marsilio, and knew any wrong word uttered in their presence might come back to haunt her in some fashion. This was a dangerous game with men who were killers. Her greatest desire was for both of them to rot in Hell. She shook her head and said, "I do not know."

Fiordespina nodded and stared at her feet. "I also wonder what my fate will be."

"What happened to you?" asked Doralice.

Fiordespina spoke in hushed tones. "I am no longer a maiden. I took a man to my bed."

"Were you in love?"

Fiordespina nodded as tears spilled down her cheeks.

Doralice hugged her and whispered, "I envy you. I wish I knew what love was."

Mandricardo had been a generous lover, but he demonstrated how selfish he could be the last time they coupled. He grabbed her without warning and unloaded his lust into her with as much sentimentality as an animal passing dung. Her needs were only important to him when they served a purpose. She could be rid of him, but then she would be at the mercy of Rodomont.

She clung to Fiordespina to provide some strength and comfort to her friend, but felt a lump rise in her throat as she fought an urge to cry. She could not allow her emotions free rein, lest she be unable to stop sobbing. Her fate would be sealed that night and she had to keep her wits about her. Or else, it might be the last night of her life.

Doralice broke her embrace of Fiordespina when she heard a rustling of the tent flap. Her father towered over her and his face appeared solemn. He held out a hand, beckoning her to stand.

"Amir Akramont wants to avoid bloodshed between all of his best commanders and would rather this disagreement be settled without a duel," said her father. "Your cycles have returned so there is no worry of your carrying a child by Mandricardo. This allows you to be free to marry either man, and tonight you will be asked to choose your husband. Amir Marsilio and I are in accord on the matter."

Doralice swallowed hard, afraid of what was coming next.

"You will choose Rodomont," he said. "Both are dangerous men, but Rodomont can summon armies of men from the Maghreb in a heartbeat whereas Mandricardo's armies are thousands of miles away. The security of my people is at stake."

She understood. Doralice remembered the day she made a wish to return to having decisions made for her. Her father gave her a directive, making her wonder if he considered her welfare and happiness when he selected her husband in the first place. She summoned the courage to ask a question vexing her for weeks.

"Tell me father, why was I brought here? I thought my marriage was to be after this war?"

"It was," he nodded. "However, things changed after the battle of Toulouse. I nearly died at the hands of Orlando."

Hearing the name Orlando sent a shiver down her spine. She had seen his fierce countenance and knew how lucky her father was to be alive.

"Rodomont saved my life," said her father. "He insisted that his reward be marrying you as soon as possible. I sent messengers with the orders for you to be brought here. Had I not done that, you would be in Granada and still a maiden."

The tent flap opened again and Amir Marsilio entered. "Governor Stordilano, you and your daughter are wanted in the royal tent."

CHAPTER TWENTY-FOUR

Akramont dismissed Gradasso, Sacripant, and Ruggiero. Their disputes had been dispatched for the time being, but he still had to resolve the issue of Doralice. As he stared into Mandricardo's eyes, he saw a smug attitude as if the Khan of Tartary thought he was superior to everyone else. Mandricardo returned from his fortnight away from the war looking well-fed and happy with himself. The man's red beard was trimmed and he no longer showed any signs of exhaustion from the long ride to Paris. Mandricardo provided nothing to this war; he came only with his title and his temper. Akramont wished Mandricardo had died in the planned duel with Rodomont, but unfortunately this redheaded miscreant was alive and still a continuing source of discord.

"I tried settling your dispute by a duel, but further disruptions regarding swords and horses made that impossible," said Akramont. "I changed my mind on how the matter should be resolved."

"How so?" asked Mandricardo.

"There is one person who should settle the matter," said Akramont.

Mandricardo and Rodomont looked bewildered.

"As you swore to me earlier today, I want you to affirm that you will honor the decision made in this matter and respect the wishes of the person who will determine which man will be recognized as Doralice's husband."

"Who will be the judge?" asked Rodomont.

"You must swear to me first," said Akramont.

"I swear on Doralice's honor," said Rodomont.

"I also swear on Doralice's honor," said Mandricardo.

Akramont exhaled. "It is fitting that you should both swear on her honor. For she is the one who will decide."

A look of panic crossed Rodomont's face. "What happens if she chooses him? Am I to be without a wife? After all I went through to become betrothed to her?"

"Should the need arise, there is another young woman who will be your bride," said Akramont.

Rodomont cocked his head. "A beautiful young woman of noble birth?"

"Of course."

"As long as I am provided with a comparable replacement, I will agree. However, I still want Doralice."

Mandricardo appeared calm. "I have no quarrels over her making the decision."

Akramont gestured toward his seneschal. Marsilio entered the tent followed by Stordilano and Doralice. The old man guided his daughter by the arm until she stood before Akramont. This was the first time Akramont had seen the woman up-close who caused such strife. She was a fair-skinned beauty with long black hair falling in waves. She had soft feminine curves and a quiet grace about her as she stood with her head held high.

"Doralice, two men claim you as their bride," said Akramont. "Both claims have merit, but only one man can be your husband. Since you will have to live with the decision, it should be you who makes that determination."

She gave him a slow nod never once looking at either Rodomont or Mandricardo.

"Before you announce your choice, you should hear both men plead their case," said Akramont. "You will first hear from Governor Rodomont."

He stepped forward and went down on one knee before her, taking her right hand in his. By the light of the oil lamps Rodomont's dragon hide armor gave a greenish cast to his dusky-colored skin. His time away from the camp had not been good for his health. His cheeks were hollowed out and he appeared gaunt. Rodomont's expression was so often in a scowl that his eyebrows appeared to be fused into one. His lips twitched into what looked like an attempt at a smile.

"My dearest lady, you stole my heart the first time I saw you. I was but one of your many suitors. I bargained with your father for over a year when he held a tournament to allow the victor to win your hand in marriage. With you as the prize, I was determined to win at all costs. I could not bear to lose, lest I lose my reason for living."

Akramont remembered hearing rumors about a death and several maimings at the tournament in Granada. Rodomont's winning at all costs was likely to have been an ugly spectacle to witness.

"My victory guaranteed my future happiness," said Rodomont. "To proclaim my love for you to the world, I changed my standard to display your beautiful face."

Doralice turned toward him, but she did not meet his gaze.

"I wanted our life together to begin this spring, but your father was concerned with your safety. He insisted our wedding be held after the conclusion of this war." Rodomont swallowed hard. "Yet, I insisted you be brought here so you would be here to share in our victory. Had I known you would not be protected properly, I would have met your ship when it docked on the western coast of Francia."

He bit his lower lip. "As soon as your man servant came to me and told me you were in danger, I left on your rescue. I abandoned the battle here in Paris to defend your honor. I did not rest until I found you. It grieves me that I was unable to stop you from being abducted and ravished," his voice cracked and he paused to recover. "In time, all that unpleasantness will be forgotten as we are surrounded by our children. You shall be exalted as my wife and live in a palace overlooking the sea." Rodomont strained to give her another smile. "We shall visit your father frequently so he may be a doting grandfather."

Rodomont stood, walked to the table and picked up his sword. Three guards followed him, ready to draw their own weapons. He shook his head, "I want to pledge my love and wish to do it on the one possession I hold most dear. I already swore on her honor to Amir Akramont that I would not attack Mandricardo."

Akramont nodded and the guards allowed Rodomont to keep his weapon. He returned on bended knee before Doralice.

"I, Rodomont, Governor of Sarza, pledge to Doralice of Granada my eternal love, my devotion. I swear on the sword of my noble ancestors that ensuring your safety and happiness will be my most solemn duty."

Stordilano bore a satisfied look upon his face. Akramont was surprised at the depths of feelings expressed by Rodomont. He was more than a godless commander with a bloodlust for revenge, he was also a man wounded by the torture of love. However, this outpouring of emotion did not create even a flicker of a response on the face of the woman he adored.

"It is now time to hear from Mandricardo," said Akramont.

Rodomont nodded, sheathed his sword, and walked over to stand between Marsilio and Stordilano.

Mandricardo stepped forward and stood a few feet in front of Doralice. He gave her a rakish smile. Her eyes narrowed as if she were challenging him.

"Doralice," he said, his voice as soft as silk. "I remember admiring your image on Rodomont's banner. I wondered how it measured up to its model. I realized once I saw you that no artist could ever capture the full essence of your beauty in an object. I have known many women, but none can compare to your beauty, grace...and passion."

A blush arose on her cheeks.

"That fateful day when I came upon your escorts, my first thought was to spend the night and a meal with fellow soldiers. Then I learned their mission was not as reinforcements for the war, but to safeguard your passage. I asked to make your acquaintance so I could judge the quality of your likeness to the silken replica. I did not expect a simple request would be received in a combative manner. Nor could I have known how I would react when I finally saw you. I realized then, that I would have moved Heaven and Earth to call you my own. The happiest moment of my life was the first morning when I woke with you in bed by my side."

Mandricardo gave a long sigh, shifted his weight, and locked eyes with her. There was a subtle change on Doralice's face. Gone was the stony resolve she bore when Rodomont spoke, it was replaced by the familiarity of a woman gazing at her lover. Akramont knew from her reaction that Doralice had *not* been ravished by Mandricardo; she had been seduced. His boasting about his prowess in bed was not done merely to goad Rodomont, but was a crude explanation of the nature of his relationship with her.

Stordilano looked shocked, while Rodomont's teeth were bared. Doralice appeared not to notice their reactions as her attention was focused solely on Mandricardo.

"I swore to honor and respect your decision if you should choose Rodomont as your husband." He gave her a sad shake of his head. "However, I hope that does not happen, for your sake and for mine. I do not wish for you to be in the arms of a coarse, ugly man who lacks the ability to be tender with a woman. As for me, my heart would have to subsist on memories of our too few days and nights we spent in each other's arms. I would spend the rest of my life searching in vain for another woman who could match your beauty, charms, and grace."

Mandricardo licked his lips. "I miss having you by my side and in my bed. I hope you choose to share your life with me. You know *I* can be a gentle and generous lover. I vow as your husband to satisfy all of your wants, needs, and desires."

He stepped back and stood far apart from where Rodomont stood. Doralice's eyes followed Mandricardo.

"You heard from both men," said Akramont, "it is time you announce your decision."

She turned and looked at him. "Is this truly my decision to make?"

"Yes, it is."

A pained expression came over Doralice, before she covered her face with her hands. Her breathing became labored. All eyes were upon her, but she refused to look at anyone.

This was not going as planned. Doralice was supposed to follow her father's orders and choose Rodomont. Instead, it appeared she was deciding her own fate. *Look at your father, look at your father,* willed Akramont.

Doralice took a deep breath, opened her eyes, and brushed tears from her cheeks. "I stand by the decision I made two weeks ago when I agreed to become Mandricardo's wife and queen."

He placed an arm around her shoulders as they walked out of the tent together.

CHAPTER TWENTY-FIVE

Akramont waited for Rodomont to explode. A simmering fury shone in his eyes, but the governor kept his temper in check. Stordilano quailed at the look on Rodomont's face, bowed his head, and left the tent without saying a word.

"Who is the replacement bride you spoke of?" said Rodomont. "Bring her to me."

"It has been a long day, perhaps we should save that subject for the morning," said Marsilio.

"No!" roared Rodomont. "Mandricardo is going to bed Doralice tonight. I insist on the same right to bed a bride tonight."

Marsilio furrowed his brow. He turned and spoke with his stern looking attendant who left the tent. "Your bride is being sent for."

"Who is she?"

"My eldest daughter, Fiordespina," said Marsilio.

"What? That lifeless girl moping around your tent? How can you possibly think she is a fitting replacement for Doralice?"

"She is my daughter," Marsilio said, with a warning tone in his voice. "She is my pride and joy. Fiordespina is a beautiful and charming young woman. Any man would be lucky to have her as his wife."

"The entire camp knows she played the harlot with a Frank and her belly is filled with a bastard."

"There are ways to clear a blocked womb," said Marsilio. "After her courses are restored, as long as only your seed is planted in her womb you will be assured that you are the father of her children."

Rodomont scoffed. "Her reputation is already in question. You cannot remove such tarnish."

Akramont's previous opinion of Rodomont came flooding back. The man who professed a deep and abiding love for Doralice was gone and replaced once again by a rude, boorish man with no respect for anyone but himself. Akramont pitied any woman having to lie with Rodomont. Stories abounded of how rough Rodomont had been with Frankish women during the looting of villages. Some women had been beaten to death when they resisted him. Fiordespina deserved better.

"She is a beautiful and fertile woman," said Marsilio. "By marrying her you will be allied with the Amir of Al-Andalus. No one will dare question your choice in brides."

"I would accept her if she was still a virgin," said Rodomont.

"If she was still a virgin, she would not be offered to you."

"Why? Am I not good enough for her?" asked Rodomont, his fists clenched.

"She was to have been Akramont's third wife."

"Now I understand. Since your daughter whored around, she is no longer suitable for an amir, but is still worthy of a lowly governor." Rodomont shook his head. "No. I will not take your scraps. I insist on the finest maiden available."

"Queen Marfisa will not marry you," said Akramont.

"Bah! Not that harridan, I want the little bird you paraded around earlier today. I want Hala."

Akramont opened his mouth to speak, but no words came out. The thought of his little sister with Rodomont was horrifying. A gentle and pure soul as Hala would be destroyed by his cruelty.

"Well? How much do you value my loyalty and contributions to your war effort?" asked Rodomont. "This afternoon you told the entire army I was your most stalwart ally in this campaign and if there was only one Muslim warrior the people of Paris knew by name, it was mine. Do I not deserve the best bride? Am I not good enough to marry your sister? Or, do I only rate being offered used up whores?"

Marsilio held his head high.

Akramont swallowed hard. "Hala is not old enough to marry, she is still a child."

"Then let us become betrothed and after her first courses, we will be married."

"No."

"I see," said Rodomont. "You promised her to a toothless old man who played with chicken bones and uttered superstitious prophecies, but you will not let her enter into a betrothal with me. Maybe you are saving her for your Golden Boy." He shook his head in disgust. "That whelp is not worthy of carrying my banner let alone marrying your sister. My loyalty means nothing to you."

Fiordespina entered the tent. She was a petite young woman with a curvaceous figure and long black hair. Akramont could see she had a pleasing face, but red and swollen eyes marred her beauty. She was led to stand near her father.

"Fiordespina," said Marsilio, "you will marry Governor Rodomont of Sarza."

She convulsed as if she was about to be sick.

Rodomont looked at her with disdain. "You offer me half a woman as a bride. She weeps for her lover. Have him marry this slut."

"That is not possible."

"Why not?"

"I had the infidel put to death by fire," said Marsilio.

Fiordespina wailed in agony, the tent became filled with the sounds of her anguish. She slipped to the ground, wrapped her arms around her knees, and began sobbing.

"What else would I have to do for you in order to be offered at least one and a half wives?" demanded Rodomont. "You were proud to show the entire army your two beautiful wives. Why am I not being offered this half of a woman *and* Hala?"

"This is our offer," said Akramont.

Rodomont snarled.

"Fiordespina," Marsilio commanded. "Rise and meet your husband."

She remained kneeling, her forehead touching the rug. She lifted her head slightly to speak, but did not meet anyone's gaze. "I would rather die than marry that man."

"As you wish," said Rodomont.

He unsheathed his sword and beheaded Fiordespina.

CHAPTER TWENTY-SIX

A kramont was in shock. Blood gushed out of Fiordespina's neck and pooled on the floor of the tent. Marsilio said the word "no" and the sound hung in the air as he went toward his daughter, but it seemed as though he was moving through water.

Rodomont sneered at the dead girl's body before turning on his heel. Two guards drew their swords, but were cut down by him. One guard lost his right arm, the other his head.

Vomit rose inside Akramont's mouth. He swallowed it down and found his voice to yell, "Stop him!"

Rodomont left the tent and could be heard running. Other guards followed in pursuit, while the wounded soldier was led away to the surgeons' tent.

Marsilio was on his knees, weeping and cradling his daughter's lifeless body as her blood covered him from head to toe. Akramont fought the urge to weep. The morning began with such promise, and he had been filled with anticipation of the glory awaiting him with victory over the Franks. Now he feared he was no longer in control of an unruly group of warriors. For the first time since the war began, he wondered if he had been wrong to call for this campaign. Perhaps he lacked the leadership skills of his father and his ancestors.

Sabri entered the tent and stood at the opening, surveying the scene. "Rodomont?"

Akramont nodded.

A single tear fell down Sabri's cheek as he bowed his head and said a prayer under his breath. After a long pause he said, "Durindana has been secured for now." He placed a comforting hand on Akramont's shoulder. "Come with me, we should allow Amir Marsilio to grieve for his daughter in private."

Akramont followed Sabri into the cool night air. They walked through rows of tents, and made so many turns Akramont thought he would be unable to find the way back to his own tent. Not that he wished to return to that place of death.

"Here we are," said Sabri as he ushered Akramont inside a tent. "Make yourself at home. I shall have tea brought to you while I go see what happened with Rodomont. My seneschal will bring your wives and your belongings here. My tent will now be yours as well. If you need anything, my personal guards stationed outside will assist you."

The tent was not as large as his, but there was a comforting feel about it. There were carpets on the floor, a table with four chairs, and a curtain to provide privacy for the sleeping area. Akramont sat down and placed his head in his hands and stared absentmindedly at a pattern on a rug until his eyes lost their focus. He had lost Allah's favor in this mission and blamed it on Rodomont's sacrilegious acts in a church in Paris. Rodomont even bragged about wanting to go to Rome and devour the beating heart of the pope. Those acts must have offended Allah.

A young man quietly entered the tent, placed a tea set on the table, and poured a cup for Akramont. The young man then bowed and left the tent without saying a word.

Akramont closed his eyes and savored the taste of mint as he sipped his tea. He allowed his mind to wander, imagining he stood on a beach near his palace in Bizerta. The rhythmic lapping of water on the seashore had a calming effect. It reminded him of the eternal nature and power of God. His mission was to help spread Islam throughout Europe. It was a noble cause and its worthiness could not be disputed.

Staying within the walls of his palace and playing the role of administrator of the Maghreb for the caliph was insufficient to demonstrate his devotion to Allah. That type of complacency also defied his family's heritage and legacy of amassing power through the conquest of war. Akramont felt compelled to initiate this war by the frequent recitations of the heroic tales of his father, Troiano, his uncle, Almont, his grandfather, Agolant, and especially those of his noble ancestor, Alexander the Great. He thought back to the day when he gathered all the governors of the Maghreb and announced his plans to invade the Frankish Empire. Rodomont was the first to respond. He stood and vowed to raise his army that same day and pledged his undying support for the effort.

Akramont realized too late that Rodomont was a bloodthirsty maniac. Perhaps Allah would once again show His favor if the campaign were rid of godless warriors. A plan began forming in Akramont's mind.

He was startled when Sabri returned and sat down in the chair next to him.

"Rodomont is an evil *jinn* who cannot be contained," said Sabri. "Before I returned to your tent I saw Mandricardo walking arm-and-arm with Doralice. I knew then that our plans did not work out as expected and Rodomont's temper would be a threat to the entire camp." He poured himself a cup of tea and drank. "I found an empty tent for Mandricardo and Doralice to stay. One where Rodomont would not find them easily." Sabri gave a long sigh. "Rodomont left the camp."

A sense of relief washed over Akramont. "Praise be."

"He left on the horse claimed by both Ruggiero and Sacripant."

A stabbing pain in Akramont's temple made him wince.

"Rodomont killed five other soldiers during his escape," said Sabri. "Sacripant stationed his own guards over the horse and when the king learned what happened, he set off in pursuit of Rodomont. So we lost two of the warriors you honored earlier today."

"And Sacripant's troops? Did they leave as well?"

"No, they are unaware their king has left them behind," said Sabri. "Hopefully we can convince them to remain here and wait for word from their sovereign, which might never come."

"Two down, two to go," said Akramont under his breath.

"It will not be long before Gradasso forces your hand regarding Durindana," warned Sabri. "And with Marfisa's insubordination tonight regarding Brunello, I think it would be wise to rid ourselves of the many disputes with Mandricardo."

"What do you propose?" asked Akramont.

"Mandricardo should face one warrior who will fight for the honor of all who have quarrels with him."

"See to it. The duel shall happen at noon," said Akramont. "There is only one warrior we can ask to be our champion."

Sabri nodded. "I shall handle all the arrangements."

CHAPTER TWENTY-SEVEN

Rodomont kicked his horse again, urging it to run faster in the dark night. The dirt road in the countryside was rough, but he could still find his way by the light of the nearly full moon. No matter the speed or how far he rode from Paris, he could not put any distance between himself and his troubles.

He made a vow on Doralice's honor, but discovered she had no honor and was a faithless, disloyal whore. He would make her understand the pain she caused him and regret her betrayal. Revenge was his new mission in life. He would get his revenge against Mandricardo, Doralice, and that insolent child, Ruggiero. Rodomont's fortunes changed that fateful day when he first met the young whelp outside Toulouse. He would go to his grave before breathing a word of the humiliation he suffered by Ruggiero. He almost avenged himself when they met again in the Frankish village, but their fight was interrupted.

Ruggiero nearly died fighting over a damned horse. The horse he was still riding. Rodomont cared nothing about animals. They were beasts to use and replace. Ah, but Ruggiero cared. The boy was a fool about this horse and that is why Rodomont went out of his way back at the camp to retrieve Ruggiero's prized mount instead of taking the nearest horse to make his escape. He had killed more soldiers in seizing Ruggiero's horse.

That disrespectful child will come running when he learns I have his precious Frontino. The thought made him smile. He would have his revenge. He would have his revenge on Mandricardo, on Doralice, and on Ruggiero.

Rodomont knew Mandricardo would soon tire of the war and leave for his kingdom of Tartary. Akramont's war had been incidental for Mandricardo's mission to avenge the death of his father. Now that he had Doralice, there was no need for the Tartar to stay and fight the Franks. Mandricardo would journey back to his kingdom with Doralice as his prize while Rodomont would be waiting for them to pass his way.

In the distance, a tavern stood on the outside of a small village. It represented a warm meal and a place to spend the night. As he slowed his horse to a canter, he heard hoofbeats behind him. He looked back and recognized the rider was King Sacripant. Rodomont turned his horse around and withdrew his sword.

"Surrender that horse," yelled Sacripant as he drew near. "Frontalatte is mine."

"He is a fine animal, but is he worth dying over?"

"Take this horse, I want Frontalatte back."

"No," sneered Rodomont.

"He is mine!" bellowed Sacripant as he withdrew his sword.

"He was yours, but a damned dwarf stole him while you were fighting with a girl. You want him back? You must kill me."

Rodomont narrowed his eyes as he prepared for Sacripant to strike. He no longer cared if he lived or died. Doralice's rejection removed his desire for a future. He once dreamed of a life with her, raising sons to continue his family line, but now those hopes were gone. Should he die in a duel of honor, he would be put out of his misery.

Sacripant swung his sword and Rodomont deflected it with his shield. The contact lit a fire inside of him. He channeled his fury and frustration into a series of sword strikes causing sparks to fly into the night sky. Engaging in a fight lifted the darkness over his heart. He felt alive again.

"You are too old to fight!" said Rodomont.

Clang.

"I am a veteran warrior," said Sacripant.

Clang.

"You are fat."

Clang.

"Give me my horse back."

Clang.

"No."

Clang.

"Why? You care nothing about him."

Clang.

"True, but I want revenge."

Clang.

"What did I do to you?" asked Sacripant.

Clang.

Rodomont hooked the crosshatch of his sword onto Sacripant's blade, causing them to pause in the fighting.

"I seek revenge against Ruggiero. He will honor your claim for this horse, but he cannot abide the thought of me having the horse."

He released the hold and swung again at Sacripant.

Clang.

"Ruggiero will come after me," said Rodomont. "Then I will have my revenge."

Clang.

"What did he do?"

Clang.

"He insulted my honor."

Clang.

Sacripant snorted. "You have no honor."

Rodomont saw his opponent become distracted and slashed his sword across Sacripant's throat.

"Neither did you," said Rodomont as he watched his rival fall to the ground.

He dismounted and dragged the body off the road. Rodomont grabbed Sacripant's leather purse and two golden rings before walking the two horses to the nearby inn where he would enjoy a meal and a room for the night.

CHAPTER TWENTY-EIGHT

*D*oralice's heart was paralyzed with fear at the sound of thundering hoofbeats. Somehow she knew Rodomont was coming for her.
Ka THUMP. Ka THUMP. Ka THUMP.

A cold breeze chilled her. She stood in the moonlight, barefoot, and wearing only a thin linen shift. Mandricardo was dressed in his armor, mounted on his horse, and held his sword aloft as he circled around Ruggiero on horseback. They were engaged in a dance of death.

"He is coming," Doralice said.

Mandricardo either did not hear her or did not care. His sword clashed against Ruggiero's in midair.

"Rodomont is coming to kill me," she said, her voice beginning to rise.

Mandricardo and Ruggiero exchanged blows again and again. The galloping horse became visible as it rode through a thick mist. Rodomont held his massive sword aloft with one hand and a bag in the other. He bore an evil grin on his face as the standard attached to his saddle fluttered in the wind. It was in tatters and the painted image of her face on the silken banner appeared to have blood stains smeared on it.

She trembled as Rodomont stopped his horse in front of her. Doralice turned to plead for help from her husband, only to watch Ruggiero use a knife to stab Mandricardo. Blood coursed from the wound as well as Mandricardo's mouth. He dismounted, took three steps toward her before falling down dead.

Doralice screamed. Rodomont's eyes glowed like red-hot embers. As he turned his bag upside down, a head bounced on the ground, rolled and stopped on Doralice's bare feet. She screamed again as she recognized the face of Fiordespina.

"What is it?" asked Mandricardo.

Doralice opened her eyes. She was lying in bed next to her husband.

"What is wrong?" he asked.

Her heart still pounded. She sat up and tried to speak, but could only manage shallow breaths at first. Tears welled in her eyes as Mandricardo took her hands in his.

"Tell me what disturbed you, my love." His voice was warm and comforting.

"Rodomont," was all she could say.

Mandricardo pulled her into his arms. She wore the simple linen shift in her nightmare, but her husband was nude. The heat from his body warmed her and the fear from her dream began melting away. He began touching her curves in an intimate fashion as she sensed his arousal taking shape.

"He came back for me," she said, breaking the mood. "He was about to kill me."

Mandricardo kissed her forehead. "I shall protect you, so let your worries take their leave."

She closed her eyes, trying to calm her fears, but the image of her husband's dead body flashed before her. "I also saw..." she choked, unable to speak about his death in her dream.

He began kissing her neck. Her visions meant nothing to him and any further mention of them would serve as a distraction from his lovemaking.

"Pardon my intrusion, Khan Mandricardo," came a voice from outside the tent, "but I have important news for you."

"Can it wait?" he asked.

"No, I bear an urgent message from Amir Akramont."

"Give us a few moments." Mandricardo threw off the covers, put on breeches and a tunic. Doralice began making the bed.

"Why bother?" said Mandricardo with a rakish smile. "After hearing the message, we shall continue where we left off and consummate our marriage again. Leaving no doubts as to the legitimacy of our union."

Doralice nodded and sat in a chair. She wanted to change into a proper dress, but knew her husband would disapprove of the time it would take.

Mandricardo opened the tent flap ushering in the morning light and Governor Sabri. The elderly man appeared exhausted and bore a somber look on his face.

"*Salaam*, Mandricardo. *Salaam*, Doralice."

"*Salaam*, Sabri," said Mandricardo. "Thank you once again for finding a tent for us."

Sabri nodded. "It would not have been proper for you and your wife to stay with me in my tent. I shall arrange for your belongings to be brought here." There was a long pause before he said, "Before I deliver my message to you from Amir Akramont, I must tell you what transpired last night. Both Governor Rodomont and King Sacripant left the camp. I doubt either will return."

"Why did Sacripant leave?" asked Mandricardo.

"Rodomont stole Sacripant's horse."

Mandricardo nodded, as if that reason made sense. Doralice knew Sacripant had dozens of horses, and to abandon his army over one horse seemed sheer madness.

"Why did Rodomont leave?" she asked.

Sabri turned his attention to her. "Rodomont was upset by your rejection."

"I thought there was a replacement bride for him," said Mandricardo.

Doralice was surprised at that pronouncement.

"There was," said Sabri, "but it was not an acceptable match for either party."

Mandricardo appeared nonplussed.

"Who was she?" asked Doralice.

Sabri did not answer.

"Fiordespina?"

"Yes."

There was a sharp stabbing in her heart. Doralice needed to comfort her friend. She reached for the red and green silk dress she had worn the day before, as it was the only other item of her clothing in the tent. She made a move to put it on. "I must see how she is faring."

"You cannot," said Sabri.

"Why not? Is she in seclusion?"

His eyes looked sorrowful. "No. Rodomont reacted badly to being rejected twice in one night."

"What happened?" she asked, setting the dress aside as her throat became dry.

"She said she would rather die than marry him," said Sabri, who paused before taking a deep breath. "Rodomont granted her wish."

"Noooooo," she wailed as her knees buckled. Mandricardo caught her before she fell on the ground and laid her on the mattress.

Doralice looked up at her husband's concerned face. "I saw Fiordespina's severed head in my dream."

"It might have been you," Mandricardo whispered in her ear.

He laid down next to her. She shivered as he stroked her hair, trying to calm her.

"She was my friend. We played together as children," said Doralice.

"I offer my condolences for your loss," said Sabri. "It is a great tragedy for Amir Marsilio."

"Thank you for telling us," said Mandricardo. "Now if you will excuse us, I need to comfort my wife."

"I will take my leave soon, but there is more I must tell you."

Dread filled Doralice's stomach. She sensed the news would bring about the other half of her dream.

"Amir Akramont recognizes the disputes surrounding you remain unsettled and will likely cause strife within the ranks, especially as to the rightful ownership of Durindana," said Sabri. "Therefore, he decided you will fight in one duel with a champion who will represent the grievances of Gradasso, Marfisa, Ruggiero, as well as Sacripant."

Doralice closed her eyes and chanted under her breath, "Not Ruggiero. Not Ruggiero. Not Ruggiero."

"When will this occur?" asked Mandricardo.

"After today's noontime prayer in the old Roman arena."

"And who will I be fighting?"

"Ruggiero," said Sabri.

Doralice's heart sank. Her nightmare was becoming reality.

"I accept," said Mandricardo.

"I will notify Amir Akramont."

"I demand Durindana be restored to me for this fight."

Sabri shook his head. "Not possible. Once this fight is over, the sword will be awarded to either you or Gradasso. Depending on the victor."

"I insist Ruggiero not be allowed to use his sword, since it was stolen from Orlando. If I cannot use a sword owned by Orlando, then he cannot either."

Sabri nodded. "That is a fair request. Both of you will be given equal swords for the fight." He bowed and left the tent.

"Husband," Doralice said, as she sat up. "Please do not fight Ruggiero. I would rather we leave right now for Tartary."

Mandricardo kissed her on the forehead. "I cannot leave without Durindana."

"It is just a sword. You can get another. You won my hand in marriage, please let us start our life far away from here."

"Need I remind you I set out on this mission without any weapons, any armor, horse or money? I vowed to seize whatever I needed on my way to avenge my father's death. On my journey I won the armor once worn by Hector of Troy, as well as his famous sword Durindana, and a renowned destrier once owned by the great Almont." She felt his warm hand through the thin fabric of her nightgown. He cupped her left breast with one hand and teased her nipple with his thumb. Her body began responding to his touch. "I have everything in the world to live for; Ruggiero has nothing. I am a powerful khan of a vast kingdom; he holds no title or lands. I married the most beautiful and sensuous woman in the world. I doubt that man-child has ever been with a woman. Without lands, money or title, he has no chance of marrying a woman of nobility. The boy has no means or purpose. I am not worried."

She looked away. How could she make him understand that she foresaw his death?

"I am thinking of you and our future together," he said. "A king is only as strong as his reputation. Should I run away from this challenge, the word will be spread far and wide. I will be thought of as weak and a coward. Tartary would suffer from repeated invasions. I will fight this young cub out of the love and respect I hold for you. After Durindana is returned to me, we shall leave for Tartary. I care nothing about Akramont's war."

He removed his clothing and tugged at the bottom of her shift.

"What if you die?" she asked.

"I bested Gradasso and Orlando. I will not die fighting a boy."

"But what if you do? What will become of me?" she swallowed hard. "I am your wife. I am now the Queen of Tartary, but being your widow will mean nothing if you die here today. I do not even know where Tartary is. I miscarried after that long ride, so I am no longer carrying your heir. It is too soon for me to conceive again, so I cannot become a regent."

His mood darkened. "If by some miracle Ruggiero kills me, you would be free to marry again."

Doralice gave a hysterical laugh. "Who would marry me? I would be a young widow with a reputation of being abducted, ravished, and returned to my father only to defy him. No one would want me as his wife." She bit her lip before continuing. "Last night my father ordered me to choose Rodomont as my husband. If you die, I could be put to death for disobeying my father."

He rolled his eyes. "I told you, I am not going to die."

She took his face in her hands. "I saw you die in my dream," she said, her voice cracking. "I watched you fight with Ruggiero, and you were killed."

He gave her a patronizing smile. "It was only a dream."

"It was a prophetic dream! I saw both Fiordespina's death and yours in that dream. I beg of you, let us leave here while we can. Maybe we can change our stars."

Mandricardo removed her hands from his face and placed them under the covers. "If I am to die this day, let me first demonstrate to my wife how much I love her."

Doralice choked back tears as he pushed her down on the bed and parted her legs with his knees. His pride prevented him from listening to reason and she would once again surrender herself to his desires. It might be the last time she ever did.

CHAPTER TWENTY-NINE

Ruggiero sat on a prayer rug in Gradasso's tent absorbing the news from Governor Sabri. Fiordespina's murder devastated him. He failed Richardet. She died believing her lover was dead. He could not even summon anger toward Rodomont, instead he felt numb. That man was a demon who needed to be driven to Hell.

Hopefully Sacripant would see that through. Ruggiero understood why Sacripant left the camp to reclaim his horse, Frontino. Ruggiero had been fortunate to ride such a fine destrier, and recognized Sacripant as the rightful owner. Rodomont's theft of Frontino as he left the camp showed his contempt for others. He ignored Sacripant's claim to ownership while trying to provoke Ruggiero to follow him. And he showed utter disrespect toward Akramont's ruling on the proper ownership of the horse.

However, Ruggiero needed to focus on his duel with Mandricardo in a few hours. He ignored Gradasso who droned on about the two times he dueled with Mandricardo.

"Mandricardo must not be allowed to use Durindana," said Gradasso as he paced. "That sword belongs to me. I won it by force when I took Charlemagne hostage last year. You may have his armor after you kill him, but I shall be awarded Durindana."

Ruggiero closed his eyes and imagined himself in the center of the old Roman arena. Mandricardo was dressed in the antique bronze cuirass adorned with a silver eagle on a field of blue. Their swords clashed in mid-air.

He said a silent prayer asking for divine guidance in his upcoming fight. Ruggiero also sent a mental message to Bradamante. "My beloved, today I will be fighting for honor. I will duel against a man without honor who bears the standard of my noble ancestor Hector of Troy. Inshallah, I shall soon find a way to break my bonds to Akramont allowing us to be married."

CHAPTER THIRTY

D oralice sat alone on a stone bench in one of the boxes reserved for nobility. She was wearing the same red and green silk dress she wore the day before. The previous day had started out as a festive occasion, even though she had been filled with dread and uncertainty. At least she felt comforted by sitting next to her father. Now her father sat elsewhere. She dared not look for him, for she did not want to see disappointment in his eyes.

The overcast sky reflected her mood. Her woolen shawl was no match for the cold wind whipping through the arena. Fear gripped her heart. She had difficulty taking deep breaths as the details of her nightmare flashed before her eyes. Nothing she said to Mandricardo made any difference. He was unyielding. All she could do was wait and hope her husband survived the duel.

Governor Sabri walked out in the middle of the arena, raised his arms signaling the gathered crowd to be quiet. "Amir Akramont called us to Francia to further the spread of Islam and the wisdom of the Prophet Muhammad, peace be upon him. We are not here to fight with each other, yet as was demonstrated here yesterday — there is bad blood between our most valiant warriors. These conflicts threaten to disrupt our mission. Therefore, we must put an end to them so we can concentrate on our unified fighting of the Franks. Before rumors spread, I will acknowledge that two of the honored leaders from yesterday's celebration left the camp during the night."

A wave of murmuring washed through the crowd.

Sabri motioned for silence. "Both Governor Rodomont and King Sacripant left for personal reasons. The amir is grateful both commanders' forces have remained and are committed to fulfilling our honorable mission. Today, Ruggiero shall serve as champion for four separate disputes against Khan Mandricardo. This will settle all of the remaining conflicts between the aggrieved parties."

A ripple of excitement moved through the crowd. It was as if the sand of the arena eagerly awaited another blood offering to the old pagan gods. Doralice felt bile rise in the back of her throat. She placed her hands over her face and tried to settle her breathing.

The crowd roared its approval and she instinctively lowered her hands to see her husband ride into the center of the arena on the back of Orlando's black horse Brigliodoro. Mandricardo basked in the adulation as he raised his sword in the air to a rousing cheer from the men in the stands.

Ruggiero came out of a tunnel riding on the back of a pitch-black stallion. Doralice felt there was something disturbing about Ruggiero's horse. It snorted and she could have sworn red flames flickered out of its nostrils. She rubbed her eyes to clear her vision. Ruggiero's sword and shield were at the ready, but he did not engage with the crowd. He appeared focused on the task at hand. The crowd roared again knowing there would soon be blood spilled.

Squires handed the two warriors lances. Doralice bowed her head and said a quick prayer for Mandricardo's safety hoping she still had some grace in the eyes of Allah. She raised her head in time to see the fight begin and the horses charge against one another.

The lances shattered against the shields with pieces of wood flying high.

The men threw aside their broken lances and drew out their swords. Doralice flinched with every clink of the swords against one another and every clank of swords against shields. Mandricardo raised his right arm above his head as he prepared to bring his sword down upon his opponent's head. Ruggiero seized the opportunity and stabbed Mandricardo under his arm, an area not covered by his bronze cuirass. Doralice winced as blood gushed from the wound.

Mandricardo cast his shield onto the ground as he bellowed, "You will die!"

Ruggiero turned his horse around and had a defiant air about him. "You threw my noble ancestor's shield away, proving you do not have the honor to bear that eagle."

Mandricardo charged his horse and brought his sword down with a two-handed strike on Ruggiero's back. The young knight dropped his sword and slumped forward as his horse bore him away to the other side of the arena. Mandricardo kicked the flanks of his horse in pursuit.

Doralice stood up straining to see what was happening on the other side of the arena. Tall men stood in the rows before her, blocking her view. She climbed on top of the stone bench and could see Mandricardo's back as he repeatedly struck his opponent. Ruggiero fell from his horse. The crowd roared their approval as Doralice raced down the stone steps to congratulate her husband. As she ran across the sand in the center of the arena, her eyes welled with tears. Mandricardo had dismounted and walked towards her. As her tears fell, her vision became clearer. It was then she saw blood streaming down the front of his armor and the handle of a dagger near his collarbone.

She screamed as he faltered and collapsed on the ground. Doralice fell to her knees, and cradled his head in her lap. His warm blood soaked her dress.

"I won," he said. He smiled at her before his eyes lost their focus.

"Husband, husband," she called to him, "I am here, I am here. Do not die."

Governor Sabri knelt. "To Allah we belong and unto Him is our return," he said as he closed Mandricardo's eyes.

Two soldiers lifted Doralice to her feet as her husband's body was placed onto a stretcher. Sabri laid a large white cloth over Mandricardo. Grief overcame her as she wept while being led out of the arena. She turned as Akramont's voice rang out over the din of the crowd.

"Surgeon! Come quick! My champion Ruggiero is still alive!"

⚜

CHAPTER THIRTY-ONE

Hearing was the first sense restored to Ruggiero after he had blacked out. He heard sounds, then voices before he could distinguish words. Amir Akramont called for a surgeon. Ruggiero began feeling the weight of his body, but could not move a muscle. He was face down on sand. Then came the pain. Overwhelming, excruciating pain.

Hands turned him over and he gave an involuntary gasp when his back touched the ground. His eyes fluttered open. He saw light and slowly images came into focus. Then he remembered he was in the old Roman arena of Paris.

Akramont's face appeared above him. "Be strong, you will survive."

Ruggiero's eyelids slammed shut. It took too much effort to keep them open. As he tried taking a deep breath, he felt a stabbing pain in the right side of his chest. Breathing was limited to shallow breaths through his mouth.

He was lifted onto a stretcher and carried away. With each step made by the men carrying him, Ruggiero felt new pain. There was soon a pattern to the pain, like waves on the sea. The pain became a swirling eddy and Ruggiero's mind consumed by the rhythmic ebb and flow of agony. His mind drifted away as he re-lived the duel. Mandricardo brutally pounded on his back knocking the wind out of him, causing Ruggiero to drop his sword. He knew he would be dead unless he used his dagger to kill Mandricardo. Ruggiero refused to black out until after he plunged his knife into his enemy's neck. The image of blood erupting from Mandricardo's chest appeared again and again inside Ruggiero's mind, until the men carrying him stopped. Ruggiero opened his eyes. He was lying on a table inside a large tent.

A man with a full black beard smiled. "*As-salaam-alaikum*, Ruggiero. I am Ibrahim, personal surgeon for Amir Akramont."

"*Wa alaikum...* " croaked Ruggiero.

"You are hurt. Do not worry about niceties or protocol. Speak only when there is a need."

Ruggiero gave him the barest of nods and closed his eyes.

"Your armor must be removed so I can treat your injuries," said Ibrahim. "I will have two men help you sit up before they lift the hauberk off your shoulders."

Two men on either side of Ruggiero started to move him, causing a shooting pain on his right side. Ruggiero gasped when a man gripped him under his right arm.

"Here is sandalwood to bite down on," said Ibrahim as he placed a stick in Ruggiero's mouth.

As his right arm was lifted above his head, Ruggiero clenched the wood with his teeth. The pain was excruciating as the two men worked to remove his shirt of mail. Spots danced before his eyes. He felt nauseated and fought the urge to retch.

"Roll him onto his belly," said Ibrahim.

Ruggiero laid with his head turned to one side and the stick in his mouth. A warm wet cloth was applied to his lower back.

Ibrahim hummed and sang in Arabic as he cleansed the wounds. The rhythmic sound of the surgeon's voice helped calm Ruggiero and reminded him of his mentor Atallah's ministrations to him as a youth. Warm hands gingerly touched his back, allowing him to relax somewhat.

"Ruggiero," said Ibrahim. "I need to wrap your chest with bandages, so you will need to sit up again."

One soldier worked on Ruggiero's left side and lifted him upright. Without the heavy mail armor on his shoulders and chest, he found the pain to be less intense.

Ibrahim offered him a wooden cup. "This is a tea made from poppy seeds and will ease your pain. Drink it all."

It had a bitter taste, but Ruggiero did his best to finish the liquid in one smooth motion. After downing the medicine, Ruggiero put the stick back in his mouth to brace himself for having his chest wrapped with linen. His lower back throbbed, but the pain was beginning to be manageable. Still, he could not take a deep breath.

Akramont entered the tent. He locked eyes with Ruggiero and gave him an encouraging smile. "Tell me Ibrahim, how is he?"

"He has serious wounds, but it appears the ribs in the small of his back are only cracked and not broken. He will need pain medicine for several weeks, but should recover in time. I see no reason why he will not be at full strength after a month or so of resting."

Ruggiero gave a feeble smile. That was the best possible news he could have heard. He would live and recover to his former strength.

"Is Mandricardo dead?" he asked.

"Yes," said Akramont sounding pleased. "At first, when you fell off your horse everyone thought you died and Mandricardo had won. Thankfully, you delivered him a death blow before you blacked out."

Ruggiero tried nodding, but his head started spinning.

"The patient needs his rest now," said Ibrahim.

"Yes," said Akramont. "I want Ruggiero to know Mandricardo's armor will be waiting for him. It once belonged to his noble ancestor, Hector of Troy, and will now be worn by a worthier man."

"And Durindana?" asked Ruggiero.

"Belongs to Gradasso," said Akramont. "He laid claim to that sword years ago and you are in no shape to challenge him. Be satisfied with Balisarda and Hector's armor."

"I shall," whispered Ruggiero as he struggled to finish his thoughts. "And you may have Mandricardo's horse."

He closed his eyes and drifted off to sleep.

PART TWO:

SPURNED LOVERS

Doralice felt dazed as she followed behind Mandricardo's corpse being carried out of the arena. She knew what needed to be done and somehow summoned the strength to speak up.

"Governor Sabri," she announced and stood her ground until he turned his head in her direction.

He made a motion for the men carrying the corpse to halt.

"I am Mandricardo's wife, and I shall prepare him for burial. Have my husband brought to the tent we shared together along with shrouds."

Sabri nodded and led the procession to the tent where Mandricardo spent his last night. "Bring a large table in here," he said to a soldier. "She will also need soap, pitchers of water, a basin, cloths for washing as well as three cloths for his shroud."

The man bowed as he left.

"Governor Sabri," said Doralice, trying to keep her voice from cracking. "Mandricardo is a martyr. He does not need washing. He should be covered in a shroud and buried as he died."

There was a look of sadness in Sabri's eyes. "I am sorry for your loss my child, but your husband is not a martyr. As his wife, you have the right to ready his body for burial, but he did not die in battle. He died from a duel predicated on prideful disputes. He will be stripped of his armor, washed, and buried according to our customs."

With that pronouncement, soldiers began unfastening the ancient bronze cuirass Mandricardo wore.

Doralice stomped her foot. "No! He should be buried in that armor."

Sabri shook his head. "His armor is said to be enchanted and once belonged to Hector of Troy. I am loathe to provide temptation for anyone to commit the grievous sin of desecrating a grave."

Men entered the tent bearing a basin, soap, a box of cotton cloths, two empty barrels, and three pitchers of water. More men followed carrying a large table into the tent. A wooden incline was placed on it before being covered with a sheet. They placed the corpse on the table with the chest elevated above the legs.

"That is so the water will flow down and not stay on the body," said Sabri. "The last pitcher contains lotus leaves for the final wash."

"I remember," said Doralice. "I helped prepare my mother's body for burial. I would prefer to perform this sacred duty by myself. I believe I am the only person in this entire camp who is saddened by his death."

"Very well, but first we must strip the body," said Sabri.

Fresh tears welled in Doralice's eyes as she watched soldiers pull and prod her husband's lifeless body to remove his armor and padding. Sabri pulled out the jeweled dagger lodged near Mandricardo's collarbone. A dark trickle of blood trailed the knife. Doralice extended her hand, indicating she wanted the weapon.

"No," he said. "This belongs to Ruggiero. He will want it back. Tell me, does Mandricardo have any outstanding debts?"

Doralice's anger flashed again. "How dare you ask me that at this time?"

"It is required by our faith. Souls remain on this earth until their debts are paid."

She shook her head. "I do not know of any debts. You should have asked him that question before you started the duel costing him his life. Especially if you knew his immortal soul hung in the balance."

"You are right, I should have." Sabri placed a cloth over Mandricardo's pudendum, extending from his navel to his knees. "To cover his shame."

Doralice crossed her arms to silently tell Sabri to leave.

"There will be guards stationed outside your tent," he said. "Send a message to me once you are finished. Your husband will then be dressed and shrouded while you cleanse yourself. I shall have your attendants draw a bath for you. We shall await for your arrival before starting his funeral prayer."

Sabri and the men left the tent. Doralice was alone with her thoughts and Mandricardo's corpse.

❦

Doralice began the ritual of *wudu* on herself by saying, *"bismillah."* She poured water into the basin and washed her hands, face, and feet three times in the ritualized manner she had been taught to do before every prayer. She felt a pang of guilt when she thought of how her prayer life had been disrupted by Mandricardo.

"You were not a good Muslim," she said as she wrapped a cloth around her right hand and wetted it. "How could you be? That would mean submitting to a higher authority than yourself."

She began wiping the dried blood from Mandricardo's corpse by cleansing the wounds on his chest and under his right arm. She discarded the dirty cloths into a barrel and continued the process until all the blood was removed.

"You are dead because of your foolish pride," she said as she pressed upon Mandricardo's abdomen. She wrinkled her nose at the smells created by that act. "You ignored my warning. Had you shown respect for my wishes, we would be miles away from here finding a place to spend the night in each other's arms. Instead, you are dead and I...," she reached between his legs and wiped away the filth, "...am cleaning your mess."

She tossed the dirty rag into a barrel and cleansed the area twice more. "The day you entered my life and upended my world, I was a mere child. One who did as she was told and minded her manners. You changed that. You made me into the woman who stands before you and is furious with you."

The cloth covering his pundendum was stained yellow. Doralice cleansed his thighs and placed a fresh cloth over his private parts.

"I warned you," she said as she threw those soiled cloths into the barrel. "I foresaw your death, but you would not listen to me. Have you ever listened to anyone besides the old man who challenged your manhood because you had not avenged your father's death?"

Doralice scrubbed her hands with soap. "What if you ignored him? You would have stayed in Tartary and never entered my life." The thought made her laugh.

Grabbing fresh cloths she wetted and soaped them before wrapping them around her hands. She looked down at his face. It was dull and lifeless, the same as her heart. "You set off on a mission to kill Orlando, but he is still alive. You seized his sword and horse, but that Frankish warrior is alive while you are dead." She washed his nose, mouth, face, beard, and his hair. "You accomplished nothing in your life. No one will be singing your praises. Instead, you shall either be forgotten or remembered as the son of the mighty Agrikhan who set off to avenge his father's death and failed."

She used more fresh cloths to wash Mandricardo's right side starting with his chest, arm, leg, and ending with his foot. "You will be remembered as a failure, while I shall be known as Mandricardo's whore. You bragged of your sexual prowess and of my responsiveness. Your pride determined both of our legacies." Doralice moved to the other side of the table and washed his left side starting once again with his chest.

She emptied the water into the second barrel before pouring a fresh pitcher of water into the basin. Doralice repeated washing Mandricardo's face before repeating the cleansing of his right side.

"I knew what you were that first day when you ruthlessly murdered all of my escorts. I was terrified of you and terrified of dying. Had I shown more courage, I would have found a way to anger you and died a virtuous death. Instead, I allowed you to abduct me, confuse me, and seduce me. You were a good lover, but my pleasure was always laced with guilt."

With fresh cloths, she began the second washing of his left side. "I am alone with no one to protect me. Rodomont will hear of your death and return to claim me. My father will have no choice in the matter because he will not want Granada invaded by Rodomont's army. I may be allowed a mourning period before he takes possession of me, but it would only serve as a waiting period before he tortures me. I have seen what he will do to me in my dreams — in my nightmares. Knowing what is in my future, I have nothing to live for."

She tossed the used cloths into one barrel and dumped the water into the other barrel. Doralice began rummaging through her belongings, which had been brought into the tent as Governor Sabri had promised. On the bottom of the small casket filled with jewelry was a dagger taken from a Frankish lord's castle. She returned to Mandricardo's side and withdrew the blade from its scabbard.

Doralice held the dagger above her heart. "If only I had such a weapon the day you came into my life. I would have killed myself and died a virgin. You are damned to Hell, as am I. Your sins of pride and murder as well as your refusal to perform the prayers required of our faith all condemn your soul. I am also damned for disobeying my father and for the crime I am about to commit. Your third washing shall be in the blood of your wife. Until we meet again in Hell."

CHAPTER THIRTY-THREE

Aistulf was weary after spending the entire day flying above lands in North Africa. The sun was setting and he found a secluded hilltop with a pool filled with fresh water to spend the night. He took out the magical piece of cloth from the enchantress Melissa. It had the deceptive appearance of linen with a single gold thread woven into its border.

He held the four corners of the cloth together with his left hand, closed his eyes, took a deep breath, moved his right hand in a circular motion three times. "Nourish my body, nourish my mind, nourish my spirit."

Once he felt weight inside the cloth, Aistulf opened his eyes and examined his food. The cloth conjured meals and no two meals were alike. One night he had roasted venison and another night was grilled fish. This night held a small feast of black bread, a flaky pie filled with pheasant and root vegetables, a dessert made of baked apples, and white wine. As he dipped a piece of bread in honey, he wondered what else Melissa expected of him. Perhaps since he now had information gleaned from flying over Hispania and North Africa, she might permit him to fly northward and rejoin Charlemagne's army.

Aistulf had discovered a magic spell in the book Logistilla gave him that created loyalty in the hippogriff to him. This gave him peace of mind. He allowed the flying beast to go off and hunt without worrying about becoming stranded. It also relieved any worry he might have of theft, as the spell was powerful enough for Kamal to break iron chains and return when called.

Kneeling near the still pond, Aistulf spoke aloud. "Melissa, what more do you want from me? May I now fly northward to be with my liege, or my father?"

He stared in disbelief as the shadows in the water shifted and Melissa's face appeared.

The elderly woman gave him a warm smile. "Hello, Aistulf. I congratulate you on the courage you demonstrated when you faced Atallah's sorcery and secured Ruggiero's freedom."

"How do you know about that?"

"I veered Rabican's course into the Gresigne Forest so you would come upon that enchanted castle."

"How is Ruggiero? Where is he now?"

"Ruggiero rejoined Akramont's war effort and is in Paris. He is wounded, but should recover. I am grateful to see you claimed the golden ring Atallah wore."

"This belongs to Ruggiero," said Aistulf as he lifted the hand wearing the ring. "I will return it to my friend when I see him again."

"I gave Ruggiero that ring on Alcina's island."

Alcina. The mere mention of her name made Aistulf shudder.

"She used her magic to create a false world of enchantments," said Melissa. "Once Ruggiero wore the ring, he saw the ugly truth surrounding him. He saw Alcina's former lovers frozen in time as statues, trees, and bushes. Ruggiero could also see Alcina in her true form."

Aistulf remembered the transformation of Alcina from a beautiful blonde woman to an ancient hag as her magical powers broke. The memory caused bile to rise in the back of his throat. "I feel shame for having been intimate with someone so hideous."

"That ring will allow you to see the truth, devoid of enchantment, and will be vital for your next adventure. Tell me, what did you learn on your journey?"

"The cities of Hispania and North Africa seem to be populated with mainly women, children, and the elderly. Soldiers stood guard at their gates, but far fewer than can hold off an attack. The Muslim lands are vulnerable to an invasion. However, that information will not be of use to Charlemagne since his army is at war with Akramont's army."

"Yes, the armies are locked in a siege."

Ripples through the water caused the image to show the Muslim army surrounding the walls of Paris.

"Am I to lead an army to make Akramont retreat to protect his lands? If so, how will I find enough soldiers to make such an army?"

"An army is headed for the Maghreb," said Melissa. "Those forces will cause Akramont much strife."

The sight of thousands of soldiers marching with banners fluttering in the breeze appeared in the water. Then the focus shifted again to the face of a well-dressed man astride a fine horse. There was intensity in his eyes, making Aistulf recognize this was not a man to cross.

"Who is that?"

"Caliph Harun al-Rashid."

A drop of fear rolled down his spine. "The Caliph of Baghdad. Why is his army on the move? Will they be reinforcements to Akramont?"

"That will depend on what he learns from spies and reports on the war. The caliph's original intent was to punish the amir for beginning an unsanctioned war."

Aistulf rocked back on his heels. "Akramont acted on his own?"

"Yes. This is a vainglorious campaign attempting to succeed where his grandfather failed at expanding the Muslim Empire into Francia. None of Akramont's various commanders questioned the idea of invading the Frankish Empire and assumed the caliph called for the war."

His mind reeled at this knowledge. "So if the caliph learned Akramont was winning the war..."

"He might bring his army northward to help the effort," Melissa said, finishing his thought.

"How do I influence which fate will come to pass?" asked Aistulf.

"There are a large number of Coptic Christians in Africa who would be natural allies to Charlemagne's cause. Ethiopia has a positive history with Muslims after giving refuge to some of the first followers of Muhammad who were persecuted in Mecca. Because of this history, it is likely an appeal from the Ethiopian king to the caliph will be given respectful consideration. To gain such a letter of introduction, you must first gain the king's confidence. This will require much bravery and a spiritual journey on your part."

"A spiritual journey?"

"Yes, Aistulf. First you must discover how to remove curses plaguing King Senapo."

CHAPTER THIRTY-FOUR

Rodomont sat on a trestle bench near a long table outside of a tavern, staring at the road coming from Paris. The sun had set, but the sky still held daylight. He took another long drink of stout from his cup. It was a dark, bitter brew, but he found the alcohol soothing. It allowed him to calmly reflect on the betrayals committed against him and plot his revenge.

Mandricardo and Doralice would soon be passing this way on their journey to Tartary. He would be waiting for them. Mandricardo would die first and then he would make Doralice regret rejecting her most ardent suitor. She would be humbled. Repeatedly. Doralice would not be held in reverence, but in submission with no one to rescue her.

Rodomont's lips curled at the thought of Doralice on her knees begging him for mercy. And then on her back as he showed her none. She had turned his heart to stone.

He took another sip of stout and noticed riders in the distance. He squinted, trying to determine if they were the despised couple. No, this was a group of men riding fast.

Rodomont stood, withdrew his sword, and picked up his shield. He walked over to the road and waited while they approached. If Akramont sent soldiers after him, he would kill them all or die trying. He would never return to serve or be punished by that spineless excuse of a man.

As the soldiers came to a halt, Rodomont stood in an aggressive pose ready to strike at the legs of the first horse that came near him. Ten riders were in the party. The two front warriors raised their right hands in a gesture indicating they meant him no harm.

"*As-salaam-alaikum*, Governor Rodomont," said a dark-skinned man with a fierce countenance.

"*Wa-alaikum-salaam*," replied Rodomont, without lowering his guard.

"My name is Bambata. We left the camp to find and join you. There is nothing left there beside certain death with Akramont."

Rodomont was surprised and suspicious at the pronouncement. "Whose ranks did you desert?"

"None really. Brunello was our governor. Akramont sent him on two lengthy missions, so he was rarely there. Now he is dead, at the hands of Queen Marfisa." Bambata spat on the ground. "Akramont allowed this murder to happen. We lost all respect for Akramont and his handling of this war. After the burials today — none of whom died at the hands of the Franks — we left in the hopes of finding you."

"Come, dismount," said Rodomont, as he lowered his stance. "The innkeeper has enough beds for everyone and dares not refuse us anything lest we burn his buildings to the ground."

The horses were put in the stables and the soldiers joined Rodomont at the outside table. He jangled Sacripant's purse filled with coins and commanded the innkeeper bring supper and pitchers of stout for the men. Platters of brown bread and a hearty mutton stew with carrots and onions soon covered the long table.

Rodomont heard each of the ten men introduce themselves. He soon forgot the names except for Bambata and Abdul, a large man with a crooked scar running across his left cheek.

"It was a mistake for Akramont to be named Amir of the Maghreb," said Bambata after he finished his first cup of stout. "He may come from a long line of esteemed commanders, but he lacks instinct when it comes to strategy. Akramont's first attempt at conquest was to attack an emperor with more years in battle than he has been alive."

"If the caliph were closer, the leadership decision would have been different," said Abdul. "Instead, Troiano extracted promises of allegiance from all the governors for his son to be his successor. The caliph should have ignored Akramont's claims and appointed someone else after Troiano's death."

Rodomont enjoyed hearing criticisms reflecting his own thoughts. "How widespread is this discontent?"

"There is a lot of grumbling in the ranks," said Bambata. "After his disastrous choice of Brunello as our governor, we had no desire to see who Akramont would saddle us with next. Brunello was a lying thief and given the title of governor as a reward for stealing something Akramont wanted. The most that little rat deserved was a slave girl to warm his bed."

Rodomont poured more beer into Bambata's cup. The gruff soldier nodded his thanks and downed his drink in one swift move.

Bambata wiped his mouth with the back of his right hand. "Akramont dithered ever since you penetrated the walls of Paris. After that night, the army has done nothing. All due to Sacripant's advice. The Franks are starving while our men grow bored and angry."

"Sacripant left the camp last night," said Abdul. "You should be on the look out for him."

Rodomont waved his hand. "He found me and tasted my blade."

Bambata smiled. "You are the leader we needed. You deserved being named amir, not Akramont the Unready. The only victories in this war were due to your leadership. You breached the walls of Paris and led your men inside. They gave their lives for you."

"Damned infidels," said Abdul. "The firey trap killed your men. We pledge to follow you from now on. We all want to be your servants."

"I accept," said Rodomont.

"Akramont even disavowed your destroying their pagan house of worship," said Bambata. "He went so far as to apologize for your act of bravery."

Rodomont felt a bitter taste in his mouth. "Any difficulty leaving the camp?"

"No," said Bambata. "I told the guards we were sent on a mission to find and bring you back as a prisoner for killing Marsilio's daughter."

"Did Akramont send anyone on such a mission?"

"Doubtful. The man in charge of the horses responded with 'What took him so long?'" said Bambata.

"I think Akramont hoped Sacripant would return to his side with the news that he killed you and won his horse back," said Abdul.

Rodomont snorted with laughter as he took another drink.

"Akramont finally had a duel today that he tried so desperately to have yesterday," said Bambata. "Yet instead of uniting the army, it only served to weaken his war effort."

Rodomont leaned in closer. "What happened?"

Bambata poured more beer for himself. "Ruggiero served as a champion to settle all of the remaining disputes against Mandricardo. It was a brutal fight. Everyone thought Ruggiero died when he fell off his horse, but he somehow survived and taken away on a stretcher."

"And Mandricardo?" asked Rodomont.

"Dead."

Rodomont smiled. "That is the best news I have heard in years. Mandricardo is dead and the Golden Child is close to death." He finished the beer in his cup, sat back, and thought of Doralice. She was his for the taking. He would not wait for any damned mourning period either. He licked his lips. "Did Doralice weep and wail as Mandricardo was buried?"

Bambata shook his head. "No. She killed herself and was buried alongside him in the same grave."

Rodomont was in disbelief. "Doralice is dead?"

He felt an unexpected pang in his heart. He picked up his empty cup and drained the remaining drops. Mandricardo was dead. Doralice was dead. Ruggiero was nearly dead. Akramont had lost the confidence of his army. All those who had wronged him were either dead or humiliated. His need for revenge was gone, leaving him without purpose in life.

"What now?" asked Abdul.

Ten sets of eyes stared at Rodomont. He poured more stout into his cup and passed the pitcher down the table. "Tonight we drink. Tomorrow we set out for a new adventure. Our forces have a stronghold in Arles. Perhaps we can spill more Frankish blood there before we return to the Maghreb where you shall all serve in my palace guard."

Bambata gave him a crooked smile. "Brunello spied for Akramont. Before we left camp, I stole maps from Brunello's tent. Those should help us find our way to the fortified city of Arles."

CHAPTER THIRTY-FIVE

Bradamante finished adjusting the saddle straps for her father's horse. As she began packing the saddlebags with clothing and personal items, the dread in the pit of her stomach grew.

"Do not look so melancholy, my dear," her father said as he handed her his drinking cup and spoon to be packed. "I will only be a few days' journey away. I will assess the progress of my new castle, but not remain there long. Building sites are uncomfortable and at my age I cannot abide rustic surroundings. After my inspection, I will give further instructions to the master builder, and return here." He winked at her. "With any luck they will be so far along your mother will soon start decorating the interior."

Bradamante managed a small smile.

"There's my girl," he said. "I know it will be difficult, but do your best to humor your mother while I am gone. She is at her most joyful when she is making plans and commanding others. It would serve you well to not question any of her grand plans."

As she led his horse out of the stall, a commotion of kicking and braying came from the far end of the stables.

"Pardon me, father," she said, handing him the reins. "I must go and settle Rabican."

"You are the only one who can tame that hellion." He turned and led his gray roan out to the courtyard. Bradamante calmly approached the stall where the black horse reared and shook his long mane.

"Shhhhh," she soothed. "I know, I know. I made promises to you before, but today I will take you for a long ride."

She stepped out of the shadows so the angry stallion could see her dressed in a tunic and breeches. "I know you hate being confined, but unless you behave I cannot allow you out."

The horse snorted approval as she bowed to him.

"I must see my father off, then I will return and take you for your long awaited ride."

Walking out into the courtyard, the bright morning sunshine blinded her at first. As Bradamante's eyes adjusted she saw her mother, Beatrice, rushing about shouting orders to servants readying packhorses for the trip. Clarice stood in a shaded spot holding baby Aymon while young Bernard defended himself with his wooden sword against shadow opponents.

Once the assemblage appeared ready to depart, the official goodbyes to Duke Aymon began. The servants queued up, according to their position and gave respectful nods as he walked past.

"Bernard, come here," called Clarice.

The young boy walked over to his mother and placed his wooden sword in a belt loop. Bradamante slipped in near Bernard, but that soon changed.

"Here," said her mother. "You should stand between myself and Clarice."

This placement made Bradamante wince. She towered over her mother and was several inches taller than Clarice, and her mother's withering glance made her feel improperly dressed. Both Beatrice and Clarice wore their finest attire for the departing duke, while she was dressed in riding clothes. Beatrice wore a purple silk gown with an ermine collar and Clarice was bedecked in a dark green linen dress adorned with lace.

Duke Aymon smiled at Bernard. "You and your baby brother are the only males of our family left at our ancestral home. I trust you will make your father proud."

"Yes, grandfather," Bernard said, standing straight as a rod.

"Clarice," Aymon said, nodding approval. He then gave Bradamante a kiss on the cheek. "Stay strong, my dear."

He grasped hands with his wife, looked her in the eye, and smiled. "I shall return with good news as soon as I can."

Once those formalities were over, Duke Aymon mounted his horse and left with his party of men. As the portcullis closed, Bradamante felt as if she were being locked inside a dungeon. She shook her head to dispel such ominous thoughts and saw another look of disapproval on her mother's face.

"Change out of those boy's clothes. Those are not suitable for a lady."

"Did you raid Richardet's trunk?" smirked Clarice. She returned to the castle without waiting for a reply.

Bradamante took a deep breath and addressed her mother. "Aistulf entrusted me with his horse. Rabican needs to run and I have been unable to attend to him since returning home. I planned on taking him for a ride today. Breeches are more practical than skirts for that purpose."

Her mother gave a dismissive wave of her hand. "Have someone else do that for you. There is a painter waiting in the garden. Our last portrait of you was when you were nine. It is high time we have a portrait made of my daughter as a lady."

Bradamante nodded and headed inside. The thought of wearing armor crossed her mind until she heard her mother say, "I placed the dress you will wear on top of your trunk. Make haste while there is still morning light."

As she climbed the circular stairs, a sense of doom increased with each step. A dress. She did not want to wear the hideous dark green dress Clarice made for her. Currently, it was her only dress as she had outgrown the others and had not been home long enough for more to be sewn. Bradamante would rather a portrait depict her true nature: a warrior maiden. She wanted to wear her armor and helmet, maybe holding a sword.

Entering her chamber, she was surprised to see the light blue silk gown and blonde wig given to her by Atallah. She had placed those treasures on the bottom of her trunk underneath a woolen blanket, because she did not want to explain their origins.

She removed her tunic and breeches and set them aside. After donning the gown, she gazed at her reflection in the polished metal mirror. Her cropped hair had started to grow back a little, but it was still short and boyish looking. Bradamante bent over, placed the wig on her head and stood upright causing the tresses to fall over her shoulders. Tucking stray hairs underneath the cap, she looked at herself again in the mirror. It was like looking at a stranger, but this was how Ruggiero saw her just a few days before when they pledged their love for one another.

Her mother entered the room and gave her a rare smile. "I always knew you would grow into a beauty. You resemble your Aunt Gisela when she was your age."

"Thank you," said Bradamante, feeling herself soften a little.

Beatrice helped cinch the lacing in the back of Bradamante's gown. "This is fine silk. My mother insisted that I and my sisters have new silk gowns every year." Her voice sounded strained as if holding back tears.

"Then I was married off to a poor knight and such luxuries were no longer possible. Now at long last, you have your first silk dress."

She turned Bradamante around and nodded her approval. "It is an amazing fit, better than this dress my brother gave me to honor my being named a duchess. We have waited far too long to have the proper appearance of relatives of Charlemagne. Hopefully with your father's recent elevation to being a duke and his increased land holdings, we shall have more of what is due us."

Beatrice began brushing the long hair of Bradamante's wig. "This is like your hair not that long ago. It was so lovely, I will never understand why you cut it off."

Bradamante said nothing. She lied to her mother about her hair being cut. It was easier to proclaim she surrendered her tresses due to the oppressive heat under the summer sun rather than admit a louse-ridden hermit cropped them to tend to her head wound sustained in battle. The lie was told to mollify her mother, but any lie was a sin. Bradamante did not want to commit that same sin by restating her lie. Besides, she also knew her mother was not expecting a reply.

"Where did you get this wig and gown?"

The question was inevitable, but Bradamante hoped it might not be asked. The truth could not be told. She could not admit an Islamic wizard conjured them by magic. Her mother distrusted magic in all forms, but the idea of sorcery being performed by a Muslim would give her fits of hysteria. It would be far better to offer a plausible lie for her mother's benefit, even if it meant committing more sins of bearing false witness.

"Gifts from Geoffroi, the Count of Foix."

Beatrice smiled. "I never met him, but have heard of his fine reputation. I seem to recall him being a widower."

"He was a fine man," said Bradamante. "However, he died last month while fighting in Marseille."

Her mother's smile vanished. "Such a shame. He must have been fond of you to give you such expensive gifts."

"He was. There was a letter found in his quarters addressed to Father...." She could not finish her thought, as it was too painful. Had her father received such a letter from a nobleman, Bradamante would have been betrothed to someone other than Ruggiero.

Her mother grabbed a few rose petals from a vase. Rolling the petals in her fingers a few red drops stained her fingers before she brushed the juice on Bradamante's cheeks and lips. "Now you have some color."

Bradamante placed the Visigothic eagle pendant around her neck.

"Another gift?" asked her mother.

"Yes." Bradamante did not elaborate. She could not say the necklace came from Fiordespina, the daughter of Amir Marsilio. By not clarifying, her mother would likely assume the necklace also came from the Count of Foix. Perhaps it would only be half a sin since this was a lie by omission, rather than a lie by commission.

Her mother motioned Bradamante to follow her downstairs. There would be no more delaying. The artist was waiting and the morning light was not. They walked out a door leading to the small garden behind the castle. A man with a medium build had his back to them and stood in front of a prepared panel board resting on an easel.

"Signore Roberto, this is my daughter Bradamante."

The man turned and gave her a warm smile.

"I am charmed to meet you," he said with a small bow.

He positioned Bradamante to stand under the trellis covered with pink roses. She tried to sit on the nearby stone bench, but Roberto was against the idea.

"I will lose the gentle curve of your waist if you are seated. No, you must be standing for this."

His brown robe was splattered with paint spots and his wavy brown hair had a few splotches of paint in it as well. Bradamante guessed he was in his early thirties as he appeared older than her brother, Renaud.

Roberto grinned as he started sketching on the canvas. "The colors are a delicate mix, and such a beautiful subject to paint. This will be a joy for me."

"Have you painted clients who were a painful chore?" asked Bradamante.

"Many of the elderly cardinals in the Vatican," he said with a low voice. "Ugly and unpleasant men with little patience, even when I allowed them to sit while I painted. They were also displeased if their portraits reflected their true likenesses."

"You worked at the Vatican?" asked Beatrice.

Roberto nodded as he mixed egg yolk with pigments on his wooden palette. "Yes, for many years. I was there that Christmas Day at St. Peter's when the pope crowned your brother emperor."

"You were? Tell me about that day."

"Charlemagne had a magisterial presence overwhelming the pope and all the cardinals put together. He looked like a Biblical figure filled with the glory of God. My fortunes changed that fateful day. I sought out Charlemagne as a patron and offered to paint his coronation scene to capture that historical event for future generations. Later, I painted portraits of him, his sons and daughters, and dignitaries of his court."

Beatrice examined the colors on his palette. "You should make the color of her dress a darker shade of blue."

"I can certainly do that my lady," said Roberto. "However, I would like to say the color complements her fair complexion beautifully as if it was designed for her. And my lady, see how the light shimmers off the silk folds presenting an even lighter blue to the eye. Anything darker might cause her coloration to become washed out."

"Then compensate by adding more color to her hair or her cheeks and lips, while taking care she not look like a painted harlot."

Bradamante felt her cheeks begin to burn. Talk of her complexion and dress embarrassed her. She would much rather be riding Rabican far away from the castle and her mother.

Beatrice's tone of voice turned icy. "This portrait will last for many years. While you may consider pale blue to be a flattering color on my daughter, it suggests poverty as if we skimped due to the expense of dyes. You will use darker paints on this portrait."

Bradamante groaned inwardly about her mother's obsession with money and stature. Beatrice still wore the dark purple gown trimmed with ermine, even though the day was warm and the head of the household had departed. Purple was a color reserved for royalty and she must have wanted to emphasize to Roberto that they were members of the royal family.

He lowered his gaze, avoiding her mother's glare. "As you wish, your grace." Roberto added more blue pigment onto his palette.

CHAPTER THIRTY-SIX

Aistulf took to flight on the back of the hippogriff in the morning. Having a set destination in mind made him anxious to meet whatever challenges awaited him. Melissa did not elaborate on the curses afflicting the king of Ethiopia, but she did say where he could be found.

"Follow the Nile River southward. You will pass over the desert land of Nubia and see where the great river splits into two lesser rivers. Continue your flight over the smaller of the two rivers. There may be more times that rivers will come together, but listen to your heart and follow the Blue Nile to its origin. It will climb into the sky, bending and snaking through jungles. Once you see where the water begins to smoke as if on fire, you will see a great lake. King Senapo can be found on the largest island there."

Aistulf thought he would find the king by midday, and was surprised at the length of the journey. He had become accustomed to seeing vast expanses of sand after flying over North Africa. The greenery clinging to the banks of the Nile expanded and became lush and verdant jungles. There were trees the likes of which Aistulf had never seen before along with birds sporting colorful plumage flying alongside him. Following the river became hypnotic as the hippogriff banked and turned in the sky. He followed the river south, then after the major split the river went east, then north, then...Aistulf lost track of all of the directions the river took as it climbed into the sky winding its way through the greenery.

As the day wore on, Aistulf resisted stopping for a midday meal even though he was hungry. The jungles teemed with life and he was unsure what kind of animals might emerge if they thought he or the hippogriff were prey. There was also the matter of offending his future host if he arrived with a full stomach. Courtesy demanded nobility offer a banquet for guests. Aistulf wanted to fully partake in a multi-course meal and appear grateful for the king's hospitality. So he continued flying, even though his hunger grew.

He was relieved to finally see a waterfall as Melissa had described. The lake and the large island appeared soon afterward. A reflective glint in the sunlight guided his way. Aistulf pulled on the reins and made the hippogriff fly lower, peering through the treetops, allowing the villagers to see the magical sight of a man riding atop a flying beast. The people pointed fingers to the sky. A large wooden building was surrounded by an enclosure of poles whose tops had been sharpened to vicious looking points. Sensing he should be invited inside the walls, Aistulf landed outside the gates of the building.

As he landed, Aistulf looked around at the dark-skinned people surrounding him. He felt very pale and overdressed. He wore his custom armor made of chain mail covered with an iron cuirass dipped in gold. His helmet and shield were also dipped in gold and adorned with pearls. This was his style. Normally he was greeted by looks of bemusement because of his opulent attire, instead the Ethiopian people appeared to be in awe.

He dismounted and a collective gasp came from the crowd. Their sounds changed to murmurs and then words in a foreign tongue Aistulf had never heard before.

He looked skyward and muttered, "Dear Lord, give me strength and your guidance," before making the sign of the cross.

The reaction from the people was swift. They knelt before him and bowed their heads. He realized they viewed him as an angel sent from Heaven. With his fair skin, blond hair and golden attire riding a golden flying animal, he resembled descriptions of angels.

Knowing that Coptic Christianity held ties with Constantinople, Aistulf made an announcement in Greek hoping someone might understand his words. "I am Aistulf, son of King Odo of Essex in Britannia and a paladin of Emperor Charlemagne of the Western Roman Empire. I am seeking an audience with King Senapo."

The name Senapo echoed through the crowd as people shook their heads and looked at one another. It may have been the only word Aistulf spoke that was understood. He considered repeating himself in Frankish, but doubted anyone would speak that tongue. Greek was one of the languages he studied when he attended the Palace School in Aachen along with his cousin Renaud. He learned a little Arabic, but not enough to be conversant in that language. Movement came from within the crowd as an old man worked his way to the front. The man wore filthy rags, had stooped shoulders and used a walking stick. Once the man drew near, Aistulf felt pity for him. His eyes remained closed, and he was so painfully thin that he resembled a living skeleton.

"You seek King Senapo?" said the man in perfect Greek.

"I do," said Aistulf.

"Did you come down from Heaven as the people say?"

"I have a flying steed, but my origins and purpose are of this earth."

The beggar nodded. "Come with me."

Aistulf followed the beggar to the closed wooden gates. The old man spoke a few words in his native language to the guards before they were allowed inside. They stood inside a large courtyard that seemed to be a gathering place for an army. A well-dressed dark-skinned man in a white cotton tunic approached and bore a look of surprise on his face at the sight of Aistulf and the hippogriff. The beggar once again said a few words in his native tongue and the well-dressed man led them inside to the palace door.

Aistulf paused before entering the building and wrapped the reins to the hippogriff around the saddle. "Go hunting my friend. I shall call when I need you again."

The hippogriff spread his wings and took off in flight. As Aistulf walked inside the palace, he was puzzled by the lack of servants found in royal households. Instead, it felt like being inside a tomb.

They were led into a small chamber with a table and four chairs. The walls were decorated with mosaics of Jesus on the cross, but in a style different than he had seen before. The well-dressed man lit a few oil lamps, poured wine into a goblet for Aistulf, nodded to both Aistulf and the beggar before leaving and closing the door behind him.

The old man sat at the dimly lit table with his hands crossed and had a beatific look on his face. "I apologize I cannot offer more hospitality. You will understand why after hearing my story and confession. I am King Senapo. I hope you will be my personal savior that was promised and will remove the curses that have made me the wretch you see before you."

CHAPTER THIRTY-SEVEN

Bradamante grew weary of holding the same position for what seemed like hours.

"How much longer is this going to last?" She asked the painter.

Roberto gave her a warm smile and placed his brushes in a small clay pot with water. "We are done for the day. We will start again tomorrow after the morning meal, so that I may take full advantage of the morning light. Please try to remember the position of your pose for tomorrow's session."

Bradamante gave a sigh. Portrait sitting was an ordeal that would occupy her mornings for the foreseeable future. She did not have the heart to ask him for a timeframe. She was about to return to the castle when Hippalca called to her.

"Milady, I have a message for you."

A flicker of hope raised her spirits. Might there be news from Ruggiero? She restrained herself from running to Hippalca's side. Bradamante walked in a deliberate manner toward her handmaiden and fought a rising sense of irritation when Hippalca turned her back and walked away.

Bradamante quickened her pace as she realized Hippalca was entering the stables. Once inside, Bradamante looked around to see if anyone else was there.

"We are alone my lady," said Hippalca. "The stable hands are all eating."

"What news do you bear for me?" asked Bradamante. "A message from my beloved?"

At the sound of voices, Rabican responded by kicking his stable door again and again.

"No, milady. The message is from me. Earlier I heard you make a promise to Rabican. If you go inside the castle, your mother will occupy you until the end of the day. I heard her speaking with a monk. She used your name several times."

"What does he want with me?"

"I do not know."

Bradamante's heart sank. "What do you suggest?"

"You should always keep your word when possible. I brought your riding clothes for you to change. Should you ask for your mother's permission to go on a ride, I am certain it will be denied. So it may be best for you to keep your word for the ride while you can. For tomorrow, if you know of your mother's plans for you from sunup to sundown, it would be rebellious for you to leave."

Bradamante felt a surge of warmth and tenderness toward her hand-maiden. "Help me change."

The young women worked in concert and soon Bradamante was dressed in the riding clothes from earlier.

"I packed some bread and cheese for you," said Hippalca. "Try not to be gone for too long. She will be angry."

Bradamante nodded and headed for Rabican's stall. "Here I am," she announced to the stallion. "We shall soon ride as fast as the wind will take us."

Rabican settled down and allowed Bradamante to enter the stall and place Aistulf's saddle on his back. Wasting no time, she left the stables and the castle grounds. As the portcullis closed behind her, Bradamante felt as if she had been released from captivity. She did not need to kick Rabican's sides to get him galloping away.

They were on the road headed west. The sun was directly overhead and beat down on her back, but the breeze of riding on horseback cooled her off. This was indeed a magical horse, one that could ride hundreds of miles in a day. Thankfully, the saddle felt like a cushion, the repeated jostling while she rode brought about no discomfort. She surmised the enchantress Melissa must have performed a charm on the saddle for Aistulf.

Bradamante was filled with joy as she rode. For the first time in weeks she felt alive and happy. They rode past rolling hills waving with wheat and barley almost ready for harvest. The speed of their journey was in stark contrast to the plodding of the merchants transporting their wares in the wagons. She could only imagine the open-jawed looks on their faces at the sight of the horse riding at such speed.

She had no destination in mind, and only came to a stop as they approached the Atlantic Ocean, glistening in the afternoon sun. Bradamante marveled at how quickly they arrived. The trip, which should have lasted several days with many breaks for her horse to rest, was accomplished in an hour or so. She looked at the sun in the sky and realized time had passed, but not much. Rabican slowed to a canter. The horse sniffed the sea air and began to relax.

A fleeting thought of riding to Paris to join the war crossed her mind. All she wanted was to find Ruggiero and run off with him. As if that was possible. She shook her head. No, she would have to return to Montauban and await his promised return to her side and have him claim her hand in marriage.

Bradamante had not developed a strong tie with Rabican yet, and did not want to risk him bolting from the site and leaving her stranded. To avoid that, she did not dismount to eat her meal. Instead, she pulled the food from her saddlebags and remained on horseback as she broke bread and ate hunks of cheese. Her momentary sense of contentment would be fleeting for she knew she would be punished for having left the castle grounds without her mother's permission. She might not have an opportunity like this again for a long while.

CHAPTER THIRTY-EIGHT

Aistulf studied King Senapo. He was emaciated, but upon closer inspection did not appear old. There were no lines of age, just cheeks sunken from starvation. His eyelids remained closed, but the eyes themselves protruded from the sockets resembling large grapes. His hair was thin, brittle, uneven bald patches, and turning white.

He remembered tales of kings donning clothes of commoners and walking among them to better understand his people. Aistulf doubted King Senapo lived on the streets for that reason. He fought the impulse to retrieve his magic cloth and produce a meal for King Senapo. The man was cursed, and to help this king he must first listen and understand before offering help.

Senapo licked his parched lips. "I became king when I turned twenty. As a child, I lived in the royal palace and studied with the best tutors my father could find. I learned to read and write in Arabic, Latin, and Greek. I studied scripture as well as classical texts. I was taught the art and history of war, but rarely saw my father as he traveled throughout our kingdom. My mother died after delivering a stillborn when I was only three. My memories of her are vague. Once I turned fifteen, my father took me along with him on his travels. That was when I learned about the responsibilities of being a king. I became obsessed with expanding Ethiopia's power and wealth.

"My first act in that goal when I became king was ignoring my late father's wishes. He brokered a marriage for me with the daughter of a wealthy Ethiopian nobleman. The girl came from a respected family and reported to be a devout Christian, beautiful, virtuous, but not yet old enough to wed. That arrangement was not advantageous enough for me. I saw no benefit for my ambitions. Instead, I began negotiations with the King of Nubia for his eldest daughter. Many suitors vied for her hand, but no one else could make her Queen of Ethiopia.

"I extracted a sizable dowry including valuable border lands with gold mines. Those concessions were ceded to me without any blood being shed in war. We held the royal wedding in Nubia and many welcoming celebrations throughout Ethiopia. My people expressed joy over having a young and beautiful new queen. My wife, Malia, and I shared a bed until she conceived and began to show. I moved her into my late mother's set of rooms in the palace, far away from mine. This was for her health and to assure a safe delivery. I did not want to cause her any injury, and I could not resist temptation if she were in my bed. That began Malia's banishment from my life. Once she gave birth to a healthy son, I had no more use for her as a wife."

"I do not understand," said Aistulf.

"She fulfilled all of her necessary functions. She provided me with a lucrative dowry and an heir. I had no more need of her, other than to serve as a mother to my son. If she given birth to a daughter, I would have tried again for a son."

"But she could have bore you more children."

"Yes, but any subsequent pregnancies would be fraught with risks. I did not want her to die in childbirth and leave my son motherless — or — she might have borne another son."

"Would that be bad?" asked Aistulf.

"History is filled with examples of brothers turning on brothers to seize thrones or lands. I wanted to prevent any possibility of fratricide. Your own emperor inherited half of his father's empire. It was divided between himself and his brother Carloman. Have you heard the many rumors and suspicions regarding Carloman's unexpected death at a young age? Charlemagne benefited from consolidating his brother's lands into his own. Malia was still my queen, but no longer my consort. I eliminated the risk of my son being murdered by a relative trying to steal his throne."

"Do you have a family history of this?"

Senapo nodded. "My uncle plotted to kill my father, when I was ten. A stable boy's mother worked in the kitchens. She would sneak food to him, before meals were served. Or so he thought. In actuality, he was an unknowing royal food taster. One night he became ill right after eating. His death spared my father's life. After an inquiry, my uncle and his sons were executed as well as a servant who poisoned the food."

"I am sorry to hear about treachery in your family," said Aistulf. "Did your father have any other children who challenged you for the throne?"

"I know of no other children and no one has dared challenge me."

"Did you father any other children?"

"I had concubines who bore children. However, I have never claimed any of them as mine. I would only take a woman as a concubine when I was at one of the many other castles, but never at the royal palace. I would not dishonor my queen in that manner. I left before the birth of any of those unclaimed children. The mothers are kept on as members of the servant staff so they are not destitute. I do not care to know about any illegitimate offspring as they will not inherit anything."

"How did your queen feel being ignored by you?"

"I think it slowly killed her. Two years ago, word came to me that she was dying and wanted to see me. I hurried back to the palace. It would upset my people if they heard their king refused their dying queen's request. She had lingered on her deathbed for days, but clung to life waiting for my arrival. I had not seen her for at least five years." His voice began to falter. "She begged for my forgiveness. She thought she displeased me. For years she prayed to God to learn what sins she committed and how she could return to my side. Tears flowed down her cheeks as she told me this. I wanted to set her mind at ease, and reassured her that she was blameless. I told her of my desire to prevent fratricide. I also confessed I would not allow myself to love her or anyone. To love another is to be vulnerable. That is a weakness enemies can exploit. It made for a stronger kingdom if their king concerned himself with his people and not with his family."

"How did she respond?"

"She became possessed and spoke in a deep voice. 'Unless you change and allow love to enter your heart, you must never touch a woman again.'" Senapo held his head in his hands. "If only I realized she spoke a warning, I would not be cursed. Six months after my wife died, a new woman began working in the palace and caught my eye. I never desired a woman as much as her."

A smile crept on his face. "Fana had a regal air about her. One look and anyone could see she was not a commoner. I became entranced by her grace and beauty."

"Did you take her as your wife?"

Senapo sighed and shook his head. "That would have gone against my ambitions. Wives provide dowries and political alliances, Fana lacked both. She had come from a good family, but her father lost his fortune. By the time she came to work at the palace, she was destitute. For me to marry her would solely be for love itself. I never considered such an idea. She was a reluctant lover because she was devout and insisted on following her late father's wishes to remain untouched until marriage. But she could not refuse her king."

Senapo opened his eyes and revealed milky white orbs welled with tears. "A few months after she conceived, I heard news I sought for years. My explorers found what they thought was Terrestrial Paradise. My life's obsession centered on finding the earthly entrance to Heaven and see God the Father for myself. An expedition of men was assembled and because I adored Fana, I brought her along as well — against her wishes. She warned me. She thought God would be upset at any mortal arrogant enough to enter Heaven while still living.

"I refused to listen, just as I refused her repeated pleas to sanctify our intimacy by being married in the Church. The journey was strenuous. One night as we camped on the mountainside, she again begged me to marry her. I then told her about my worry of fratricide and offered that as a reason against marrying. She asked me if her child was a girl, would I then marry her? I refused again. She wept and told me the secret she kept hidden from me. She had been betrothed to me to years before. After I married Malia, it ruined her father's reputation. Our marriage contract had been known far and wide in Ethiopia, and he became a wealthier merchant when he held the status as the future father-in-law to the king. After the announcement of my marriage to the King of Nubia's daughter, Fana's father was ruined. Then years later she became my concubine and suffered another marital rejection from me. She was good enough to bed, but not rich enough to wed." He pounded a fist against his forehead. "If only I listened to her. My father wisely chose a suitable woman for me, but I refused to allow love to enter and change my selfish heart."

He began pulling at the remaining patches of his hair. "Fana could no longer climb the mountain. I left her in the care of several attendants. I hoped to see her again after I explored the summit. I wanted to tell her of my meeting with God, except that night I dreamt of Saint Michael the Archangel. He was furious with me and said I was blinded by greed and an insatiable appetite for power. I repeatedly rejected the love of those who needed me the most: my wife, my son, and Fana. He would see me suffer in this life and not wait until my death to go Purgatory or Hell. I realized then that the deep voice I heard from my wife on her deathbed was from Saint Michael. He warned me then, but I did not change my ways. He said I was cursed and needed to atone for my sins. My dream changed and I saw Fana. She had gone into labor early, but the baby had not turned and was breech." Senapo's face twisted with the memory as tears spilled down his cheeks. "One leg went down the birth canal, but the other leg was bent at the knee and would not descend. There was blood everywhere and she screamed in agony. No one knew how to help her. My physician tried cutting her open, and she died calling for me.

"I awoke calling her name and found I was blind. I called off the expedition and we immediately returned down the mountain for Fana. We were too late. She had died as I saw in my dream. I am to blame for her death. She became pregnant due to my lust, she went in early labor because I insisted she come on an arduous journey. If I had respected her wishes, she would be alive today as my wife."

Senapo put his head down on the table and wept. Aistulf sat there, wishing he knew how to help ease Senapo's pain and guilt. The man's curved shoulders shook as he sobbed. Once the king recovered his composure and raised his head, he looked as if he had aged another ten years.

"Only in the evening did my other curse reveal itself" said Senapo. "It is a thousand fold worse than losing my sight. I am denied the peace of enjoying a meal or the pleasure of a full belly. I had been so determined to reach Fana's side and then despondent when I saw her dead body, I refused all offers of food. After her burial, I finally sat down to eat. As I took my first bite of food, A terrifying screech split the night air. Three winged demons swooped down and snatched the food with their talons. During their rampage they left behind droppings so foul everyone lost their appetite."

"Did anyone try to chase those demons?" asked Aistulf.

Senapo nodded. "A few archers tried their luck at first, but no arrows could hurt these creatures from Hell. Many witnesses described these events and what my tormentors look like. They have the head and breasts of ugly women with the body and talons of vultures."

"Sounds like the Harpies from Greek legend," said Aistulf.

"Perhaps. For the ease of our conversation, I shall call them Harpies henceforth."

"How long has it been since you ate a meal?"

"Fana died one year after Malia died. Today marks one year since Fana's death."

"A year without eating?" Aistulf was aghast. "How did you survive?"

"I learned by trial and error how not to call the Harpies. I can only eat the most meager of food. I must scrounge for scraps in the streets and fight dogs for crumbs and gnawing of bones from garbage mounds. I cannot even accept food offered to me out of pity because it will cause the Harpies to descend. I asked to be brought to this remote island so my shame would be hidden. My seneschal returned to the royal palace and is acting as regent for my son. I am known for traveling throughout my kingdom, so my absence has not been recognized yet. I am still thought of as king, so my neighbors and enemies do not see this kingdom as vulnerable. If it became known that Ethiopia's king cannot rule, we would be attacked."

"Pardon my interruption," said Aistulf. "Vulnerability to foreign armies is why I am here. Amir Akramont led a vast army from throughout the Maghreb to invade the Frankish Empire. I used my own winged creature to fly over northern Africa and saw how vulnerable the region is to attack."

"Are you are here to ask for my army to attack your enemies' lands?"

"No. There is another army already on the move."

Senapo sat up straight. "Which army? The Nubians?"

"The Caliph of Baghdad's." Aistulf paused to allow that statement to sink in with the king. "Akramont started a war without the knowledge of his liege. Caliph Harun al-Rashid could punish Akramont and the governors who followed him into war or his army could act as reinforcements in Francia."

Senapo started pulling on his lower lip as if deep in thought.

"Or perhaps," said Aistulf, "they would invade Ethiopia if they learned it is vulnerable."

Senapo turned and blindly stared in Aistulf's general direction. His demeanor shifted from a grieving man to one of military strategist. "Saint Michael visited me again in my dreams last night. I saw you descend from the clouds on the back of a magical flying creature. He said I repented enough for my sins and promised you would remove my curses. Afterward I am to help your noble cause."

"Tell me more of what Saint Michael showed you and, God willing, I shall do my best to make your dream a reality."

"I saw the two of us seated at a table in the courtyard. Food was set before us. The moment I touched a morsel of it, the accursed Harpies descended and stole it from my hands. You hopped onto your winged steed and flew after them."

"Did I kill any of them with my sword?"

Senapo's eyebrows knitted. "No. They are spirits sent by an archangel. I do not think they can be killed, only contained."

Aistulf pondered that statement. "Did I catch any and put them in a cage?"

"No, you blew a horn which frightened them. They flew away and you followed."

"Now I know what I must do," said Aistulf. "Let us go to your courtyard and have food brought to us. I will call my hippogriff and then pray I can work a miracle."

※

CHAPTER THIRTY-NINE

Renaud's stomach grumbled. It had been hours since he and his small troop of soldiers had stopped for their midday meal. They were traveling northward on an old Roman road tracking through a forest. He was always alert for dangers, but going through woodlands made him feel more on edge. Brigands were notorious for hiding behind trees to attack travelers. Renaud had expected they were about to be ambushed earlier in the day when an oak tree blocked their path. As it turned out, the dead tree had simply fallen over as attested to by the large uneven splinters on the stump where it used to stand.

His party rode through a stretch of blackened trees, silent reminders of a fire that had swept through long before. New growth blanketed the forest floor surrounding the charred remnants serving as a testament of life springing from death.

He realized they would not get through the vast forest before nightfall. There was not a castle, tavern, abbey or a commoner's hut to be seen. Renaud had hoped they would come upon a dwelling where they could spend the night and be offered a warm meal. Even peasants were expected to follow the customs of hospitality. They might wind up slaughtering an animal being raised for the next Christmas feast to feed seven warriors who were their unexpected guests. To ignore the needs of a travelers at your door was dangerous. That discourtesy might result in terrible and immediate retribution by those seeking food and shelter. As he looked at the lengthening shadows of the trees from the setting sun, Renaud resigned himself to sleeping out-of-doors and either using their food stores or finding game.

His party would continue their march throughout the night without complaint if asked, but the horses needed their rest. Renaud saw several sparkles in the darkness and recognized water. He raised his right hand in signal and brought his horse to a halt.

"We shall pitch camp for the night," he announced before dismounting. "Maugis and Vivien will prepare the site, Emile and Richardet will see to the needs of the horses, Alard and Guichard will join me hunting."

He led his horse from the road to a small clearing in the woods. "This will serve as our camp. Maugis, I want you and Vivien to gather a large pile of sticks. More than we would need for a fire."

His cousin nodded, a quizzical look on his face. "As you wish."

"Richardet, there should be a stream not too far from here," said Renaud. "Be certain when you feed the horses to only give them one cupful of oats and to balance the amount taken from either side of the saddle-bags."

"Are you going to give me instruction about how to brush them as well?" grumbled Richardet.

Renaud walked over, placed a hand on Richardet's left shoulder, and spoke in an undertone. "Little brother, I did not train you as a squire. Until I have confidence you will perform all the tasks expected of you, I shall give you detailed instructions as I did with Emile. He caught on quickly and within three days there was no need for me to give him any orders."

Richardet bore an insolent look upon his face. "Why only one cup's worth of oats? The horses will still be hungry."

"The oats are to supplement their grazing and keep them healthy," said Renaud. "However, we might end up needing oats as food. Once we arrive in Paris, we may discover the denizens have descended to eating rats. At that point, you will wish we had been stingier in feeding oats to the horses."

Richardet gave a nod.

"And, the reason I specified removing oats equally from both saddle-bags is to ensure balance on the horse's back. Would you want to be the one to tell Bradamante that the horse she lent us has difficulty walking because of your mistreatment?"

"No."

"I thought not," said Renaud. "Once you and Emile have fed, watered, and groomed the horses, you will come back to the campsite."

Vivien smirked as he walked by gathering firewood. He seemed to enjoy the sight of Richardet being scolded.

"I know you would rather join me in hunting than see to the horses," said Renaud.

Richardet nodded, looking a bit sheepish.

"This will not be festive hunting you engaged in before. We do not have a pack of trained dogs to flush out our game and we will not be riding in pursuit of quarry. Instead we need to employ stealth and attempt to stalk our prey as if we were lions." Renaud opened a saddlebag, removed a woolen blanket, and stashed his golden helmet. The blanket had a large slit in the center and he slipped it over his head and shoulders. "Once I finish talking to you, there should be no words spoken until after your brothers and I return with hopefully something for supper. To be successful in the hunt, we need to avoid being seen, heard or smelled by the animals.

"There is a small breeze coming from the north. Your brothers and I will be heading where the wildlife will be upwind of our smells. You should walk the horses in the opposite direction to the stream. That way the sounds of the horses should not scare off the animals we are hunting."

Richardet scowled as he led two horses away. Renaud chuckled. His youngest brother had not been fostered because Richardet and his twin Bradamante were inseparable as small children. Charlemagne ordered Bradamante trained as a warrior, but Beatrice insisted the training be done in Montauban to assure the maiden's virtue and reputation. Therefore, Richardet also remained at home. Only after their sister was given her first command was Richardet sent to Duke Namo for training. Renaud was confident his youngest brother would become a capable squire in time, but the process was coming with a fair amount of resistance. He assumed Richardet had expected praise rather than criticism and instruction from his eldest brother.

Guichard handed Renaud a drawstring leather bag. "Inside is a new lure I made from the last stag we killed. The scent is strong, and should attract other bucks trying to defend their territory. This is the perfect time of day when the deer migrate to their sleeping spots. We saw some tracks headed northward. Give us a head start before you follow us."

His brothers were skilled archers and would bring about the kill while Renaud would attract the animals to come in range of their arrows. Renaud agreed with the plan, then spotted Emile waiting to speak with him.

"Pardon me, my lord, but I am confused," said Emile.

Renaud smiled at the young man. "How old are you?"

"Fourteen, milord."

"And how long have you been fostered?" asked Renaud.

"I was sent to the royal court in Aachen when I was seven."

"We had similar trainings. Tell me, is this mission your first real experience away from a large army?"

"Yes, milord."

Renaud nodded with understanding. "We were fortunate during that fortnight to always find a place to stay indoors for the night and a warm supper."

"This is a warm evening with no threat of rain," said Emile. "Sleeping outside should not pose any hardship for us."

"It is not the weather concerning me, it is the dangers of sleeping outside protective walls."

"I slept in tents before without worry," said Emile, sounding puzzled.

"Has that always been with Charlemagne's army?"

"Yes."

"There is a vast difference between travelling with a large army and a party of our size with only seven members. We shall take turns standing watch for attacks by dangerous animals," said Renaud.

"Wolves?" asked Emile.

"Yes, wolves are one of the predators to watch for. A wolf pack can destroy a horse in a few moments' time," said Renaud. "However, I am more concerned with threats posed by two-legged animals."

"Pardon?"

"Brigands," said Renaud. "Woods are notorious shelters for brigands. We must stay vigilant to prevent the theft of our horses and from being attacked in our sleep."

Emile's brow furrowed as he absorbed the dangers. Renaud gave the lad a wistful smile as he nostalgically remembered his own days of youthful innocence.

Renaud took a clump of moist soil and smeared it on his face. "This is to help hide my otherwise pale face. You should join my little brother in watering the horses. Refill our water skins as well."

Emile nodded and led two horses away. Renaud set off after Guichard and Alard taking care to be as quiet as possible. The woolen blanket on his shoulders served to dampen the rustle of the chain mail as he moved. Soon the area surrounding him no longer appeared touched by fire. The underbrush was abundant with delicate ferns and wood sorrel's heart-shaped green leaves while the scent of pine filled the air.

He traveled about two miles before he saw his brothers hiding. Alard held his bow in front of him while perched on a large Y-shaped branch of an old oak tree. Guichard stood among a cluster of bushes. Renaud opened the leather bag and withdrew a piece of fabric bound with a length of thin rope. As he unwound the rope, the stench of the lure made his eyes water. Guichard had mentioned a strong smell, but not how overpowering it was.

Renaud dragged the cloth behind him as he imitated the gait of a deer. He took steps on his toes and did a few hops, all the while trying to be light on his feet and avoid seeming like a clumsy two-legged man. He picked up the fabric a few times and smeared it against the bark of trees at the height where a deer would mark territory by rubbing his glands. Renaud was grateful to be wearing leather gloves, for he was fearful of touching the putrid smelling cloth with his bare hands.

As his nostrils burned, Renaud knew the smells of three hunters would be masked and the animals of the forest would either be attracted or repelled by the foul deer musk. He drew near where Guichard was hiding and tied the lure to a branch of an oak tree. Renaud performed his deer hop-walk to a hiding place and waited expectantly in hopes trickery would entice stags to come their way.

Renaud's stomach rumbled again. He regretted not taking a bit of jerky before beginning this hunt, but he knew the others would have followed his lead. That action would run counter to his efforts to conserve their food stores. Deer were known for having keen sense of hearing; he wondered if the sound of growling stomachs would cause them to become wary. Perhaps that could be an excuse in the future for him to eat jerky, along with Alard and Guichard, but not the others.

He closed his eyes and listened to the sounds of the forest. There was a distant croaking of frogs, occasional chirping of birds, and a sneeze.

A sneeze!

He turned to Guichard and then to Alard. Both of his brothers bore angry looks on their faces.

If Richardet decided to follow us...

He did not get a chance to finish that thought as an eight point stag emerged from behind a tree. Alard waited patiently for the deer to walk into range and then let an arrow fly. The aim was true and the point was buried in the neck, but the stag turned and bounded away. Renaud removed his sword from its scabbard and ran in pursuit of the wounded animal. Guichard followed him as they crashed through the forest hoping to finish the kill.

The deer ran over a small hill and disappeared from sight. Renaud panted as he made his way over the incline and smiled to see the fallen deer. His joy evaporated when an unknown warrior stepped from behind a tree bearing a knife intent on claiming their prize.

CHAPTER FORTY

Bradamante saw the stone towers of her childhood home of Montauban in the distance. The sight made her stomach clench. Fear was a stranger to her on the battlefield, but her mother's wrath made her nervous. She brought Rabican to a canter as she approached the gates.

The guardian at the gate recognized her and gave the signal to raise the portcullis. A horn was blown, signaling her return. With the clanking of the chains as the barricade lifted, the tension inside her grew. Her mother's secretary waited for her inside the grounds. He was a tall, humorless man whose face seemed fixed in a perpetual scowl.

"Lady Bradamante, your mother demands your presence. You will follow me."

She dismounted. "I will obey, but first I must tend to my horse's needs."

The man lifted his chin and was about to utter a retort, when Rabican reared on his hind legs. Bradamante struggled to maintain a grip on his reins. Fear crossed the man's face as all the guards stepped three paces backward.

"Or does anyone here wish to take Rabican to the stables, unsaddle, and then brush him?"

The guards shook their heads as if they were afraid of saying anything aloud.

"Very well," said the secretary. "I will remain here waiting to escort you to your mother while one of the guards informs her that you will soon be on your way."

"Whoa, whoa," Bradamante soothed the agitated stallion.

Rabican settled down and walked across the courtyard to the stables. Bradamante suppressed a smile, and was grateful no one dared come near her magical horse. Rabican pranced as she led him into the stables. Eos, Bradamante's pure white mare, nickered as the stallion passed by on his way to the end stall. Bradamante latched the door before she let go of the reins.

"I enjoyed our ride today," she said as she unbuckled the saddle. "You are an amazing horse. I can see why Aistulf values you."

Bradamante spoke to Rabican as if he could understand the Frankish language. He was a magical steed, and perhaps he could sense the thoughts of his riders. She displayed confidence with him and he behaved well for her. Knowing her mother was waiting, Bradamante did not give Rabican a leisurely brushing, but he nonetheless appeared to enjoy the attention paid to him by a young woman.

While leaving the stall she said, "I look forward to our next ride." She was careful to not specify when that might be. Bradamante had no idea when she could slip away for a ride again and did not want to make a promise she could not keep.

Three guards and her mother's secretary were waiting for her outside the stables. They escorted her through the gardens behind the castle. At first she expected to see her mother sitting on the stone bench, but was instead led to the chapel. It was a small wooden building abutting the sheer wall of the mountain framing the rear boundary of the fortified property.

With her heart lodged in her throat, Bradamante opened the door of her family's private place of worship. Her mother bore a look of frozen anger on her face and still wore the purple silk gown trimmed in ermine. Beatrice sat next to an elderly monk.

"My wayward daughter has finally returned. I have waited here for hours wanting to hear your confession as to why you disobeyed me."

Bradamante had difficulty swallowing. "I apologize for my delay in responding to your summons. However, there is no one else here who can handle Aistulf's stallion Rabican. I had to return him to his stall."

"That is not the disobedient act I meant. Have you nothing else to say for yourself?"

Bradamante attempted to maintain a look of innocence. "This morning I planned on riding Rabican. That was before you told me about Roberto painting my portrait. I postponed my ride in accordance to your wishes. I have felt guilt over not fulfilling the promise I made to our kinsman, Aistulf, in seeing to the needs of his horse. It had been five days without Rabican having a good run. Our other horses are gentle enough to be tended by our groomsmen, but there is no one else here who can see to Rabican."

Her mother turned her face away and nervously twisted a ring on her left hand.

Bradamante changed tack. "I rode west and did not see any signs of enemy soldiers. I believe their forces have left the area and are concentrated in Paris and in Arles."

Her mother's demeanor seemed to thaw a little. "You said before that the infidels are no longer in Marseille?"

"My efforts helped drive them away from that port city."

Beatrice gave a small nod. "That is good news. However, your disobedience was not spending mealtime with your family. My husband left this morning. All of my sons are off at war. You are my only child at home, and you left the grounds without any thought or consideration of my feelings."

Bradamante lightly bit her tongue.

"Without a single word to me, you left like you did in your last visit. That same day your twin went missing for over a month. At least your father knew of your plans to leave that morning and so I had to release my sense of..." she paused and her lower lip trembled, "...abandonment by you. You are a soldier with orders, but no one knew where Richardet went. I was sick with worry over him."

Bradamante marveled at her mother's expert use of guilt as a weapon; she wielded it with far more skill than Richardet showed with a blade.

Her mother turned to the monk who had been sitting in silence. "Fra Galen, this is my daughter, Bradamante. She is a commander in my brother Charlemagne's army, but she will be here at Montauban for the foreseeable future. Bradamante, this is Fra Galen."

The man stood and gave her a warm smile. Upon closer inspection, he appeared to be in his mid-forties. He had a natural tonsure and his hair and beard were mostly gray, but had once been brown.

"Friday when you remained here," said Beatrice. "I sent for Fra Galen from the Abbey at Saint Antonin. You will spend your afternoons with him after your portrait sessions are over. While it is admirable that you can read and write Latin, you still have not mastered Greek."

Bradamante's stomach sank. Greek. She saw no need to learn that language. Arabic would be a more helpful language for her to learn.

Galen bowed and spoke with a voice sounding like a tenor in a choir. "It is my pleasure to meet you, my dear young lady. We shall begin by refreshing you with the basics of my mother tongue. Knowing I would be tutoring a warrior, I also brought my own personal copy of a Greek classic."

"Is it *The Iliad*?"

Fra Galen shook his head. "No. I have yet to procure a copy of that book. It is however, Homer's second poem, *The Odyssey*."

"I — I cannot read about the villain Odysseus."

"Villain? How can you be so ungrateful?" snapped Beatrice.

Bradamante took a deep breath. "Odysseus used guile and deceit to defeat the city of Troy. *The Odyssey* follows this dishonorable man after the Trojan war ended. After twenty long years, he finally returned home to his wife who had remained faithful. But during his time away from his wife, he took lovers."

"While I agree with your opinion regarding marital infidelity, wives must ignore such indiscretions committed by husbands," said Beatrice through gritted teeth. "However, I sense there is more to the cause of your rebelliousness in this matter."

"Yes, Mother. Through your father's lineage, we are descended from the Royal House of Troy. Hector — the paragon of the perfect knight — is one of our noble ancestors. I cannot devote time into studying a text used to glorify a man who sought to end our bloodline."

Beatrice looked confused. "We are descended from the House of Troy?"

Bradamante clasped hands with her mother. "I learned that recently and am proud of our heritage."

There was a period of silence as Beatrice stared at her daughter before Fra Galen cleared his throat. "I also brought Aristotle's *Poetics*. Hopefully that should not cause my pupil any distress."

"That will be fine," said Beatrice. "The lessons will start on the morrow. Come let us enjoy our evening meal. It has been delayed for far too long."

CHAPTER FORTY-ONE

The hippogriff waited nearby in the courtyard as servants began setting a low table for dinner. Clay bowls were filled with colorful foods: mounds of brown paste, chunks of meat covered in a red sauce, chopped green vegetables, and two round flatbreads. Aistulf had never eaten anything foods like these before, but his mouth watered at the smells wafting up to him.

Servants brought forth bowls and pitchers of water. King Senapo held out his right hand for water to be poured over it. The servants caught the excess water in a basin and dried his right hand with a towel. Another servant performed the same hand washing ritual on Aistulf. The two men sat on short chairs before the table. Aistulf was reclined, but not relaxed as Senapo touched one of the flatbreads.

A loud screech cut through the air as silhouettes of three birds with massive wingspans appeared in the sky. As they approached, Aistulf saw them in all their hideous glory. The heads were hags foaming at the mouth with disheveled hair, while their bodies were of vultures. Aistulf grabbed his flatbread from the table and stuffed it into his satchel as the first Harpy's talons seized food from Senapo's hands. The king fell on the ground as the other two birds swooped down and knocked the bowls off the table. They turned in mid-air and the three birds wrestled over the prize of Senapo's bread.

Aistulf jumped on the back of the hippogriff and surveyed the carnage. The table was in disarray and the food strewn about the courtyard. The Harpies began defecating as they flew around squawking at each other. The stench made his eyes water. Aistulf understood why Senapo practically starved himself to death to avoid his subjects seeing such a grotesque display.

Taking his ivory horn, Aistulf sounded a blast. The servants covered their ears as they ran away. Senapo cowered in place as the Harpies dropped the shreds of food they had been fighting over and flew away. Pulling back on the reins, Aistulf kicked the sides of the hippogriff as they took off in flight.

Clearing the walls of the wooden palace, they began their chase. The retreating forms of the Harpies flew in a southeasterly direction. Aistulf leaned forward onto the hippogriff's neck to urge the creature to speed up the pursuit of the evil spirits and held out hope the Harpies' lair would not be far away. He reasoned it must be nearby since they appeared so soon after food was set before King Senapo.

A large tree covered hill loomed in the distance. The Harpies disappeared as they flew over the treetops. Aistulf was taken by surprise after clearing the hilltop when the Harpies attacked him from three different directions. One had its fierce talons aimed at the hippogriff's head, another attacked from below, and the third Harpy flew headfirst at Aistulf. The hippogriff bolted upward and the three Harpies hit each other in mid-air. Once Aistulf caught his breath, he grabbed the horn strapped to his side and blew. The piercing sound once again made the Harpies react with panic. The demon birds plummeted, almost hitting the ground before they recovered and flew away. The strokes of their wings had become imbalanced as if they forgot how to fly.

Aistulf sat upright in the saddle with one hand on the reins, the other on his horn. He would not hesitate to blow it again. This was his only weapon against them and he would not stop until he trapped them with no hope of escape. The Harpies followed the contours of a river before plunging into the face of a rocky out cropping. He pulled back on the reins in time to avoid colliding into a stony wall. The hippogriff hovered in mid-air as Aistulf's eyes adjusted to the twilight. There was a hole large enough for a man to enter, but not large enough for his flying steed. He brought the hippogriff down for a landing near the rock.

"Go hunting," said Aistulf. "I will call you when I am ready to leave."

With that, the hippogriff left him alone on the banks of a river. Aistulf crept toward the opening. Suspecting the Harpies might be lying in wait for him, he gave another fierce blast on the horn. He peered inside and was surprised to see a faint orange glow illuminating the floor of the cave. Putting one hand to an ear, he heard what sounded like thousands of souls in agony. He knew then it was an entrance to Hell.

Spotting several boulders nearby, Aistulf had a fleeting thought of blockading the hole but quickly dismissed the idea. Caves frequently had multiple entrances and, if this was the case, the Harpies could simply escape elsewhere and continue tormenting King Senapo. His face burned at the thought of his humiliation if the Harpies attacked again when the king tried to eat a meal. He could not risk such failure. It would be more than personal embarrassment, but could spell the defeat of Charlemagne if King Senapo did not give him assistance with Caliph Harun al-Rashid. Instead, Aistulf knew he needed to venture inside the cave and discover how to trap the Harpies within the confines of Hell.

Aistulf dangled his feet inside the opening and dropped down to the hard floor. He rounded his shoulders and ducked his head as he followed a cramped passage. After about fifty paces, the cave opened up into a large vaulted ceiling with countless icicle shaped rock formations looming over his head like the famed Sword of Damocles. Water dripped from those shadowy pointed rocks onto the ground where companion rock formations rose upward. The ground was slick, so he walked with a deliberate pace.

The cave was illuminated by thousands of glowing embers each creating a cloud of thin black smoke. As he came closer he realized those clouds were in the shape of men and women, but thinner than a sheet of parchment. While there was a cacophony of murmurs, he could not discern any words. Then from deep inside the recesses of the cave, came wailing sounds of the damned. He shuddered as a sense of gloom descended upon him.

Continuing onward, he came upon a river snaking through the cave and another access to the outside world. That opening was large enough a team of horses could enter without difficulty. This confirmed his instincts about more than one passage to Hell. He wondered if the Harpies chose a small entry so Aistulf could not fly the hippogriff inside.

In the distance, a hooded man stood in a small boat bearing passengers and using a pole to approach the cave. Aistulf spied a large dog lying down near the entrance. He rubbed his eyes, but his vision did not change. The dog continued to have three massive heads. Remembering what Melissa said about the ring he wore, Aistulf removed it from his finger. The orange glow surrounding him disappeared along with the spirits and the only light inside the cave came from the glistening of moonlight upon the river. There was still a dog, but with only one head. The boat had disappeared. Magic concealed the true nature of this place, and only because he wore the ring could he see things as they truly were. He wondered how many people had stumbled upon that cave and if they had been able to return to the land of the living. Then again, he mused, the dog would probably scare people away if it had a menacing bark.

Aistulf worried about being stuck in Hell ambling around forever and not knowing where to go. He needed a guide. Deciding to take a gamble, he spoke up loudly.

"Greetings, spirits. If anyone is willing to share companionship with me, I am in want of a guide."

There was a jostling within a clump of shadows as one came forward.

"I will serve as your guide," came a female voice. "My name is Lydia."

✳

CHAPTER FORTY-TWO

The unknown warrior was on his hands and knees with a knife out and about to slaughter the deer when Renaud pointed the tip of his sword into the back of the man's neck. "Give up your weapon."

The man swallowed and said, "I am at your mercy."

Guichard walked forward and accepted the surrendered knife. Renaud shifted his stance to see the man's face. The youthfulness of the warrior surprised him. He had a boyish face, similar to Richardet, but with black hair and brown eyes. There was a familiarity about him, but Renaud was certain he never met this man before.

"The woods and all the game within it belong to the nobility," said Renaud. "This forest is controlled by Duke Aymon of Dordogne, my father." The youth flinched and a small trickle of blood formed at the sword's edge. "Poaching is a crime, punishable by death."

"I am not a poacher," said the warrior. "I have a right to be in this woods and I have a right to this stag."

The calmness of the young man's voice impressed Renaud. He looked at Guichard and drew a circle in the air. Guichard nodded as he quietly went in search of accomplices hiding in the woods.

"It is my brother's kill," said Renaud. "That arrow is his, not yours."

"Yes, his arrow wounded the deer, but if you will allow me," said the youth, "I will show you that my arrow killed it."

Renaud took a step backward as the young man grabbed the deer's antlers and lifted the head revealing a second arrow on the other side of the neck. The shaft had been driven deep into the flesh and likely crushed the windpipe.

"I have as much right to this stag as you," the youth said looking straight at Renaud with a touch of defiance in his voice. "More, since I actually killed it."

"He is right, Renaud," agreed a warrior who emerged from the forest walking alongside Guichard. "And, from the looks of it, there should be more than enough meat for all of us to share."

The warrior's long black hair was tied back. As the man came closer, Renaud recognized a friend and sheathed his sword. "Aquilant, why did it take you this long to arrive back in Francia?"

Aquilant laughed. "We shared a few adventures on our journey homeward from Cathay delaying our return. We will regale you with those tales over a good meal and wine. It includes having met up with Queen Marfisa along the way."

"Indeed? I look forward to hearing your stories," Renaud said as he embraced his friend.

"I feel blessed," said Aquilant. "My little party of four shall join forces with yours."

"Where is your worthless brother?" joked Renaud.

"Where else? Grifon is tending the horses, but here comes the last of my companions. Say hello to Sansonetto." Aquilant gestured toward a warrior coming towards them wearing a red surcoat covered with white flowers.

Aquilant thumped Renaud on the back. "It is a good thing you did not harm our friend Guidone Selvaggio for it is a sin to commit fratricide."

"Speak plainly," said Renaud.

Aquilant tipped back his head and laughed. "Guidone has as much right to hunt in this forest as you because he is the fifth son of Aymon. Say hello to a brother you never knew you had."

The young man stood and lifted his chin in a defiant manner.

"What is your name again?" asked Renaud, feeling stunned at the revelation.

"I am Guidone Selvaggio."

Renaud regarded the young man. He had broad shoulders, a full build, and was as tall as his other brothers. Guidone resembled Guichard. They shared a similar jaw line and shape of their noses. The difference was Guidone had black hair and brown eyes, instead of the fair hair and blue eyes that marked the House of Lyon. Renaud now realized why this young man had a familiar look about him; Guidone was family. He nodded to demonstrate acceptance of Guidone's claim.

"Selvaggio? You are named Guidone the Savage?"

The young man clenched his jaw. "My mother thought it a better name than Guidone the Bastard."

Renaud was taken aback by the defensive tone. "And from where do you hail?"

"I grew up in Reggio Calabria, on the toe of the Italian peninsula."

"Yours is a story I want to hear." He clapped him on the back. "But it should be told in front of all of your brothers tonight after we feast." He turned to Sansonetto. "I trust you know how to properly dress a deer."

"Of course."

"Good. My brothers Guichard and Alard shall stay and assist you, then help carry it back to our camp. We should have a campfire ready with red-hot embers by the time you arrive. Aquilant, go find your brother and help him lead the horses to our camp. We are west of the road, east of the stream and about two miles downwind of here. If you cannot find us, you are not the skilled huntsmen I took you to be."

Aquilant laughed. "We shall find you."

"Renaud," said Alard, "please do not let Guidone start his story without us."

"I promise. I do not want anyone mentioning Guidone's parentage until the end of our meal. I want to see how Richardet reacts when he discovers he has yet another brother." He looked at the young man. "How old are you Guidone?"

"Eighteen."

"Yes, another *older* brother."

CHAPTER FORTY-THREE

Aistulf felt grateful a spirit agreed to serve as his guide. He had no idea how it might impact her punishment, but that was not his worry.

"Follow me," said Lydia as she glided forward into the recesses of the cave. As she spoke, her shadow began to expand and glow from the spark of her soul.

The shadows of other spirits surrounded Aistulf. He brushed them aside as if clearing cobwebs, but rather than becoming covered with a silken residue he became covered in soot. Fearing the worst, he reached for his horn.

"Please, do not sound your horn again," pleaded Lydia. "It is terrifying."

Lydia's ghost had transformed into the shape of a woman wearing a tunic. There was an overall orange glow about her making it impossible to know the tone of her complexion or her hair color in life. She appeared to have been a young woman whose hairstyle of ornate braiding and curls denoted being of a noble class.

Aistulf let go of his horn and continued following Lydia. The shadows left his side the moment he touched his horn. Perhaps the threat was all he needed. She led him into a narrow passageway alongside the river.

"Take care not to fall into any of the waters here. They have magical powers and I do not know what would happen to someone still living."

Aistulf slung his shield across his back, removed his gloves, stuffed them into his satchel, before finding handholds and footholds along the wall to make his way sideways along the river's edge. His mood brightened ever so slightly as he thought of himself as an overgrown crab.

"You must not eat or drink anything here," added Lydia.

His mood darkened again and his stomach grumbled at the suggestion of food and drink. "I have some bread with me. I could eat that, if I become really hungry."

"No, you will need that for when you leave. You will need food to distract the dog's three heads allowing you to run to safety."

"Is there only one entrance?" asked Aistulf.

"No, the world is vast and therefore there are many places for the dead to enter the Underworld, and they are all guarded by Cerberus."

"How can that be?"

"The Underworld is a vast magical domain. The guard dog appears where and when he is needed. While Cerberus guards one entrance, the others are closed."

Aistulf paused, his cheek pressed against the cool rock wall. He reminded himself that he was brave enough for this journey.

"What brought you to the realm of the dead?" asked Lydia.

"I am in pursuit of the Harpies. It is my quest to confine them so henceforth they cannot torment anyone."

Lydia lowered her voice. "You are a brave man. There are many, even here, who would rejoice should that come to pass. You are fortunate the spirits marked you before we enter the next chamber."

"Marked me?" Aistulf was puzzled and renewed his sideways movement.

"Your golden armor is blackened as is your face. This will allow you to move in the Underworld without being seen. You will blend in with the many shadows. It is best that certain spirits never learn you are here."

"What spirits are those?"

"I will not speak their names, lest I call their attention to us."

Aistulf nodded as he continued his tedious, one handhold and one foothold at a time. He resisted looking toward Lydia and instead focused on the area before him. He needed to concentrate on not falling into the water lapping the side of the cave.

"What is your story, Lydia?"

She gave a long sigh. "I have not spoken a word since being condemned to spend an eternity amongst the legions of dead. Silence has been my greatest punishment. Your request for a guide has given me a welcome reprieve from such tedium, I thank you for this rare opportunity." Her voice began to crack. "I am in Hell because I was cruel and heartless to a man who loved me beyond reason. I rejected him and his love, when I should have graciously accepted him."

Aistulf's fingers began to go numb from clutching the cold rock wall. He tried using Lydia's faint glow to help guide him since his could no longer feel.

Sniffing, Lydia began again. "I am named after the kingdom my father ruled. My beauty was praised far and wide. One suitor was a brave knight by the name of Alceste. He came to my father and offered his services. Alceste soon distinguished himself as not only a strong fighter, but a keen strategist. My father had become too frail for war and my brother, the heir to the kingdom, was inept at strategy. In three years, Alceste doubled the size of our kingdom and proved his loyalty to my father. He was a handsome man and we shared many happy moments when our eyes locked during banquets. I dreamt of marrying him, but we were never allowed to be alone together or even speak with each other. Alceste approached my father and asked for my hand in marriage. My father rejected him without hesitation. I was a princess and expected to wed a king or an heir, not a mere knight."

"How did Alceste respond?" asked Aistulf.

"He became angry and his pride wounded at being dismissed so readily. Alceste left without a word and joined the forces of our enemy, the King of Armenia. He began a campaign seizing town after town, citadel after citadel. Countless people died and my father kept us on the run, escaping by secret passageways until we were at the last castle. We were sheltered on a rocky plateau and the castle thought to be impregnable. Our walls stood firm with the long siege, but our food supplies dwindled. Surrender became the only option. Only then, did my father admit why Alceste turned traitor. All because of his love for me."

Aistulf noticed the water level of the river began fluctuating similar to a tide rushing to the shore. He wanted to ask why this was happening, but did not want to interrupt Lydia's story.

"As each of our towns fell, terms were offered that my father ignored. Alceste wanted my hand in marriage. My stubborn father refused to admit he was wrong until faced with starving to death. He sent me along with a few knights to discuss terms of surrender. My father was to be set free, I would marry Alceste, and my dowry would be half of what remained of my father's kingdom."

"What happened?" Aistulf glanced toward Lydia and was relieved to see a large chamber ahead. His slow trek on the water's edge would soon be over.

"As soon as I stood before Alceste, I realized for the first time in my life, I had power over another. He trembled with love and adoration at my feet. I saw that as a weakness, and sought revenge for a year of living in fear of him. I cursed him for not having enough faith in his love for me to remain loyal to my father. He should have pressed his case over and over, because my father was stubborn and never granted a first request for anyone. Had I known, I could have pleaded with my father as well, begging to marry my favored champion. Instead, Alceste betrayed our love by abandoning my father and siding with our enemy. My love for him changed to fear and then to hate. I told him I would rather be torn limb from limb than submit to his ardor."

"How did he react?"

"He wept. Begged my forgiveness. He handed me his sword and asked I take my revenge then and there."

"Did you strike him dead?" asked Aistulf.

"No. That would have been merciful. I had a grander scheme for revenge. I lied to him. I let him hope that he could win back my heart by demonstrating loyalty to me. He was to restore the borders of my father's kingdom and rid him of enemies. He first had to get the King of Armenia to give up all the recently gained lands. Alceste hired mercenaries to accompany him when he approached the king. After his entreaty was rejected, Alceste killed the king. Within a month my father's lands were restored. Yet, I kept making new conditions before consenting to marriage. Finally, after he had made enemies of everyone who once fought alongside him, I revealed that I despised him and would never marry him."

Aistulf stopped on a wide ledge before entering the large chamber of the cave. "Please tell me the rest of your story, before we have to watch out for other beings."

"My cruelty killed him. Alceste died from a broken heart within weeks of my rejection. I cast aside the one man who loved me and devoted his life to me. I used my beauty as a weapon, and I had plans of wielding it for years to come. Except, I died from a fever that swept through the land before I could manipulate any other man. Please learn from my sins, do not treat love with callousness."

Aistulf thought of his own history with romance. He had bedded many women, but never loved any of them. He vowed to atone for his sins and to allow his heart to experience love in a manner that both Lydia and King Senapo had not.

"Have you seen Alceste here?"

Lydia shook her head. "I learned Alceste was in Purgatory, but would eventually be allowed to enter Heaven. That is because his heart was pure, though his actions were not. All of his sins were committed in service for my love. Whereas I am condemned to be here for eternity." She paused. "We are about to enter the portion of Hell where the worst sinners are punished. Remember to not eat or drink anything, no matter how tempted you are."

"I shall resist."

"Good. The creatures you seek have a nest inside a small cave a short distance from the entrance to Tartarus. I expect they will be hiding in there, hoping you will abandon your pursuit of them. Keep your horn handy, but do not use it unless absolutely necessary for it will bring unwanted attention of other spirits. I shall point in the direction you should head, but I will not say another word and will wait for you on the other side of this chamber. I will then direct you out of this place."

Lydia stepped aside and allowed Aistulf to enter an enormous cavern.

✳

CHAPTER FORTY-FOUR

Renaud led Guidone Selvaggio back to their camp. They walked in silence. There was no need to risk alerting bandits hiding in the woods of their position. He was grateful Guidone followed his lead and did not try to make conversation. Besides being concerned about security, Renaud was absorbing the idea of his father having an illegitimate child. He wondered whether or not his family's standings would change should it become known. Kings could sire bastards, but it was an altogether different matter for the husband of a king's sister. The king might take it as a personal insult, especially since Charlemagne never wanted his sister to marry in the first place.

He wondered if Charlemagne was aware of Aymon's infidelity. If Guidone was conceived during a long military campaign, perhaps Charlemagne knew about the liaison at the time. Charlemagne might have turned a blind eye to the affair, similar to his apparent ignorance of Maugis' magical powers.

As the trees began to appear blackened again, Renaud's thoughts returned to finding the camp. Soon he saw the glow of a campfire. Maugis and Vivien had placed large stones in a circle and started a fire in the center. Richardet and Emile tethered the horses to trees in an area not too far from where they would be sleeping.

"Who is with you?" asked Vivien.

Renaud smiled, indicating his approval of the stranger. "This is Guidone and he is the first of four additional warriors I found in the woods. They will be joining us in our travels to Paris."

"Is there anyone I know in the group of four?"

"Yes, Oliver's sons, Aquilant and Grifon, as well as a young man named Sansonetto."

A broad smile crossed Vivien's face. "Where are those scoundrel brothers?"

"They should be on their way along with their horses."

Maugis did not share the same enthusiasm. His face was stone-like. "While I am pleased you found more reinforcements for Charlemagne's war effort, I am wondering if you found any game while in the woods. Or will we be using our food stores to feed even more mouths?"

Renaud was tempted to apologize to Guidone for his cousin's boorish behavior, but thought better of it. This would give him a chance to gauge his half-brother's manner when challenged.

"We will feast on venison tonight," said Renaud. "Alard and Guichard are helping Sansonetto dress the kill. They will be bringing it back here soon."

Maugis nodded, walked around Guidone looking at him from head to toe before grabbing his hands. Guidone looked uncomfortable, but did not flinch.

Renaud knew his cousin was using magical powers attempting to read the young man's mind. He had seen that trick done many times before, sometimes leading to Maugis being punched in the face. Guidone clenched his jaw, but said nothing.

Maugis stared at him. "You are honorable...but I also sense you are filled with bitterness and resentment." His voice sounded threatening. "You are hiding something from me."

Guidone pulled his hands free. "Everyone has secrets."

Maugis smirked. "I *will* discover yours."

"This is cousin Maugis, a powerful warrior, paladin of Charlemagne, and a man with more secrets than anyone else I know," said Renaud. "Perhaps after a good meal and a cup of wine, we can persuade Guidone to share his story with us."

He then introduced Guidone to Vivien, Richardet, and Emile. The beginning of a light-hearted conversation was cut short at the sound of movement amongst the trees. Soon the black-haired Aquilant and his brother, the white-blond haired Grifon, appeared and both were leading two horses.

"Have you twins been knighted yet?" asked Vivien.

"Not quite," said Aquilant. "Our knighting ceremony was to be after Charlemagne's Pentecost Tournament last year. After the chaos ensued, we followed Orlando to the east in pursuit of the fair Angelica."

"You have stories to tell," said Vivien. "Squires! See to their mounts."

Emile rushed forward and took the reins from Aquilant.

Richardet grumbled, "Why am I to play squire to others who have not been knighted? Why do they not tend their own horses?"

Renaud made a quick motion for Richardet to be quiet and follow Emile.

"They have been fed and watered," said Grifon, "all they need is to be secured with the other horses."

Richardet gave the barest of smiles as he took the reins from Grifon. "Welcome to our group of soldiers, I am Duke Aymon's youngest son, Richard."

Renaud laughed. "Not until you have killed a man, little brother. Until that time you are to be called Richardet!"

His youngest brother turned his back on the group of men and led the horses away.

Renaud spoke to Maugis in an undertone designed so no one else would hear. "Once Alard, Guichard, and Sansonetto bring the stag here, I want you to secure our surroundings."

"Is that what all the twigs are for?" asked Maugis.

"Yes, I thought you needed something physical to create a protective barrier."

Maugis gave him a knowing smile and nodded. "I know just the spell. It will keep out all entities from our circle including humans, animals, and spirits. We will be safe until the circle is broken when someone steps outsides its confines."

"I shall designate an area within the circle and away from our sleeping area for the men to relieve themselves during the night."

Maugis and Renaud set out to scour the area for more twigs while Vivien began an animated discussion with his friends, Aquilant and Grifon. Once the slaughtered deer was brought back to the camp and roasting over the open fire, Renaud made an announcement.

"Listen up, and take notice down near that bush is where everyone will relieve themselves. We shall remain in an area soon to be defined by Maugis. He will be setting traps for those intending on harming us. Respect the barrier or you will be chastised. It will be hard for you to ride on the morrow, should you cross me."

"Is he jesting?" asked Sansonetto.

"Renaud never jests in matters of strategy or security," said Vivien.

Maugis tied a blanket around his neck making a large sling allowing him to carry a large number of sticks. He muttered strange words under his breath as he placed the twigs on the ground in a large circle. Renaud helped him in this endeavor by bringing more armloads of sticks, so there was no pause in the creation of the protective barrier. By the time their task was complete, the air was filled with the smell of roasted meat as Vivien carved the deer.

Renaud tore into the venison in a manner that would have made his mother and wife scowl. The meat was lean with a sharper flavor than fatted cattle slaughtered for feasts. The texture was a bit stringy, but Renaud enjoyed eating fresh game. He preferred gorging on food in the wild over eating course after course of elaborate dishes served at formal banquets. He poured himself a large share of red wine as the last of the men sat down with their food.

"Emile and Sansonetto, you will take the first watch," said Renaud. "Sit near the horses and be certain no one is lurking nearby in the darkness waiting to steal them."

"I thought Maugis set traps?" asked Sansonetto.

"He did, but I insist on having some eyes serve as lookouts," said Renaud. "Be certain to stay within the boundary or I shall beat you."

"Yes, my lord," said Sansonetto as he and Emile walked away with their plates of food to be near the horses.

"Now that is taken care of," said Renaud, "Guidone Selvaggio promised to tell his story and why he is joining Charlemagne's army."

With that pronouncement, the remaining men sat up with rapt attention.

"My story begins with my mother," said Guidone. "She is a beautiful, intelligent, and talented woman, but most of all, she is a survivor. She survived betrayal and abandonment, and raised me to be a respected warrior. I would be nothing if not for her." He took a long drink of wine. "I am about to share her secrets with my brothers in this group, but only if you swear not to tell anyone. Her life, her reputation, and her marriage would be jeopardized if the truth were known."

He looked at each face staring at him around the fire. "Swear it!" Guidone commanded.

One by one they raised their hands in the air and repeated the words, "I swear to keep your secrets."

CHAPTER FORTY-FIVE

Aistulf gaped at the sight before him. The ceiling was at least fifty feet high and filled with stone icicle formations. In one corner it looked as if a waterfall had been frozen in midair. He was surprised several areas were well-lit as if bathed in the glow of moonlight. Lydia pointed to the far wall with a large hill, and made a gesture indicating the Harpies' lair was behind the hill.

Directly in front of him was a massive tree laden with ripened fruit. It was covered with apples, plums, and pears as well as other fruits he did not recognize. His hunger overruled his sense of reason. Aistulf walked toward the tree while holding out his right hand. A juicy red apple was almost within his grasp when the limbs moved upward out of his reach.

Aistulf almost complained aloud at such teasing and trickery when he saw movement within the river. An emaciated man stood up to his neck in water with his arms outstretched trying to grab a plum inches from the man's fingertips. There was agony in the man's eyes. His arms flailed as the branches moved enough to be just beyond his reach.

The skeletal man lowered his arms and opened his mouth as he tried to take a drink of water. The river receded as the man lowered himself. Not a drop of water touched his lips. While on his knees in the riverbed, the fruit-laden tree once again lowered its branches. A peach dangled in front of the man's face. He reached his hand out, but once again was denied food as the water flooded up to his neck. Aistulf realized this man's punishment was the cause of what he previously thought of as tidal action of the river.

The lure of the forbidden fruit had been so potent Aistulf forgot Lydia's warning about eating or drinking while in the Underworld. With a fresh resolve, he turned his back on the accursed wretch and walked toward the large earthen hill in the distance. A bearded and muscular man pushed a boulder up the hill. Other boulders were piled in a heap at the bottom. Aistulf watched the man's progress as he made his slow ascent. The man wore only a loincloth, allowing the rippling muscles on his arms, back and legs to be easily seen. His skin appeared to be as dark as the earth he walked on. As the man neared the top of the hill, the boulder slipped out of his hands and rolled and bounced its way down. The man turned around and plodded downward with a look of resignation on his face.

Aistulf glanced behind himself to see the river recede from its banks only to return when the skinny man stood again. Then he remembered the names of the legendary men: Tantalus and Sisyphus.

He continued walking toward Sisyphus in a slow, deliberate pace as he did not want sudden movement to call attention to himself. A slow moving shadow should be an unremarkable sight in the Underworld. He passed by a mound topped with a tall wooden pole bearing leather straps illuminated by a moon-like glow. A palpable sense of misery hung in the air near the mound.

By the time he made his way past Sisyphus, the boulder had crashed to the ground at least three times. Aistulf became so enthralled by this repetitive scene, he almost stepped into large round droppings at the bottom of the hill. The foul stench was the same at Senapo's fortress. He followed the trail of filth to a small opening in the nearby rock wall.

Aistulf surveyed the pile of rocks at the bottom of the hill and spied one appearing large enough to block the Harpies' lair. He pushed with his arms, back, and legs. The boulder barely budged, rolling less than a foot when it stopped. It was heavier than he could manage. A sense of desperation came over him. He could not fulfill this task by himself. The urge to weep was strong, but he resisted. He needed to find a way to move that boulder.

He looked around, hoping to find some tool to aid in this task, and saw a larger opening in the rock wall. Evil rolled out in waves, and he realized this was the entrance to Tartarus, mentioned by Lydia. Being in the Underworld was driving him mad. Aistulf needed a solution and fast. The boulder Sisyphus was moving rolled once again to the bottom of the hill. The man had a look of resignation on his face.

Aistulf decided to take a chance. "Hello, Sisyphus!"

"What do you want?" the man grunted.

"I need your help. I thought you might take a short break from pushing that rock up a hill, and instead roll a boulder across a small cave."

Sisyphus put his shoulder and hands against his boulder and began pushing it up his well-worn path. "Why should I help you?"

"I am not strong enough to move it myself."

Sisyphus snorted. "You did not answer my question. I am condemned to perform this task for eternity without stopping and with no possibility of fulfilling it either."

Aistulf followed alongside Sisyphus up the hill, standing in the man's shadow. Somehow he needed to find a way to persuade this dead soul to help. An idea began to form in his mind when the air was split by inhuman laughter.

Three winged forms flew overhead. At first Aistulf thought they were the Harpies, but he soon realized these beings were far more frightful. These women wore black tunics, had wings on their backs, and snakes for hair. Aistulf cowered as he kept close to Sisyphus.

"Who are they?" he whispered.

Sisyphus gave a small smile. "You must not be dead. Any dead spirit would know. Those are the Erinnyes, better known as the Avenging Furies."

Aistulf shuddered as the three hideous women flew around the enormous cavern. "They are uglier than what I expected from legend."

Sisyphus chuckled. "They are even uglier up close. They cry tears of blood when they laugh. Those three immortals torment the living and the dead, but only those who committed heinous acts. They are returning from their earthly rounds and will devote their attention to those evil souls condemned to Tartarus."

The Furies emerged from Tartarus pulling on a rope tied to the hands of an ancient woman. She was naked, covered in wrinkles with only a few wisps of hair on her head. The woman fell and wailed in agony as they dragged her across the rocky floor.

Aistulf had a fleeting sympathetic thought toward the woman, but it was quickly replaced by a sense of familiarity. After another loud cry of protest, he recognized her.

"She is new here," said Sisyphus. "After awhile, she will accept her punishment as I have."

"Her name is Alcina. She earned every stripe she gets," said Aistulf.

"It sounds like you knew her," said Sisyphus.

Aistulf nodded as Alcina's hands were bound to a pole before the Furies took turns whipping her. Her screams mingled with the hyena-like laughter of her tormentors and the chilling sounds echoed throughout the enormous cavern. The witch's back became criss-crossed with red gashes. Aistulf's sense of underlying terror for being in the Underworld was mitigated by a sense of vindication at seeing punishment being meted out for the evil sorceress.

Aistulf turned his attention back to Sisyphus as they made their way up the hill. "You have pushed this same boulder up this same hill for how long?"

"Forever it seems."

"And it always slips away?"

"Always."

"If you moved a different boulder in a different place, you might actually feel a sense of accomplishment instead of futility."

Sisyphus cast him a skeptical look. "Did the gods send you to tempt me?"

"No, I am here because the king of Ethiopia had a prophetic dream. Saint Michael predicted I would chase the Harpies away from his kingdom and imprison them in Hell."

Sisyphus appeared startled and the boulder slipped from his hands about two-thirds of the way up the hill, far earlier than normal. "You want me to trap the Harpies in their lair?"

"Yes, will you help me?"

A grin spread across his face. "Of course. You should have said that from the beginning. I despise them. They fly about my head pecking my ears with their beaks and leave droppings on my hill for me to step on." He turned and began his slow walk down the hill. "I hope the boulder you want moved will stay put, but I have no confidence it will."

"If you can get it started, I shall give the final push to set it in place."

"That might work."

Aistulf walked behind Sisyphus and noticed pale streaks on his back from sweat rolling down his dirt-coated skin.

They reached the bottom of the hill and Aistulf pointed out a large rock. "This is the one I want moved."

Sisyphus grunted and leaned in with his shoulder and arms while Aistulf helped push the boulder. Working together, they rolled the immense stone across the floor of the cavern. Aistulf felt hope rise within him.

Squawking came from within the small cave, but the Harpies did not try to escape. Just as the boulder was about to come to rest, Sisyphus stood back and allowed Aistulf to give the final push. The two men stood there waiting and watching. The boulder remained in place.

Sisyphus smiled. "Thank you. I shall be forever grateful for this reprieve from an eternity of wasted effort. Now, you must leave before you are discovered and forced to stay here forever."

Muffled howls came from within the Harpies' blockaded lair.

Sisyphus turned his back and began pushing his boulder up the hill once again. Aistulf needed to make his way to the other side of the cavern where Lydia waited for him. To get there, he would have to go around Sisyphus' large hill. His momentary elation for having successfully entrapped the Harpies disappeared when he realized he could either walk by the opening of Tartarus or in front of the Furies torturing Alcina. Both options filled him with dread. Continuing to stand at the bottom of the hill seemed dangerous as well. He needed to move before the Furies spotted him. Even if he had not committed evil acts, he was trespassing in the Underworld and that might be enough of a crime to warrant punishment. Sisyphus made his slow climb to the summit of the hill once again.

"Or I could go a third way," Aistulf mumbled to himself.

Scrambling his way back to Sisyphus's side, he mimicked the strong man's movements as if he were his shadow.

Sisyphus turned his head and frowned. "Why are you still by my side?"

"I thought it might be safer to go down the backside of your hill rather than go around it."

"You can try. I will do another favor for you. As we near the top, go ahead and wait on the other side. As this boulder begins to slip from my hands, I will speak aloud. That will be your signal to begin your descent. I advise against trying to run or walk down. You do not want to risk breaking a leg if you fall."

"How else should I go down the hill?" asked Aistulf.

"Use your shield as a sled."

The suggestion horrified him. His shield was expensive, and would be destroyed if he used it in such a manner. Then he realized replacing a shield was better than losing his life.

"I am grateful for your help and advice," Aistulf said.

His heart began pounding in his ears like a drumbeat. Escaping notice of the Furies was his immediate goal as well as getting past Tartarus without malevolent spirits claiming him. He paid close attention to the well-worn groove on the hill. As they neared the position where the boulder would slip from Sisyphus's hands, Aistulf bolted away and headed for the backside of the hill. He almost fell as he teetered over the summit.

Aistulf removed his shield slung on his back and placed the design facing the ground. He sat down on it with his knees tucked inward and his hands holding onto the side of the hill. He held that position until he heard Sisyphus exclaim, "Not again!"

Giving a push forward he wrapped his arms around his chest and slid down the steep hill. He bounced a few times, but did not crash. Thankfully, the sounds made by Sisyphus's boulder concealed the noise from his rapid descent. No spirits seemed to recognize anything was amiss in the realm of the dead. Once he was at the bottom, Aistulf spotted Lydia beckoning him from a far wall.

✳

CHAPTER FORTY-SIX

Renaud looked at his brothers and two cousins. They sat at rapt attention waiting to hear Guidone Selvaggio's tale. Aquilant and Grifon leaned back against large rocks with knowing smiles on their faces. Emile did not need to learn family secrets. Renaud hoped the squire was far enough away to not overhear conversations around the campfire.

Guidone took a deep breath and began. "My mother's name is Costanza and is a daughter of a wealthy nobleman in Palermo. She was famed for her beauty and had many suitors. Her father chose a duke's son to be her husband. Her betrothed was said to be handsome, brave, and a hero. The Saracens invaded the southern part of the Italian peninsula, and he led the defense against the infidels. After that victory, the Duke of Reggio Calabria made an odd request. He sent a ship to Palermo and asked for my mother to return the next day to Reggio. She was to be married, but none of her family members would be allowed to attend the wedding. My grandfather was not in a position to argue with such a powerful man, so she left her family never to see them again."

Guidone stared at the fire. "She arrived with fanfare, but had been instructed to wear a veil over her face when she left the ship. They placed her in a small room in the palace. All of her luggage, including her bridal dress was taken from her. The next day she was given a simple black dress to wear and taken out the back gate into a carriage. During the ride, the duke's seneschal warned about threats made against her life. He was taking her to a safe place where she would not be harmed. This frightened her, but she trusted him." His voice turned bitter. "He enrolled her in a convent and told the Mother Superior my mother was to be called Maria Antonia and had taken a vow of silence for a year."

"A year?" blurted out Richardet.

"My mother was confused, but realized she was not to speak," said Guidone. "After a week of being in isolation, she was allowed to be with other postulates, but none asked any questions because they knew she was to remain silent for a year."

"Did she ever find out who wanted to kill her?" asked Richardet.

"It was all a lie. She discovered later that the duke's son married another woman the same day she entered the convent. Everyone thought the bride was Costanza of Palermo, but the woman he married was a Saracen. The duke used my mother's good name to fool his people into thinking a godless Saracen temptress was a proper Christian noblewoman." He kicked a few stones with his boot. "My mother wept when she realized she was imprisoned in the convent and could not send a message to her father. Six months later the Saracens attacked again. This time they seized the city, killed the duke, his two sons and the harlot Saracen woman who used my mother's name. It was madness, blood in the streets."

Guidone stopped and chewed a little more on a piece of meat before he continued. "After the Saracens came to power, they encouraged everyone to convert to Islam. They allowed Christians and Jews to remain with their faith, but they closed down the monasteries and convents. The nuns were made their servants. Amir Agolante ruled from the duke's palace. My mother became a laundress in the household where she was once destined to be a lady."

"What was it like for her serving infidels?" asked Alard.

"Thankfully, God protected her from harm," said Guidone. "She was almost ravished, but she fell to the ground and began twitching. One of her fellow postulates lied to the man and told him that my mother had prophetic powers of death and had similar fits twice before. The nuns who touched her during those spells, both died within a week. The man became scared and left my mother alone. Soon whispers about her spread throughout the palace and no man bothered her again."

"So when did she marry?" asked Richardet.

"I will get to that," said Guidone, taking another long drink of wine. "Later that year, after the harvest, Charlemagne's forces finally arrived and liberated us from the Saracen plague. It was a horrible war, and Charlemagne's forces were almost defeated. Then the brave young Orlando became a hero when he killed Almont and saved Charlemagne's life."

"Orlando is our cousin," said Richardet with pride in his voice.

Guidone gave a wan smile. "I met him briefly, but did not get a chance to thank him for freeing my people."

Renaud sat up. "When and where did you see him?"

"A few days ago, outside the castle of Altaripa."

"The Maganzas," said Renaud through gritted teeth.

"Yes," said Guidone. "The four of us were forced into serving Pinabel and his harlot wife. I do not want to go into that story right now. We were defending Pinabel's horrible rules against a knight when a curse befell us and everyone blacked out. When we awoke, the knight was gone, and Pinabel was found in a ravine not far from the castle. His widow ordered us to kill the man covered in blood standing over Pinabel's corpse."

"That was Orlando?"

"Yes," said Aquilant. "He was confused. He looked at Belle and called her Angelica."

Renaud gave a small smile when hearing Angelica's name because it no longer caused a surge of jealousy and obsession. All of his concern regarded finding his kinsman. The spell over his heart had been lifted. "Did you try killing Orlando?"

"We are not mad," scoffed Aquilant. "We would have been snapped in two like twigs. Besides, he is betrothed to our Aunt Alda. We think of him as a kinsman, so we refused her order."

"I refused her as well," said Guidone. "Belle ordered her servants to kill Orlando and one after another they died at his hands. We left the castle that night knowing our vow to serve Pinabel, made under coercion, ended with his death. We set out to reclaim our honor by joining Charlemagne's forces."

"What night was that?" asked Renaud.

Aquilant started counting back on his fingers. "Tuesday?" he asked Grifon.

"Yes, it was Tuesday."

Renaud shared a look with Guichard. "We must have been two full days behind him." He turned to Aquilant. "Did you see Orlando again?"

"No."

"Guidone," said Renaud, "pardon my interruption of your story. Guichard and I had been on a mission to find Orlando and bring him back to Paris. We spent a fortnight searching for him. Please continue."

"Where was I? Oh, yes, the liberation of Reggio from the Saracen menace. There was a citywide celebration. People danced in the street all through the night. It had been over a year since the day my mother was commanded not to speak. My mother chose to end her silence, a vow she never made but followed. That night she met my father. My mother fell in love with a handsome warrior who made her feel beautiful, desirable, and wanted. She had doubted all those things about herself after being forced into a nunnery."

He ran his fingers through his hair. "She gave him the name Valentina, but would not speak about her family. He knew from the way she carried herself that she was of noble birth. Charlemagne set up court in the duke's palace to stay through the winter. They left in the springtime after the snows melted in the mountain passes. My mother was heavy with child by that time. My father swore he loved her above all other women, but could not take her with him because he had a wife and children back home."

Renaud grit his teeth. His parents were not in love with each other, but he resented hearing about another woman winning his father's heart. It was disrespectful to his mother. Alard and Guichard had pained expressions on their faces.

"How sad for your mother," said Richardet.

"He tried providing for her," said Guidone. "He gave her gold coins and helped her become a part of the new Duke of Reggio's household. My father told the duke that Valentina was the widow of a fierce warrior named Selvaggio. He gave enough details to be believable, but not enough to be discovered as a lie. My mother had a pleasing demeanor and was judicious in her speaking. She became a constant companion of the duchess who was protective of her. If anyone asked my mother about her late husband, she would tear up and appear distraught. The duchess would end those conversations. So no words were spoken about that painful subject, and no new information ever gleaned. My mother's real name and my paternity is not known in the palace."

"What about the servants?" asked Renaud. "They would have known her from before."

"No. The Saracens had forced nuns and monks into servitude. Once the city was liberated, the convents and monasteries were reopened. My mother was the only one from the convent who did not return. New servants were found from the city dwellers. I was raised alongside the duke's son as if we were brothers. After the death of the duke's wife, he married my mother. It would be a scandal if it became common knowledge that the duke's second wife had borne a child outside the confines of marriage."

The men nodded and raised their hands again signifying they would keep his secret.

"Why did you come to Francia?" asked Renaud.

"I learned Charlemagne's army was facing the Saracen menace," said Guidone. "I came to join his forces. If the Saracens had not invaded Reggio Calabria, my mother would have lived a life without deceit. She would be able to use the name Costanza and she would not have been betrayed by a duke, imprisoned in a convent, and abandoned by a lover. I am here to make a name for myself and to bring honor to her."

Richardet leaned forward. "Do you know who your father is?"

"I do. One of the last acts he did was to give her his shield bearing his standard. I use his old shield, but I covered it with leather to hide its truth. Wait here, I will show you."

Guidone stood and walked over to the pile of weapons and shields. He retrieved a large shield decorated with a black design bearing a diagonal white line. Guidone used a knife to slice through the leather lacing securing the cover. He patiently pulled the binding until he removed the leather covering revealing a silver lion on a field of red.

"My father is Duke Aymon of the House of Lyon," said Guidone.

Richardet stared at Guidone. "So the rumors *are* true. Our father has a bastard of his own. Bradamante did not believe me."

"Who is Bradamante?" asked Guidone.

"Bradamante is our sister," said Renaud. "A fierce and beautiful warrior maiden whose service and leadership Charlemagne honors."

"She is my twin," said Richardet with pride.

"I look forward to meeting her," said Guidone.

A smile crept on the face of Maugis. "Honor, resentment, and secrets. Yes, I believe you told us the truth, Guidone Selvaggio. Welcome to the House of Lyon, my new kinsman."

CHAPTER FORTY-SEVEN

Aistulf made his way toward Lydia. She stood near a stone bridge crossing the River Styx. On the other side of the river was a pathway leading to a cave entrance. The three-headed dog stood watch as a small boat with the ferryman and freshly dead spirits entered the Underworld.

"After you return to the land of the living," said Lydia, "you must first cleanse yourself before you can rejoin the mortal world. You have become marked with the tarnish of death."

"A bath does sound inviting."

Lydia frowned. "After you leave, I shall return to being mute as atonement for my myriad of sins. However, it is not too late for you. It is far easier to atone for your sins whilst you are living than to do so after death. Try and cleanse your soul as well and resist temptations."

"Thank you, Lydia, for your guidance in this realm," said Aistulf.

She smiled. "It was my pleasure. Now, for your escape, you have to get past Cerebus the three-headed dog. Earlier, you mentioned you carried food."

"Yes, I have honeyed bread."

"Break it into three pieces, one for each head. You must wait for Charon to get past Cerebus, then reveal yourself to the dog. Show the food and throw the pieces behind you. Cerebus will go after the food and you can run to safety. All of this must be done while the passengers of Charon's boat are disembarking. Once his boat leaves here, this passage will close as he shifts his duties to other areas where dead souls are waiting."

Aistulf walked up the steps of the stone bridge arched over the river and waited in the shadows. As soon as the ferryman passed the three-headed dog, Aistulf finished crossing the bridge and walked toward Cerebus. Because he was covered in soot, the dog did not see him at first. As Aistulf took a few more steps, the ears on one of the dog's heads twitched. The head turned in his direction and snarled. The other two heads turned to him and snarled as well.

He reached into his satchel and withdrew the bread. "Hello, doggie. Look what I have. Honeyed bread. All for you."

The three heads stopped snarling. All six eyes focused on the food and tracked the bread as he waved it in the air. Drool formed in the three fearsome mouths.

He broke the bread into three pieces and threw them toward the bridge. "Go get it."

The dog lumbered past him, almost knocking Aistulf over. The stench from the beast was overpowering. Aistulf wasted no time and sprinted toward the cave entrance. His shield slammed against his back as he ran. He was mere steps away from the entrance when he heard the dog barking as it chased him. Fear propelled him to run even faster, and he lost his footing. He tripped, falling face down. He braced himself to be torn apart by the many jaws of Cerebus, when he felt a breeze on the back of his neck. He had gone beyond the gates of Hell.

Aistulf began laughing into the sand where he had fallen. He had made it out alive. He struggled to his feet, still laughing, and happier than he had remembered being for a long time. The moon was almost full and the silvery light illuminated the river flowing into the rock wall of the mountain. Not trusting these waters, he turned toward the mountain and walked up the hill. After putting a good distance between himself and the river, he said the charm calling Kamal the hippogriff.

The winged creature appeared in the sky a few moments later, but refused to land. Aistulf had wanted to climb on the beast's back and fly far away, but his Kamal would not cooperate. Looking down upon himself, Aistulf remembered he was soot covered.

"I understand. You want me to bathe before I can climb on your back. Would you please lead me to a pool of fresh water?"

The hippogriff turned and flew in an easterly direction. Aistulf followed and within three miles he climbed a hill and beheld a fresh water spring nestled in a small valley. He took off his helmet and his shield, dumped the contents of his satchel onto the ground and retrieved his water flask. Aistulf carefully refilled it while trying hard to keep his filthy hands out of the clean water. He drank and drank until he had his fill. His head began to clear from the depressive spell he had been under after spending so much time in Hell.

Aistulf removed his armor, before doffing his gambeson and breaches. He cupped his hands in the water and splashed his face. The cool water was refreshing and he was a bit dismayed as black droplets formed upon the water's surface. He washed his face three times. He set about cleansing his clothes and his armor. As each item entered the water, blackness covered it like a cloud. The filth congealed into dark droplets that formed into a circle; then the droplets spun like an eddy and fell to the bottom.

He placed his shield into the water with the design turned away from him. He swished the shield back and forth in the water. The filth formed another cloud, before it congealed into a halo of black droplets and spun to the bottom. Turning the freshly cleaned shield around, Aistulf was dismayed to survey the damage it sustained when he slid down the backside of Sisyphus' hill. Deep gouges scarred the surface. All of the gold plating had been scraped away, and the pearls encircling its edges were crushed. That fanciful adornment had always been impractical, but he adored the flourish. Now, it was ruined. The bronze shield would still protect him in combat, but it no longer reflected the warrior who carried it. Aistulf shrugged his shoulders; his shield's design was the least of his worries.

Turning his attention to his satchel, he paused to examine its contents strewn about the ground. He had contaminated the inside of his bag, and its contents, when he retrieved the bread to feed Cerebus. Soot coated everything except for the magical gifts given to him by Melissa and Logistilla. The book, tablecloth, and the horn were the only items held in the satchel lacking tarnish. He assumed there were enchantments protecting them from the effects of the Underworld.

He washed his belongings as well as the leather satchel in the water. He placed them on a small grassy knoll to dry. Aistulf turned to the hippogriff and said, "Guard my belongings."

Kamal slowly blinked and gave a small nod of his head. Aistulf was grateful to have such a smart and loyal beast as a companion.

Aistulf took a deep breath, closed his eyes, and jumped into the cold water. He did not want any of the Underworld grime to waft near his eyes. He used his hands to scrub his arms, legs, and body to liberate the soot clinging to his skin. As he surfaced, the dark droplets surrounded him in a circle. Fearing the effects of the forthcoming eddy, he swam to the far side of the pool. He watched as the small whirlpool formed, the muck swirled, and disappeared.

"Two more times," he said with happiness in his voice. "Did you hear me, Kamal? Two more times and I will be finished."

Aistulf swam back to the area where he had bathed himself, and repeated the washing. Once finished, he swam to the rocks again. The eddy process repeated, although this time with far less dirt in the water. Upon the third time of washing, Aistulf was pleased only a small clump of dirt remained.

He swam underwater with his eyes wide open, happy to be alive. There were schools of brightly-colored fish as well as lily pads floating on the top of the water. As his hands went in front of him, he was surprised the golden ring he wore was black. He removed it and began cleansing the dirt off with his fingers.

Something or someone tapped him on his left shoulder, startling him. Aistulf was naked, and thought he was alone in the water. He clutched Ruggiero's ring in his right hand and turned around. A beautiful mermaid with flowing seaweed hair smiled at him.

CHAPTER FORTY-EIGHT

Aistulf stared at the mermaid. She bore a friendly smile with human-like teeth, the arms and torso of a woman, but the lower half of her body bore a fishtail. Her skin had a greenish glow as did her seaweed hair that gently moved with the water's currents. Realizing he needed air, he kicked to return to the surface. The mermaid moved forward, touched the sides of his neck and kissed him on the mouth, while pressing her bare chest against his. Stars danced before his eyes as his need for air intensified. He began panicking, but the fear passed when she released him and he began breathing underwater. She had gifted him a set of gills.

The mermaid smiled again and grabbed his left hand leading him deep underwater. He wondered about her intentions, and knew he had to be wary of temptations put before him. Aistulf could not allow himself to be seduced by a sea nymph and become trapped inside a watery realm.

Aistulf was led through deep recesses of the spring until the mermaid stopped in front of two large square rocks and one large round rock. She released his hand before she reached for a handle on the first square rock. A portal opened and revealed an image of himself wearing royal clothes and sitting upon a grand throne like the one in Aachen. He was holding a scepter and wearing Charlemagne's jeweled crown. Frankish soldiers knelt before him. The scene made him feel nervous. He did not aspire to seize Emperor Charlemagne's throne. He was the heir to the throne of Essex and did not covet another king's empire.

The mermaid opened the second square door. The image behind it was of Princess Angelica lying upon a bed. She was nude and beckoning him to her side. The bedchamber was filled with silks and luxuries. Aistulf had forgotten how beautiful she was. He remembered the first time he saw her at Charlemagne's Pentecost tournament. She arrived, unexpected and unannounced, in the company of her brother and four giants. She issued a challenge to find a champion who could beat her brother in the joust and she would be the prize. Every man there burned for her and vied to win the right to possess her. Now, he was being of-fered a naked Angelica on a silken bed.

"*Resist temptations,*" Lydia's voice rang in his head.

Then the mermaid opened the round door. Inside was a darkened room resembling a cave. The only light was from a single oil lamp. Aistulf saw himself wearing a plain brown tunic, sitting on a stool at a desk while writing on a piece of parchment with a quill.

"*You must go on a spiritual journey,*" said Melissa's voice.

Perhaps visiting the Underworld was not the only spiritual journey he needed to fulfill. If that was the case, he could not think of anything more spiritual than to live like a monk. The mermaid was waiting for his answer. He needed to choose between the three doors.

Aistulf was treading water and about to point at the third door when he realized he was still clutching Ruggiero's ring in his right hand. Re-membering it held magical powers to show the truth without enchantment, he carefully slipped the ring on a finger. The first door's scene changed. Armies were gathered outside the castle ready to attack as well as assassins inside the castle attempting to poison his food. The second door's scene changed as well. There was a dagger under Angel-ica's pillow and another lover awaiting her in an adjoining room. Outside the palace was an army led by a frustrated suitor who wanted to claim her for his own.

He felt vindicated for having rejected both of those doors. Promises of power and lust were fraught with danger, and he did not want to spend an eternity suffering in Hell like Tantalus or Sisyphus. Nervously, he turned his attention to the third door. This scene, to his delight, had only one change. He was no longer present, but a pair of sandals and a tunic was on the bed waiting for him. The rest of the tableau was the same.

Aistulf swam toward that open door, once inside he found himself standing in a dry room. He turned around to wave goodbye to the mer-maid, but she was no longer there. Neither was the door. He was in a round room with no corners, no windows, no doors, and lit by the flame of an oil lamp.

He slipped on the sandals and donned the tunic. As soon as the rough fabric touched his skin, he began to scratch. Aistulf touched the sides of his neck and realized his gills were gone. His stomach rumbled with hunger and his head began spinning. It had been an entire day since he had last eaten. Looking around the room, he found the empty bowl on the ground.

"Food. I would like some food because I am hungry," he said.

Aistulf was holding out hope his basic needs would be fulfilled, if he merely asked. He sat down on the bed waiting for the bowl to fill with breads, fruit or meats. Nothing.

He heard Melissa's voice again, *"You must go on a spiritual journey."*

"And all spiritual journeys begin with fasting," said Aistulf as he fell back on the bed and wept from hunger and frustration.

CHAPTER FORTY-NINE

R odomont was jerked awake. He was sitting down and leaning up against a stack of wooden crates. He had fallen asleep while riding with his men down the Rhône River on a stolen barge. Rodomont rubbed his eyes as Bambata began barking orders to the men to tie their barge and another barge to the dock. He glanced at the sky. There were still a few hours left before sunset.

"Where are we?"

"Outside the last tavern we will visit before we rejoin the army," said Bambata with a note of excitement in his voice. "Tomorrow the war. Tonight we enjoy our last cup of wine and hopefully some tavern wenches."

The men gave a rousing round of approval at Bambata's suggestion. Rodomont could have overruled him, because it was known he had planned to arrive in Arles by nightfall. His leadership was being questioned, but he had no desire to force the issue. The war could wait until the next day. Truth be told, he liked the idea of another night of drinking and whoring.

"How far are we from Arles?"

Bambata ran a hand over his face. "It is about three miles upriver."

"We passed it?"

"We did, but I kept going because I heard about this tavern last night. The men want one more night to enjoy ourselves, before we go back to killing people and risking our own lives."

There was an expectant look on the men's faces. They all wanted to visit this tavern. No one was to blame for their appetites more than he was. The first night he met them, Rodomont introduced them to the joys of alcohol. What was his hurry in helping out Akramont's cause?

The men led the horses off the barges and onto the dock. Bambata strode out in front down a dirt lane to a large wooden building in the small village. Rodomont issued the same warning to the stable hands as he had each night when they arrived at a tavern.

"Water, feed, brush, and secure our horses. If any are stolen or mistreated, we will burn this place to the ground."

They entered the dimly lit building that held a smell of mustiness, alcohol, and sweat. There were about a dozen North African soldiers inside seated on trestle benches around a long table. Rodomont sat down near a man who looked like a commander. The man had a full beard, an expanding waistline, and finishing his last bite of stew.

"*As-salaam-alaikum.*"

"*Wa-alaikum-salaam,*" the man replied. "Who are you?"

"I am Governor Rodomont of Sarza."

"The man who singlehandedly burned half of Paris?"

"You heard of that?" Rodomont said, trying to sound nonplussed. Inside, however, he was thrilled his fame had spread.

"Heroic news such as that travels fast. My name is Hamad. I serve Governor Grandonio of Morocco, the commander of the forces in Arles."

"Grandonio is a fierce warrior. I have fought alongside him before. I respect him."

"What brings you this way?"

"Akramont did not press the advantage I created. The siege in Paris became interminable. We left in the hopes of spilling more Frankish blood in Arles. Tell me, how does it fair?"

"We control the region," said Hamad, "but the coastline is back in Frankish hands after an horrific massacre in Marseille." He described the night when almost the entire fleet of Muslim ships were destroyed by fire.

"My men and I were sent on a mission to bring back more food to the city. This is the first time in weeks we can drink. Grandonio had all the alcohol destroyed when we conquered Arles. It was a tragedy to see the streets flow red with wine." Hamad gave a sigh. "So our bringing back food will wait until we have had our fill first." He raised his cup and called out, "Ferrand!"

A white-haired man wearing an apron looked up. The man finished refilling a soldier's cup before coming over.

"Ferrand, meet my new friend, Rodomont. His men are hungry and thirsty," the commander said in Arabic.

Ferrand, the innkeeper, nodded and gave a welcoming smile revealing large gaps between his yellowed teeth. "Tonight we are serving brown bread and meat stew. You want beer or wine?"

"I'm surprised you speak our language and so well," said Rodomont.

"I am an old man. This area used to be ruled by Muslims, and then was conquered by the Franks. I grew up speaking both languages. It has served me well over the years, and it helps when I have customers such as you and your men. As long as a customer pays, anyone is welcome."

Rodomont jangled Sacripant's purse half-filled with coins. "None of the tavern owners we met on our journey from Paris could speak more than a dozen words of Arabic."

"Provence is different from Paris," said Ferrand. He turned toward the kitchen, cupped his hands and began to bellow, "Jacques! François! More customers."

Two burly Frankish men came out of the kitchen door. One man served bread bowls and wooden spoons to the new customers, and the other man ladled warm stew.

"What kind of meat is that?" asked Rodomont.

Ferrand gave him a half-smile. "With a war on and your army seizing all the farm animals for miles around, do you really want to know that answer?"

Rodomont thought of animals that were plentiful even in times of famine: cats, rats, squirrels, pigeons, and seagulls. None were appetizing, but when a man was hungry...

Hamad gave a hearty belch. "Whatever it was, I enjoyed it."

Rodomont noticed chunks of carrots, onions, and garlic along with stringy meat he did not recognize. The stew was warm, hearty, and the meat had a wild taste to it. He doubted it was *halal*, but Rodomont had no concern about the dictates of Islam.

"So? What will it be? Beer or wine?" asked Ferrand.

"How is your wine?" asked Rodomont.

"Worth staying here for another night!" said Hamad as his men roared their approval.

"We will have the wine," said Rodomont.

Jacques and François gave cups to Rodomont's men and filled them with red wine. The wine bore flavors of earth and berries. Rodomont's mood softened as he felt a slight burning sensation down his throat. He finished his cupful and motioned for more.

"Do you have any women for us?" asked Bambata.

Ferrand scowled. "No! After what my accursed wife did to me, I do not allow any woman to cast a shadow on my tavern door. This village is too small to support a brothel. If that is what you are looking for, you have to go to Arles."

Hamad shook his head with disgust. "Grandonio shut those down. At least for low-level soldiers like ourselves."

Rodomont waved his hand to dismiss Bambata's attempt to pursue this any further. He looked intently at Ferrand. "Tell me, what did your wife do?"

The innkeeper poured himself a cup of wine and drank it in one fluid motion. He sat down on the bench and filled his cup again. "I do not often tell this story, because it hurts too much. I will tell you, only because I sense you have also been harmed by a cruel and heartless woman."

Rodomont nodded.

"Anyone who would like to hear a tale of misery, gather around," said Ferrand, "because I will not repeat myself."

The men quieted down and moved to stand near the innkeeper.

CHAPTER FIFTY

Renaud was anxious for nightfall. The ever-present threat of impending death for himself and his kinsmen heightened his anticipation preceding a battle. A myriad of details paraded through his head about their forthcoming attack.

The party of eleven men sat in a small grove of trees, finishing a supper of sausages, cheeses, and stale bread. A pigeon circled in the air before landing in the midst of the men. Maugis knelt down and removed a long, narrow piece of parchment attached to one of the bird's legs. The pigeon flew away as Maugis read.

He looked at Renaud and said, "Oliver is awaiting our signal. He will lead the first regiment out of Port Saint Marcel. The other regiments will follow."

"Pardon me," said Emile, looking bewildered. "How could Maugis have gotten word from anyone in Paris?"

"Maugis used carrier pigeons." Renaud said this with a note of finality in his voice. He wanted his squire to understand there were to be no further questions on this subject. Emile was young and naïve and did not recognize Maugis' magical powers. Only a few of Charlemagne's paladins could be entrusted with the knowledge of Maugis being a wizard.

Renaud announced, "These are my last orders before we embark upon our mission. Once leaving the safety of this grove, we will not speak a word until the infidels sound the alarm of our attack. The Saracens invaded our lands, they have threatened our people, they have threatened our emperor, and they have threatened our faith. Tonight they will taste our wrath. Charlemagne is counting on us to be the force to lift this siege. We will wait here until the half-moon is directly overhead, and then we shall travel the final two miles in utter silence. Our pack horses will remain here with Richardet and Emile."

He drew circles on the ground with a stick when Richardet approached.

"Brother, I request a private audience so that I may plead my case about joining in the attack."

Renaud was about to respond when he saw the look of seriousness on Richardet's face. They walked a short distance away where their hushed voices would not be overheard. "Proceed."

"It is a matter of honor. There is a young lady in their camp whose safety I am obligated to protect. Fiordespina, the daughter of Amir Marsilio, was my lover. After we were discovered, Marsilio ordered my execution, which I am lucky to have escaped. Fiordespina was sent to her father to receive her punishment. I must try and find her to prevent her from being killed or ravished during the Frankish invasion."

Renaud was surprised and impressed to learn of his brother's love life. There was not the time to ask for details of the clandestine relationship, nor of how Richardet avoided certain death. However, Richardet's concern for Fiordespina's safety was justified. Women suffered at the hands of conquering armies.

"Yours is a noble cause, and I wish you success in finding her." Renaud turned and called out, "Sansonetto, I changed my mind. It is not wise for two squires to watch over five horses. I need you to stay here with Emile. Come the morning, you two will advance from this position joining us in a victory celebration or use your wits to survive." Renaud returned to the circles he had drawn in the dirt, and then created a line representing a road. "After leaving this grove, we will first come upon the Saracen camp represented by this circle. I saw the camp clearly the morning that Guichard, Emile, and I left Paris on our mission to find Orlando. If it has not changed, there will be a single fence with only one gate. After killing the guards, we will wave our flag to notify the guards in the tall Paris towers. Oliver and his troops will leave the walled city of Paris and join us in the bloodbath. The infidels will have no escape."

CHAPTER FIFTY-ONE

A istulf's life in the cave became a routine. Upon waking, he drank water from the cup, washed his face and hands from water in the large bowl, and then relieved himself in that same bowl. His waste would disappear and fresh water would reappear. He followed this by praying and reading the Bible. Unsure of what the parchment, quill, and ink were for, he was reluctant to touch them. He did not want to begin transcribing the Bible and discover he would remain there until he completed a full copy. There were only a few sheets of parchment, yet Aistulf felt confident more sheets and more ink would appear as needed.

Without ambient light, he did not know when a day had passed as he had no sense of time. He read and prayed for guidance until he became overcome with exhaustion. He slept and when he awoke, the process repeated itself.

His body soon became cleansed of all solid waste. Without food, no more waste could be created. Aistulf's survival was based on water and prayer. It became increasingly difficult for him to concentrate reading the Bible as the words began swimming together.

A voice called out, breaking the silence and surprising him. "Who are you Aistulf?"

The voice was deep and resonant, clearly a man's voice. The question confused Aistulf. If the voice knew his name, then the voice knew who he was.

"I am heir to the throne of Essex in Britannia. I am also one of twelve paladins of Charlemagne."

"Titles. Those are mere titles. It says nothing about who you are as a man. Reflect on that and write down what you discover."

Aistulf took a deep breath to release some of his disappointment and anger. There was no end in sight to his confinement. His stomach had long since ceased rumbling.

"Who am I?" He shook his head and began chuckling. "I am a man who serves my father and Charlemagne." He paused. "It has been years since I last saw my father. I know him now only through letters. He sent me to Aachen for training when I was seven. He wanted me to become a famous knight. My leaving Britannia was to protect me from possible assassination attempts as well as to strengthen the ties between Essex and the Franks. Neighboring kingdoms will think twice before invading our lands. The purpose of my serving Charlemagne is to further my father's power."

The statement hung in the air. His first allegiance was to his father. Did that surprise him? For years he had received lengthy missives from his father detailing his desires for Aistulf's success. The letters accompanied his healthy allowance. His father wanted him to stand out in Charlemagne's court. The security of Essex depended on Aistulf gaining fame.

Aistulf dipped the quill into the ink and began scratching out words on the parchment.

My name is Aistulf. My first allegiance is to my father. King Odo of Essex. My mother was the maiden queen until she married a nobleman with ties to the Frankish Empire. I serve as a paladin to Emperor Charlemagne. My father sent me to Aachen to reinforce the strong ties between the Frankish empire and the Kingdom of Essex to prevent wars from our neighbors.

"Why did you refuse your Emperor?" said the voice.

A chill ran down is Aistulf's spine. He had been asked this before, but never gave a full answer. He could not explain why he acted the way he had. Charlemagne ordered him to surrender Renaud's horse Bayard to Gradasso. Instead of following the command, he challenged Gradasso to a duel. He won, Gradasso was humiliated, and left the Frankish Empire that same day taking his army with him. Charlemagne's fury transformed to amazement at Aistulf's gambit.

"Write your answers using your left hand," commanded the voice.

Aistulf swallowed hard. His left hand. He did not understand why, but the idea frightened him. Nonetheless, he moved the quill to his left hand, dipped it in the ink, and began to write. His hand smudged the ink as he wrote. No priest stood over his shoulder, barking about his messy hand. Aistulf concentrated on the words and ignored neatness.

I defied my Emperor. He ordered me to surrender Bayard to Gradasso. I could not do this. To do so I would have violated my vow to Renaud.

Aistulf looked up. Tears welled in his eyes. He did not understand why, but writing with his left hand evoked an emotional response. A long dormant memory came back to him. He was a small child and a priest struck Aistulf's left hand with a cane.

"Use your right hand," thundered the priest. "Left is sinister. It is a sign of the devil."

Putting down the quill, Aistulf massaged his left hand in memory of the stinging pain created by that priest. The fear of God made Aistulf suppress using his left hand. Now he understood why lessons in writing had taken him longer than the other students at the Palace School in Aachen. The skill of sword fighting was also a challenge for him, more than the other boys.

He was left-handed. Did that make him evil? No. He shook his head. While he was not a saint, he was not evil. Favoring the left hand did not signify evilness or a follower of the devil. The priest was wrong, and Aistulf suffered because of it.

Tears trickled down his face.

"Cleanse yourself," came the echo of Lydia's voice.

His body had been cleansed inside and out, but Man was more than just a body. There was the body, mind, and spirit. Aistulf needed to cleanse his mind and spirit.

"What are the seven cardinal sins?" he asked himself.

Struggling to remember, he began writing them down.

Gluttony.

Anger.

Sloth.

Envy.

Lust.

Pride.

He frowned. The list only had six and there should be seven. He decided to start with the list and hopefully the seventh one would come to him.

Gluttony.

I have on occasion eaten too much at banquet. But I am more likely to drink in excess than over eat. Drinking softens my mood and allows me to forget my problems. I drank most with my cousin Renaud. There were times our drunkenness caused problems for us at the Palace School in Aachen.

Anger.

I was angriest with Alcina. I wanted to kill her for what she did to me and to all those other men. It was satisfying to see her being punished in Hell for her sins.

He paused his writing as memories of anger and shame from childhood surfaced. The other students at the Palace School ridiculed him because of his difficulty with writing. He had to stay late and re-copy all of the day's work to make it legible. Echoes of taunting voices flooded his senses as did images of their spiteful faces.

"Moron."

"Imbecile."

"Are you sure he's the son of a king and not a commoner who stole fancy clothes?"

"He writes like a monkey."

"No, a monkey could write better than Aistulf the dummy."

As a child I wanted to go home to Essex after being tormented by other students. They humiliated me. I am grateful my cousin Renaud came to my defense. He threatened to beat anyone who mistreated me. He was a nephew to Charlemagne and the strongest in our class.

Aistulf and Renaud first met each other in Aachen. It felt awkward being introduced to a stranger and being told he was a kinsman. After Renaud spoke in his defense, no one bothered Aistulf again. Renaud was fierce and fearless. No one wanted to cross him.

Not long afterward, Aistulf realized Renaud was mocked due to his poverty. No one dared tease Renaud directly, but sniggers were made behind his back about his clothes. Aistulf used some of his allowance to buy clothing for Renaud. However, their bond of friendship was cemented by laughter as Aistulf made Renaud laugh. They became as inseparable as twins. Aistulf learned to use his humor as a shield and finally became accepted by his peers. His reputation of being a fool was his way of coping for having been ridiculed as a child.

He looked at the list of sins again.

Sloth.

Laziness. I do not think of myself as lazy. I am not as skilled as my kinsmen Renaud or Orlando but I am not lazy. Charlemagne named me one of his paladins. So I must have some worthy skills. Perhaps I became a paladin because of my wealthy father.

Aistulf stared at the parchment. The mention of money made him consider the sin of greed, the sin he had forgotten.

Greed. I do not hoard my money. I have given gifts to my cousin Renaud as well as others in need. Any of my sins about money is my dependence on obtaining more money from my father because I have spent too freely.

Another look at the list had him continue where he had left off.

Envy.

I am envious of Renaud. He came prepared to the Palace School after years of training. My father never had time to train me and he distrusted those who could have served as my tutors. He said I would learn how to become a knight in Aachen and they would rather teach students the correct methods than break bad habits. He was wrong. I came unprepared and it showed. Every other boy had some previous training.

Renaud arrived looking like a miniature knight. He soon became compared to our cousin Orlando while they laughed at me for being slow. Becoming best friends with Renaud did not stop my jealousy of his skills. I envy Renaud.

Lust.

I am guilty of the sins of lust and fornication. I have known many women and have never been married. My first lover was Berthild the barmaid.

Aistulf stared off in the distance and the image of her curly red hair, smiling face, and ample bosom danced before him. On his sixteenth birthday, he went to a tavern with Renaud to celebrate. They drank and laughed and flirted with Berthild. He gave her extra coins and she gave him a kiss. He and Renaud returned night after night. Each night Aistulf took things further with Berthild. A longer kiss, a tickle, a touch, and finally, after a few weeks, she took him to her bed. The first and only time he ever won in a competition with Renaud. Aistulf became a man before his cousin.

He remembered the last time he saw Berthild. Tears trickled down her face. Aistulf knew he needed to finish her story as part of his confession.

Berthild told me she carried my child. I panicked and accused her of having other lovers and only being after my money. I dropped three gold coins on the ground and said goodbye. It was more money than she would have seen in a year working at the tavern. I responded with cruelty to her when she had always been kind to me. She died alone and unloved in childbirth. I am ashamed of the way I treated her.

Renaud and I started going to brothels together. We would get drunk and enjoy the company of women. There we had no worry about fathering bastards. At least we never knew.

I am ashamed of that behavior as well. But my greatest shame was having Alcina as a lover.

He clenched his right hand into a fist.

I regret everything about my time with that witch. My redemption came in aiding Ruggiero in her defeat. I saw her in the Underworld and I recognize the magnitude of her sins. I am horrified I engaged in intimacy with such a hideous soul.

He then recalled Ruggiero's restraint when Alcina's beautiful female servants arrived in Logistilla's domain. One woman threw herself at Ruggiero, but he calmly rejected her. Ruggiero explained none of those women would make suitable wives.

I shall try to be more like Ruggiero in the matter of treating women. I understand the sadness of King Senapo and I vow to become a better man.

Pride.

Aistulf took a deep breath. Pride, or vanity, was his greatest sin. His distinctive gold-plated armor adorned with pearls demonstrated his vanity and designed to make people notice him.

"Be honest," said the voice.

Aistulf began writing again.

My armor is a sign of vanity. My shield was destroyed in the Underworld. I will change the design to be more modest and resembling what other knights use. It will not be ornate.

He felt something bubbling up inside of him. A truth he had long suppressed.

I chose to use gold and pearls on my armor to make Renaud envious of me. I can afford displays of wealth that he cannot.

Aistulf reviewed all the sheets of parchment and read Renaud's name mentioned under every sin. Without thinking, he continued to write. The words poured out, ink smearing as he wrote.

I refused my Emperor because I worried about how Renaud would react and not Charlemagne. That is because I am in love with Renaud.

Tears filled his eyes. He could no longer see the letters on the parchment.

I love Renaud. It is more than love I should bear for relatives. It is a love I can never act upon. It is a love that I can never declare. It is a love that can never be returned.

I must avoid being with Renaud. That is to prevent me from committing more sins because of him. After the war is over I shall return to Essex and fulfill my duty to my father and to our kingdom. I will find a suitable bride. I hope I will find a smart and beautiful woman who will make me laugh. I will love her as best I can.

Aistulf put down the quill and laid himself down on the bed. He closed his eyes and cried himself to sleep.

CHAPTER FIFTY-TWO

R odomont consoled the innkeeper. "You are among friends. We want to hear your story."

Ferrand gave a heavy sigh. "That ungrateful woman ran off with a customer. After a lifetime of my being a good husband to her, she repaid me with betrayal."

"Is there any woman worthy of adulation?" asked Hamad.

"No," said Ferrand. "Eve is the mother of all women and her sin makes them all temptresses. Women are by nature unfaithful and untrustworthy." The innkeeper poured himself more wine. "I used to believe my wife was different. I considered myself a lucky man with a praiseworthy wife. I was wrong. All women are contemptible." He drank his wine and then poured more.

"A year ago, two customers told me an incredible tale. I thought it funny at first, and did not realize their intent. The first man was Giacondo from Rome. He was a handsome fellow, one who could turn every woman's eye. He left his beloved wife one morning to go on a journey. She begged him not to leave her, and he promised he would return in a few days. Not too far down the road, he realized he forgot something important. Upon returning home, he found his naked wife asleep with their stable boy."

Rodomont clenched his fists. "Did he kill those cheating bastards?"

"No, he held his temper in check. Giacondo was not a man of violence and wanted to find a way to make her live to regret her sin. He continued on his journey to meet Astolfo, Duke of Spoleto, another handsome man. During his stay at the palace, Giacondo discovered a hole in his bedroom wall. After hearing some amusing sounds, he spied through the hole and saw the duchess having sex with a dwarf. Giacondo felt a kinship with Duke Astolfo like never before, for both were cuckolded."

Rodomont snarled. "Any cheating wife deserves to die."

Ferrand took another long drink of wine before continuing. "Giacondo went to the duke and told him that he knew of a secret. Before telling it, he made Duke Astolfo promise not to harm anyone once he learned the truth. The duke made the solemn vow and was then shown the duchess in the act with her lover. Duke Astolfo became enraged. After Giacondo calmed Astolfo, they began commiserating about their unfaithful wives. They decided to seek their revenge by committing adultery on a grand scale. Their goal was to sleep with as many wives as they could."

Rodomont's mind drifted as the innkeeper's story recounted the two handsome men's multitude of conquests. The soldiers gathered around in rapt attention. They laughed and guffawed in response to the many tales of outrageous acts of seduction committed by those rogues. The men identified with Giacondo and Astolfo, thinking they could engage in similar acts with women willingly accepting them as lovers. Baby-faced Jamar laughed the loudest of all the men in the tavern. Women swarmed around Jamar, while they averted their gaze when it came to Rodomont.

He scowled. No woman ever flirted with him. Not even in brothels. No whore ever sat on his lap or flaunted her body to him. He was ugly. The whores he had sex with were ones he chose when paying the brothel owner directly. Rodomont also ravished women during pillages. No woman ever willingly took him as a lover.

He drained and refilled his cup of wine over and over again. His head began swimming with thoughts of Doralice and her infidelity. He had wanted a wife who would be devoted to him. After bargaining with her father for more than a year, he thought he had procured a wife. Then, she was abducted and seduced by a handsome man. Damned Mandricardo stole her virginity, her heart, and her loyalty.

"Those two scoundrels did not go after virgins," said Ferrand interrupting Rodomont's thoughts. "Girls can be tricked by flattery. No, they wanted married women who appeared to be virtuous. The greater the reputation of faithfulness, the more they lavished their attentions. They vowed they would only stop if they came upon a virtuous wife who refused their entreaties. I laughed as I listened to their story, and I mentioned my own wife. I did not consider she would become a target. How could I? They were young and handsome. She was old, wrinkled, and after having borne five children, was well-worn. I did not realize these men did not care about a woman's age or beauty. They were interested in her status as being married and having a reputation of faithfulness. My wife of forty years left with Giacondo the next morning. A few days later she returned, after being replaced by another man's wife. She was tearful and begged my forgiveness."

"Did you?"

"Hell, no!" Ferrand pounded his fist on the table knocking over his cup. Red wine ran down the wooden table and dripped onto the straw covered floor. "I barred the door and warned our children I would disown them if they helped that damned harlot."

"Where is she now?" asked Bambata.

Ferrand shrugged his shoulders as he refilled his cup with wine. "I know not, nor do I care. Nun, whore, beggar, corpse. Any of those fates for her means nothing to me. I learned there is not a woman alive who would have refused those two honey-tongued devils. They went so far as to claim to seduce a widow in mourning on the day of her husband's funeral."

Rodomont's stomach turned, he had heard enough of these two men and their conquests. The image of Fiordespina's tear-streaked face and bloodshot eyes flashed before him. "I know a woman who would have refused them."

"You should erect a monument in her honor," said Ferrand as he raised his cup. "Let us drink to this mythical virtuous woman whom all husbands delude themselves to think is their wife."

The men laughed and raised their cups.

Rodomont chafed. "She was not mythical. This woman existed and was offered to me as a bride. She was a fallen woman and in despair over being separated from her lover. She became hysterical when told her lover died. It would not matter to her about these men's looks or their pretty words. She would never have succumbed to their charms. She was devoted to her beloved and no man could have replaced him in her heart."

"You speak of her in the past tense. What happened to her?" asked the innkeeper.

"She said she would rather die than marry me. I granted her wish."

The men stared at him. The room became as quiet as a tomb.

"You are right," said Rodomont. "A woman who demonstrates that much devotion to her man deserves a monument in her honor."

"We do not need any more damned statues," said Ferrand. "What we need around here is a bridge."

"Forget this accursed war," said Rodomont. "Rather than rejoin Akramont's lost cause, we will make our mark here. Julius Caesar built a bridge over the Rhine River in ten days. We shall build a bridge over the Rhône in the same time in honor of Fiordespina. That bridge will serve to test the honor and mettle of knights who would cross. We shall derive riches and fame from such a bridge. We start building on the morrow!"

The room full of men lifted their cups and pledged their loyalty to him.

PART THREE:

MIRACLES AND MASSACRES

A light fog rolled off the banks of the Seine River and encircled the gates of the walled city of Paris. The mist crept over the Left Bank toward the Saracen camp and fell over its ten-foot tall fence. There was no defense against the advance of this magical fog, nor of the sleep that followed once inhaled. One-by-one, Saracen warriors succumbed to slumber as the small Frankish war party advanced in silence.

Renaud smiled as the enemy encampment came into view. The fog hung over the camp, but did not extend beyond it. Dark forms of men lay on the ground near the fence. Renaud turned and nodded toward his brothers Guichard, Alard, and Guidone. They let loose arrows landing deep into the necks of the sleeping guards. Renaud preferred long distance attacks on sentries because a man could not call out an alarm when his windpipe was crushed by an arrow.

His plans needed no alterations. No changes had been made to the security of the camp since Renaud saw it last. A simple wooden fence surrounded the tents and still likely had only one gate in the whole circular structure. The purpose of this fence was to prevent desertions during the night, and not protect the soldiers within.

Renaud considered this layout for a military encampment to be a sign of arrogance and laziness. During prolonged sieges, Charlemagne insisted his armies follow Julius Caesar's example in the battle of Alesia. The army surrounded the city they besieged with two rings of barricades complete with deep trenches. The inner barricade was called a vallation and it protected the invading army from attacks by the defending army sallying forth from their castle. The outer barricade, known as a contravallation, protected the invading army from attacks from reinforcements by allies of the besieged. The castle represented the bullseye on a target with two large circles of enemy fortifications.

Akramont had not taken the time nor the effort to build extensive barricades. Renaud believed this oversight would be the amir's undoing.

While Renaud had tremendous respect for his sister Bradamante's military skill, he was grateful she was not part of this attack. She would have pulled him aside and declared his strategy dishonorable and "dependent upon guile and deceit." Renaud, unlike his sister, cared not about honorability to achieve victory as long as his side won. This was war, and the poets would describe his leadership in whatever terms they desired for posterity. They could declare him to be a hero, a villain or a scoundrel; it mattered not to him. He wanted to defeat his enemy and he would use any methods to achieve that end, including magic.

Nearing the gate, Maugis lifted his arms and the fog engulfing the Saracen encampment dissipated before Renaud could count to ten. Eight sleeping guards were revealed to be sitting on the ground with their mouths agape. One man's hand rested on a large horn, while another's fingers were wrapped around a large spear. With the magical mist removed, the Frankish soldiers would not fall asleep as they entered the camp, but all within could awaken. Soon the sleeping enemy soldiers sprouted arrow shafts from their necks, making their slumber an everlasting one.

Maugis turned his attention to the fortified walls of Paris. He fixed his eyes on the easternmost gate on the Left Bank. He raised his arms again and the low hanging mist surrounding the Port Saint Marcel disappeared. Vivien waved the flag of the House of Lyon, a rampant silver lion on a field of red. The Frankish guards at the top of the thirty-foot walls waved a torch in reply. Oliver and his men would soon join them.

One more impediment remained. The gate to the Saracen camp was secured from the inside. Maugis closed his eyes, knitted his eyebrows, his hands appeared to be lifting an invisible object, and then he made a motion of throwing. A dull thud came from behind the door. Maugis opened his eyes and smiled. Aquilant and Grifon pushed the barrier open.

Renaud was the first rider to enter the Saracen camp. He grabbed a spear from a rack of weapons near the entrance. The slaughter was about to commence.

CHAPTER FIFTY-FOUR

Aistulf was having a vivid dream. He floated above his body inside the cave before passing through the stone wall into the cool night air. The hippogriff slept while still guarding his possessions alongside the spring. He looked up at the half-moon and smiled.

"Come Aistulf, it is time you joined me," said the voice from the cave.

"Where?"

"Follow the sound of my voice."

He stretched out his arms, and flew effortlessly through the sky. He soared over fields and hills faster than he had on the back of the hippogriff. The voice urged him onward as he glided through the air. A large chain of jagged mountaintops loomed ahead as he climbed upward through the night sky. The rocky peaks and outcroppings decorating the mountains had a stark beauty. Aistulf wondered if he had died. He was at peace with the thought. He was in God's hands and at His mercy. There had never been a time in his life when his soul was as ready to meet his maker.

On the summit of the mountain stood a small marble building with Ionic columns. Nearby was a water fountain and trees laden with fruit. An old man with flowing white hair and a long beard, wearing a full-length white tunic waited for him. Warmth emanated from this host.

"Welcome Aistulf."

"Am I... dead?"

"No and neither am I."

"Who are you?"

"I am the prophet Elijah."

Aistulf stood in awe. "The same prophet mentioned in the Bible? I thought you went to Heaven in a flying chariot."

"I was brought here instead. This is where I have served the Lord for many centuries."

"If this is not Heaven, where are we?"

"The closest place to Heaven," said Elijah. "We are in Terrestrial Paradise. This is the place King Senapo spent many years trying to find."

Aistulf felt a sense of tranquility as he looked around him. There were lush gardens lit by glowing lanterns lining numerous crooked pathways. Stone benches beckoned him to rest and enjoy the sight of ponds and flowering trees.

"King Senapo could never ascend this mountain and be allowed inside this sacred space. Only those who purge themselves of sin, and be invited, may enter."

"I am honored to be in such a blessed place, but why am I here?"

"The Lord chose you as one of his servants. You have three tasks to perform. The first involves King Senapo. He committed many sins, including trying to force his entry here. He was punished and has now repented. I shall give you the cure to his blindness."

Elijah walked down a flagstone path, crossed a footbridge over a brook, and entered into a gazebo. In the center was a clay pot with a small plant bearing purple and yellow flowers with heart-shaped petals.

Aistulf picked up the plant and studied it. "This reminds me of a plant that grows wild in Essex. We call it heartsease."

"Well done. The one you are holding is unlike any others. This plant was grown especially for King Senapo and would be poisonous for anyone else. To cure his blindness, take the petals and roll them between your fingers — then apply those drops to his eyes. Afterwards a tea should be made of the remaining stems and leaves that only he can drink. It will mend his wounded heart."

"I could use a plant like that myself," said Aistulf.

"Indeed. You examined your heart and discovered your unrequited love. A tea will be brewed with leaves from a plant grown just for you. It will not cure your heart, but it will ease your pain.

"What are my other tasks?"

"Work in concert with Caliph Harun al-Rashid and lastly, you must restore your cousin Orlando's sanity."

"What happened to my kinsman?" asked Aistulf.

"His unrequited love for Angelica drove him mad."

Aistulf hung his head in sadness. "I always knew they were not meant for each other. How is he?"

Elijah sighed. "Orlando is like a rabid dog. He lost all reason and cannot even understand language. Quite simply, Orlando lost his wits. We shall go retrieve them, so you can return them to your cousin."

Aistulf was confused, but followed Elijah as he continued down the flagstone path under a bower of vines. As they rounded a bend, a clearing bathed in silvery moonlight emerged. Four horses snorting flames were attached to a glowing red carriage.

"My chariot awaits," said Elijah.

CHAPTER FIFTY-FIVE

As the small contingent of Frankish soldiers entered the sleeping Saracen camp, they split into their pre-assigned tasks. Renaud, Vivien, Guichard, and Alard set off in search of Amir Akramont. Maugis waited outside the camp for the Frankish soldiers from Paris to join them. Aquilant and Grifon dismounted and quietly went about killing all the soldiers near the gate.

Richardet and Guidone Selvaggio sought the tent belonging to Amir Marsilio. Richardet spent many days riding next to his newfound brother and speaking of his love for Fiordespina. He was grateful to have assistance in his quest to find and rescue her.

Their horses walked slowly through the long row of tents toward the center of the camp. With each clip clop of the hooves, Richardet winced fearing the sound would wake the sleeping soldiers. His eyes darted back and forth looking for any sign of movement within the tents. The further they went inside the camp, the more tension he felt.

Richardet's mind flashed to Ruggiero, the man who saved his life and promised to speak with Fiordespina. Had Ruggiero succeeded and would she be expecting him? Might he also face Ruggiero during this long night? That last thought filled him with dread. He had grown fond of Ruggiero and owed his life to that brave Saracen warrior. Honor required Richardet to save Ruggiero's life if threatened, but Fiordespina's welfare came first.

In the half-moonlight, the two brothers reached the area with large cooking pits. Traversing around this, they passed more rows of tents. Each row had a different flag, signifying the different governors' standards. After passing the eighth row, Richardet saw a banner limply hanging from a pole with a dragon on a field of gold and black. This was Marsilio's family crest. He turned his horse down the line; his eyes became fixed on a large tent midway down the row. Two sleeping guards were sitting outside the tent; both men were snoring. Guidone pulled arrows out of his quiver and in a few moments, forever silenced the men. Richardet gave his brother an appreciative nod before he dismounted and handed Guidone his reins.

He lifted the tent flap and slipped inside. Richardet waited for his eyes to adjust to the darkness. A table, four chairs, and a large rug occupied the center of the tent. A man slept on a bedroll in the corner. A servant, most likely. A partition separated the room and Richardet knew Marsilio's family was behind it.

Tiptoeing across the room, he peeked behind the curtain. A sleeping woman held a small girl in her arms. He surmised she was Fiordespina's stepmother who treated her with disdain. An empty pillow lay next to the woman and in the corner was rolled up bedding. Fiordespina was not there. *Where was she?*

As he stepped back into the main portion of the tent, Richardet realized the identity of the sleeping male servant. *Neron.* The name made his lips curl. Richardet wanted to kill him, but first he needed to know where Fiordespina was.

He drew out his knife, crept over to Neron, and knelt down behind him. Grabbing Neron's hair, Richardet placed his blade against the man's neck.

"Where is Fiordespina?" he whispered.

"Who are you?"

"Where is she?" The tip of the knife cut into the skin. A drop of blood formed.

"She is dead and buried."

"You lie."

"No, the amir tried marrying her off, but she refused. Governor Rodomont killed her when she rejected him."

Bile rose in the back of Richardet's throat. "Marsilio will die for offering her to such a vile man. I will also see that Rodomont dies."

"Who are you?" repeated Neron, fear in his voice.

"I am the man who loved Fiordespina. The man you tortured and condemned to die by fire. My father is Duke Aymon of Dordogne. I am the youngest brother of Count Renaud de Montauban. My name is Richard." With that, he slit Neron's throat.

A sound made him turn. Marsilio's wife stood near the partition looking horrified. She opened her mouth and screamed.

✳

CHAPTER FIFTY-SIX

Renaud located Amir Akramont's tent in the center of the camp. It was four times as large as the other tents, but what was puzzling is there were not any guards posted outside.

He and Vivien dismounted their horses and handed the reins to Guichard and Alard. Renaud entered the amir's tent with his sword drawn and surprised to find it empty. No furniture, no bedding, and no one inside. A sense of evil hung in the air. As his eyes adjusted he saw dark stains on the fabric covering the ground and sharp edges where the stain was missing. He guessed a rug had been removed. Renaud looked up and saw splatters on the fabric walls. He knew then, someone died there and the stains were blood.

Renaud whispered. "Do you think Akramont was killed?"

Vivien shook his head. "Oliver would have told us."

"That is, if the news made it outside this camp."

Vivien shrugged his shoulders as they left the tent. He used his sword to slash the ropes holding up the entranceway. The tent hung slack on the center pole.

Renaud and Vivien remounted their horses as a woman's scream rang through the camp. She yelled in Arabic. The only word Renaud recognized was "Franks."

CHAPTER FIFTY-SEVEN

Akramont woke with a start. He had fallen asleep while sitting at a table covered with a map of Paris. He was in the new royal tent, a place untouched by Rodomont's violence. As he began getting a sense of his surroundings, he saw Amir Marsilio and Governor Sabri had likewise fallen asleep during their strategy session. Everyone was still wearing their armor, how had they all fallen asleep?

A woman's bloodcurdling scream came from across the camp. Akramont realized it was her screams that woke them.

"The Franks are here!" yelled the woman.

"Rosenda!" said Marsilio as he ran from the tent.

A cacophony of sounds could be heard: running, shouting, the clash of swords, and horns being blown as a call to arms.

"We must evacuate your family," said Sabri.

Marfisa appeared from behind the curtain, her eyes were wild. She was already dressed for combat as it was her custom to sleep in armor. She gripped her shield and had a hand on the pommel of her sword.

"Stop!" commanded Akramont. "You will protect my family from the infidels."

He grabbed an oil lamp, walked past the sleeping form of Ruggiero and went to the back of the tent. Akramont yanked on a few fabric ties and then pulled back a tent flap. "A secret gate is built into the wall behind this tent. Sabri will open the gate and two soldiers will carry Ruggiero on his stretcher away from here."

Sabri left as Alia, Anika, and Hala rose from their beds. Fear and confusion were mingled on their faces.

"The Franks are here," argued Marfisa. "I want to fight them."

"Only kill Frankish soldiers while you are protecting my family. I am entrusting you and Governor Sabri with my most treasured possessions. There is a trail that leads to a boat on the Seine River. Get on that boat and make your way to Arles. I will send Ibrahim to accompany you. My army may have to retreat there. Now go!"

"Be sure to bring my mare, Gloriosa. Otherwise there will be hell to pay," Marfisa said, grabbing Hector of Troy's bronze cuirass and forced Anika into wearing it.

"That is too heavy," she whined.

"Yes, but it may protect you from being stabbed in your belly by a Frank's sword," said Marfisa with an even voice. She handed Ruggiero's helmet and shield to Alia. "Take these."

Alia did so without complaint.

"Hala, grab his sword," said Marfisa. "Use it against any Frankish soldier who comes near you."

Hala went to retrieve the weapon. Sabri returned with two guards who stepped inside and grabbed the ends of the stretcher and began carrying Ruggiero outside.

Ruggiero tried lifting his head, but his eyes were unfocused. "I must fight," he mumbled.

"You must rest," said Sabri.

Ruggiero's eyes slammed shut.

Akramont kissed both his wives. "*Inshallah* we will see each other again soon! Now go!"

CHAPTER FIFTY-EIGHT

Richard almost dropped his dagger when the woman screamed. He felt like a small boy and his mother caught him being naughty. His cheeks burned with embarrassment as he scrambled to his feet, thrust his bloodied knife into the scabbard, ran outside, and mounted his horse. The screams continued and rang in his ears as he galloped back to the center of the camp and turned down the row leading toward the gate. Guidone Selvaggio followed close behind.

The first Saracens who emerged from their tents were half-asleep and not dressed for battle. Few wore any armor, and they appeared uncertain as to where they should go. Some responded in the direction of the screams, while others ran after the sound of galloping horses. The confusion as to where they should report led to some bleary-eyed soldiers with weapons drawn accidentally wounding their fellow soldiers.

Aquilant and Grifon rode on horseback and worked as a team to bring down tents. Aquilant's sword slashed ropes while Grifon followed with his battle-axe, whacking at the poles. Behind these two warriors came a thundering storm of Frankish cavaliers who joined the fray.

CHAPTER FIFTY-NINE

Aistulf climbed into Elijah's famous chariot and gripped the sides. "Where are we going?"

"Where all things go when they are lost on Earth; to the moon, of course."

Elijah gathered the reins and gave the command. The horses lifted their front legs into the air and bore the chariot aloft. The flames on the chariot lit up the night sky, but the fire did not consume nor did it warm the carriage. The speed they traveled surprised Aistulf. The chariot hurtled through the sky like a shooting star.

The moon loomed ahead of them. The right half enshrouded in the Earth's shadow, while the left-half shown bright white with massive dark craters marring its surface. Elijah pulled on the reins and the chariot began gliding over the rocky surface. They made several passes over various craters until Elijah gave the command for the horses to land inside one at least three miles in diameter.

"The location is hard to find, but it is all a part of God's plan."

Aistulf stepped out of the back of the chariot. The soil was gray and reminded him of sand. Elijah led the way while Aistulf walked behind him and marveled at the bizarre landscape. The crest of the crater towered in the distance appearing to be at least fifty feet tall. The sloping walls resembled wrinkles in cloth, and there were tunnels at the base.

As they approached one of the openings, Elijah paused, held up his right hand, before shaking his head. "This is not the one."

"What are they?" asked Aistulf as they continued walking.

"The Lord made cosmic storage places here on the moon for losses back on Earth. The tunnels are dedicated to different types of losses. That last one contains trinkets such as keys and jewelry long since forgotten." As they walked past another cave, Elijah gestured. "This cavern contains more serious losses such as lost hopes and dreams. The next one is filled with broken promises and lost honor."

The tone of the prophet's voice had turned solemn. Misery emanated from the openings of those caves. Aistulf did not understand how intangible concepts such as broken vows could be rendered into a physical sense to be stored, but he did not question the statement.

They passed several more cave entrances before Elijah stopped. "This is the repository of lost tempers and wits."

The prophet picked up a leather satchel and a large stick near the entrance. He touched the tip of the stick and it glowed, lighting up the inside of the cavern. The walls had multiple shelves carved into the rock face. Glass bottles of various shapes and sizes were crammed onto the shelves and covered with a thick layer of dust.

"These bottles contain the lost wits of those who were enraged," said Elijah. "Most people will lose their tempers now and again, and that accounts for the massive number of bottles here."

Aistulf picked up a bottle at random and brushed off the dust. He read 'The wits of Jean Marc of Toulouse.' He turned and stared into the darkened chasm, trying to get a sense of how far it extended. "Do these go back to the beginning of time?"

Elijah chuckled. "Thankfully no. Once a soul dies, the vessels containing their various intangible losses disappear like the morning dew under the noontime sun."

As Aistulf watched, bottles rattled on the shelves, seemingly at random, and disappeared while new bottles popped into view. Small clouds of dust kicked up, but soon settled down like a thick blanket on the various neighboring containers. Aistulf was amazed as a vessel in front of him expanded in height.

"Someone must have lost his temper again," said Elijah. "This cave is as busy as a beehive."

"How will we ever find Orlando's amongst all of these?" Aistulf began panicking. He worried they might spend weeks searching the cave.

Elijah offered a comforting smile. "The ability to find what I need here is another gift from the heavenly Father." He lifted his stick higher. "Come, I sense what we seek is near at hand."

They walked a few more steps when Aistulf saw a large round flask sitting prominently on a shelf. It glowed. Another flask nearby had a similar glow, although it was much smaller.

"We found them," said Elijah as he picked up the bottles.

"Why are there two bottles?" asked Aistulf.

"The smaller one belongs to you. After all you have been through, and for what you have yet to do, you deserve your full wits about you." Elijah picked up both bottles and placed them in the satchel. "And now, we must return to Earth where you will continue on with your special journey."

Elijah left the cavern and strode purposefully toward the chariot. Aistulf knew his time with the prophet was nearing an end.

"Who should I help first? Orlando or King Senapo?"

"You must first return to King Senapo's side," said Elijah. "Trust that the Lord will cause you and Orlando's paths to cross in due time. King Senapo will provide you with the key to your meeting with Caliph Harun al-Rashid. You will then provide the caliph with information helpful to his army utterly defeating Akramont's supporters in the Maghreb."

"I am confused. Is the Lord our Father on the side of Charlemagne and Caliph Harun al-Rashid?"

"Yes, it is Amir Akramont who lost God's favor."

Aistulf pondered the implications of God favoring both the Christian and Muslim armies, but opposing Akramont's campaign.

"Why would the Lord choose me?" asked Aistulf.

"Despite all of your self-doubts, you have a good heart. You also passed every test put before you since your rebirth as a man."

"Do you mean after having spent time as a tree?"

"Yes. Everything that has happened to you since you were abducted by a whale has been fantastical. No one would believe your stories if you told them. The sole exception would be Ruggiero Tazeem."

"You know about my friend, Ruggiero? Do you know how he fares?"

"He rejoined Akramont's army and was badly wounded in a duel with a fellow soldier. He is healing and should regain most of his strength."

"Is he doomed to die in this war?"

Elijah shook his head as he entered the chariot. "Ruggiero has the Lord's favor, but his fate is uncertain. However, Ruggiero's fate will determine the outcome of this war."

"What do you mean?"

"The Lord works in mysterious ways, but the free will of Man plays a role in determining what comes to pass." Elijah placed a comforting hand on Aistulf's shoulder. "You must ensure the care necessary to subdue your kinsman completely in order to save him. Orlando has the strength of ten men. If he is not under your complete control, he will swat away the bottle containing his wits. Should that happen, all hope will be lost for him and he would be condemned to die like a rabid dog." He gathered the reins and gave the signal for the horses to fly once again.

The idea that Orlando's fate depended on Aistulf was disturbing, but worrying about that could wait. In the meantime, he felt overcome by the beauty of the Earth as they sped toward it through the night sky. It resembled a blue glass ball with white streaks.

The next thing he knew, Aistulf was in the cave, in bed, lying on his back, and clutching a bottle in each hand. Holding them up, he recognized the bottles from his dream. Or, was it a dream? Had he gone to the moon? He sat up and noticed his sandals were coated with a fine gray dust.

CHAPTER SIXTY

As dawn broke, Amir Akramont surveyed what remained of the Muslim camp. He sat in his saddle, disheartened at the large number of tents trampled by the rampaging Franks; some still with people inside of them. Mounds under the fabric were stained with dark splotches. A tattered flag lay on the ground near a tent. The design was red and white quartering, but the white portions were covered with bloodied hoof prints. Akramont's heart sank as he saw a child's hand peeking out from under that tent. The small fingers were curled and still.

His fears were confirmed when foot soldiers lifted the fabric and revealed the lifeless forms of Daniso's widow and son. His late cousin's family had perished at the hands of their enemies. Akramont failed his kinsman yet again. He said a silent prayer that his own family had fared better on their way to safety.

A man's voice emerged through the chaos of the battle, catching Akramont's attention. The Frank spoke in broken Arabic with bad pronunciations, but the man's message was understandable. "I challenge Akramont to fight. I am Renaud de Montauban."

Akramont looked in the direction of the shouting and tried in vain to see his famous challenger.

"Mine! He is mine!" roared Gradasso. The king of Sericana made his way through a throng of mounted Muslim soldiers. His face reddened as he pounded his chest. "I have been waiting over a year to claim his warhorse that I won by right of conquest. Renaud must surrender Bayard!" He withdrew Durindana from its scabbard. "You may dismember his corpse when I am done with him."

Gradasso passed by without slowing. Akramont nodded at the back of Gradasso's head, as if his approval was necessary. "Your claim for a duel with him precedes his challenge to me."

His words hung in the air, but no one seemed to care.

"Renaud, you are a lying son of a painted whore," Gradasso bellowed as he brandished his sword. "Surrender your horse or die!"

A rush of Muslim warriors followed after the brash king of Sericana. This duel promised to be an exciting one to watch.

Akramont sat in his saddle, staring ahead, uncertain as to his next move. The Franks poured into the encampment by the one northeastern gate as a steady stream of Muslim soldiers retreated out of three exits created in the southern fence.

Marsilio's voice broke through the mental fog. "It is time. You must leave with your men."

Akramont wanted to argue with his wazir, but he also wanted to leave. He hesitated in replying, because what he wanted most of all was to retain the respect of his forces. That desire stood in stark contrast with the reality of abandoning supplies, leaving behind dead soldiers who needed proper burials, while more soldiers were fighting and dying at the hand of their enemies. How could he flee and not be regarded as a coward?

"If you do not leave now, you will die and this entire campaign will have been for naught," said Marsilio. "The army needs to rally around you as their leader. Retreat is a part of war. I have been forced to retreat more than I care to admit. Charlemagne is my oldest rival, and I know him well. I shall remain here with my troops and we will delay the Franks. Seek refuge in Arles and send to the Maghreb for more reinforcements. Now go, before it is too late."

"What of your family?" asked Akramont. "Shall I take them with me?"

"No, my son Matalista has taken them from the camp and is guarding them. They are in hiding and are safe for now. We shall meet again soon, *inshallah.*"

"*Ma'a salama* my friend," said Akramont as he gave an appreciative nod to his advisor.

"*Ma'a salama,*" replied Marsilio.

Richard regretted having left Marsilio's tent. He panicked when the woman screamed, and left the one place the amir of Hispania would go during this battle. Hours later, he had killed many enemy soldiers but felt he failed his beloved.

He aimlessly wandered around the Saracen camp, uncertain where to go next when he heard his brother Renaud's challenge to Akramont. A flicker of hope sprung up when a few moments later, a voice responded in anger and a horse charged through the camp. Renaud's gambit worked. Perhaps a similar ploy would work for him.

"Marsilio!" yelled Richard. "Come meet the man who loved your daughter. The man you ordered to be executed. She is dead because of you. I challenge you to a duel in Fiordespina's honor."

There was no reply at first, then came a sharp horn blast. A delegation of Saracen soldiers appeared. In the center was the silver-haired amir, flanked by men bearing his standard. A breeze caused the flags to flutter in the air. Richard smiled, thinking the amir responded to his summons.

"Bring me to Charlemagne," announced Marsilio. "We shall discuss terms of surrender."

Another sharp horn blast came, this time from the Frankish forces.

"Cease fighting," thundered a voice.

Even before Richard turned, he knew it was Oliver who spoke. The paladin had a commanding presence about him, in keeping with his position of being one of the twelve peers of Charlemagne. No Frankish soldier would dare defy an order given by this fierce warrior.

Oliver's shield bore a golden gryphon on a field of green, and his sons, Aquilant and Grifon, rode on either side of him. These three warriors represented a wall of power.

"Christian soldiers, you may take Muslim prisoners, but not any more lives," Oliver announced. "There is now a truce."

More blasts of horns sounded throughout the camp to spread the message.

"Amir Marsilio, follow me. I will take you to the emperor," said Oliver.

With that announcement, Richard knew he lost his chance to challenge Fiordespina's father.

✳

CHAPTER SIXTY-TWO

"**R**enaud, you lying son of a painted whore. Surrender your horse or die!"

"Gradasso, you are more obsessed with my horse than a newborn with his mother's teat!" taunted Renaud as he signaled Bayard to advance. He rode through the camp with a burning need to find the accursed King of Sericana.

"Stop hiding. Meet me on the field of glory," yelled Gradasso.

"Hide? I never turn down a challenge to prove my worth and superiority."

Saracen foot soldiers cleared a path for Renaud to make his way through the camp. Soon he was glaring at his nemesis.

"You never avoid a challenge? Tell me why you sailed away from our fight," snarled Gradasso.

Renaud's blood began to boil. "I did not leave there on my own accord. We were both victims of sorcery. If I wanted to avoid a duel with you, I would not leave my horse behind."

"Surrender Bayard to me," barked Gradasso. "Your emperor ceded that horse when I conquered this damned city last year."

The gathered crowd murmured and jostled one another. They wanted to see blood spilled between these two renowned warriors.

Renaud cracked a smile as he began teasing his enemy. "Funny, I heard you jousted with my kinsman, Aistulf, over Bayard. After one pass, you were on your back staring up at the sky. Then you ran away like a little dog with his tail between his legs."

Gradasso bore his teeth as gales of laughter erupted from both the Franks and Saracen soldiers standing around.

"To claim my horse you must prove you are superior to *me*," continued Renaud. "We must conduct our duel away from spectators who might seek to aid their favored warrior."

A horn blasted in the distance, followed a few moments later by further horn blasts. The words "surrender" and "truce" echoed through the camp. The Saracens put down their weapons before the Franks.

"Our dispute is not hindered by any truce between the armies," insisted Renaud. "We must leave here and find a place to fight."

"Not along the banks of the Seine. I will not allow you to escape onto a ship again."

"I told you, I did not escape. I was tricked and abducted. Enough talking, follow me and we will settle this."

Renaud led the way out of the camp past scores of Saracen soldiers now trapped inside at the mercy of their enemies. He took Gradasso near the woods where Sansonetto and Emile were hiding. At least he would have allies who could provide him with a horse should Fate deal him an unkind blow.

CHAPTER SIXTY-THREE

The events of the night before confused Aistulf, but he shook his head with a smile. He was a mere servant of God and should stop trying to make everything fit into a logical pattern. After all he had seen and done, he needed to accept matters and not worry about comprehending God's will.

He rose and walked over to the desk. The quill, inkwell, parchment, and Bible had vanished. The oil lamp bore a flame blazing with enough intensity to make the cave appear to be lit by sunshine. The flowering plant from Terrestrial Paradise sat on the desk along with a cup of steaming hot tea.

Aistulf placed the two bottles he held in his hands on the desk and sat down to drink the tea. It had a bittersweet flavor and a sense of melancholy washed over him. He drained the cup before he brushed the dust off the small bottle revealing the words "The wits of Prince Aistulf of Essex." Uncorking the vial, he placed it under his nose, and inhaled a sharp essence making him wince. Then, a sense of peace and contentment settled in his heart and mind. For the first time in his life, Aistulf felt whole. He closed his eyes and took several deep breaths, trying to capture this sensation as a lifelong memory.

Upon opening his eyes, he was surprised to see the bowl at his feet contained flatbread and soft cheese. Aistulf nearly cried at the sight of food. He tore a hunk of bread and dipped it into the cheese. He savored the tang of the cheese and the chewiness of the bread. This was a simple meal, but he cherished every bite.

As he stood, the wall of the cave opened to reveal a large square door. It led to the meadow where Kamal the hippogriff stood next to a pool of water. The eagle-like head caught fish jumping in the air.

Aistulf doffed his sandals and rough tunic and left them on the bed where he found them. He left the cave naked and walked out into morning sunshine feeling like he had been reborn. His clean breeches and gambeson lay on the hillside. He donned them before strapping on his armor.

After gathering his belongings, he placed them in his leather satchel along with the plant and the bottle of Orlando's wits. This was a magic satchel, and everything would be secure inside. No need to worry about breakage of the bottle or damage to the plant.

The last item Aistulf picked up was his battered shield. He gave a bemused smile as he examined the deep gouges in the front rendering the design unrecognizable. It was still functional, but the cover would need changing before he went into battle again.

Aistulf mounted Kamal. "Time we return to visit our friend, King Senapo."

CHAPTER SIXTY-FOUR

Charlemagne was surprised by the news Amir Marsilio was surrendering. Amir Akramont commanded this war effort and by all rights it should be Akramont surrendering and not an ally. Nonetheless, Charlemagne was more than willing to discuss terms of surrender with one of his oldest adversaries.

He called for a pavilion be erected outside the Saracen encampment for this purpose. Oliver escorted Marsilio inside. Charlemagne gathered as many of his champions and advisers as he could muster on short notice to demonstrate his strength and power. Namo, the Duke of Bavaria, stood at his right side with Namo's four grown sons nearby. Ogier the Dane, Archbishop Turpin, Vivien, Aquilant, and Grifon, stood guard as well.

Marsilio entered the tent flanked by a few burly soldiers. He was haggard and appeared as if he had suffered sudden weight loss. His eyes lacked their normal sparkle of cunning and intelligence. He bore the look of a beaten man.

"We meet again, my old friend," said Charlemagne. "But where is your leader Akramont? Why is he not pleading for my mercy?"

"Akramont fled along with his troops."

"So this is not an end to the war, but only a partial surrender limited to you and your groups?"

"Yes," said Marsilio, followed by a heavy sigh.

"Why did you stay behind? Why did you not flee with Akramont's men?"

"Because I lost faith in his leadership and do not want any more of my men to die in a doomed cause."

Charlemagne suppressed a smile. He wanted to learn more about his enemy's weaknesses in leadership, but thought it best to coax information out rather than ask Marsilio directly. "Why did you join forces with Akramont?"

Marsilio shrugged. "He amassed a large army and there was a chance I could reclaim lands you seized from me. I would love to once again have Barcelona and the Pyrenees Mountains in my domain. I had hoped to expand into Toulouse, Narbonne, and Bordeaux. You expanded your empire over the years, surely you can understand that desire."

Charlemagne smiled. "Of course. Tell me, where did Akramont go?"

"I will tell you, but only after we have agreed upon the terms of surrender."

"Go ahead."

"First, I request my men be allowed to provide proper burials for our fallen."

Charlemagne gave a quick nod.

"I would ask for assistance by your men to help dig graves while we prepare the bodies. We will set aside any Christians who died in the battle and, if you wish, ready them for burial as well."

"Setting their bodies aside will be sufficient. Our priests will oversee their burial preparations. Now, let us discuss your tribute. You will send twelve chests filled with gold each year to my palace in Aachen before Pentecost." He paused to allow that large amount of treasure to hang in the air. "This war has lasted three months so far. Therefore, I demand three of your family to serve as hostages to ensure you comply with the terms of this surrender."

Marsilio hung his head. "Agreed."

Charlemagne began ticking his fingers. "The first hostage will be your son, Matalista. The second hostage will be your daughter, Fiordespina. I heard she is as beautiful as the rising sun."

Marsilio gave a strangled sob. The amir's eyes welled up with tears. "If only that were possible," his voice cracked. "My beloved daughter is dead. Akramont is to blame for that as well." He covered his face with his hands.

Charlemagne waited. There was more to this story, but his rival needed to regain his composure.

"Akramont convinced me to agree to the marriage between my daughter and... and..." his face twisted, "the foul Governor Rodomont of Sarza. If you find him, do me the favor of disemboweling him for his crimes."

Charlemagne made a fist. "Is he the same man who desecrated one of my churches?"

"Yes." Marsilio's eyes were downcast. "Rodomont was spurned by his betrothed. Akramont tried mollifying that man's temper by offering my daughter as a replacement bride." He gave a long pause as he recovered his voice. "My daughter knew of his cruelty and refused to marry him. A second rejection was too much for that bastard's pride. He murdered her in front of me." His hands once again covered his face.

Charlemagne was horrified. He turned to his seneschal. "Audulf, have some chairs, a table, and tea brought here. My old friend needs comforting."

CHAPTER SIXTY-FIVE

R enaud and Gradasso finished securing the reins for their horses on separate large branches of an immense oak tree. It stood alone on a field west of the city of Paris. Gradasso's mare and Bayard were near each other, but not close enough to make physical contact.

"Terms first," barked Gradasso. "I cannot trust you to fight with honor."

Renaud scowled as he looked over his opponent head to toe. The man wore a vivid blue vest with a bend of gold over scale armor and a golden crown on his helmet. A long scar ran down one cheek.

"A fight to the death," said Renaud. "Whoever lives owns both horses. We fight alone, on foot, armed only with a sword, shield, and dagger. No matter what happens with the armies, we shall continue this fight until our dispute is settled."

"No interference from any allies," said Gradasso.

"None."

"Now we begin," said Gradasso as he withdrew his sword from its scabbard. Renaud stared as he recognized his opponent's blade.

"Durindana? How did you get Orlando's sword?"

Gradasso flashed a wicked smile as he began moving. "I claimed this after Mandricardo died."

"Did Mandricardo kill Orlando?" asked Renaud as he drew out his sword and began his own dance of Death.

"Mandricardo was an arrogant bastard who bragged about every aspect of his life. He brandished this sword as well as the horse he seized from Orlando. He did not speak of how he beat that famous warrior. Knowing Mandricardo as I did, I believe he was hiding something about his duel with Orlando."

Renaud needed to ignore any thoughts of worry about his kinsman. Inattentiveness could be deadly. He lunged at his enemy. Gradasso was ready and their swords clashed in the air.

CHAPTER SIXTY-SIX

Charlemagne nodded as his chamberlain poured tea for Amir Marsilio. He knew the quality of the beverage would not be as good as the amir was accustomed, but it was an attempt at showing hospitality. Marsilio sat at the table with a faraway look in his eyes. He was not the same man Charlemagne had known for over thirty years. Marsilio raised the cup to his lips and drank without any change of expression on his face.

"Can you name another family member to serve as a hostage?"

"My sister, Lanfusa."

Movement out of the corner of his eye made Charlemagne turn. Vivien clenched his fists and his nostrils flared. Charlemagne then remembered Maugis and Vivien had been held hostage by Lanfusa. He would have tried to help release them, but only learned of their captivity after his forces were under siege in Paris. Charlemagne considered Lanfusa a worthy prisoner and thought her evil would be easier to contain if she was under his lock and key.

"I would also like her son, Feraguto," said Charlemagne.

"You may have him as a captive, but I cannot surrender Feraguto to your forces."

Charlemagne arched an eyebrow.

"He left with Akramont."

"Where did they go?"

Marsilio cracked a bittersweet smile. "As I said earlier, I will tell you, but only after we have agreed on terms."

Charlemagne sighed and gave a motion for the amir to continue.

"The length of confinement for the hostages. After five years of tribute payment, they will be returned."

"During that time there will be no military campaigns by the Emirate of Córdoba against my Frankish troops," added Charlemagne.

"Emirate of Córdoba, Hispania, or al-Andalus. Three wonderful names all to describe my beautiful lands. Yes, I agree. My men will not engage in combat against your men during this time, if you likewise agree on no more incursions into my lands by your troops."

Charlemagne nodded.

"After five years of my paying tribute and no wars between us, you will return my family members to me."

"Agreed. However, the tribute will last for ten years in total."

Charlemagne's scribe, Einhard, sat nearby dutifully recording the details on parchment.

"Matalista is to be treated as one of your own family. He will be allowed to eat meals in your presence and housed in your palace at Aachen. He will improve his language skills at your renowned Palace School."

Charlemagne tapped Einhard on the shoulder and shook his head. "Those details are not to be recorded. I cannot guarantee where Matalista will be housed, but I guarantee he will be extended the same courtesy shown to Ogier the Dane." Charlemagne gestured to a tall blond knight standing next to Duke Namo. "Ogier's father had been in arrears for his tribute and his son was surrendered to ensure future compliance. Ogier became like a fifth son to Duke Namo."

The elderly Duke of Bavaria nodded and smiled at the handsome warrior.

"Yet, Ogier's father still refused to send his tribute as required," said Charlemagne. "Because of that, he has not seen his father since the fateful day he was surrendered. However, Ogier proved himself worthy in battle many times over. He is now one of my twelve paladins."

"Would you take Matalista into battle?"

"Certainly not against Akramont's forces," said Charlemagne. "However, should the Saxons or other enemies give me trouble again…" He stopped speaking when Marsilio winced. Perhaps the prospect of the death of another child was more than the amir could handle in that moment. Charlemagne decided to change the subject. "Should Feraguto become a hostage he will also be treated with similar hospitality, but the two will not be held at the same household."

"I will agree to those terms," said Marsilio. "As for my sister, Lanfusa —"

"She will be kept in a comfortable tower, be well-fed, and allowed fresh air each day. More than that, I shall not guarantee. Lanfusa has a poisonous reputation."

"Fine. I will send my seneschal to bring my family out of hiding."

"Ogier take some men with you and accompany Marsilio's seneschal. Bring his family to me."

One of Marsilio's attendants walked out of the pavilion escorted by Ogier.

"Once our agreement is written down and signed by both of us, I will tell you Akramont's destination. In the meantime my men should start preparing the dead for burials, while yours begin digging the graves."

Charlemagne turned to his seneschal. "Audulf, see those things are done."

CHAPTER SIXTY-SEVEN

Renaud was weary of fighting. His arms and back ached, his stomach growled with hunger, his throat felt parched, and yet he could not rest until his duel with Gradasso was over. The king of Sericana was a brutal opponent. One of the fiercest Renaud ever fought. Their swords clashed many times, but neither found an advantage nor had there been any stumbles.

The sun had risen in a cloudless blue sky. Renaud was anxious for his secret weapon to be revealed. The golden helmet he wore would soon be hit by the sun's rays. Balls of light would dance before Gradasso's eyes, obscuring his vision. Once Renaud noticed his opponent flinch, it would signify his opportunity to go in for the kill.

Just as Gradasso's eyes began squinting, darkness blanketed the sky. Renaud had no time to consider the cause, when a sound like the screech of one hundred eagles assaulted his ears. He and Gradasso stopped fighting as an enormous blackbird with the wingspan of over thirty feet flew over their heads. As the colossal bird swooped downward, its gigantic talons brushed Gradasso's helmet knocking him to the ground. Renaud saw his rival in a vulnerable position and realized he could behead his enemy or try to save his beloved horse from a demonic creature. He could not accomplish both.

Renaud ran with his sword held high and swung at one of the claws clamping down on Bayard's belly. Using all of his might, Renaud severed the bird's leg that was as large as a man's thigh. Another loud screech sounded as thick green blood coursed out of the wound and sprayed down onto Renaud and Bayard. The warm fluid burned where it came in contact with bare skin, mostly on his neck. The mammoth bird turned in the sky and glared at Renaud with glowing red eyes. An overpowering smell of sulfur filled the air. He lifted his sword in defiance as Bayard kicked and reared, breaking the reins, before galloping away.

Renaud almost called out to his horse when Gradasso rode by and banged him on the helmet with Durindana. He fell to the ground and all went black.

CHAPTER SIXTY-EIGHT

T he return flight to King Senapo's secret island was a leisurely one. Aistulf found himself slowing down the process so he could enjoy the fresh air and sunshine. After having been in the Underworld followed by confinement in a cave for what felt like weeks, he savored the simple joys such as a soft breeze on his face and the warmth of a summer's day.

This time when they arrived on the island, he directed the hippogriff to land inside the courtyard of the fortified wooden palace. A clamor of servants soon surrounded him. Aistulf repeated the instruction to Kamal to fly away and return when called. Senapo's courtier stepped forward and ushered Aistulf inside the building. He was taken to the small chamber decorated with religious mosaics.

King Senapo sat at the table, his eyes still milky white and looking in Aistulf's direction with a large smile on his face. "My friend, you finally returned."

Aistulf was surprised at the dramatic changes in the king. Senapo no longer looked like a beggar. He was thin, but no longer emaciated and wore a clean tunic with a rich embroidered design accented with golden thread. The blind king held out his bony hands in the air. Aistulf grasped them.

"I have eaten full meals again, thanks to your bravery," said Senapo, his voice thick with emotion. "You saved my life."

Aistulf sat down next to him. "I have something for you. It comes from the place you dedicated your life trying to find."

The smile on Senapo's face faltered. "Terrestrial Paradise?"

"Yes. It is beautiful, but it can only be entered when one has been cleansed of all sin, and only if invited. You became cursed, because you tried forcing your entry. That is forbidden, but since you have atoned for your sins, I have something to make you whole."

He reached inside his satchel and removed the plant.

"Your heart is troubled. As a small child you were deprived of a mother's love due to her untimely death and denied a father's love due to his absence. You were raised with cold, calculating principles and devoid of love and compassion. Later, when your wife, your son, and your lover needed your love, you failed them because of your closed heart. Because of that, they suffered and in the last year you suffered." Aistulf rolled the purple and yellow flowers between his fingers and squeezed a few precious drops onto Senapo's sightless eyes. "As I apply the drops from heartsease to your eyes, it will restore your vision."

The king blinked and then rubbed his eyes. After a few moments he opened them. Their color had changed to brown. He looked at Aistulf and tears welled in his eyes.

"Thank you, my son," said the king. He began laughing as tears ran down his face. "I can see again and what a beautiful face to behold. You look like an angel from Heaven."

Aistulf shook his head. "I am but a flawed man. Please have the stems and leaves of this plant dried and then made into a tea. This heartsease plant was created just for you and the tea will mend your heart, and allow you to feel love and to love others. However, should anyone else taste that tea, it would poison them."

Senapo handed the plant to his attendant and spoke to them in their native tongue. After the man left, the king said to Aistulf, "My kitchens will prepare a royal banquet in your honor. I cannot think of anyone who deserves it more. Come, let me show you a room where you can rest."

CHAPTER SIXTY-NINE

Bradamante took a deep breath as she headed across the garden toward the chapel. She could no longer delay another insufferable Greek lesson. Her nephew, Bernard, stood almost hiding behind his mother's skirts until Clarice pushed him forward.

"Auntie, could you give me a lesson today?" He asked in a plaintive tone.

Bradamante felt warmth spread in her heart. She knelt down and smiled at him. "I would like nothing better than to spend my day with you. However, I do not control what occupies my day, your grandmother does. Perhaps," she said, dropping her voice to a whisper, "if you ask her sweetly, she will allow it."

He threw his small arms around her neck. "I will! I will!"

The hug made her feel happy until she saw the triumphant look on Clarice's face. Clarice would make her life miserable if Bernard's needs were not addressed that day. Bradamante banished the thought as she walked hand-in-hand with her nephew through the garden. Upon entering the chapel, Bradamante's nerves were on edge. Her mother sat at the table with Fra Galen.

Beatrice affixed her signet ring to a wax seal on the outside of a rolled piece of parchment, looked up and smiled. "My darling boy, what brings you here?"

Bernard wiped his hands on his pants and bowed his head as he spoke. "Hello Grandmother, my father told me on the morning he left that my aunt would teach me how to be a knight. She has not done that yet. I wanted to know if we could start my training today."

Beatrice nodded to the monk and handed him a coin before walking toward her grandson. "Dear Bernard, of course Bradamante will help you. Today is a perfect day to start your lessons. Fra Galen has been called back to the abbey and will be leaving this morning. Bradamante will not have more lessons with him until he returns. Roberto is finishing up the final details on her portrait and he will be unveiling it tonight."

"Does that mean we can start now?" Bernard squealed.

Beatrice gave him a wide smile. "Yes."

He jumped up and down with joy.

"You may show me your gratitude," said Beatrice, leaning down.

Bernard planted a kiss on her cheek, before turning to Bradamante. His face split in a grin.

"Let me first change out of this dress," she said, "and then we will begin working on your swordplay in the park."

❧

"Hold your shield higher," Bradamante said, tapping her wooden sword on Bernard's practice shield. "Swing your arm as you deflect the blow."

"But I want to use my sword, not my shield," whined Bernard.

"Have you ever tried to pick up a real sword?"

"Yes, it was too heavy."

"Exactly. You need to first learn to defend yourself from attack while you are unable to wield a weapon. That was how I learned. In my first lesson, someone hit my little shield. My father expected me to run away in tears, but instead I became angry."

Bernard's jaw dropped. "Really?"

"Have you never heard your father telling the story of how I became trained as a warrior?" asked Bradamante.

He shook his head. "No. I wish my father was home more. I love hearing his stories, but it seems he is always away in battle. Could you tell me that story?"

Bradamante smiled and nodded. "Come, let us sit down on the bench. I cannot tell a story well while I am fighting."

Bernard climbed up on the stone bench and gazed at her with admiration.

"I have heard your father tell this story so many times I cannot remember where my own memories end and his embellishments begin."

"How old were you when you started training?"

"Three years old."

Bernard eyes grew wide. "I am four. Am I too old?"

"No, dear heart, of course not." She patted his hand. "Your Uncle Richardet and I are twins. That means we were born on the same day. As babies we did everything together. We ate together, slept together, and we became inconsolable whenever we were separated. If two different people held us and we could not see each other — we cried."

"You really loved each other."

"Yes, and we still do. But, when we were young, Richardet and I did not feel complete if our other half was missing. We would cry until we saw each other again." She smoothed the hair out of Bernard's eyes. "Our family traveled to the Royal Palace in Aachen to attend the formal knighting ceremony of our cousin, Orlando. He had been knighted informally a few years earlier when, as a squire, he saved Charlemagne's life during the liberation of Reggio Calabria."

"A squire saved Charlemagne?" Bernard said with awe.

"Yes, at the same time Orlando also avenged the death of his father, Milon, and of our grandfather, Bernard of Lyon. You are that great man's namesake."

Bernard swung his feet under the bench. "Tell me about the celebration."

"As Orlando turned eighteen, Charlemagne wanted to hold a lavish celebration in honor of his nephew who had become a famed warrior. Our family arrived and my mother hoped I would spend time with Charlemagne's daughters. Richardet was to be given his first lesson with a practice sword."

"They tried separating you," said Bernard, "and you cried."

Bradamante nodded, happy he was following the story. "Oh, we wailed and screamed. Guards came running to see what was happening. They thought children were being tortured." She tickled Bernard until he screamed with laughter. "My father suggested they find another practice shield and sword for me. He thought I would cry and run the first time someone hit my shield. My mother held out hope I would go and play with my girl cousins."

"What happened?"

"A man laughed at me and said training a girl to fight was a joke. He made me mad. Fighting mad. Your father loves to describe the fierce look on my face saying, 'I am from the House of Lyon, I was born to fight.' Charlemagne was so impressed he commanded my parents to train me as a warrior alongside my brothers."

"How old were you when you first went off to war?"

"Thirteen. That was after your father's knighting ceremony. He had been trained at the Palace School in Aachen along with our cousin, Aistulf, so the family had not seen him for several years. I wanted to impress my famous brother with my skills, so I challenged him. He thought it was a jape at first, until we started our duel. Then, he discovered it was no laughing matter. A crowd gathered to see the spectacle, including Charlemagne. After it was over, he commanded I join his forces that very day."

"Have you been knighted?"

"No," she said, shaking her head, "that honor is reserved for men."

Bernard's brow furrowed. "But my father said you are more skilled than most of Charlemagne's paladins."

Bradamante was about to reply when the expression on his face gave her pause. She was forcefully reminded of the image the enchantress Melissa showed her of the future child she was to bear with Ruggiero. Her eyes watered at the memory and the hopefulness she once felt at the promise of being a wife and mother. For the thousandth time, she regretted leaving Ruggiero's side to seek her revenge against Pinabel of the House of Maganza. Had she stayed with Ruggiero, he might now be baptized and be fighting on the Christian side.

"Come let us return to your lesson," she said, forcing herself to smile as she stood.

Bernard scrambled to his feet and crouched with his shield at the ready waiting for her to strike. His face filled with intensity as he blocked the blow of her sword.

"Good," she said as she lifted her sword into the air before hitting his shield again.

Her attention became broken when she heard, "Bradamante, is *that* you?"

The tone in the man's voice made her wince, as if she was caught doing something wong. She turned and saw Roberto, the painter, walking toward her. Bernard seized the opportunity and stabbed her in the stomach with his practice sword.

"Take that," he said.

"Ow, yes Bernard, you won this round," she said. Bradamante turned to Roberto. "Good afternoon."

"What happened to your hair?" he said, sounding worried.

Bradamante gave him a sheepish smile. "It was cut months ago. I wore a wig for my portrait. At least it resembles how long my tresses had been, so it is not a total deceit."

"I heard the servants talk about you being a warrior, but I thought it was a jest. I have never seen this side of you before." He gave her an appraising smile as he examined her from head to toe.

Bradamante looked down at her attire. She was dressed in a quilted gambeson and riding breeches. There had been no need for her to don the heavy chain mail armor, but she regretted that practical decision because she felt immodestly dressed. The heat of a blush grew on her cheeks.

"I regret I finished your portrait. I would love to capture this powerful aspect of yours," he said.

"I would have rather sat for you wearing my armor than finery."

"That would have been a portrait for the ages."

Bradamante swallowed hard. "Are you not intimidated by the thought of a woman warrior?"

"On the contrary, I find it intriguing," Roberto said, as he ran a hand through his dark tousled hair. "Alas, I cannot remain here and paint a second likeness of you. Other clients are awaiting my talents. I doubt I will ever have another subject as beautiful and gracious as you."

She was uncomfortable with hearing praise about her appearance. Averting his gaze, she nodded and said, "Thank you for your kind words."

Bernard stood between them and pointed his wooden sword at Roberto. "Stand back from my auntie! I will protect her."

Roberto raised his hands in a mock surrender. "Young man, I would not dare make a move toward your aunt, but I recognize I may have spoken with too much familiarity. I offer my apologies, if I have offended you."

She lowered her eyes and waved a hand to dismiss his concern.

"As you asked, milady, I set up an easel near the trellis and set aside a pallet and some pigments for you. Might I ask what you will create with this?"

"I am going to paint a new design for my shield."

He gave a low chuckle. "Of course, my fierce warrior lady. What else could it be for? It is time for the unveiling of your portrait. We should make haste as your mother is not someone to be kept waiting."

✳

CHAPTER SEVENTY

Renaud's head throbbed. As he woke, he was confused. He did not recall going to sleep in a bed. He was lying on an ornate four-poster bed in a grand chamber. After a few moments, he realized this was the same room in the ducal palace where he stayed once before.

His cousin, Maugis, sat nearby. "Our illustrious leader is awake."

Renaud sat up, feeling groggy. "What happened?"

"Sansonetto and Emile were watching your duel from inside the woods. They came to your aid after you were knocked out. They brought you here where I tended your wounds and removed a poison that would have killed you." Maugis handed him a cup of warm broth.

He took a drink of the salty brew. "Where is Bayard?"

"I knew you would ask, so I poured a pan of water and scried on the matter. For all of Gradasso's harsh words about sorcery, he knows a few things about magic," said Maugis looking amused. "He wears enchanted armor, which is why it was impenetrable to your sword. He also had herbs in his saddlebags allowing him to tame Bayard and to treat his wounds. Your horse is fine, but Gradasso does not have the horse's loyalty. To answer your question, Gradasso is on his way to rejoin Akramont's forces."

"I must go after him," said Renaud as he started to pull back the bed covers.

Maugis pushed him back down on the bed. "Not today. You must allow my medicine to work. Here, have some meat and cheese."

Renaud took the wooden plate on the bedside table and bit into a cube of brown meat. It had a strange taste, like game but unlike anything he ever tasted before. "What is this?"

"Something to increase your strength and endurance. Do not ask any more questions." Maugis gave an enigmatic smile.

"Did you send that monster to steal away Bayard?"

"You think me a fool? You almost castrated me over my previous intervention with Gradasso."

Renaud stared at his cousin. His face was like a stone. No nervous twitching, no movement of any kind. "If you were not responsible, who was?" asked Renaud. "That bird must have been summoned by magic. Gradasso?"

Maugis shrugged his shoulders. "Maybe, but I did not see any sense of that from my scrying. Perhaps he hid his powers from me."

Renaud thought about the sequence of events from the morning. "Gradasso had no compatriots. He had motive, but there was no time for him to cast spells."

"Perhaps there is another wizard who wants to hurt one of Charlemagne's famed paladins."

"Perhaps."

Renaud finished eating the strange meal his cousin Maugis prepared and felt a wave of exhaustion roll over him. His loss of sleep the previous night as well as all the exertion spent in combat caught up with him. He settled back on the bed and was about to close his eyes when there came a knock on the door.

"The hero of Montauban has returned," said Oliver, as he entered. "Your company's attack was well planned and executed. The siege is broken. Our enemies panicked and left behind all their food and supplies."

Renaud sat up again. He was happy to hear such tidings, especially from a well-respected warrior. Oliver was one of the heroes Renaud admired when he was a child.

"I am grateful you found and brought back my sons," said Oliver. "I worried that I would never see them again."

"You should be proud of Aquilant and Grifon. They are fine cavaliers."

Oliver sat down in the chair next to the bed. "Amir Marsilio surrendered and will be returning to Hispania."

Renaud smiled. "That is better news than I expected."

"Yes, and Charlemagne was shrewd in arranging the terms. Marsilio is only allowed twelve wagons to transport their tents, weapons, and supplies. That is the same number of wagonloads of tribute they will owe Charlemagne for the next ten years. Namo's sons will lead a battalion to serve as an escort to the Pyrenees to assure Marsilio does not try to rejoin Akramont."

"When will our forces leave?"

"Because of all of the burials and the time it took to finish the terms of surrender, Marsilio's troops will not leave until the morrow. Our forces will not leave for at least three days. Charlemagne wants a full accounting of the tents, horses and other supplies left behind by the Saracen army. He also sent an expedition eastward to gather more food for our journey. He wants our forces to be prepared for the upcoming siege."

Renaud almost asked where Akramont's forces were headed, when Oliver stood. "There are two people you should meet." He beckoned toward the open doorway as a man and woman entered. The man, dressed in bronze scale armor carried his helmet and a shield slung across his back. The warrior was tall with a good-sized build and a full head of black hair. The woman wore a long white dress with golden brocade at the hem and neckline. She was thin with blonde hair falling past her shoulders.

As the couple came closer, Renaud rubbed his eyes.

"This is the newest paladin," said Oliver. "I would like you to meet—"

"Brandimart," finished Renaud, "and his lady, Flordelis. I am overjoyed to see you again my friends."

"You know each other?" said Oliver.

"Yes, we shared many adventures together in the East," said Renaud. "Let me stand so I can welcome you properly."

Maugis put his hands on Renaud shoulders. "You must rest," he insisted. "If you try to leave this bed again, I will have your arms and legs bound."

"This is my meddlesome cousin, Maugis. He is also a paladin," said Renaud, trying hard not to lose his temper in front of a lady.

"You may still have poison in your veins," warned Maugis. "Allow my medicine the time it needs to work."

"Poison? Oh, please rest," said Flordelis, her voice trembling. "I could not bear it if you were harmed because of me."

Renaud leaned back against the headboard of the bed and smiled at her. "I cannot refuse a lady's request."

She gave him a weak smile in return. Flordelis had never appeared so frail.

Brandimart put a comforting arm around her. "Since we last saw each other, Flordelis and I were married. She also learned she was the lost daughter of the King and Queen of Liza in Armenia."

"I was stolen from them as a small child and grew up in the castle of Rocca Silvana."

"We passed through the kingdom of Liza on our journey westward," said Brandimart. "We heard their story of a stolen daughter and realized it was Flordelis. Her unique birthmark proved who she was."

"Congratulations on your marriage," said Renaud. "And for finding your family. I always knew you had a noble bearing. I have never seen a couple as devoted to each other as you are."

She gave him another weak smile. "This dress was a gift from my parents."

"I sense there is something vexing you, my lady. What is it?" asked Renaud.

"I paced the ramparts all night long and throughout the morning until Brandimart returned to my side. While I am happy with the turn of events, I am devastated Orlando was not with you."

Brandimart nodded. "We hoped we would share a victory celebration with our dear friend, Orlando. We are heartbroken you did not find him."

Oliver chimed in, "Because of your success in putting our enemies on the run, Charlemagne agreed to another mission to seek out my childhood friend Orlando. The three of us will be leaving at dawn."

"Renaud cannot leave that soon," said Maugis.

"You misunderstand," said Oliver. "The party will consist of me, Brandimart, and Flordelis. We came here to learn what Renaud discovered during his search."

Renaud took another drink of broth before telling them of the events of his search starting with Orlando being dressed in black. He followed the trail of a tearful knight who asked everyone he saw about Angelica. The farther south from Paris, the more disturbing the tales of the Black Knight seemed to become. The search ended near the village of Saint Antonin, but only because Renaud ran out of time.

"I do not believe Angelica loves Orlando," said Flordelis. "The four of us left Cathay on our way here. We became separated, but in the short time I spent with her, I did not like her. Angelica's eyes did not glow when she spoke with him, nor when she looked at him. I do not trust her, and I hope Orlando will relinquish his dreams of a life with her." She paused and looked down at her hands. "Angelica is cursed. Death and destruction surround her. She has an unnatural power over men that drives them mad. Orlando deserves better than that witch."

"I agree," said Oliver. "He deserves the love of a fine woman, such as my sister Alda."

Renaud did not want to say anything about Angelica. He was finally rid of her from his own heart. "I am compelled to voice my objection to Flordelis leaving on this journey. It would be safer for her to stay here, behind the strong walls of Paris."

"I cannot," said Flordelis in a firm voice. "I would escape any confines to seek out my husband." She cast Renaud a pleading look. "You know my part in our many adventures. If I had not summoned help, Brandimart would still be a prisoner in Falerina's enchanted garden and you would still be a prisoner of the fay Morgana." She began wringing her hands. "I cannot be left behind. I would become worried to death about his safety."

"She made a similar case in front of Charlemagne," said Brandimart. "He could not deny her request to stay by my side."

Flordelis lifted her chin. "I was trained by the herbalist at Rocca Silvana, who had the gift of Sight. She taught me to recognize magic in all its forms." She cast a long look at Maugis, "and to be wary of them. The wise woman knew of many magical realms in the surrounding lands and told them to me as bedtime stories. Only after Brandimart and I left that kingdom, did I realize her tales would not for amusement. Her knowledge saved all of our lives. I will be a help on this mission, not a hindrance."

"Very well, I remove my objection. But I suggest before departing that you attempt to alter your appearance, for safety's sake."

Flordelis looked confused.

"You cannot disguise your beauty, but you can change your dress. Ask the Duchess of Paris for a frock from a serving girl. By wearing the clothes of a commoner, you will disguise your station and not appear to be worthy of a large ransom."

Maugis nodded. "As someone who was recently held for ransom, I must concur with my cousin. You should also cover your beautiful blonde hair."

CHAPTER SEVENTY-ONE

A small crowd gathered in the main hall awaiting the portrait unveiling. Clarice patted her sleeping baby on her shoulder, Bernard rocked back and forth on his heels, while Bradamante's mother had an inpatient air about her. Bradamante resisted the urge to chew her nails by pressing them into the palms of her hands. She glanced at her handmaiden, Hippalca, and received a reassuring smile.

Roberto bowed to Beatrice. "I wish to once again extend my gratitude to the Duchess of Dordogne for granting me the honor of capturing the beauty of your daughter onto canvas. Your hospitality was as gracious as Bradamante's modeling."

Bradamante gave Roberto a polite nod, while Clarice gave him a tight-lipped smile.

"Here is Lady Bradamante," Roberto said as he removed the drape covering the easel.

Bradamante stared at her image, as if she was looking at a stranger. She recognized the wig, the dress, and the Visigothic eagle pendant, but it was hard to believe she was the beautiful woman in the painting. The woman's confident smile on her face suggested that she bore a secret. Bradamante was captivated by the portrait and wondered if Ruggiero saw her in such a positive light.

"Do I really look like that?" she asked Hippalca.

"Yes, milady."

"My daughter," said Beatrice, her voice thick with emotion. "The colors are in perfect balance between the dark blue of the dress and the bright pink roses of the bower to just the proper amount of blush on her cheeks and lips. Thank you, this is exactly what I needed." She pressed a small bag of coins into Roberto's hands.

Clarice appeared astounded. "Master Roberto, you are a skilled painter. You have accomplished what I did not think possible. You brought out a feminine side to Bradamante."

Roberto furrowed his brows. "I believe any man who sees her portrait will undoubtedly fall in love with her."

Bradamante began to squirm at the scrutiny being paid to her likeness. She had always felt uncomfortable when attention was paid to her appearance, rather than her martial skills.

Bernard jumped up-and-down. "My auntie looks pretty."

"Thank you," Bradamante said smiling. She leaned down and gave him a hug.

CHAPTER SEVENTY-TWO

Aistulf was restless about his continued presence as a guest at King Senapo's remote palace. He was eager to begin the tasks the Prophet Elijah told him about. Guilt nagged at his conscience every time he thought about Orlando, but the king insisted that Aistulf remain until further notice. He was being treated with every possible courtesy, and to criticize anything would be ungracious and disrespectful. So Aistulf waited for more than a week, while trying not to show any sign of impatience with his host.

One night, Senapo invited Aistulf to join him in the chamber with mosaics adorning the wall. A servant poured honeyed wine into cups. The king gave a nod as more servants entered the small room and placed Aistulf's helmet and shield upon the table.

"My tinsmiths finished the repairs you asked for," said Senapo. "The pearls, crushed or whole, were all removed and the design has been changed."

Aistulf examined the shield. The damages to its surface during the slide down Sisyphus's hill in the Underworld had required sanding. All the gold plating that had once made him so proud was gone. In the center of the shield was a large image of the full moon made of silver. His fingers gingerly touched the grooves cut into it and he smiled as he considered that over time tarnish would highlight the carvings of craters on the moon. Along the edges of the shield, where once had been pearls, small silver circles echoed the lunar design. The helmet had its pearls removed and similar silver circles adorned its rim.

"This is remarkable workmanship," said Aistulf. "My compliments to your artisans."

"I will have your sentiments conveyed to them." Senapo gave him a smile. "You looked frail and starved when you first came back here. It is good to see a more robust appearance after a week's worth of meals." He waved his hand and sent the servants from the room. "Tell me, when you were at Terrestrial Paradise, did you meet God? Your hair and beard are white, yet you are youthful. I am reminded of Moses having his hair turn white after he saw the hand of God."

Aistulf ran a hand over his beard. "You are right. My hair had been golden in color, and I did not have a beard — only a mustache. Those in Charlemagne's court will be startled at my new appearance. I decided to keep this new facial hair until I return to my father's court in Essex."

Senapo stared at him without amusement.

"No, I did not see the Lord our Father."

"What happened on your journey? You have yet to tell me. All I know is that you chased the Harpies away and returned a week or so later."

Aistulf kept the tone of his voice light. "You have had your own brushes with the fantastical, between losing your sight overnight to being tormented by Harpies. Those types of curses are frightening to even contemplate, let alone experience. Most people would recoil in horror and doubt the sanity of anyone who told such tales if they did not see the beasts from Hell themselves. You moved and hid in this remote island fortress, because you feared how your subjects would react if they realized their ruler was cursed. My story after chasing them is no less fantastical. I am having a difficult time understanding what all transpired, and at times I feel that it must have been a fevered dream. I doubt anyone would believe what happened to me if I told him. Rather than have you ponder if I have lost all of my wits, I shall keep my own counsel on this matter. Perhaps, one day, while making a confession to Archbishop Turpin, I will tell him my tale. As a paladin of Charlemagne, he has also experienced some fantastic events in his life. But even if he did not believe me, he would be bound by the sacred seal of the confession to keep my secrets." Aistulf then sipped his wine, signifying he had nothing further to say on the subject.

Senapo steepled his fingers. "Tomorrow we shall both leave this island. I am returning to my capital where the first order of business will be to re-establish a relationship with my son. He deserves a father's love as well as my strategic advice for ruling and expansion of power. Skills he will need once he becomes king. And as for you, I have at last heard from my spies about the movements of Caliph Harun al-Rashid."

Aistulf set his cup down. "What did you hear?"

"The caliph's army set sail a few weeks ago from Tyre. By this time, they should be about a fortnight or so from Bizerta. It will not be difficult to spot the vast fleet in the Mediterranean. However, to find the caliph's ship, look for the grandest one that bears a solid black flag. That is the symbol of the Abbasid dynasty."

Aistulf began imagining the route he would direct the hippogriff to find the caliph's forces.

"If the caliph aids Akramont and attacks the Frankish army," continued Senapo, "I will view it as an act of aggression against Christendom. I will respond accordingly to protect my interests."

"What do you mean by that?"

"My army will secure control of the Nile and its port in Alexandria."

Aistulf's jaw dropped. "That would split the caliphate."

"It would. Ethiopia's trading power would also increase tenfold." Senapo gave a slight smile that did not reach his eyes. "The Maghreb being so distant from the capital of the caliphate, it has always been wayward and hard to control. The Abbasids overthrew the Umayyad dynasty more than fifty years ago. There was a massacre, but one member of that family, Abd al-Rahman, escaped and hid for five years amongst Christians."

"Here? In Ethiopia?"

Senapo shrugged his shoulders. "Perhaps. My country has a long history of sheltering religious refugees, especially Muslims. Abd al-Rahman eventually made his way to al-Andalus and found sanctuary there. That is why the westernmost portion of the Islamic empire broke off from Abbasid rule and became its own caliphate under the last Umayyad. If the caliph does not punish

Akramont for this unsanctioned war against the Franks, then he risks having his vast empire divided further."

A gnawing suspicion grew stronger with Aistulf that Senapo was not acting like a man who had been made whole. The ruthlessness displayed by the king made him doubt that Senapo drank tea made of the heartsease plant. That meant the king, while cured of his curses, was not healed of the deep wounds suffered for not allowing himself to feel love.

Senapo placed a rolled piece of parchment bearing his royal seal into a leather tube and handed it to Aistulf. "An army will be attacking the Maghreb. If not his, it will be mine. Give this to the caliph."

CHAPTER SEVENTY-THREE

Duke Aymon returned unannounced to Montauban. Bradamante was surprised, but relieved to once again have the company of her beloved father. To mollify her mother, Bradamante changed into her wig and blue silk dress for the leisurely noontime dinner in honor of her father. Afterward, Bradamante strolled with him through the garden while holding onto his arm.

"I hope your time here without me, or any of your brothers, was not too trying on your spirit," said her father.

Bradamante gave him a wistful smile and shrugged.

He laughed. "Beatrice is a tenacious woman. Once she has a plan in mind, she clings to it as desperately as a starving dog with a bone. She told me all the details of the activities of yours she controlled from sunrise to sundown."

Bradamante nodded, trying to keep her face impassive. She did not want to outwardly express discontent toward her mother.

"Well, you will soon be given a reprieve. I will be taking your mother away from here, so you will not be subjected to her demands for a while."

"How does the construction fare for your new castle?"

"It is almost complete and ready for your mother's touch. The size is twice that of this castle, and the view is spectacular. The fortress sits atop a large hill and overlooks the beautiful Dordogne River. I do hope that the duchess will finally be satisfied and feel I have earned something worthy of her station in life." He sighed and shook his head. "Who am I fooling? She will continue to try and persuade her brother into giving her a grand stone castle somewhere else."

"When can I visit?"

He patted her hand. "That must wait until after your mother finishes her decorating, for I would not inflict the torture of enduring that process upon anyone I care for." He plucked a white rosebud from the nearby bower and handed it to her. "Speaking of which, she expressed her disappointment that you did not assist in the creation of a tapestry to hang in the new hall. She said you were insistent on making fabric instead."

"I have an urgent need," said Bradamante, not wanting to explain further.

He chuckled. "Finding an excuse for being at a separate loom from her, I believe would qualify as an urgent need."

She shared an affectionate look with her father. This levity at her mother's expense was unusual and perhaps heralded Bradamante as being accepted into adulthood.

"I received a letter from Renaud," he said.

Her mind shifted to the war. "Yes?"

"His little party wreaked havoc on the Saracen camp and preceded an all-out assault by the Frankish army. Our enemies deserted the area and fled to Arles."

"Arles?" she said, taken aback. "That is far from Paris, it makes no sense."

Her father shrugged. "It was their only other stronghold, but perhaps this demonstrates that Akramont is not a military strategist to be feared. Renaud wrote of the Saracens' vast casualties in Paris and of the loss of Amir Marsilio's troops."

"Pardon?"

"Marsilio surrendered to Charlemagne. He and his forces are returning to Hispania and will be paying tribute to the emperor for many years. Renaud expects the war to be over soon with our enemies killed or driven from our shores."

Bradamante felt as if the cloud covering her heart was lifted. Perhaps the prophecy about Ruggiero bringing about the destruction of Christendom was nothing more than a superstitious belief by a well-meaning but delusional enchantress. Just as her spirits began soaring from the good news for the Frankish army, they plummeted as she wondered about Ruggiero's welfare and whether or not he had been killed or wounded.

"Charlemagne's forces are expected to arrive outside of Arles in the next few days and finish the effort." He glanced over his shoulders, both left and right, before lowering his voice. "I realize you must feel restless watching over your brother's castle while there is a war raging. Your talents are being wasted here, so I instructed a few of my men at the Dordogne River site to come here in a few days time. By then, I will have spirited Beatrice away, and you may leave the security here in their capable hands."

Bradamante's mind reeled. Did she want to rejoin the war?

"You set off from here alone once before without incident," he said. "I have confidence you can do so again. If you take your cousin's fierce stallion, I doubt any brigands could cause you harm. I would not worry about Clarice voicing any objections to your leaving. After all, without you or Beatrice here, she will be the sole mistress of this estate. I believe she has been craving that distinction for many years."

CHAPTER SEVENTY-FOUR

Aistulf rose before dawn. Even though he had been treated as an honored guest, he felt unsettled by the King Senapo's demeanor and did not wish to interact again with the mercurial monarch.

After gathering his belongings, Aistulf undressed and placed the sandals he had worn under the bed, and folded the long white cotton tunic King Senapo had given him. His fingers traced the intricate embroidery as he gave a wistful sigh. It was exquisite, but Aistulf did not want to burden himself with worldly possessions. Leaving this finery behind was his first test to see if his purified soul could resist the temptation to backslide.

Aistulf then donned his armor and leather boots. Being dressed for battle made his heart beat faster. He slung the magic bag over his shoulder and snuck outside into the quiet courtyard. The compound was still asleep. Guards were stationed at the gate, but their backs were toward him. The darkness of the night was beginning to give way to the first rays of dawn.

He whispered the enchantment three times that would summon the hippogriff. It was not long before the winged creature appeared in the sky. The beast had barely landed when Aistulf mounted and pulled on the reins giving the signal to fly away. They cleared the outer walls and were gliding over the vast lake when Aistulf heard bells being rung by King Senapo's guards.

"Just try to catch me," he said under his breath.

They climbed higher into the air and flew past the waterfall where the water appeared to smoke, before following the Blue Nile as it snaked its way northward to the Mediterranean Sea. Leaving without official leave may have been discourteous, but Aistulf had convinced himself that King Senapo had never drank the tea made of heartsease. This thought made him both sorrowful as well as wary of the king and his intentions. Since Aistulf now had the letter of introduction required to meet the caliph, he no longer needed to remain with the Ethiopian king.

The letter's contents were a mystery, leaving Aistulf to hope the message was what Melissa and the Prophet Elijah had expected.

After flying for what seemed like a hundred miles or so, Aistulf had the hippogriff land on a verdant hillside near a stream.

"Never again will I arrive somewhere and not have a full stomach."

He dismounted and began to remove items from his magic satchel. The leather tube and the book of enchantments were placed on a large flat rock. Aistulf paused before he withdrew the cloth of plenty. Closing his eyes Aistulf pictured roast beef, carrots and onions with bread and honey. He opened his eyes and saw soft cheese with flatbread.

"That is not what I had in mind," he said to the sky.

Kamal the hippogriff cocked his head.

Aistulf gave a little laugh as he broke off a hunk of bread and dipped it in the soft cheese. As he tasted the tang of the cheese, a sense of melancholy rose up within him as he remembered this was the same meal that broke his long fast in the cave. He shook his head, trying to cheer himself when his attention was drawn to the leather bound book.

"Perhaps I could find a spell to ease my worries," he muttered. "There are hundreds of spells in this book and I have only used a few of them."

He looked up at the hippogriff as he thought through the problem.

"Logistilla gave me this book while on her deathbed, but Melissa showed me how to use it. I simply concentrate on the spell I need and the book opens to the proper page. The first spell she had me cast was to enchant this cloth into a source of plenty so I would not worry about food on my long journey." He licked his lips remembering some of the piping hot meals he devoured thanks to this magical fabric.

"The first spell I cast on my own was to cushion the saddle I used with Rabican," he chuckled. "It only took one morning before I sought help from the book to preserve my bottom. Riding through the air on your back is far gentler on my backside than traveling on the back of the fastest stallion on earth." He chewed on another hunk of bread. "I needed a spell to release Ruggiero from an enchanted castle. Later, when you became my magical steed, I found an enchantment for you to return when I called."

The hippogriff blinked and began preening feathers on a wing.

"There are hundreds of pages in that book, I expect there must be a spell that could translate Arabic into Latin. Then once I understood what King Senapo wrote, if I disagreed perhaps there would be another spell, allowing me to change the wording... then of course, a spell to re-instate the wax seal."

The hippogriff let out a large screech and shook his head. He scratched the ground with a claw.

Aistulf hung his head. "You are right. I am only a messenger. I was not given the responsibility to craft the message to be delivered. To alter that pact, I would risk pride becoming my downfall. This must be one more divine test to see if I would succumb to temptation. The tome of spells was given to me for necessity and nothing else, even if I try and justify it as serving the interests of Charlemagne."

CHAPTER SEVENTY-FIVE

Akramont's spirits soared as his men cheered the appearance of the walled city of Arles in the distance. His army had been on a forced march for nearly two weeks and they were glad their destination was in sight. They left Paris in haste without tents, gear and other equipment necessary to engage in war, but this also allowed them to move with greater speed and to cover longer distances in a day. This was the fourth day of the holy month of Ramadan adding a further layer of guilt to the day's journey. Muslims are obligated to fast and consume meals only before sunrise and after sundown. However, walking up to thirty miles under the hot sun without being able to drink any water could be dangerous. This was a recognized exemption from the mandatory fasting obligations of healthy adult males. The army would be deferring their obligations to fast until after the war was over.

They were traveling on the old Roman road of *Via Agrippa* that followed the banks of the Rhône River. Centuries of neglect had taken its toll on the road where many stones had been pilfered, making it painful for horses or footmen to traverse on its surface. Even when the all the stones were present, there were grooves worn into the stones from centuries of wagon wheels traveling over them. At times, it was less arduous to walk on the muddied pathway next to the road.

A small contingent of about a dozen men on horseback from the city of Arles rode toward them. Black banners were flapping in the breeze. As the horsemen drew nearer, the design of a golden bear as a sigil could be discerned. It was a fitting standard for Governor Grandonio of Morocco for he was a bear of a man. Grandonio was taller and broader than most men and sported a full, untrimmed beard and an unruly head of black hair.

"*As-salaam-alaikum,*" said Grandonio, as the men came to a stop in front of Akramont.

"*Wa-alaikum-salaam,*" replied Akramont.

"We have been waiting for your arrival. There is a large meal ready for your men as soon as the sun sets and we have beds for them throughout the city."

Grandonio gave a signal and his men turned to lead the forces past the western edge of the city. The walls appeared to be at least fifteen feet high and made of dingy yellow stones.

"I have grown fond of Arles or the 'little Rome of Gaul' as it was once known," said Grandonio. "The city sided with Julius Caesar back in his war against Pompey Magnus. Marseille chose the losing side. After Caesar's victory, he rewarded Arles and punished Marseille. The city has many Roman monuments, and even though three centuries have passed since the Roman Empire fell, many are still in decent condition. I only wish the aqueduct was still functional, but alas it is not."

"Punished by the Romans," said Akramont. "I know that legacy. Bizerta made the mistake of siding with Carthage in its rebellion against Rome. All of her monuments were dismantled in retribution. I wonder if Marseille suffered as much as my fair city."

Grandonio shrugged his shoulders as they passed a large gate on the western wall. Guards inside the round turrets on either side of the gate waved at the army, but the portcullis remained steadfastly closed. "Not far inside that entrance is the old Roman amphitheater. Some of the heathens barricaded themselves inside before we took the city. That was over two months ago. Many are still trapped inside there and refuse to leave. They have no fresh water, no sanitation, and no way to deal with their dead other than throw the corpses over the top for us to bury. The stench is overpowering. I did not wish to bring you, or your men past that pile of filth."

"Thank you," said Akramont, swallowing hard. "That is something we can do without on our first day." He then noticed a shadowy place lined with trees in the distance. "What is that over there?"

"The old Roman burial grounds. That is where we have been burying the infidels."

The procession turned right to follow the road around the fortified city. Akramont was happy to see there were fewer gates than the walls of Paris, so there would be fewer places for the Frankish army to attack. The southern gates were open and horns blared as the army entered the city.

Akramont basked in the roar of the assembled crowd. He looked around and was surprised his wives were not there to greet him. "Where is Governor Sabri?"

"He is with your family. Their journey here was a difficult one. I will take you to them after you eat. I have much to tell you."

PART FOUR:

MESSAGES AND MESSENGERS

Aistulf fought to stay awake. The glare of the sun in the western sky was blinding him and he squinted to lessen the harmful rays. He had been tempted to close his eyes for a nap and was close to giving up the search for the day. Sleeping while flying on the back of the hippogriff was not safe, he might lose his balance and fall into the Mediterranean Sea. Being weighted down in full armor would signify his certain death by drowning. He shook his head, willing himself to stay awake as he continued his search as images appeared on the horizon. He blinked again and then let out a whoop of joy.

"Finally!" he said to his winged companion. "The fleet is up ahead."

There was a vast array of ships, some with oars and sails, some only with sails. Aistulf flew on the southern edge of the flotilla rather than flying directly over the fleet because he wanted to avoid any risk of being shot down by archers. He soon gave up counting the ships and instead concentrated on finding the grandest ship out in front.

Once his flying steed had flown past all of the ships, he turned to face them. With the setting sun at his back, he could finally see the ships without difficulty. The full scope of the fleet was a sight to behold. It was as if every merchant ship from the ports of Marseille, Barcelona, Naples, and Alexandria had all come together for one grand purpose.

King Senapo had told Aistulf to look for the black flag of the Abbasid dynasty. He scanned the ships and finally saw that standard high upon the mast of a large ship. As he drew near, he could hear the excited voices of sailors who were reacting to the fantastic sight of a warrior riding on the back of a magical flying creature. He circled the ship three times and motioned to the sailors below that he wanted to land on deck. Sailors gathered together, but left an area for Aistulf to bring down the hippogriff. The men were staring at him with wide eyes.

He nodded to the men before dismounting. He whispered "stay" to the hippogriff. In Arabic he announced, *"As-salaam-alaikum.* I bear a message for Caliph Harun al-Rashid."

Murmurs went through the crowd as the men looked at one another.

Aistulf cleared his throat and repeated himself with a louder voice. "I bear a message for Caliph Harun al-Rashid."

A man stepped forward. He wore a full-length black robe and a black turban. The man was dark-skinned and appeared by the way he held himself to be of the ruling class. "*Wa-alaikum-salaam.* I am the Caliph."

Aistulf was unconvinced. He remembered the image of the caliph that Melissa showed him weeks before. That image was a handsome light-skinned man. He remembered thinking that power rolled off the caliph like waves. The man standing in front of him had to be an imposter. He scanned the faces of the sailors and saw one man looking the other way who was also dressed in a full-length black robe. Excusing himself as he made his way through the crowd, Aistulf bowed in front of the man he sought.

"I bear a message for you."

The man turned to face Aistulf, a hint of a smile played on his face.

"Who are you? Who do you serve?" the man asked in Arabic.

"The message is from King Senapo of Ethiopia. I am Prince Aistulf of the Kingdom of Essex and I am a paladin for Emperor Charlemagne." He bowed as the men applauded.

Caliph Harun cracked a smile and spoke in Arabic, but whatever he said was beyond Aistulf's limited knowledge of that language.

"I apologize," said Aistulf in Arabic. "I only know a few phrases in your tongue. I speak English, Frankish, Latin, and Greek."

Harun nodded. "I have translator," he said in broken Greek.

The air was split by the sound of a man singing the call to prayer. The sailors began moving around the deck responding to that call and forgetting about Aistulf's intrusion.

"Time to pray. Come, you will give me message, we will eat supper and you will meet Isaac. He is like you, from Charlemagne's court. Isaac will translate."

CHAPTER SEVENTY-SEVEN

A kramont was grateful when he could finally sit down to eat and drink. The journey had taken a toll on him and his men. After their evening prayer was concluded, male servants brought out platters of black seasoned olives, unleavened bread, and roasted mutton. The men were gathered in the old Roman forum and waited their turn in line to take their fair share. Some of the soldiers were leaning up against trees or brick walls as they ate.

Grandonio and his advisors were seated at one of the few tables in the large open area of the city that served as the market center. Akramont was seated in a position of honor framed by the two remaining Corinthian columns standing behind him. He looked at the many men standing as they ate and felt fortunate that he was able to sit while enjoying his meal.

"I have some news for you," said Grandonio as he wiped his mouth with the back of his right hand. "Marsilio surrendered to Charlemagne. He and all of his forces are returning to Al-Andalus."

"Marsilio promised to delay the Franks, but did not mention surrendering," said Akramont. "Do you know the terms?"

"A large payment each year for ten years with the agreement that Marsilio will not take up arms against Charlemagne's lands again. Hostages were taken to ensure compliance. One was supposed to be Feraguto, but he came with you."

"So I have lost one of my closest advisors and all of his forces. I should have expected that as the outcome when he stayed behind in Paris." Akramont picked up a shriveled black olive and bit into it. He was rewarded with an intense flavor. He removed the pit before taking another olive.

"There is some good news. More reinforcements from Morocco, Egypt, and Tunisia arrived two days ago. The construction of the new bridge across the river is finished and my men have gathered the crops from farms for miles around. We will have plenty of food to last for several months, while the Frankish army will have to travel great distances for food." Grandonio stood and brushed crumbs off his lap. "It is time that I show you to the palace. That is where your family has been staying. Governor Sabri is waiting for you there."

Akramont followed Grandonio's lead through the paved streets of Arles and felt relieved as he saw a large stone building in the distance with Ionic columns adorning the façade and a Roman arch over the doorway. It was not as grandiose as his palace in Bizerta, but it was far more civilized than a tent. Servants opened the door and Akramont sighed with relief to feel the coolness of the house compared to the stifling heat outside. He was pleased to see the floor of the atrium decorated with an ornate mosaic depicting images of various Roman gods. Mosaics were a sign of culture. He was beginning to share Grandonio's fondness for Arles.

Grandonio gestured to a small room on the left. "Governor Sabri is inside here."

Akramont entered the darkened room. Sabri was seated in a chair with his head in his hands. There was a sense of gloom hanging in the air.

"*As-salaam-alaikum.*"

"*Wa-alaikum-salaam,*" replied Sabri.

"Where are my beautiful wives?" asked Akramont, adding a note of cheerfulness to his voice. "I expected them to be at the gates to greet me."

Sabri struggled to stand. "I have some sorrowful news to bear. Anika did not survive the journey here."

"What do you mean Anika did not survive?"

Sabri took a deep breath. "The hike to the river in the middle of the night was arduous. The person who suffered the most at the beginning was Ruggiero. All attention was paid to him as the jostling with the stretcher brought about intense pain. Ibrahim and Marfisa were devoted to Ruggiero's plight and no one noticed that Anika suffered as well."

The old man poured a cup of tea and handed it to Akramont. "Anika had carried heavy armor in the escape and became injured. She was terrified when she began bleeding, and feared she was losing your child. Hoping that the power of prayer would be enough to heal her, she kept this knowledge to herself and prayed for Allah's intervention. It was only days later, when she lost her balance and fell overboard from the barge, that attention shifted to her."

"Did she drown?"

"Almost. After she was fished out of the water, Ibrahim discovered she had miscarried and was feverish. Alia blamed herself for not recognizing Anika's pain. She performed a vigil at Anika's side and ignored her own needs for food and rest. Anika lingered, but never recovered, and she died the day after we arrived here."

Akramont closed his eyes as grief washed over him. His beautiful wife Anika was dead. Dead. He swallowed hard before finding his voice. "Where is Alia?"

Sabri cleared his throat. "She grew ill. Her throat became sore and swollen. Her voice was gravelly and hoarse. A fever struck and she became covered with red spots."

"Can I see her?"

He gave a pained smile, but did not move. "She succumbed to the fever late this morning. I thought she was strong enough to see you one last time."

"Alia is..." Akramont could not finish the thought.

"Awaiting burial."

"This cannot be," said Akramont his voice rising. "They were healthy not ten days ago. How can they both be dead?"

Sabri nodded. "It is hard to accept. I never wished to bury my daughter, yet it is my duty. We should proceed before dark, we must bury her outside the city walls." He guided Akramont down the hallway to a room. Alia was lying on a table wrapped in a shroud with only her face exposed.

Tears filled Akramont's eyes as he looked upon Alia's once beautiful face that was now disfigured by small red bumps. "My love," he said in a strangled voice. "I should have left you and Anika behind in Bizerta. It was selfish of me to bring you to war. My selfishness cost me the lives of those most dear to my heart. I thought I could protect you from harm. I am sorry. I failed both you and Anika."

He moved to kiss her forehead, but Sabri placed a hand on his shoulder. "It is not safe. Ibrahim thinks she may be contagious. Hala prepared her body for burial and she will be held in quarantine for ten days."

Akramont felt his temper flare even further. "Are you telling me I cannot see my sister either?"

"You may speak to her through a curtain." Sabri covered Alia's face with the edge of the shroud. He then placed a comforting hand on Akramont's shoulder. "It is time."

Four strong men entered the room. Two men gently lifted Alia's body from the table onto a stretcher. The men proceeded outside and placed her body onto a flower-strewn wagon.

Akramont gripped Sabri by the arm. "Why was I not told of this news before? Why did you not send a messenger to me? Or have me brought here as soon as I arrived?"

The elderly governor gave him a sorrowful look. "This kind of news blocks out the sun and the moon. I advised Grandonio to give you his counsel about the forces in Arles, and to do so before you learned of these tragedies. This news could wait, because it cannot be changed."

CHAPTER SEVENTY-EIGHT

Aistulf sat at a small square table in the caliph's quarters and wondered who would break the silence at supper. He had expected it to be the caliph, but instead it was the imposter.

Isaac, an elderly Jewish man with a full gray beard, translated the question into Frankish. "Jafar wants to know why you doubted him when he announced he was the caliph. They have played that trick many times and rarely does it fail. You have never been to the caliph's court before, how did you know who the real caliph was?"

Aistulf took another bite of salted fish while he considered his answer. After taking a drink of water he said, "I had a vision of the caliph and Jafar did not resemble the vision."

Isaac then translated Aistulf's answer. Aistulf studied Jafar. The wazir was close in age, height and build to the caliph, but lacked the raw sensuality that his leader possessed. Instead, Jafar seemed to possess a cunning streak making Aistulf wary.

The caliph asked a question that Isaac translated. "What do you make of King Senapo as a ruler?"

"He is obsessed with power and expanding his kingdom. King Senapo feels that insurrections must be punished, otherwise it is a sign of weakness in the ruler. He is aware that Amir Akramont's campaign was done without your approval or knowledge. If Akramont's actions do not result in retribution, then King Senapo will exploit your weakness, before others have the chance."

The caliph raised his eyebrows when he heard Isaac's translation.

Aistulf then added more thoughts. "I believe controlling the port of Alexandria is attractive to King Senapo. I do not know how he hopes you will react to his letter. He might prefer you join Akramont's campaign, allowing for an expansion of his own kingdom."

Isaac continued the translation. Caliph Harun al-Rashid posed another question that Isaac translated. "King Senapo suggested you could be our spy in the sky, providing an eagle eye's view on the city of Bizerta."

"You saw the hippogriff," said Aistulf. "I will do whatever is needed to help defeat Charlemagne's enemies."

Aistulf helped himself to the bowl of figs while he waited for Isaac to translate another question from the Caliph.

"Why did you seek out the king of Ethiopia for a letter of introduction? Why not have someone in your court write one instead?"

Aistulf took a long drink of water while he thought of an answer. He did not want to lie, but he could not reveal he was sent to Senapo by the enchantress, Melissa.

"Charlemagne is at war and does not travel with his full court. I was sent on a mission to survey the defenses of Hispania as well as cities in the Maghreb, this was before I sought out King Senapo." Aistulf finished his statement and felt relieved. He had spoken the truth, but knew the caliph would interpret the answer as if he had been sent on the mission by Charlemagne.

The next question was easier for him to answer. "How do the defenses appear?"

"Vulnerable. Any army could easily overthrow the meager defenses left behind."

The caliph exchanged looks with Jafar. "Thank you, Aistulf," said Harun in Greek. "I will speak with you and Isaac on the morrow."

Isaac stood and motioned for Aistulf to join him. They had been dismissed.

CHAPTER SEVENTY-NINE

Bradamante had not dreamt of Ruggiero for weeks. This was deliberate on her part. She drank wine before going to bed to ensure a dreamless sleep. She did not want to bear witness, even in the dream world, to the massacre of Frankish soldiers or death of a family member. However, after her father informed her of the routing of the Muslim army in Paris, she actively sought to restore the dream connection she once had with her beloved.

"Were you hurt?" she asked while thinking of Ruggiero before drifting off to sleep.

She saw a weakened Ruggiero lying on a bed. A shadow at his bedside gave her an unsettled feeling.

Ruggiero gave her a warm smile. *"My Lady, I have missed you. I was wounded in a duel, but I am almost recovered. I long to see you again. My love for you is eternal."*

The scene changed and Bradamante saw events from Ruggiero's eyes. He was grappling with another warrior and grabbed a knife. She felt a sharp pain in her back while Ruggiero plunged the blade into his opponent's neck. The scene began to blur as Ruggiero fell from the back of his horse, but Bradamante could see the man was not Rodomont. Instead, he had a bright red beard. She did not know who this enemy was, but he was a dangerous man.

She awoke finding it difficult to breathe. Bradamante sat up and had to remind herself to inhale. Her throat tightened as she muttered, "wounded, but alive."

Clarice rubbed her eyes. "Did you say something?"

"Sorry, I must have talked in my sleep."

Bradamante rolled over and hugged herself. She was relieved to learn Ruggiero was still alive and loved her.

CHAPTER EIGHTY

A istulf enjoyed the cool sea breeze on his face as he stood leaning against the railing of the ship with Isaac, grateful to share elderly Jewish man's wine. The night sky was lit with only three stars and a crescent moon, but before long the constellations would be visible. They could speak Frankish freely and not worry anyone else on board would understand what was said.

"Tell me Isaac, what is it like in Baghdad?"

"I do not know. The caliph moved his court to the city of Raqqah to be closer to his greatest adversary, Empress Irene."

"Of Constantinople?"

"It is only a few days ride from Raqqah to the border separating the caliphate from the Byzantine Empire."

"Why would Empress Irene be his enemy? I thought her son, Constantine, had come of age and was the ruler?"

Isaac gave him a smile. "While it is true that Emperor Constantine wears the crown, it is still his mother, Empress Irene, who wields the scepter. She became regent for her son after the death of her husband, and while Constantine has come of age — she refuses to release her grip on power. The Greeks are viewed as the caliphate's most dangerous enemies. Your mention of the port of Alexandria being a target for attack is not unfounded. He saw the vulnerabilities when we docked for more provisions. He left two hundred men behind as reinforcements, lest it be overrun before this mission was over."

"Do you think the caliph would join Akramont's campaign?" asked Aistulf.

Isaac pulled at his beard. "I hesitate to predict how any ruler will decide on matters of conquest and expansion of their empires, but I doubt he will choose that path. It is too risky to allow his enemies to attack the Maghreb, which Akramont bled dry of soldiers. The caliph was furious when he learned of Akramont's disobedience. It contradicts his own diplomatic gestures and exchange of gifts with Charlemagne."

"Did the caliph decide immediately to turn his army against Akramont?"

Isaac let out a sigh. "It was not as easy as that. First he had to stop the planned annual raids on Empress Irene's border towns, and then assemble this fleet. That was a challenge that took far longer than he wanted." He took a drink from his cup. "Your warning about how the king of Ethiopia views an insurrection as a sign of weakness is most likely the topic of tonight's conversation between the caliph and his wazir. He would not want either the Ethiopians or the Byzantines taking over any part of the Maghreb."

Aistulf looked at his companion. Isaac's long beard was mostly white with some remaining dark brown hairs hinting at what he looked like in younger days. Crow's feet circled his eyes, his shoulders were starting to round, and his knuckles were enlarged.

"How did you become an ambassador for Charlemagne?"

"I was a successful merchant and traveled extensively to bring back goods for our emperor. Over the years, I learned to speak many languages. Charlemagne honored me when he asked me to go on a mission with two other men, Lantfrid and Sigimund."

"Where are they? On another ship?" asked Aistulf.

"No," he said, his voice cracking. "They died on this journey. We left Aachen five long years ago. I wonder every day if my wife is still alive."

Aistulf patted Isaac's hand on the railing. "While I have not been away from my home as long as you have, I understand what it is like to yearn for family. It has been more than a year since I last saw my father. I hope he is as strong and stubborn as ever."

Isaac gave a small chuckle as he poured more wine in their cups. "My wife is also stubborn. I should imagine her refusing to die until she can scold me one last time for being away for so long and making her worry."

"Let us drink to that."

CHAPTER EIGHTY-ONE

R odomont was about to finish his morning beer when he surveyed his men sitting at the long benches in the tavern. He stood and raised his mug. "Men, I have a feeling that today will be our best day since Fiordespina's bridge opened."

The soldiers raised their cups in salute. Rodomont threw coins on the table as payment for their meals and lodging.

Ferrand, the innkeeper, nodded at him. "I may need to cross your bridge today."

"For you, there is no toll," said Rodomont. "Everyone else must pay."

The soldiers followed him out of the dusty inn and into the bright sunshine. The road leading to the bridge was muddy from a light rain the night before, but nothing dampened Rodomont's spirits. He had a sense that he would soon be facing a prominent foe and was excited at the prospect. Near the entrance to the bridge was a large wooden wall emblazoned with Fiordespina's name written in both Arabic and Latin. Armor from conquered foes adorned the structure with plaques bearing the names of the vanquished. There were cuirasses and hauberks from Christian and Muslim soldiers and a prominent empty spot where Ruggiero's name was to be hung.

Jamal brought forth Frontino from the stables. "Here is your horse, my lord. He is fed, watered, and brushed."

Rodomont grabbed the reins and mounted the steed. He had grown fond of Frontino and admitted to himself that this was a destrier worth fighting over. In the end, King Sacripant of Circassia died trying to reclaim this horse. Rodomont's dispute with Ruggiero was a different story. He despised the boy for humiliating him after the battle of Toulouse and for being Akramont's favorite. Rodomont had confidence that once the Golden Boy recovered and learned about this bridge being only a few miles away, that the spoiled child would come to reclaim his beloved horse. The promise of revenge against Ruggiero warmed Rodomont's cold heart.

A stolen barge was released from the dock and positioned under the middle of the bridge to retrieve anyone who fell into the water, while Rodomont's soldiers settled in their stations for the day.

A merchant with a wagonload of wicker baskets waited patiently behind the barricade to cross the river. The old man had a shock of white hair and a face that reminded Rodomont of an old shriveled apple, wrinkled with reddish cheeks.

The man bowed his head and extended a hand holding a silver coin. "My lord, I ask permission to cross your bridge. Here is a token in the hopes you will grant your approval."

Rodomont accepted the offering and added it to his leather pouch filled with coins. "Permission granted."

The guards on the west bank moved the barricade aside as the peddler climbed into his wagon and the mule began walking across the wooden structure. The narrow bridge was of simple construction, without railings, and built in only ten days. There were no other functioning bridges near Arles making Rodomont's a godsend for merchant traffic and thus a great source of income for him and his men.

He was about to signal Frontino to walk upon the bridge when he heard a commotion. A naked man was running toward them. His hair and beard were matted, his skin was brown from the sun and blackened with filth. The soldiers lunged at the wild-man with their swords and shields, but the man was not cowed. Instead, he launched himself, knocking down a guard. The feral man banged the soldier's head on the ground causing blood to pour out of the helmet. Other guards helplessly swung their swords at the wild-man's back, without any effect. The blades appeared to bounce off his skin.

Rodomont leapt off his horse, dropped his sword and shield, and ran onto the bridge.

"Over here!" he yelled. "Come and fight me!"

The beast of a man looked up and stared at Rodomont. He dropped the bloodied warrior and lumbered onto the wooden structure.

"I see him!" came a man's voice from the distance. "Orlando is on that bridge."

Rodomont saw, out of the corner of his eye, three people riding on horseback.

"Orlando, stop!" called the voice again. "We will help you. We are your friends, Oliver and Brandimart."

Rodomont stared at the savage man's face, trying to find any resemblance to the warrior he fought in the past. There was no reason left in the man's eyes, but Rodomont recognized a similar fierceness to that of the famed Frankish warrior. Orlando snarled as he continued his slow approach onto the bridge as if stalking prey. Rodomont bared his teeth and held out his arms, ready to wrestle with a madman.

CHAPTER EIGHTY-TWO

R odomont and Orlando locked arms with one another in a deadly
embrace. Orlando squeezed so hard, Rodomont was afraid his
ribs might crack. He grappled, trying to get Orlando into a head-
lock, but could not manage it. As Rodomont was lifted into the air, he
hooked his left foot behind a leg and caused Orlando's knees to buckle
sending both of them tumbling over the side of the bridge. Before hitting
the water, Rodomont took a deep breath. He knew drowning was a possibility if he did not keep his wits about him.

Once in the water, Orlando released his grip. Rodomont delivered a
large kick to his opponent's midsection hoping to move himself as far
away from Orlando as possible. He then sank like a stone to the riverbed
and watched as Orlando thrashed about. A stream of bubbles escaped
Rodomont's lips as the urge to take a breath began to overwhelm him.
He pushed himself upward and was able to stand. His face was barely
above the waterline as he gulped for air. Rodomont was grateful it was
late summer and the river level was not as high as it would have been in
the spring.

A rope with a large loop appeared in the water in front of him. He
grabbed the lifeline, wrapped it around his chest, and gave a tug before
he was dragged toward the barge. Rodomont was pulled onboard by
Bambata. As he lay on his back and struggled to catch his breath, his
heart pounded in his ears. He might have died, had his men not been
there. As his heart began to slow, another commotion could be heard
from the west bank of the river.

"Let me pass," a man bellowed.

"No! You must earn the right to cross," said Abdul. "My commander
is being brought here by that barge. No one crosses this bridge without
his permission."

"Orlando needs my help. It cannot wait," he said in broken Arabic.

Rodomont sat up and watched as Abdul and the other guards pointed
their spears at the man's horse standing behind the barricades. The

Frank pulled back on the reins causing his horse to rear on its hind legs. Abdul tried stabbing the horse in the belly, but missed.

"Oliver, stop!" yelled a woman in Frankish. "Orlando is out of the river. We can wait. Do not endanger your horse."

Rodomont turned his attention to the woman. It was hard to see her at first, but as the barge came closer he could make out some details. She wore clothes of a commoner, but was riding a fine looking horse. That aroused suspicion in Rodomont's mind about her class as well as knowing that servants would never speak in such a familiar manner to their lords, not without being punished. Oliver withdrew from the barricades and spoke with the other knight.

As Rodomont stood, water poured out of his dragon hide armor. His quilted gambeson was soaked with cold river water and as he pressed his arms across his chest more water fell onto the deck of the barge. It had been the first time he had fallen into the river and he felt his temper begin to boil. The two Frankish warriors waiting to cross the bridge would serve to wipe away any humiliation he suffered at the hands of mad Orlando.

The barge was getting close to the riverbank as Rodomont began to shout. "You wish to cross Fiordespina's bridge? You must earn that right by agreeing to a duel. If you are victorious in the joust, you shall be allowed to cross. However, if you lose — you shall belong to me."

Oliver's brows furrowed. "What do you mean?"

"You forfeit your horse and your armor will be added to my collection." Rodomont gestured toward the wall covered in hauberks and cuirasses. "I look forward to adding the name of a famous paladin of Charlemagne to that wall. Once you are defeated, you will be given three choices. You can swear undying allegiance to me and join my forces, you can become a slave and serve me back in my palace in Sarza, or you can choose death. To help you decide, you will join my other conquered foes on an island until I return to my domain."

Oliver turned and spoke with his fellow knight. There was a brief exchange before he responded, "And, if I refuse those terms?"

"Then you cannot cross." Rodomont snapped his fingers and one of his men left to retrieve a lance for the joust. Jamal brought forth Frontino again and handed the reins to Rodomont.

"Do you accept my challenge?" asked Rodomont.

"Under duress," said Oliver.

The barricades were removed and a lance was presented to Oliver who couched it under his arm.

Rodomont then delivered his well-rehearsed speech. "We shall begin. Because I am defending the bridge, I will start on the other side. Upon Abdul's mark we will start and meet in the middle. If you fall in the river, you lose. If I fall in the river, you win." He pointed to the barge headed away from shore. "Once it is stationed in the center and ready to catch the loser in its net, we shall begin."

Rodomont rode across the bridge and grabbed the lance offered to him by a guard. Waiting for the signal to start his charge was maddening. Finally, the sound of a horn was heard and he kicked Frontino's sides. The hooves thundered across the planks of the bridge as he rode toward his opponent.

Oliver did not stand a chance. The lances offered to challengers were made of pine and easily broke, while the lances reserved for Rodomont were made of oak and delivered a stronger, forceful blow. His lances were also two feet longer, providing him the advantage of his opponents' weapons never being able to touch his shield. His victories were unfair, but he never cared about fairness. Rodomont had also developed the strategy of riding down the middle of the bridge and not allowing any room for his opponent's horse. This made some of his opponents compensate by trying to veer to the right rather than have the two horses crash into each other. A few men actually rode off the edge of the bridge without any help by Rodomont's lance. A large net cast upon the water waited for the losing warriors and their mounts to be rescued and brought upon the barge.

Near the center of the bridge is where they met. Rodomont's lance smashed onto Oliver's shield. The paladin's horse had flinched and veered to the right side of the bridge. The impact caused Oliver and his horse to go flying into the awaiting net. Rodomont let Frontino gallop to the other side of the bridge to where the other warrior and the woman were waiting behind the barricade.

"Is it your wish to join your friend in servitude or death?"

"No! It is my wish to rescue both my friend Orlando and to liberate my friend Oliver," said the man in perfect Arabic.

"Who are you?" asked Rodomont.

"I am Brandimart, son of King Manodante and newest paladin to Emperor Charlemagne."

Rodomont shook his head. "You were raised a Muslim and now serve an infidel?"

"I have been baptized a Christian, and I serve the most powerful monarch to ever live. Now, should I prevail in this duel, I demand not only have the right of passage across the bridge, but the right will also be extended to my female companion."

Rodomont nodded his assent.

"And you will release my friend, Oliver."

"It will not come to that, but I will agree to his release should the impossible come to pass."

Rodomont repeated his journey across the bridge and awaited the signal to advance. Once again, his opponent was defeated by the inferior lance and by the crowding of the horse on unfamiliar terrain. He let out an exuberant laugh as he heard the splash of his second Christian prisoner of the day. Only upon reaching the west bank of the river, did he discover the woman had vanished. He felt a pang of disappointment, for she would have served as relief for both him and his men.

CHAPTER EIGHTY-THREE

The black banner of the Abbasid dynasty flapped in the stiff sea breeze. Aistulf secured its pole onto the side of the hippogriff's saddle in the new holder he created. It was fashioned after the one made for his ornate saddle that transported Argalia's golden lance. This new leather attachment was not as well designed, but the journey carrying the banner would not be as long, or as arduous, as his trips to and from Cathay.

Isaac handed him a horn dipped in gold that glinted in the midday sun. "Sound your approach long before you are in range of the archers' arrows. Once you have everyone's attention, make your pronouncement. Do you want to practice it one more time?"

Aistulf shook his head. "I know what I am to say, but I wonder why this message is to be delivered today when the fleet will not dock in Bizerta until tomorrow. Would it not be better to arrive unannounced? Giving our enemy warning may allow them time to prepare."

Isaac chuckled and patted him on the shoulder. "The caliph does not share your perspective. You see Amir Akramont as an enemy, while the caliph views him as a wayward vassal. The people of Bizerta are the caliph's subjects. Imagine if the Pope were to travel in the Frankish Empire. Would any city refuse him hospitality?"

"Of course not."

"What if Charlemagne came to visit?" said Isaac with a twinkle in his eye. "Would any duke or count dare to deny the emperor's entourage food and lodging?"

Aistulf shook his head. "That would be unthinkable."

"The caliph is not only a military leader like Charlemagne, but also a spiritual leader like the Pope. That combination means he should be welcomed throughout the caliphate. Your message giving the city notice of their obligation to their rightful leader will ensure that the gates will be open tomorrow to welcome him and all of his troops."

"Ah, now I understand," said Aistulf. "It is a great honor and a burden to host a royal entourage, but a noble cannot refuse to extend hospitality to his sovereign."

"Exactly. It is customary to give at least a month's notice of a visit so that the noble can make the necessary preparations, but a sovereign needs only to assert his authority to receive his due deference. However, without notice being given, the noble would perceive a fleet of ships appearing on the horizon as enemies and defend against them."

Aistulf tested the horn by making a sharp blast. He was pleased with the sound, but the men on the ship's deck turned and shot him puzzled looks. Isaac handed him a leather tube bearing a letter from the caliph that Aistulf stashed inside his magic satchel.

"Your silver and golden appearance will be seen as an angel from Heaven landing in their midst," said Isaac. "Even if the man left in charge of Bizerta wants to deny entry to the caliph, you will make that impossible. The people will hear your pronouncement, become excited at the prospect of a visit from their caliph. There will not be any refusal."

"Perhaps, I do need to practice the wording with you once more," said Aistulf. "The proclamation should include notice that Caliph Harun al-Rashid will arrive on the morrow."

Isaac gave him a broad smile. "A minor change that will take only a few moments for you to learn."

Aistulf flew on the hippogriff westward over the Mediterranean Sea to Bizerta. He kept the northern coastline of Africa visible to keep his bearings, but preferred not to fly overland. He thought once again of Logistilla's last words to him, *"You are meant for great things, Aistulf. Do not hurry back to be a mere soldier of war; you must use your tools and gifts, and set off for the skies."* He wondered how much the enchantress had seen of his future and how much more this mission entailed for him.

The bottle filled with Orlando's wits weighed heavily on his conscience. Aistulf had no idea when his path would cross with his troubled kinsman as had been promised by the Prophet Elijah. He was anxious to have the caliph release him from duty so that he could set out in search of his cousin and finally restore Orlando's sanity.

As land appeared in the western horizon, Aistulf veered the hippogriff to fly northward. It was not long before he saw the city of Tunis and the ruins of Carthage in the distance. He would soon arrive in Bizerta and the fate of this mission rested on his shoulders. Isaac's encouraging voice competed with the negative voices from childhood that continued to ring in his head in periods of self-doubt.

"You went to the moon and back," he reminded himself. "You can deliver a memorized message in Arabic."

A narrow strip of large rocks rose out of the sea about half a mile from the shore. Similar strips of land framed the entrance to the bay. Spiked chains would be strung across those manmade barriers in times of war to stop enemy ships from gaining access to the city's port. Several ships were navigating their way in and out of the barriers, so it signaled that Bizerta was not expecting an invasion.

As he neared the city walls he pulled out the golden horn and began making a series of short blasts. He needed to call attention to himself and draw a crowd. Inside the walls behind the gates was a courtyard where a contingent of soldiers began amassing. As he flew in a circle, high above the city and well beyond the reach of the archers, he continued sounding of his horn. People began streaming out of their homes and through the narrow alleyways into the courtyard. Once the commoners outnumbered the soldiers, Aistulf felt he could speak.

"*As-salaam-alaikum,*" he spoke his message in Arabic with a loud and clear voice. "I bear the banner of the Abbasid dynasty and of Caliph Harun al-Rashid. He is the Commander of the Faithful, the leader of the *ummah,* and the rightful heir to Prophet Muhammad, peace be upon him. The caliph will arrive on the morrow for a visit to your fair city of Bizerta."

The crowd erupted in shouts of joy as the people began dancing down a wide street that led to the palace on the hill. Aistulf flew above the people who were singing and clapping. He gave a few more blasts of his horn that resulted in more cheers from the people.

Upon reaching the courtyard, he had a chance to admire the grand appearance of the palace. It was three stories tall with ten Doric columns framing its entrance. The frieze on the top of the building depicted warriors on horseback conquering their enemies. The stone walls of the palace were painted white with blue accents for the doors and shutters.

The large double doors opened and a man dressed in a fine white cotton tunic walked out and stood next to the guards. The people erupted in another cheer as Aistulf gave his horn a final triumphal blast before repeating his message in Arabic.

"Caliph! Caliph! Caliph!" the people chanted as he landed his hippo-griff in the center of the courtyard.

The well-dressed man made his way to Aistulf and began speaking in Arabic. Aistulf did not understand more than a few words of what was spoken, but merely gave a polite nod before handing the dignitary the message from the Caliph.

"For Amir Akramont," Aistulf said with a smile. He then re-mounted the hippogriff and took off to the skies with the approving roar of the crowd in his ears.

CHAPTER EIGHTY-FOUR

Bradamante's parents left as her father had promised. As with any event involving her mother, the departure was a dramatic production. The biggest surprise for Bradamante was how light her mother had packed. The wagon carried only one trunk of clothes, Bradamante's portrait, her parents' bedframe and mattress, and goose down pillows. Had the wall tapestry been finished, she was certain that would have gone as well.

Clarice's mood was joyful. While the master chamber still had many personal effects of the Duke and Duchess, this was the first real sign they would soon permanently reside elsewhere.

Without her mother around, Bradamante was able to spend more of her time giving Bernard lessons, as her daily review of the portcullis, gates, and the walls, was perfunctory. The responsibility of guarding of the castle was left to sentries.

Over a week passed before her father's promised additional soldiers arrived. Clarice was disturbed by the intrusion of six burly men who arrived unannounced, expecting food and shelter. Charged with the castle's security, Bradamante had to read Duke Aymon's letter aloud three times to Clarice before Aymon's men were allowed inside the gates.

Bradamante waited for Clarice to become pre-occupied in thought before broaching the subject of her leaving Montauban. The new guards sat down on the trestle benches in the main hall and began eating. Clarice had not yet touched her plate of roasted quail, and bore a look of disdain at the loud men who were laughing and gnawing on pig bones.

"My father expressed his wish that I should return to the war effort," said Bradamante. "These men were sent here to ensure your safety. With your permission, I shall leave on the morrow."

Clarice waved a hand at Bradamante and scowled at the men.

Renaud's chamberlain, an elderly man with stooped shoulders, walked over to the men and said a few words. Their laughter subsided and the men lowered their voices to a dull roar.

Once the dinner was over and Clarice had retired to her chamber, Bradamante approached the men. "I will be leaving for Arles in the morning. Did you see anything on your journey here that I should know?"

One man chuckled, "Gaston can tell you. He was stationed in Arles along with his commander, the Duke of Bordeaux."

Bradamante turned her attention to a young man with a scraggly light brown beard. "You were in Arles?"

"Yes, milady. The Saracens conquered the city two months ago. Many Christians were slaughtered, but the infidels took many of us as slaves or hostages. I am just a foot soldier, so I could not command a ransom."

"You were made a slave then?"

"Yes. Women could cook the food, but they wanted only men to serve the meals."

"How did you escape?"

"In the excitement and confusion of the arrival of Amir Akramont and the troops from Paris, I walked out the gate. It was a bold act, but I thought it might be my only chance."

"He was trying to make it home to Bordeaux," said another soldier as he slapped Gaston on the back, "but he cannot read road signs and got lost along the way. We found him and brought him with us because we thought you might want to hear firsthand about the enemy's camp."

Gaston told Bradamante about Grandonio's leadership style along with a narrative regarding the number of troops inside the walled city of Arles.

"Messengers delivered the news that Akramont would be coming to Arles. Expeditions were sent out to bring back more food. Then, a day or so later, came the first party of evacuees. Akramont's wives, his sister, Governor Sabri, a wounded soldier, and some guards. They left Paris by boat and made their way by a combination of river and overland travel."

"What was so special about this wounded soldier?"

Gaston shrugged his shoulders. "He was some important warrior. Akramont's own physician tended to his wounds. There was also a warrior queen in the party who was at his bedside everyday."

Bradamante remembered the shadow over Ruggiero's bed that had been so disquieting in her dream. "Was this Queen Marfisa?"

Gaston's face lit up. "Yes, do you know her?"

"No, but there are not many warrior queens and she is notorious."

"I had not heard of her before, but the Saracens had."

"Do you speak Arabic?"

"A bit. I learned more during my time in Arles. One of the cooks was old and she gave me some lessons. She knew the language well from times when the region was held by Saracens."

"So what was said about the special warrior? How was he wounded?"

Gaston stroked his beard. "He had been in a duel to the death. The whole Saracen army had watched the spectacle. Ruggiero won, but almost died."

She gave a sharp intake of breath upon hearing her beloved's name mentioned. "Who did he fight?"

"Mandra...or Manda...something," he shook his head. "I forget the name. The Saracens were happy he died. He was a hothead from Asia. No one liked him."

"You said Ruggiero almost died. How was he wounded?"

"Cracked ribs, punctured lung. He almost died on the journey to Arles as well. Queen Marfisa was there at his side, all day, every day." He licked his lips. "She was a sight to behold; a mixture of beauty and fury. There was talk around camp that once Ruggiero recovered, he and Queen Marfisa would become married."

Bradamante felt a stabbing in her heart. She stood and began to turn away. "Anything else I should know about Arles?"

"Akramont's wives died soon after they arrived."

She nodded. "Thank you for your report, Gaston. I shall have someone help you return to your home in Bordeaux."

Bradamante caught Hippalca's eye as she was pouring wine for the men. She gave the signal to her handmaiden to follow. Her first instinct was to go to her chamber, but Clarice was there. Instead, Bradamante led Hippalca into the small room adjacent to the main hall. Once the door was closed, she let down her guard.

"Ruggiero has forsaken me for another."

Hippalca shook her head. "Impossible, he told me of his undying love for you."

Bradamante ran a hand through her cropped hair and began laughing tinged with hysteria. "Undying? While he was on his deathbed, another woman swooped down and snatched away his love with her talons. His love for me was weak and I am..." she struggled for the words. "I am worthless."

Hippalca grabbed Bradamante's arms and shook her. "That is not true. You are worthy of love and respect. I refuse to believe he has fallen for another."

"Believe what you choose, but Gaston is a witness of Ruggiero's love for Marfisa. They are soon to be married." She began pulling at her hair. "I knew there was this risk as soon as I heard my brothers and kinsmen talking of her beauty. Ruggiero loved me for my skills and my beauty, but Marfisa has those as well. They are both Muslim, so there are no impediments to their marriage. He does not have to break his ties with Akramont nor change his faith. Nothing! All they have to do is profess their love for each other and they are married." She bit her lip and held back tears. "My heart aches as if he tore it out of my body," she withdrew the dagger on her belt. "Perhaps I should just end my agony now."

Hippalca grabbed Bradamante's hand. "No! You must not do any such thing! That would be a sin. You would be damned to Hell."

There was a small struggle over the knife. Bradamante stopped when she saw the fierce look on Hippalca's face.

Bradamante nodded slowly. "You are right, I cannot take my own life." She lowered her knife and put it back in its scabbard. If I were to die at my own hand, how would Ruggiero know that his desertion of our love killed me? I thought he was the ideal knight and a man worthy of my love. How wrong I was. If I die of a broken heart, he should be the one to drive the blade in my chest and have my blood on his hands."

Hippalca looked horrified. "What do you mean by that?"

"I leave for Arles in the morning, where I will seek out Ruggiero and challenge him to a duel."

Bradamante went to her chamber to sleep when she remembered the design on her shield. She had changed her standard from solid white to bearing a white lion on a field of blue. It was her way of taking the symbol of the House of Lyon and combining it with Ruggiero's standard of a white eagle on a field of blue.

"No, that will not do. I want the world to see the heartache he has caused me. He cut my heart in two."

She grabbed her shield and headed outside. By the light of the full moon she found a mud puddle and grabbed a handful of wet soil. As she smeared mud over the design, Bradamante attempted to make it resemble a tree stump. Ruggiero's betrayal would be symbolized as a tree cut down in the prime of its life. She stepped back and shook her head at the crude design. Artistry no longer mattered. She left the shield outside to dry near the stables, cleaned her hands, and headed back to the castle.

After returning to her chamber, Bradamante readied herself for bed. As she drifted off to sleep, she thought of the sewing project she had completed a few days before. The white linen shroud would be packed in a saddlebag on the morrow. Soldiers were expected to bring their own shroud when they went to battle because it made burials easier and hers had gotten lost after the Battle of Toulouse. On the morrow, she would set off for Arles armed with the righteous fury of a woman scorned and a shroud that would be used.

CHAPTER EIGHTY-FIVE

C aliph Harun al-Rashid waited patiently in his cabin with Jafar. All had gone according to plan, and the people of Bizerta would be rapt with anticipation for his appearance. Only after his soldiers had secured the city to avoid attacks from those loyal to Amir Akramont, would Harun leave the confines of his ship.

"I think back to when I named Akramont as Amir of the Maghreb," said Harun. "His father had been killed in battle, and he immediately called a retreat of the forces. He sought pledges of loyalty from the governors before anyone else could. His first order of business was to consolidate power. Your father warned me about Akramont and his family. I should have listened."

Jafar gave a slow nod. "My father had dealt many times over the years with Akramont's father and grandfather. While those leaders inspired loyalty in the governors of the Maghreb, they refused to follow the dictates of your father and invaded lands without permission. Because of the distance, he allowed their disrespect to go unpunished. There was a concern that Akramont would continue that pattern."

"I agreed to Akramont's supplication, because when he came to my court he appeared sincere, devout and loyal to me," said Harun. "I was concerned with the stability of this vast region and worried that if I installed a trusted man from my court, he might have been viewed as an outsider and might lead to insurrections. Continuity seemed the best course of action, but it was the wrong path to choose. Akramont's betrayal led to this night and his downfall."

"The word will spread far and wide from your actions here that your authority is absolute," said Jafar.

There was a knock on the door.

"It is time, my lords," came the voice of Masrur the eunuch.

Jafar led the way through the narrow galley and into the cool night air. The sky was turning purple and the men followed the orange glow of the torches that lit the way onto the docks. Four horses were saddled and waiting for the royal procession. Jafar rode in front. Harun's two other favored companions, Masrur the eunuch and the poet Abu Nuwas, rode side by side behind Jafar. Harun would be the last horseman. This arrangement led to confusion from the crowd as to who was the caliph, especially since both he and Jafar dressed alike in black attire and looked similar to one another. Harun was acutely aware that a single arrow could end his life. Being in public left him vulnerable to such an attack, so there was security in having Jafar appear to be the ruler. They would be following hundreds of armed soldiers, loyal to the caliph, who were marching to the palace.

Once the royal entourage passed the gates and entered the city, the assembled crowd gave their roar of approval. The people of Bizerta clapped and cheered. Women threw flower petals into the air as soon as they saw Jafar. Harun bore the faintest of smiles on his face. The adulation from the crowd renewed his sense of purpose, but he was always wary.

Drums beat out a rhythm marking the time as hundreds of marching soldiers made their way through the city. Aistulf flew overhead of the vanguard while blowing his horn. The crowd gave cheers of "bless our caliph." All these sounds combined together and created a statement of triumph.

The main street through the city was made of ancient paving stones, but there were no familiar monuments associated with Roman civilization. He did not see a theatre, arena, baths, or temples. The side roads were unpaved and appeared to be filled with a jumble of buildings constructed without any planning.

As they neared the palace on the hill, the street opened into another courtyard. Harun shook his head when he surveyed the three-storied palace. While its size was impressive, he thought it was a pitiful attempt at Greek-styled architecture. The palace was painted white to appear as if made of the purest limestone, but flakes had fallen off in parts revealing yellow stone beneath the paint.

Harun smiled as he passed by a small temple with four Doric columns in the public square. A statue of a warrior stood in its center.

"That will serve my needs," he said under his breath.

The double doors of the palace opened and an imposing man wearing white cotton robes emerged. "*As-salaam-alaikum.* Welcome to the city of Bizerta. My name is Bucifar."

Jafar was the first of the four men to dismount his horse. "*Wa-alaikum-salaam*," he replied.

Harun followed Masrur and Abu Nuwas up the steps. They turned to face the crowd and waved in unison. Another cheer filled the night as the men entered the palace.

Oil lamps were lit down the long hallway and gave a warm glow to the interior. The entrance had several marble statues on pedestals of the same warrior who was depicted in the city square. The man had a confident look on his face.

"I am Abu Nuwas, the poet to the court of the Commander of the Faithful. Who are these statues honoring?"

Bucifar surveyed the poet. Abu Nuwas was a man who did not appear threatening. He was of medium build, wore a full beard, and had a soft-spoken demeanor.

"That is Amir Akramont's famous ancestor, Alexander the Great," said Bucifar. "He is proud to have descended from such a powerful warrior who conquered most of the known world in his day. There are murals on the wall in the throne room depicting various episodes of Alexander's life. Amir Akramont loves to tell those stories."

"I would very much like to hear them," said Abu Nuwas. "Perhaps I could include aspects of those stories in some of my future poems."

"Come let me show you to the throne room," said Bucifar as he began walking down the hallway. "We have regional delicacies prepared for you."

Harun and his three companions followed and entered into a stately room with a ceiling painted in gold. At the end of the room were five steps leading to a platform with a golden throne. There were five long tables to accommodate a banquet of over a hundred people. Bucifar led them to the center table heaped with roasted meats, breads, and fruit. He began pouring tea from a silver pot.

Masrur stepped forward. In many ways the old eunuch looked like a woman with a soft rounded face and musical voice. "Pardon me, my name is Masrur. While it is a kind and hospitable gesture to provide us refreshment, it is not possible for the caliph to partake." The small statured man gave Bucifar a wide smile. "It is my responsibility to oversee the preparation of all of the caliph's food and drink, for he has many foods that make him ill. It is a shame, but for his health's sake, he must decline your offer. Therefore, none of his companions can partake because that would be insensitive to the Commander of the Faithful."

Bucifar had a startled look on his face. "But - but - there is bread and fruit as well."

Masrur gave him a patronizing smile. "I must oversee and personally approve all that is set before the caliph. If you would please direct me to the kitchens, I will see to having his special tea made." He patted a satchel that rested on his hip. "In the meantime, you are welcome to enjoy your tea and the repast set out."

Bucifar appeared stunned, his mouth hung open. Harun turned away to cover a smile and walked over to one of the walls covered in colorful mosaics. He had known Masrur for many years and appreciated how the eunuch was a master at verbally undercutting enemies. The risk of being poisoned was too great to eat a meal without having control of the food preparation.

Abu Nuwas linked arms with Bucifar. "You were going to tell me about these stories of Alexander the Great. We have time while we are awaiting our tea."

"Y-yes," he stammered. "This first scene is of Alexander as a boy. A horse trader brought a magnificent stallion to Alexander's father, King Philip of Macedonia. The stallion was wild and unbroken. None of the king's men could get near the animal. King Philip was about to turn the man away when Alexander boldly announced he wanted the horse. He stepped forward, grabbed the reins, and turned the horse to face the sun. Alexander had noticed that the horse was startled by its own shadow. After this calmed the horse, Alexander mounted its back and named the stallion Bucephalus."

"That is a nice story and these mosaics are impressive," said Abu Nuwas. "They remind me of the artistry I have seen in churches in Constantinople. Are those tiles made of gold?"

"You have a good eye," said Bucifar. "Amir Akramont's grandfather, Agolante, hired Greek artists to create these mosaics to honor his noble ancestor so that future generations could behold his glory and the glory of this family. And yes, some of the tiles are made of gold and other precious metals."

Harun pointed to another scene further down the wall. Alexander was enjoying a banquet in a large palace surrounded by men and beautiful women. There were stone horses and oversized statues that appeared to be of an ancient Persian style. Then a further scene showed the palace in shambles. He thought he recognized the story behind the art, but wanted confirmation.

"Tell me about this mural."

Bucifar walked over and beamed. "That is Persepolis. Alexander the Great defeated Darius, King of Persia and then conquered and destroyed the city."

"I thought as much," Harun said. "I have been to the city of Persopolis, or what is left of it. The people of Persia have never forgiven the Greeks for that assault. I doubt they ever will."

Bucifar's eyebrows knitted. "I apologize for not being properly prepared for your visit. I had my servants work diligently since yesterday when your messenger sent word of your coming."

"One should always be prepared to bestow hospitality to a pilgrim or stranger. Indeed, you never know when the humble soul seeking refuge for the night might be an angel in disguise."

Masrur came bearing a tray with a pot and four cups. The men sat down at one of the empty tables while Masrur served the tea. Bucifar sat on one side, while Abu Nuwas, Jafar and Harun sat on the other. Bucifar was not served. Harun's private guards came into the room and stood near the entrance.

"Which one of you is the caliph?" Bucifar asked looking back and forth between Jafar and Harun.

"Does it matter?" responded Harun. "One of us is the caliph and the other is his most trusted advisor. You are to treat both of us with the utmost respect and courtesy."

"Where is your leader?" asked Jafar.

"Why the Commander of the Faithful is my rightful leader," said Bucifar.

"Clever, but try again to answer my question. Where is your direct commander? The man who left you in charge of Bizerta."

"Amir Akramont is not here," said Bucifar, averting his eyes.

Harun sipped his tea waiting for Jafar to tighten the noose around this traitor's neck.

"That much is obvious, otherwise he would be here instead of you," said Jafar, his voice dripping with sarcasm. "I will ask you again, where is he? Where has he gone?"

Bucifar's hand trembled as he turned his cup in a circle. "He has gone on a hunting expedition."

"Hunting," said Jafar with a mild nod. "Perhaps you could send a party of men on the morrow to find and escort him back."

"I-I shall see to that."

"Spare me this pretense. We both know that Amir Akramont is not off hunting. He is waging war against Charlemagne. I could go out in the streets tonight and ask any fishmonger where their amir had gone. I would be told their amir has gone off to war. So tell me what I do not know."

Bucifar hung his head low. "Amir Marsilio asked Amir Akramont for help fending off Charlemagne's army. Last year, al-Andalus was invaded by King Gradasso's army and Amir Marsilio worried that Charlemagne would invade his lands this year in an effort to expand the Frankish empire. Amir Akramont is supporting fellow Muslims."

"Bearing false witness is a sin," said Jafar, "but bearing false witness to your caliph is a grievous sin punishable by death."

Bucifar gulped.

"Furthermore," continued Jafar, "even if your tale were true about your amir's reasons for waging war against Charlemagne, it would still be unforgivable. The amir in al-Andalus is a descendant of Abd al-Rahman of the overthrown Umayyad dynasty and is therefore a rival Islamic ruler and not an ally. Even if the leader of the Maghreb was sympathetic to the security of al-Andalus, he did not seek approval, or alert the caliph before going to war. His actions and all those who followed him in this unsanctioned war are also punishable by death."

Bucifar left his seat, walked around the table and fell to his knees in front of Jafar. "I did not know that Amir Akramont was disloyal to you. I simply followed his commands. Please, I beg of you to spare my life."

Jafar turned his head toward Harun. "What say you about this wretched man's fate?"

"He knowingly bore false witness in two different sets of lies," said Harun. "He has therefore condemned himself twice over. However, the people of Bizerta have shown me their adoration and therefore will be spared. They are not to suffer due to the sins of their misguided rulers." Harun cast his eyes upon the murals once more. "The amir is proud of his ancestor Alexander the Great. He has shown me how best to exact a lasting punishment. This palace shall suffer as did the great palace of

Persepolis. Tonight we shall slumber in its luxury, and my troops will strip it bare of its wealth in the morning. Then, it shall be razed to the ground."

Bucifar had come forward on his knees with his face buried with his hands clasped in prayer. "I ask for your mercy."

"While you are not responsible for the sins of your commander, you are responsible for your own sins," said Harun. "Atonement must be made. An example must be set so that there are no further acts of insubordination. Your execution will serve the greater good."

He snapped his fingers. "Guards, put this man in chains and find a cell for him. On the morrow a lesson will be made in the city square for all to see."

CHAPTER EIGHTY-SIX

The morning sky was turning from dusky shades of blue to pink, heralding the forthcoming sunrise. Aistulf and Isaac sat on the rooftop of the palace.

"Why did you choose to break our fast here?" asked Aistulf as he withdrew the magic cloth from his bag. "We could have enjoyed the pre-dawn feast with the caliph and his men."

Isaac sat down on his knees. "This place will provide us the vantage point to observe what will become of the city as well as be safe from the crowd."

Aistulf was puzzled, but decided to wait and see what Isaac meant rather than ask. He sat down on the hard stone roof, closed his eyes and held the four corners of the cloth together with his left hand. He took a deep breath, moved his right hand in a circular motion three times over the cloth and said, "Nourish our bodies, nourish our minds, nourish our spirits."

He felt the cloth become heavy with food, opened his eyes, and dropped the corners. There was a mouth-watering array of baked white fish, fresh bread, a bowl of dates, and a jug of wine.

"It is kind of you to offer to feed me with your magical cloth," said Isaac looking disappointed. "I only wonder, why fish? Could you not have conjured lamb or beef?"

"What day of the week is this? I have lost track."

"It is a Friday."

Aistulf nodded. "There is your explanation. I have no control over the food that appears. Fridays are considered 'fast days' for Christians and we are not allowed to consume any meat, poultry or even milk and cheese. While I may have forgotten the day of the week, the magic cloth did not. Be grateful that it did not bring forth shellfish, which would be against the dictates of your faith."

Isaac chuckled as he used his knife to cut off a piece of fish. "As a guest, it was inappropriate for me to say anything other than express my appreciation for your hospitality. For that transgression, I apologize. It is simply that I have grown weary of fish having been on a ship for over a month and I have a craving for roasted lamb."

The rays from the rising sun broke on the horizon as Aistulf took his first bite of fish on warm bread. He was beginning his meal at the time when all devout Muslims were ending *suhoor,* their pre-dawn meal, and would begin their required daily fast during the month of Ramadan from sunrise to sunset. Soon, sounds of a commotion came from within the palace. Aistulf walked close enough to the edge of the roof to see what was happening below. A stream of soldiers carried off tables, chairs, tapestries, and burlap bags filled with unknown riches and headed for the ships.

Isaac stood next to him. "The caliph ordered the looting and destruction of the palace. The men of Bizerta will soon gather in the streets expecting the Commander of the Faithful to lead them in the Friday prayers. I suspect the excitement of their spiritual leader visiting their city will soon give way to apprehension."

The two men sat back down and enjoyed their meal. Once finished, Aistulf turned to the hippogriff patiently waiting several paces away. The cloth then conjured voles that scampered across the roof before falling prey to the winged beast.

Yelling came from the courtyard below. Aistulf and Isaac walked close enough to the edge to see a gathering crowd shoving one another as tempers flared.

"What are they saying?" asked Aistulf.

"They are upset that the palace is being looted and are demanding to hear from the caliph."

Men were shaking their fists, but their arms stopped in mid-air at the appearance of an elderly man with a long beard wearing black robes who made his way through the crowd. The man climbed the steps of the small temple in the center of the courtyard as the men turned their attention to him.

"This is a good sign. Basheer will calm the people," said Isaac. "He speaks with the voice of God."

Basheer's commanding baritone filled the air and brought the men to their knees. Aistulf recognized the man's voice as belonging to the *muezzin* who called the faithful to prayer every day on the caliph's ship.

"Will the caliph also speak to the people?" asked Aistulf.

Isaac listened to Basheer, waiting for the *muezzin* to pause before answering. "No. His message is being delivered by Basheer. It is likely that the caliph is down there in disguise. He and his companions have a habit of mingling with commoners. It may be risky, but the caliph gets a more honest sense of what the people think rather than reports given to him in the royal court."

Aistulf scanned the crowd and at first was disappointed. Then he closed his eyes and sought out the caliph by sensing the man's power. His head turned and as he opened his eyes, Aistulf saw the caliph dressed in the simple tunic of a merchant. The sensuality rolling off the leader was undeniable to Aistulf, making him wonder how the men standing near the caliph seemed oblivious. Further examination of the crowd showed Jafar, Abu Nuwas, and Mansrur standing a few feet away from the caliph.

Isaac translated Basheer's speech. "The Commander of the Faithful was pleased by the warm reception shown to him last night...It demonstrated the piety of your great city...However, the caliph was angered to learn he was betrayed by the man who had been entrusted as his emissary in the Maghreb...The leader of Bizerta lied to you, his own people, as well as to the governors of the Maghreb...His lies led to a war of vanity and went against the wishes of Allah."

There were gasps followed by rumbling from the people. Basheer raised his hands to settle the crowd.

"The Commander of the Faithful cannot allow betrayals to go unpunished...He recognizes that the good people of Bizerta are not to blame for the sins of their disloyal leader...Therefore, the Commander of the Faithful will not punish the people of Bizerta, but he will take revenge against those who acted against the *ummah*."

"What is *ummah*?" asked Aistulf.

"It means the community of the Muslim faithful," said Isaac.

The assembled men in the crowd became restless as they looked around and realized that the caliph's soldiers had quietly surrounded the square. A line of soldiers muscled their way through the crowd and made a path from the palace to the temple.

"What do you think will be his revenge?" asked Aistulf.

"His plan will soon be revealed."

Six soldiers came forward carrying a wooden casket. The men walked up the steps to the small temple and laid the box at the foot of the *muezzin*. Basheer motioned for the box to be opened. A dummy dressed in an elegant tunic and robe of midnight blue silk was brought out and held up for the crowd to see. There was a beard attached to the face and it wore a golden turban. Aistulf understood this was meant to represent Amir Akramont.

Basheer spoke with an ominous tone in his voice.

Isaac swallowed hard before translating. "If the traitor does not die in the war, this shall be his fate. This will also be the fate of his supporters and allies."

The soldiers threw a rope over a beam in the temple, fashioned a noose and then tightened it around the neck of the dummy. The men hoisted the Akramont's replica into the air allowing it to swing and twist in the wind. The *muezzin* again spoke to rapt attention. The men in the crowd bowed their heads in a sign of respect and submission.

"This traitor's greatest ambition was to become legendary like his famous ancestor," translated Isaac.

The soldiers then toppled the marble statue of Alexander the Great. As it fell, the head broke off and rolled away. The caliph and his companions placed black bandanas on their faces and then made their way through the crowd to enter the line of soldier carrying looted treasure to the ships.

"Why is the caliph leaving?" asked Aistulf.

Isaac waved his hand in a dismissive manner as he concentrated on what Basheer was saying. Isaac then translated, "The greatest punishment for the traitor will be that he and his family will be forgotten. Any mention of him and his family will be removed from all ledgers, all accounts, and all buildings...From this day forward, his name shall not be uttered under penalty of death."

A man wearing chains on his wrists and ankles was led from the palace towards the ship. Aistulf squinted and then realized this was the same man who had greeted the Caliph the night before. More gasps were heard throughout the crowd. Basheer made another pronouncement that brought about silence.

"Bucifar has been condemned to die," translated Isaac. "His execution will wait until Ramadan is over. The Commander of the Faithful has appointed his trusted advisor Sharif as the new Amir of the Maghreb. The governors who supported the traitorous amir will all be removed and replaced with those who have proven loyalty to Caliph Harun al-Rashid."

Basheer made one more statement causing Isaac to walk away from the edge of the roof. "It is time for our escape. We need to fly away on your hippogriff."

"Why?"

"The palace is about to be set ablaze to destroy the monument to that traitor's family. We need to return to the caliph's ship before the skies are filled with smoke and flames."

CHAPTER EIGHTY-SEVEN

Bradamante rose at dawn and Hippalca assisted dressing her in armor. There was no need to bind her breasts to disguise herself as being a man. This mission would soon be over and she did not have the same concerns as the last time she left Montauban without company.

After eating a large helping of herring and bread, she went to the stables. Rabican snorted and moved his head up and down as she placed Aistulf's ornate saddle on his back. After packing the saddlebags with her new shroud and attaching the golden lance in the holster on the saddle, Bradamante soothed the horse.

"Yes, we are leaving. You can run as fast as you wish as we ride toward the sun."

She could sense the horse's excitement as they left the stables and awaited the rising of the portcullis. Rabican rocked rhythmically back and forth while somehow not moving forward. She knew the horse would spring forward as soon as he was able. Choking back tears, she vowed to find a way to confront Ruggiero and Marfisa. There would be a reckoning and a death by the end of the day. Ruggiero swore to love and marry her and his inconstancy would not be borne.

As soon as the portcullis was raised, Rabican galloped like the wind toward the east. Bradamante's gaze was on the road and she tried hard to avoid looking at the harsh rays of the rising sun. Magical spells on the saddle made it seem as if Bradamante were simply sitting on a cushioned chair rather than riding on the back of a charging stallion. The golden lance was attached to the saddle in a manner that did not interfere with the horse or rider. If Aistulf could carry this weapon for thousands of miles, she could carry it for a few hundred miles.

This ride reminded her of the mission to rescue Ruggiero when he was trapped in an enchanted castle in the Gresigne Forest. Both trips started at daybreak and covered hundreds of miles in a single day, but the previous mission was to rescue while this one was to destroy.

Nearing the Rhône River, she brought Rabican to a canter. Finding a place to cross would be a challenge. On her travels to and from

Marseille, she had used a bridge many miles south of Arles, but had hoped she would not have to go too far out of her way when her destination was only a few miles as a bird flies.

She scanned the area, and saw a new wooden bridge spanning the river. A woman on horseback waved her arms. Curious, Bradamante directed Rabican toward the woman who wore a dark woolen dress of a commoner, but had the air of a noble.

"Aistulf, thank heavens that our paths have crossed once more," said the woman. "I must impose once more for your help."

As Rabican came to a halt, the woman stared at Bradamante. "You are not Prince Aistulf, yet that is his horse and saddle. Have you vanquished him?"

Bradamante tried to reassure the woman by giving her a warm smile. "Do not fret about the welfare of my cousin, Aistulf. He left his horse in my safe keeping while he set off on a new adventure on a flying steed. Perhaps, I can help you in his stead. Tell me what is wrong."

The woman gave a sigh of relief. "If Aistulf is your kinsman, than I know you must come from a trustworthy family. A knave rules the bridge over yonder. Merchants are allowed to cross after paying a monetary toll, but warriors are levied with a far more precious toll. They must engage in a duel and every man has lost thus far, including my beloved husband."

"What happens to those men afterward?"

Tears welled in the woman's eyes. "They are stripped of their weapons and armor, and then stripped of their freedom. They are taken prisoner and will be forced to serve that scoundrel."

"Where are they being held? Perhaps I can liberate them."

"If only you could. They are taken to an island about a half-day's journey from here. The boat has returned for more prisoners."

"Pray tell me your name and that of your husband."

"I am Flordelis and my husband is Brandimart, the newest paladin of Charlemagne."

"Paladin?" said Bradamante, feeling startled. "Do you know Count Renaud de Montauban?"

A smile spread across the woman's tear-streaked face. "Oh yes, we adore Renaud. My husband and I shared many adventures with that bold warrior back in Cathay along with Aistulf. That is also where we met our dearest friend, Orlando. We were baptized by Orlando and traveled with him to the Frankish Empire. Oliver, Brandimart and I were on a mission to find and return Orlando to Charlemagne's service when we saw him near this bridge."

"Was Orlando taken prisoner?"

"No," said Flordelis as she hung her head. "He has gone mad. Orlando did not duel as much as wrestle like a wild animal and he escaped on the other side of the river. Oliver and Brandimart tried following him, but they were forced to duel with that tyrant and lost."

"I will help you. While I have never met your husband, I have great respect for Oliver and my kinsman Orlando. If you have befriended my brother Renaud, then you have a friend in me." Bradamante removed her helmet and smiled.

Flordelis' eyes grew wide. "Are you the Maid? I heard your brother sing your praises many times."

Bradamante gave a small bow. "I shall do my best to defeat this monster and return your husband and Oliver to Charlemagne's service."

CHAPTER EIGHTY-EIGHT

Amir Akramont enjoyed the comforts of the city of Arles. While he missed the opulence of his palace in Bizerta and the sea breezes off the Mediterranean, he was growing accustomed to the idea of Arles being his new capital. He felt the palace that had once belonged to Frankish nobles was worthy as his new center of power.

His favorite room in the palace was the enclosed garden, known as the peristylium. As Akramont sat under a shaded awning, he gazed at apple trees laden with ripened fruit. There was a tranquility that set him at ease. If he closed his eyes, and allowed himself, he could almost forget about the war. That daydream was like a Siren's song, one he could not succumb to lest his entire mission end with a whimper.

He turned his attention to his advisors who sat around a long table covered with parchments and wax tablets. They were discussing troop levels and how long the food supplies were expected to last. Once again, he felt a pang of regret that it was Ramadan and therefore he could not enjoy a tea service during this daily meeting. He could have deferred the days of fasting until after the war was over, but since he was in mourning, not engaged in combat or guarding the city, and not traveling, he felt morally obligated to participate. Akramont gestured to Grandonio, the gruff leader of the forces in Arles, to begin the session.

"My spies returned with a disturbing report. The Franks have finished fortifying their camp two miles from here. They have two walls surrounding the camp with trenches dug in between them."

"So they are hiding behind wooden walls while we have ten-foot tall stone walls," said Akramont with a wave of his hand.

"The Franks will soon begin their siege," said Grandonio. "They will blockade the river and build a wall around the city to ensure we do not get any more supplies. However, time is Charlemagne's greatest enemy as the seasons will be changing soon. In about four weeks, the first snows will fall in the mountain passes. He will become nervous as to whether his forces will have to remain here through the winter."

Sabri nodded. "Adding to the emperor's worries is that his longstanding enemies, the Saxons, have started another rebellion. They are headed for his palace in Aachen. A messenger arrived three days ago alerting us about this news, something Charlemagne may already know. I believe he will want to minimize his losses and be ready to concede this area to us."

"In the meantime, we should attack their camp before they begin their siege," said Akramont. "Any thoughts as to who should lead the attack?"

Grandonio stroked his beard. "Rodomont has finished his bridge. Perhaps he would want that glory."

"Rodomont is nearby?" Akramont exchanged a nervous look with Sabri.

"Yes, the bridge you had authorized finished its construction the day you and your troops arrived," said Grandonio.

"I did not authorize the building of any bridge," said Akramont.

Grandonio looked puzzled.

"May I speak candidly?" asked Gradasso, who had been sitting quietly at the table.

Akramont nodded.

Gradasso stood and began to pace, his boot heels clicking against the tiled floor. "Rodomont is a despicable man and while I do not miss him on a personal level, I recognize that he provided your war with the only significant damage to the Frankish forces. Besides of course, Grandonio's capturing of this great city of Arles."

Akramont massaged his temples.

"Your fortune changed for the worse after he left," continued Gradasso. "Rodomont singlehandedly killed hundreds of people in Paris before abruptly leaving on a mission to rescue his lady. He provided the only damage to Paris and to the Frankish army, before Renaud arrived with reinforcements and slaughtered our troops in the rainstorm."

"Yes, I remember that night."

"Rodomont returned to Paris, but lost his bride to Mandricardo. After that humiliation, he left Paris again," said Gradasso, a pedantic tone to his voice. "A week or so later, Renaud's men slaughtered our troops in their sleep."

"What do you suggest? Besides killing Renaud?" asked Akramont through clenched teeth.

"I agree with Grandonio. You should send word to Rodomont and ask him to lead the assault on the Franks."

"Why should I reach out to someone as unpredictable as he? I had hoped that you, the famed Gradasso, would have volunteered for this honor."

Gradasso shook his head. "I have what I came to the west for. I have Durindana and Bayard. I do not have a death wish."

"But you are here, in my campaign, and you should accept whatever role I give you. Especially since you now possess the best sword and horse in the world. Think of the fame you will gain by defeating Charlemagne."

"I have already defeated him once." Gradasso smirked and shrugged his shoulders. "I do not have to do that again. I will not risk my life unnecessarily. Instead, I will stay here as an advisor and then triumphantly return to my kingdom of Sericana with the remainder of Sacripant's troops that you promised me."

Akramont glared at Gradasso. He was a smug, self-serving man who expected treatment as an honored guest, yet offered his host little in return. Having such a man around was a burden and Akramont was unsure if any of his enemies were intimidated by knowing Gradasso was in Arles.

"Then again, perhaps Feraguto would wish to redeem the reputation of al-Andalus since his uncle, Amir Marsilio, surrendered to Charlemagne," said Gradasso.

Akramont, tired of Gradasso's excuses, turned to Sabri. "What of Ruggiero?"

Sabri looked pensive. "Your surgeon, Ibrahim, feels that the young man has healed and Ruggiero has been in light training. However, that was without wearing armor or wielding his heavy sword. Ruggiero might be strong enough for a duel, but I question if he is strong enough to lead a mission where he would be surrounded by enemies. I believe without hesitation that Marfisa could perform such a feat. She would relish that honor."

Akramont shook his head. "I cannot place a woman in the position of being the tip of my spear."

"I would like to speak in regard to Gradasso's suggestion," said Grandonio. "I know Rodomont. I was one of the judges at a tournament in Granada where the men fought to earn the hand of Doralice. There were dozens of famed warriors who competed in the mêlée, including Feraguto. There was a death and three men were maimed. All of that was by Rodomont's hand. He will be the ruthless killer you need to lead an assault on the infidels' camp."

"Rodomont will never agree to return to my war."

Gradasso cast him a patronizing look. "You must give him what he wants, then he will return."

Akramont's stomach turned as if he had swallowed a live eel.

"Our victory may depend on him," said Sabri. There was sadness in his eyes and voice. "War requires many sacrifices. Some are harder to bear than others."

Akramont knew that he had little choice in the matter. "Call forth a messenger."

CHAPTER EIGHTY-NINE

A soldier holding a large blue flag with three golden spindles rode up to the bridge on the east bank of the river and waited. Rodomont recognized the standard as that of Amir Akramont. He nudged Frontino to walk toward the soldier.

"Are you the renowned Governor Rodomont of Sarza?" asked the man.

"I am."

"I bear a message for you from Akramont, son of Troiano, and Amir of the Maghreb."

Rodomont shifted in his saddle. "What does his exalted eminence wish to convey to a lowly servant such as myself?"

Guards pointed their spears at the messenger who held his head high. "Amir Akramont asks that you join him inside the fortified city of Arles. There you will be treated with respect and honor. He wants you to lead the fight against the Franks who recently arrived in the area and have set up camp north of the city. It is expected that they will soon lay siege upon the city of Arles."

Rodomont stroked his beard. "Does Akramont have any words of apology to be delivered about his treatment toward me in Paris?"

The man furrowed his brow. "He did not convey any such sentiments. He did, however, wish to extend his acceptance of you as his brother. He offered his sister, Hala, to be your bride, once she is of marriageable age."

"Liar!" Rodomont spat. "That is nothing but a stalling tactic. Akramont will never allow me to marry his precious little bird. He considers me to be beneath him. He would have me waiting until she has gray hair and swear she was still awaiting her first menses."

He turned to his guards. "Seize him."

The messenger was pulled off his horse.

"Show him the treatment we gave to the innkeepers who refused us hospitality."

The guards pummeled the man with their fists to his face and stomach. The man groaned in agony as he fell and then was kicked all over his body.

"Enough," said Rodomont. "I want him to deliver my message."

The guards picked the man up and helped him onto his horse. The man had a bloodied nose and facial wounds that would bloom into ugly bruises.

"Tell your master," said Rodomont, "that if he wants to earn back my service and loyalty, he must speak to me in person. That is the only way I can trust his message is not a ruse to use me as a hostage in negotiations with Charlemagne."

CHAPTER NINETY

B radamante growled when she recognized the warrior on the bridge from his dragon hide armor and Frontino. No other incentive was needed to persuade her on challenging the bridge master; nothing would stop her from punishing this miscreant.

Upon reaching the edge of the bridge, she examined the large wooden wall covered with armor. Oliver and Brandimart's names were emblazoned on plaques hung in a prominent place near the sign that proclaimed this to be Fiordespina's bridge. Bradamante stared in disbelief at seeing her friend's name.

"Do you wish to cross Fiordespina's bridge? You must earn the right by jousting with me," said Rodomont as he rode toward her.

She attempted to use as much Arabic as she knew. "Is she the daughter of Amir Marsilio?"

"The same."

"I thought you were betrothed to Doralice of Granada. Why did you not dedicate the bridge to her?"

Rodomont's face twisted. "Doralice was faithless toward me, just as all women are faithless toward men because it is in their nature. The only exception was Fiordespina."

"I am a friend of Lady Fiordespina. Do not tell me that such a gentle soul is betrothed to you."

"She is not. Her father attempted to arrange a marriage between us, but she refused. She was loyal and steadfast to her lover, even after hearing he had been executed. The young woman disobeyed her father's wishes and was put to death. This bridge is dedicated to the memory of the only woman I know who was faithful to her man."

Bradamante felt as if she had been punched in the gut. Her friend, Fiordespina, was dead and Rodomont confirmed she had loved Richardet. Tears stung her eyes. "Tell me how she died."

"She said she would rather die than marry me. I helped her join her dead lover on the other side, that is if there is one."

"Murderer," said Bradamante as she removed her helmet and switched to speaking in Frankish, not caring if he understood what she said. It was too difficult to speak in a foreign tongue, especially when she was furious. "You dare defame Fiordespina's memory by instituting a system of cruelty on travelers. You are wrong many times over. Her lover was rescued and still lives. He is my twin brother, Richardet. You murdered a woman who was kind and honored me with friendship even though we were on opposing sides of a war. If you wish to blame anyone for turning her against the likes of you, *blame me.* I warned her about you, long before her father ever thought of marrying her off to you. I cannot blame her for choosing death over a living hell that would be for any woman to be intimate with you."

Rodomont's eyes narrowed. "And you are?"

"My name is Bradamante, better known as 'the Maid.' Renaud de Montauban's famed sister. I fought against you twice before. Once on the plains outside of Marseille when you became frustrated for not besting me in a fair fight. So you attacked and killed my horse, leaving me for dead. The second time was in Toulouse. I took over a fight when my cousin, Orlando, was grievously wounded. Later, you refused to end the fight after the battle ended for the day. Ruggiero, the noblest of all knights, offered to take my place in that duel, so I could rejoin Charlemagne's forces. It is a disgrace to see you defile his horse, Frontino, by your mere touch."

Rodomont's face turned purple. "I remember you now. I did not realize that I fought against *a girl.*"

The diminishment of her skill added to her hatred of him. She tossed her head as if she still had long tresses. "It is fitting that you shall be defeated by *a woman.* Fiordespina was an honorable lady, who was treated dishonorably by the men around her. I shall fight in the memory of my friend and cause your downfall."

Rodomont rode closer, his eyes boring into hers. "How could I have been so blind to not recognize your rosy cheeks and girlish blue eyes. It would be a small honor for me to defeat you, but it would be humiliating to be defeated by a girl. You, my beautiful child, will not cause my downfall, but I shall claim you as my own. Your toll will be far more personal than all of the men who came before you on this bridge."

Rabican began to paw the ground and snort. Bradamante felt a similar surge of restlessness. "I accept your challenge to a joust, but on my own terms. I not only wish to cross the bridge, but I demand that your unjust regime be ended. You will surrender the horse Frontino, who you obtained by force from my handmaiden."

Rodomont gave a smirk and nodded.

"Your men will release all of your Christian hostages; those who are in a cave nearby and those who were taken elsewhere. Their weapons, armor, horses and personal property shall all be returned to the rightful owners. Whereas, your armor will be hung prominently on this wall and no one will be forced to pay any toll to cross this bridge again. You will crawl away from here like the snake you are. You will live with the stain of humiliation knowing that you lost to the warrior maiden Bradamante, daughter of Duke Aymon of the Dordogne, sister to Count Renaud of Montauban, and niece to Emperor Charlemagne of the Frankish Empire."

Rodomont sneered. "I agree to your silly terms, but it will not matter. For you will no longer be referred to as a maiden after this day. You will be my lover or, if you refuse, you will be awarded as a prize for my men to share. You will not have the option of death. You will be kept alive for a long time."

"Do not risk this, my lady," shrieked Flordelis. "I shall find another way across the river and ask your brother to challenge Rodomont on behalf of my husband."

Bradamante donned her helmet and turned to Flordelis. "Do not fear for me. I shall make him pay for his crimes against all women."

"We shall begin. Because I am defending the bridge, I will start on the other side. Upon Abdul's mark we will start and meet in the middle. If you fall in the river, you lose. If I fall in the river, you win."

As Rodomont rode to the other side of the bridge, the barricades were removed and a lance was presented to Bradamante. She shook her head.

"I brought my own. Flordelis, please unfasten my lance from the saddle."

The young woman dismounted. Flordelis released the multiple leather straps holding the weapon in place and then handed it to Bradamante. She couched her golden lance under her arm, waiting to give Rabican the signal to charge.

CHAPTER NINETY-ONE

Akramont waited in the enclosed garden with his advisors, standing at the table studying the map of Arles when his seneschal walked onto the patio.

"The messenger you sent to Governor Rodomont has returned."

"Bring him forth."

The seneschal motioned to two guards who helped carry the young man into the garden. The messenger was covered in blood and could not stand on his own.

Akramont was alarmed at the sight.

The man sputtered a few words. "Rodomont...wants you to...." then he wheezed and coughed up blood.

"Yes? What does he want?" asked Akramont.

"Come...to...him." The man's head lolled backward. His body twitched a few times and then grew still.

"Fetch my surgeon!" commanded Akramont.

A blanket was spread out on the tiled floor and the guards lowered the wounded man onto it. Akramont knelt next to the young man, unwilling to believe he was dead.

Sabri put a comforting hand on Akramont's shoulder. "We have Rodomont's answer."

"Why did I ever decide to turn to such a man? I should have known better," Akramont glared at both Gradasso and Grandonio.

"Rodomont is a killer, and that is what you need to defeat the Franks," said Sabri.

Ibrahim came running onto the patio. His eyes popped at the sight of the bloodied soldier. He knelt down and began shaking the man's shoulders.

"Wake up! Wake up!" he said. Then he put his hand near the man's nose and mouth. A pained look came over his face when he turned to Akramont. "What happened to him?"

"He delivered a message for me. The recipient vented his anger toward me on this poor young man."

Ibrahim opened the man's eyelids one at a time, before closing them again. He crossed the man's arms on his chest. "I am sorry, but there is nothing to be done except prepare him for burial."

"That will be arranged," said Akramont as he stood. "Ibrahim, I have another task for you. I want you to help assess Ruggiero's strength and determine whether he has recovered enough to rejoin my war."

CHAPTER NINETY-TWO

Bradamante squeezed her knees, signaling Rabican to charge. The stallion bolted and galloped down the center of the wooden bridge. She was lit with the fire of righteous indignation and wanted Rodomont to die for his crimes. With each of Rabican's strides her fury grew. Frontino was galloping down the middle as well, but began veering to the right as Rabican dominated the center of the bridge.

She had ridden farther than the halfway mark of the bridge when the two riders met head-on. Bradamante aimed her lance at the part of Rodomont's shield that covered his little, black heart. As her lance touched his shield, he flew out his saddle propelling him through a large arc in the air and splashing in the river below. Somehow, Frontino nimbly avoided crashing into Rabican and was sure-footed enough to remain on the bridge.

Rabican did not slow until he reached the end of the bridge. Bradamante brought him to a stop and turned behind to see what had become of her enemy. Men were shouting as they tried getting a rowboat into the area where Rodomont had last been seen. The barge and its net were also moving toward the east side of the river since he had not fallen where all of the other riders had.

She pulled on the reins and directed Rabican to cross the bridge to return to the west bank of the river. The men on that side were in a state of panic.

"You heard the terms Rodomont agreed to. I am granted ownership of his horse, Frontino, as well as my right to travel on this bridge."

The men looked at her with a mixture of fear and disbelief on their faces.

"No one will ever again be forced to pay a toll to cross this bridge. You shall begin by releasing your prisoners in the nearby cave."

Flordelis ran up to her, beaming. "You defeated that monster! You are as brave and as skilled as your brother."

Bradamante smiled at her. "Please grab Frontino's reins."

The lady approached the horse when one of Rodomont's men raised a fist threatening to hit her.

"Enough!" shouted Bradamante. "I am the victor and I claim the spoils. I can and will kill every last one of you, if necessary, to enforce the terms Rodomont agreed to."

Flordelis shouted in Arabic, repeating what Bradamante had said. The men bowed their heads in Bradamante's direction and allowed Flordelis to climb onto Frontino's saddle. Bradamante then gave a list of orders for the men to fulfill including removing all of the armor from the Christian soldiers on display. She created her own plaque that stated: "Rodomont of Sarza was defeated by Lady Bradamante of Montauban." Flordelis served as a translator and the men reluctantly followed the orders.

"I will be forever in your debt," said Flordelis. "If there is anything I can ever do for you, please ask."

Bradamante looked at Frontino when an idea came to her. "There is a small task that will not take long."

"Anything."

"I wish to have that stallion delivered to a specific warrior in the Muslim camp along with a message."

Flordelis agreed. Bradamante announced that the boat to retrieve the first round of Christian prisoners would have to wait for Flordelis before leaving. That was a message the young woman appeared overjoyed to translate.

"I should be in my husband's arms by nightfall," she said.

Bradamante gave her a wistful smile. "If only I could share in such happiness with the man I love."

The two women rode across the bridge with Fiordespina ponying Frontino behind her. Bradamante felt vindicated when she saw Rodomont's lifeless body on the shore. His skin color had a bluish tinge to it. His dragon hide armor lay in the sunshine while Rodomont was wrapped in blankets and men desperately tried reviving him. One man wailed in the background.

"I did that in your honor, Fiordespina," she said as she took one last look at the wall dedicated to her deceased friend. "Thank you for your friendship. I will remember you with fondness for all of my days."

She blinked away tears as she kissed the Visigothic eagle pendant Fiordespina had given her as a gift. Bradamante grabbed a few lances from Rodomont's stockpile. During the ride to Arles, Bradamante finished planning how she would challenge Ruggiero. She stopped in the shade of the Circus Maximus and admired the size of the old Roman monument. It was about a quarter of a mile in length and three hundred feet wide. The structure had an uneven appearance with about a third of the Roman arches remaining as the practice of harvesting stones had made its mark over the centuries, but its utter destruction had not been completed.

"If you close your eyes and listen, you might hear the ghosts of chariot racers trying to relive their glory in front of adoring crowds."

Flordelis nodded. "It is a shame so little of it remains."

"I shall wait here for Ruggiero. This is a notable landmark and is far beyond any archer's range. Do you remember the message to deliver?"

"Yes, milady." Flordelis took the reins of Frontino and made her way to the main gate. *"As-salaam-alaikum."*

"Wa-alaikum-salaam," replied the guard. "What can I do for you?"

"I have a gift and a challenge to be delivered to the famed warrior Ruggiero."

CHAPTER NINETY-THREE

R uggiero was surprised when armor was brought to his room. "The amir asked that I assist you in donning the armor you won from the duel with Mandricardo. I am to judge the progress of your recovery," said Ibrahim. The tone of his voice sounded weary, as if he was given an order that he did not wish to follow.

Ruggiero's fingers glided across the raised design of an eagle on the ancient bronze cuirass and the matching design on the shield made of metallic inlay. He was filled with pride at the idea of wearing armor created for his noble ancestor, Hector of Troy. He donned his gambeson and then Ibrahim helped him into the cuirass. Ruggiero turned and twisted to get used to the feel of wearing a metallic breastplate and back plate, it was far different than a shirt of mail. He attached the greaves to his shins and slid his hands into the gauntlets. The metal gloves felt like a second skin.

"Incredible," said Ibrahim. "This looks as if it was made for you."

"Mandricardo said this armor was held for centuries in a magical realm by a fairy and he earned the right to wear it by proving his valor. Perhaps there are magical spells tailoring the metal to the wearer," said Ruggiero.

Ibrahim scowled. "Magic? I have yet to see anything I could not explain by the laws of nature."

Ruggiero looked down at his waist to hide a smile as he attached his belt and scabbard. He decided against mentioning anything about life with Atallah or having flown on the back of a golden hippogriff.

"Come," said Ibrahim. "The amir is waiting for you. He wants to watch you spar with Queen Marfisa in the gardens."

Akramont, Sabri, Gradasso, and Grandonio were seated at a long table in the shade, appearing as if they were a panel of judges awaiting a tournament to begin.

Marfisa stood in the middle of the garden showing why she had earned the nickname "Queen of the Amazons." Her helmet bore a fresh yellow plume, her shirt of mail reached down to mid-thigh while her leather boots rose to her knees. She gripped her shield with the standard of a golden phoenix on a field of green in her left hand, while her matching sword was held at the ready in her right hand. There was a look of intensity in her eyes that warned of her lethality. This was an opportunity to prove that her fame was warranted before these powerful male spectators.

"Remember this is only an exhibition," said Ibrahim. "You must use the flat edges of your swords. I do not wish to be tending wounds on either of you today."

Marfisa charged at Ruggiero while screaming as if her hair was on fire. He blocked her attack with his shield. The rhythm of their swords hitting the other was similar to a heartbeat. There was no time for thinking. All of his moves were by instinct. The weeks of inactivity had not caused his skills to rust. While he had practiced once before with Marfisa, it had been with wooden practice swords and shields. She had gone easy on him at that time. This session was different because they were wearing armor and, more importantly, had spectators.

Ruggiero found sparring to be invigorating. Marfisa was a strong warrior and he felt they were evenly matched in skill. As he was about to bring his sword down on her helmet, Akramont shouted, "Stop!"

Ruggiero's arm froze in mid-air while Marfisa growled and took a step to the right.

Akramont's seneschal came into the garden. "My lord, there is a messenger at the front door asking for Ruggiero."

"Bring him back here," said Akramont.

The man shook his head. "I cannot, my lord. His message includes the gift of a horse."

There was a collective gasp as the group jostled their way through the hall to the front door. It seemed that everyone was curious to see the horse and hear the message.

Ruggiero stepped outside the palace and was astounded to see his beloved horse Frontino. Tears stung his eyes as he patted the horse on the side of his neck. He murmured a greeting to the horse that nuzzled him in return.

"Who sent this to me? What was their message?"

"A woman came to the main gate and did not leave her name," said the soldier. "She bade that this horse be delivered to you and said there is a warrior who accuses you of breaking your faith. That warrior challenges you to a duel by joust. Your accuser is waiting for you outside the Circus Maximus."

"Who was the warrior?" asked Ruggiero.

"No names were given. The woman said this horse would allow your duel to be a fair fight."

"This has to be from Rodomont," said Sabri in an undertone to Akramont. "He stole Frontino when he left Paris."

Ruggiero continued to stroke the neck of his horse, hearing Rodomont's name caused a deep-seated anger to rise again to the surface.

"I forbade him and Ruggiero from fighting over that horse since we learned it belonged to Sacripant," said Akramont. "Perhaps, he thinks he can still have a duel to the death with Ruggiero if the dispute is about honor and not over the horse."

"I am feeling fit," said Ruggiero. "I will accept his challenge."

"No, that is final. If Rodomont wants to duel with someone, I will send another in your stead."

Marfisa spoke up, "I will defend Ruggiero's honor."

Sabri whispered into Akramont's ear. The amir nodded and said, "No, Marfisa. You are too valuable to me. Let me send someone else who has been known to have a quarrel with him. Send for Feraguto."

CHAPTER NINETY-FOUR

Bradamante was tired of waiting. Her lance rested in the saddle holster while she kept her eyes fixed on the main gate. Movement on the ramparts threatened to distract her, but she kept her focus. Ruggiero would come and accept her challenge.

Finally the portcullis was raised and a lone rider emerged. Bradamante squinted to see details of the warrior. Once she saw a dark brown horse, she knew it was not Frontino. As the rider came closer, she made out the standard of three golden moons on a field of green rather than Ruggiero's silver eagle on a field of blue. Someone else was coming in his stead.

By the time the warrior came close enough to speak with her, her anger was simmering. She couched her golden lance under her arm.

"You are not Ruggiero," she said in her best Arabic. "I challenged Ruggiero to a duel."

"No, I am Feraguto," he said in broken Frankish. "I am fighting on his behalf."

Her lips curled as she stared at his ugly, rat-like face. "You disgust me," she said in Frankish. "I remember hearing of your duel with Argalia and how you refused to accept defeat. You then killed him in a dishonorable fashion."

Feraguto smiled, showing his pointed teeth. "You have heard of me, but who are you? I thought I was to fight Rodomont."

"I am not that despicable louse, but I do not to care to reveal my name to the likes of you. I have no desire to fight you. Go back and send out Ruggiero, it is he that I challenged to a fight."

"Sorry, but I was commanded to fight you. I cannot return until we have jousted."

"So be it. Take one of those lances from the pile and then ride back to the mile marker," she said. "You will start your advance when I give the signal."

Feraguto rode back to the old Roman mile marker where he couched his lance under his arm.

Bradamante yelled, "Go!" as Rabican galloped toward her enemy.

Feraguto's horse had not gone far when Bradamante's lance touched his shield. He sailed off the saddle and crashed on the ground. Bradamante brought her stallion to a canter as she used her lance to threaten her vanquished foe, while he lay on the ground trying to catch his breath.

"I do not care to take prisoners today. Go back and send for Ruggiero to joust with me. Agree to that condition or die."

CHAPTER NINETY-FIVE

It was late in the afternoon as Ruggiero stood on a narrow parapet, overlooking the southwestern lands surrounding the fortified city of Arles. The tops of the walls were designed for sentries to stand watch or to defend against armies, but it was not designed to accommodate spectators gathered to watch a spectacle. The duel near the Circus Maximus was the most excitement to happen in weeks, and nothing could dissuade soldiers from continuing to crowd onto the walls.

He watched Feraguto's joust, but was unable to discern the challenger's standard. There was a loud gasp when Feraguto was defeated so easily. This led to a buzz of speculation as to who the rider was.

The man's jousting skills and his impressive horse seemed familiar to Ruggiero. Beams of sunlight glared off the saddle and lance, making him wonder if it might be Aistulf on Rabican. The thought gave him pause as they had parted as friends, and he could not fathom why Aistulf would make such accusations against him.

Feraguto returned on horseback, while clutching his side in obvious pain. Ruggiero and Marfisa followed Akramont and Sabri as they made their way down a dimly lit spiral staircase. Patches of blinkered sunlight in the arrow slits were the only source of light. They emerged into bright sunshine that made them shield their eyes at first as they walked to the opening near the main gate.

Akramont grumbled as to why it was taking Feraguto so long to report back. Finally, the warrior appeared before the amir.

"Well?" asked Akramont. "Was it Rodomont?"

"No, but I discovered the man is a Frank."

There was another gasp from the assembled crowd.

"He spoke in broken Arabic," said Feraguto. "I switched to Frankish and he spoke without problem, showing it was his mother tongue."

"Who do you think it might be?" asked Akramont.

Feraguto shook his head. "I am unsure. It might have been Oliver or Renaud or someone else."

Ruggiero could not think of why either of those two famed paladins would even have heard of him, let alone challenge him by name.

"I have fought Renaud," said Marfisa. "Send me. I will verify if it is him."

"I also know Renaud, Oliver, as well as many other Frankish heroes," said Grandonio. "I would be happy to defend Ruggiero's honor."

Sabri leaned toward Akramont and said in a voice not designed to carry, "Perhaps this Frank was defeated by Rodomont and forced into doing his bidding. All to draw out Ruggiero."

"Perhaps." Akramont snapped his fingers. "Ibrahim, see to Feraguto's wounds."

The surgeon helped Feraguto through the assembled crowd and out of sight.

Akramont said in an undertone to Sabri, "He must be a rogue Frank and not anyone of significance. Any paladin would know that Charlemagne had negotiated Feraguto as a hostage with Marsilio. The Emperor made that painfully clear in his first message once his army arrived."

"Ahem." Marfisa cleared her throat. "You have not acknowledged my offer to defend Ruggiero."

Akramont nodded at Grandonio. "Find out who this man is and why he is doing this."

Marfisa clenched her fists and gave a low growl at being ignored again.

Ruggiero's nervousness did not allow him to remain in one spot. The crowd began to overwhelm his senses, so he walked away from Akramont and Sabri. He had no more interest in trying to overhear their whisperings. They were as ignorant as he was in identifying the man who bested Feraguto in the joust.

The identity of his accuser was nagging at him. The only Franks who knew him were Bradamante's kinsmen, but he had rescued three of them so it made no sense that any of them would be his challenger.

He leaned against the wall and peered through the open space in the crenellations. Perhaps by viewing the man at a different angle he could determine his accuser.

"If Akramont insults me one more time, I swear I will switch sides," hissed Marfisa. "He sent Grandonio! An old fat man who is at least thirty years and fifty pounds past his prime. Arrgh. Look at how his mare strains to walk carrying his massive girth. No horse could gallop and achieve any power in jousting with him as a rider."

"Fair point," said Ruggiero as he watched Grandonio riding slowly to where the warrior was waiting. "Akramont did not care if Feraguto was taken hostage and was surprised that he was not. Apparently this Frank is not taking hostages as is his right by conquest. Therefore, if Grandonio cannot possibly win, Akramont must only care about Grandonio's ability in identifying the man."

Marfisa grunted. "If a third warrior is sent out in your honor, it will be me. This time, I will not wait for the amir's approval. Afterward, he can send out the entire Muslim army to view the corpse if he cares so much about identifying that scoundrel."

"Thank you for the offer," said Ruggiero, "but I have recovered my strength and can answer the challenge myself."

Grandonio had finally arrived in the vicinity of the warrior. Words were exchanged, but Grandonio cocked his head to one side as if he had trouble hearing. He rode closer to the Frank. More words were exchanged. Grandonio repeated the motion and rode forward again until it appeared the two were only a few feet apart. While the overweight governor would likely lose in a joust, he had a distinct size and weight advantage if the two engaged in a hand-to-hand duel. He then turned his horse and rode back to the nearby mile marker.

Both horses began to gallop, but there was no question as to which ran faster. The Frank's horse flew while Grandonio's seemed to plod in comparison. As the two riders approached each other, the golden lance hit Grandonio's shield. The massive man slammed onto the ground and laid flat on his back without moving while his opponent rode circles around him.

There was a roar from the assembled crowd at the sight of their leader being humiliated and grumblings from men wanting to charge the lone Frank. Some men began rushing toward the towers to go down and out of the gate.

"Silence!" thundered Akramont, halting men in their tracks. "We shall await Grandonio's account before we attack. This man is deceptive and I will not jeopardize my men due to trickery." He pointed toward a few guards. "Go forth with a stretcher to bring back Grandonio. No, wait, make that a wagon and fetch a surgeon to go with you."

The men nodded then worked their way through the crowd. Akramont and Sabri followed.

"Make way," commanded Marfisa as she elbowed her way through the crowd. Ruggiero followed in her wake. After considerable effort, they made their way through the throng of soldiers on the parapet into the nearest tower.

They once again emerged into bright sunshine as they walked to the opening near the gate. Dozens of soldiers were standing around and talking. The duels with an unknown Frank had served to break the monotony of the long occupation of Arles. Money changed hands as bets were made about the identity of the Frank as well as the next warrior the amir would send next.

Akramont looked as if he was ready to snap. The men around him ceased talking after he glared at them. Sabri whispered to the amir, which was greeted by a shake of the head and a dismissive wave of his hand.

The portcullis was raised to allow the wagon transporting the wounded Grandonio into the city of Arles. The governor was lying on his back, swaddled in blankets and a surgeon sitting next to him. The fallen commander bore a grimace on his face.

A hush fell over the crowd as Akramont stepped next to the wagon. "What did you discover?"

"I did not recognize the warrior, but it is not Oliver or even Renaud."

Groans were heard in the crowd as many men had wagered on those paladins.

"I pretended to be hard of hearing, so I could get closer to see my opponent," Grandonio chuckled, and then winced with pain. "I saw the most beautiful blue eyes and a blush on her cheeks."

"*Her* cheeks?"

"Yes, while I have never met her before, I believe the warrior is Renaud's famed sister, Bradamante."

A murmur of excitement rippled through the crowd. Ruggiero turned away to hide his embarrassment as he felt his cheeks begin to burn. He had not considered that it might be his beloved. Then he remembered the letter he had written to the Maid, promising he would sever his bonds of allegiance to Akramont in one month's time. It had been written more than a month ago and because of his duel with

Mandricardo and his slow recovery, he had not been able to keep that promise. The truth was, he had not even tried.

Remorse and regret cascaded over him. He felt ashamed. After taking a deep breath to clear his head, he resolved to ride Frontino out of the gate and meet with Bradamante. She deserved to hear from his own lips what had transpired and why he had been unable to fulfill his promise. He still intended on marrying her, after he could find a way to honorably separate himself from his vows of allegiance to Amir Akramont.

As Ruggiero cast a glance to view Bradamante in the distance, he saw Marfisa on her horse galloping away on a mission to defend his honor.

CHAPTER NINETY-SIX

Bradamante wondered how much longer it would be before Ruggiero, or another warrior, would emerge from the gates. Her resolve on exacting revenge upon him was unshaken, but her patience was running thin. Just as she was about to look away out of boredom, a rider galloped toward her. The sudden approach demonstrated no interest in parlay before fighting. The opponent's horse was dark red and the rider's shield was green and gold. Clearly it was not Ruggiero.

She responded to the aggressive approach by couching her golden lance under her right arm and giving Rabican the signal to charge. They flew across the road at the opponent whose right arm held a sword aloft. The tip of Bradamante's lance hit the warrior's shield and her adversary flew through the air.

Turning Rabican around, she saw her latest opponent lying on the ground. The helmet, sword, and shield were scattered on the road. Bradamante stared at the warrior's long ornate braid and beardless face. It was then she realized her opponent was a woman and likely the romantic rival she came to kill. A coldness settled over her heart.

Bradamante placed the tip of her lance on the woman's chest. "Give me your name," she snarled in Arabic.

The woman's eyes flew open as her hands grabbed the shaft of the lance and tried wresting it from Bradamante. There was a struggle and Rabican jumped sideways putting distance between the two women.

"I am Queen Marfisa," said the warrior as she jumped to her feet. She snatched up her sword, shield, and helmet before striking an aggressive pose. There was a feral quality about her.

"How did my brothers and kinsmen find any beauty in you?" asked Bradamante with disgust. "You remind me of a wet cat."

"Climb off your high horse — you noble dog — and fight me on equal footing."

"The fight is over, oh royal one. You lost. You are my prisoner."

Marfisa ran toward Rabican with her sword raised. The stallion reared and his front hooves knocked the sword out of her hand making her howl with pain.

Bradamante leaned forward to calm Rabican. "You are magnificent. The best horse I have ever known."

Rabican pranced in a circle before Bradamante thrust her lance against Marfisa's shield, knocking the warrior queen off her feet again.

"Prisoner! You are my prisoner," shouted Bradamante to the fallen queen.

"Never!"

"Then I shall kill you." Bradamante placed her lance over Marfisa's heart. This time her aim would be true as she urged Rabican to walk forward.

"Stop! I beg of you," came a voice that broke her concentration. As Bradamante looked up she saw Ruggiero riding toward them in the distance.

Bradamante lifted her lance and yelled at Ruggiero in Frankish. "Did you only come out from behind those stone walls when your lover was in danger? Why did you send others to fight your battles for you? I thought you were striving to live up to the image of the ideal knight? Instead, you proved yourself to be a faithless coward."

Marfisa had reclaimed her sword and remounted her horse. "What is going on here?" she asked Ruggiero in Arabic.

Ruggiero ignored Marfisa and pleaded with Bradamante, "I have not betrayed your love."

Tears stung Bradamante's eyes. "Liar! I see with my own eyes the woman you cast me aside for. You will die for this." She charged, her lance pointing at his shield.

Ruggiero opened his arms wide and closed his eyes. He was no longer wearing simple chain mail, instead he wore a bronze cuirass embossed with a raised eagle. A direct hit by a lance to his neck would be fatal. He was at her mercy. As she drew near, she found that she could not bring herself to kill him. She veered Rabican to the left and struck Marfisa's shield again, causing the queen to fall for a third time and emit howls of outrage.

A rumbling came as a throng of mounted Muslim warriors rode out of the walled city of Arles heading toward her. Bradamante's attention was diverted to the vanguard. While she had not succeeded in exacting revenge on her broken heart, she had delivered her message to Ruggiero. Now, if she died at the hands of her sworn enemies, the guilt would weigh heavily on her beloved and she would not be guilty of the mortal sin of suicide.

Rabican snorted as she led him to gallop toward the approaching army. Before she died, Bradamante was determined to kill as many of her enemies as possible to further the fame and glory for her family. She rode at an angle toward the line of mounted soldiers. Her golden lance was like an extension of her right arm as she hit the shields. Riders flew backward onto the ground or onto other mounted riders. Screams were heard as men were trampled.

After riding past the line of Muslim defenders, Bradamante turned Rabican around to assess the damage. The Muslim cavalry was in disarray as the herd of horses panicked and stampeded toward the river. At least a dozen soldiers were lying on the ground, dead or wounded. Then more mounted soldiers came thundering on the plain from the north. The Frankish army had joined the fray. She was about to charge again when she realized Frontino was galloping toward her.

"Bradamante!" Ruggiero called.

Panicking, she turned her back to Arles and fled toward the cemetery.

CHAPTER NINETY-SEVEN

Ruggiero was in anguish. He urged Frontino to gallop in pursuit of Bradamante with the hope she was not heading toward any patrolling Muslim soldiers. Outside of Toulouse he had killed at least a dozen of his fellow soldiers to protect her from harm, he hoped it would not be necessary to spill Muslim blood again.

She headed south and rode alongside the tree-lined cemetery filled with large stone tombs. Beyond a copse of trees she pulled the reins as a marsh came into view. Tall reeds filled the large expanse of water.

"Bradamante!" he called. "Listen to me, I beg of you."

She turned toward him, and wiped the tears off her cheeks. "I did not have the heart to kill you, so it is up to you to show mercy and put me out of my misery."

He dismounted, knowing he could not plead his case effectively to her on horseback. "I swear upon my mother's grave that you are the only woman I have ever loved."

"If that is true, how can you marry that harridan?"

"Marry Marfisa? Impossible. You are the only bride for me." He opened his arms. "Come here, my love."

A pained look crossed her face as she dismounted. Her demeanor thawed, but before she could run into his arms, a horse came into the clearing. Marfisa wore a mask of anger.

"There you are," Marfisa snarled as she jumped off her horse. "You will pay for insulting me."

Ruggiero stood in front of Bradamante, blocking Marfisa from attacking her.

"Stop!" he commanded. "You must not harm her."

Marfisa turned on Ruggiero, lifting an arm to strike. "No one interferes with my duels."

Ruggiero reflexively used the wrestling moves he learned as a child. He twisted Marfisa's arm behind her back, then swept her legs, pinning the warrior queen to the ground. His left forearm pressed down on her windpipe. Her face was turning red as her hands clawed at his face and neck.

The ground rumbled again and was followed by a deafening roar as the earth beneath them shook. Nearby trees began swaying. The horses reared and brayed. Fearing an earthquake, Ruggiero rolled away from Marfisa. He scrambled to his feet into a crouched position, ready to run if necessary.

A voice boomed, "STOP this fight. You must not kill one another."

The shaking came to an abrupt end. Marfisa bore a look of bewilderment on her face as she struggled to her feet. Ruggiero turned and saw his mentor standing ten feet away near a cypress tree. Atallah appeared to have aged ten years since he last saw him. His long white beard appeared to have thinned and there were new wrinkles carved on his lined face.

"Ruggiero," rasped Atallah, "you must not harm Marfisa, nor should Marfisa harm you." He turned his attention to the horses, extended his hands in their direction, and gave a slow breath outward. The three horses became calm. Atallah lowered his arms as his knees gave out from under him. Bradamante rushed to his side, catching him before he collapsed.

"You look tired," she said. "Let me find a place for you to rest."

Bradamante helped him walk over to a boulder and propped him up against it. She offered him a drink of water from her flask. His hands shook as he drank.

Atallah gave her a smile. "I am more than tired, I am dying. But before I pass, I must tell Ruggiero and Marfisa the truth."

Ruggiero knelt and held one of his mentor's bony hands.

Marfisa stood nearby looking confused. "Who are you and how do you know my name?"

"My name is Atallah," the old man said in Arabic, "and I have known you ever since the day you and your brother, Ruggiero, were born."

CHAPTER NINETY-EIGHT

Aistulf stared at the plumes of black smoke billowing in the distance. He was grateful the Muslim fleet was sailing westward so he did not have to breathe that foul air. The Caliph had left behind several ships in Bizerta and one hundred loyal men to ensure his rule of law was followed. Now that a new amir had been appointed, similar new leadership would be installed in each of the provinces where governors had supported Akramont's illegal war.

The warm afternoon sun reminded Aistulf as to the passage of time. He was on deck impatiently waiting, while Isaac was below deck with Caliph Harun al-Rashid and Jafar crafting a message for Charlemagne.

Isaac finally appeared and handed him a leather tube. "This is the message you are to deliver to Charlemagne."

"Can you tell me what it says?" asked Aistulf.

Isaac shook his head. "No, but I am to tell you that according to the last reports, Charlemagne's forces are in Paris and under siege."

"Then I shall head there," said Aistulf before he uttered the enchantment to call the hippogriff.

Isaac handed him a parchment scroll. "Once you are back in Francia, perhaps you could send this message to my wife in Aachen. It will let her know that I am still alive and on my way home."

"Would you like to ride along with me?" asked Aistulf.

Isaac shook his head. "Riding on that beast with a saddle meant for one is fine for a short distance, but it would be reckless for the long journey ahead of you. Besides, I am to accompany some rather large gifts for Charlemagne from the Caliph." The two men embraced. "I am glad to have met you, Aistulf. May God bless and guide you."

Caliph Harun al-Rashid and Jafar emerged from below deck. Harun walked over to Aistulf and gave him a warm smile. "Thank you and may Allah protect you."

Aistulf bowed his head. "*Ma'a salama.*"

He then mounted the hippogriff and took off into the sky.

❀

The gentle sea breeze caressed Aistulf's face as he flew over the Mediterranean Sea on the back of the hippogriff. He was happy to no longer be the confined guest of Caliph Harun al-Rashid or King Senapo. He could decide his next destination.

"Charlemagne can wait," he said aloud. "I must find my cousin Orlando, but where do I even begin the search?"

As if an answer to his question, a white feather appeared before him in the sky. It tumbled end over end.

Aistulf smiled. Melissa had once again given him a signal. "As you wish, my dear enchantress. I shall follow your guidance."

The feather stopped tumbling and glided through the air. Aistulf pulled on the reins of the hippogriff and gave chase. Soaring through the air for hours on end, following the feather, he was lulled into a peaceful trance. His mind was free of thoughts and worries. The dream-like state ended as the feather dropped like a stone in water and was seized by a woman.

He was jolted out of his reverie as the hippogriff landed on the deck of a ship. The woman clutching the feather, smiled at him while tears streamed down her cheeks. Aistulf blinked and rubbed his eyes in disbelief.

"Flordelis? Is that you?"

"Aistulf!" she said. "You are the answer to my prayers."

CHAPTER NINETY-NINE

R uggiero was mystified by Atallah's pronouncement. "What did you say?"

"You and Marfisa are twins," said the old man. He turned his gaze to Marfisa. "I offer my deepest apologies to you, my child. I was unable to rescue you from the Bedouin raiders who stole you from me." He took another drink from the flask. "You were so small and trusting. I took the two of you to town and while in the market, you stopped holding my hand. Someone lured you from my side. By the time I realized you were missing, you were bound and gagged." Tears welled in his eyes. "After that, I held Ruggiero tightly in my arms. I was terrified I might lose him as well. I trusted no one to keep watch over your brother, while I searched for you. I ran from stall to stall until I saw several men on horseback galloping away. One was carrying you across his lap. I wept like a baby."

"Did you even *try* rescuing me?" asked Marfisa, her lips trembling.

Atallah's hands shook as he wiped away his tears. "No. After I brought Ruggiero home, I used my magic and scried in a pool of water to see what the future held for you. I saw a life of abuse, slavery, and as a young woman you would become a warrior. It would be a painful life, but one you would survive."

"I survived, yes, but..." Marfisa's voice cracked as she knelt next to him. "If you knew what I was to endure, why not try rescuing me?"

Atallah placed a hand over hers. "Because I used darker magic and saw what would happen if I tried. No matter what I did, I foresaw death for all three of us. I abandoned any hope of getting you back and concentrated on keeping Ruggiero safe from harm. I built an enchanted castle invisible to all. There was even an enclosed jungle room where Ruggiero wrestled with wild animals. I kept him inside, until Akramont learned of his existence and wanted to claim him. The amir used magic to discover where we were and drew Ruggiero outside by holding a tournament underneath the castle."

"I cannot remember anything from my early childhood," said Marfisa.

"Wait. My imaginary playmate was a real sister?" asked Ruggiero.

Atallah nodded. "I tried removing all of your memories of Marfisa, but some remained because your bond with her was so strong. I made a charm so both of you would not be so brokenhearted."

Atallah opened his shirt and untied a golden knot he wore around his neck.

Ruggiero felt a rush of memories flood his senses. He held his head until the bombardment stopped and then looked up at Marfisa with a dawning realization, "Marci?"

A smile swept over her face. "Rudy! I knew there was a reason I felt drawn to you. My brother! I have a brother."

They embraced.

Ruggiero was overcome with emotion. "To think we almost killed each other."

Marfisa broke their embrace and gave a nervous laugh. "My temper! I am sorry for striking at you in anger. I promise I shall never quarrel with you again."

"I remember playing hide-and-seek with you," said Ruggiero.

"Yes," she said nodding. "And we dueled with each other using large wooden swords."

"Then there was..." Ruggiero frowned. He remembered being a small child and pounding his fists into the old man's chest. "Atallah, I remember the day she was taken. I was furious with you."

"Yes, but nowhere as upset as I was with myself."

Ruggiero stared into the distance. "Alcina had removed all my memories, but Melissa restored them when she gave me magical waters from the spring of Mnemosyne. Why did it not bring back my memories of having a sister?"

Atallah gave him a feeble smile. "Your memories were restored to what they were *before* you drank waters from the River Lethe, but my charm still blocked your memories of Marfisa."

"But I wore a ring that nullified all enchantments," said Ruggiero. "Why did I not remember her?"

"Did you see Marfisa when you wore the ring?"

"No. I met her after you stole the ring from me."

"Had you seen Marfisa while wearing the ring, you might have known the truth. Then again, her appearance as a young woman is far different from when she was a young girl. Even with the ring that nullifies enchantments, you might not have understood why she felt so familiar to you."

Atallah beckoned Marfisa to come closer and he touched her cheek. "You have grown to be as beautiful as your mother was."

"Tell me about her," said Marfisa. "I long to know about my parents."

"You are descended from a long line of women warriors from the enchanted island of Feminoro."

Marfisa sat up straight; her eyes gleamed.

"Your grandmother was queen of that island populated by warrior women. It is protected by magic and the only time it can be found is when the island's inhabitants want a passing ship to stop there. I was with Amir Agolante when his ship was brought to Feminoro."

"Amir Agolante? Akramont's grandfather?" asked Ruggiero.

"Yes," said Atallah. "He was a renowned warrior and Amir of the Maghreb. The queen wanted the most powerful man alive to father her child."

"Agolante is our grandfather?" asked Ruggiero.

"Yes."

"Then Akramont and Hala would be our cousins," said Marfisa.

"They are," said Atallah. "Only a few warriors were selected by the queen to come ashore to mate with women on the island. Most of the men remained on board and for three nights Agolante shared the queen's bed."

"Were you one of the chosen men?" asked Ruggiero.

"No, I was not that impressive a warrior," he said. "The queen wanted a daughter, but she promised Agolante that if she bore him a son, she would send the baby to him to raise. They had no room for males on the island. Twenty years later, Agolante was surprised when a delegation of warrior women arrived in Bizerta and wanted to enter his tournament. It was led by a beautiful young woman named Galiziella, who claimed to be his daughter. Agolante's sons, Almont and Troiano, were skeptical at first. They thought warrior women were a joke, that is until they watched Galiziella compete." He closed his eyes and smiled at the memory. "She was fierce. She won the tournament and the respect of her father and brothers. The other women warriors returned to Feminoro, but Galiziella remained and lived in the royal palace. I was named as her tutor and I trained her in reading and writing of both Arabic and Latin."

Atallah began coughing. Marfisa gently patted his back, before re-adjusting his position against the rock.

"Agolante began seeking a suitable husband for Galiziella, but it proved difficult. Then her brother, Almont, advised her she should only marry a man who was stronger than she was, a man who would have the power to chastise her. He knew she would never be happy with a weak husband. She took his advice to heart and that is how she came to marry your father."

"Did our father defeat her in battle?" asked Marfisa.

"Yes. Amir Agolante's forces invaded the city of Reggio. Galiziella dueled with Ruggiero who was the chief hero for the Christian army. After a fierce exchange of blows, Galiziella was knocked off her horse. Numerous Christian soldiers surrounded her, threatening to kill her, but Ruggiero ordered them to stop. Galiziella's helmet had fallen off and her long hair had come undone. She stood there looking defiant, holding her sword in front of her, and Ruggiero was overcome by her beauty. She surrendered to him. Ruggiero's brother, Beltramo, was given the task of taking her to the prisoners' tent, seeing that her wounds were tended, and guarding her safety. Ruggiero continued to lead the rout of Agolante's forces causing them to retreat back to Bizerta."

"Did Agolante know his daughter was taken prisoner?" asked Marfisa.

"No. A rumor was spread of her dying in battle as the rest of her battalion had. No ransom was sought for her, so the rumor was believed. However, I refused to believe she was dead."

"Why is that?" asked Marfisa.

"During the time I spent giving Galiziella lessons, I fell in love with her. I could not bear the idea of her death," he said with a wistful smile. "I dabbled in the magical arts as a youth, but had not practiced it for many years out of respect for Amir Agolante. He distrusted magic. I taught his sons, long before Galiziella, and I avoided anything that might offend my sovereign. To evade being seen performing divination, I left the palace grounds and found a secluded place. I brought out a pan of water and practiced the art of scrying to see images of the past to determine the truth."

Ruggiero felt a lump in his throat. As a child he had asked Atallah many times about his parents, but had only been given scant information. This was the kind of knowledge he had yearned for.

"I learned Galiziella was alive and how she had been taken prisoner," said Atallah. "Beltramo dressed her in silks and wanted to marry her. She refused, unless he could also beat her in combat. She consented to marrying Ruggiero since he had unhorsed her, and would only marry Beltramo if he could do likewise. Beltramo feared being humiliated by a woman and gave up his demand. Galiziella was baptized a Christian, given the new name of Costanza, and married Ruggiero. They were happy together." He paused and gave a sad smile. "At least Galiziella had a few months of happiness. As soon as I realized she was still alive, I sought out my old mentor and begged to become his apprentice once more. As my powers grew, I quickly became alarmed because I foresaw her death. I became obsessed with changing her fate. I studied day and night. I was driven to learn a lifetime's worth of magical knowledge in a few months so I could save her life.

"In early spring, when your mother was six months pregnant, Agolante's forces once again invaded Reggio. I rejoined his army, but my purpose was to save your mother's life. Agolante's army laid siege to the city. Beltramo made his way to the amir's tent in the dead of night. I was brought forth to translate. Beltramo offered to help them conquer the city if, at the end, he would become Reggio's ruler with Galiziella as his wife. Agolante agreed to those terms."

Marfisa snarled. Ruggiero had known bits and pieces of his family's history and did not feel the same level of anger as his sister, since he already knew about their Uncle Beltramo's betrayal. However, the new knowledge of Galiziella being Agolante's daughter added another level of treachery to the tragic tale.

"Galiziella dreamt of the invasion as it was happening," said Atallah. "She woke her husband, warning him, but it was too late. Agolante's forces had already entered the city. A great battle lasted through the night and into the morning. Thousands lay dead. Your mother was like a tigress and killed many Muslim soldiers who invaded the palace, but she was captured. Beltramo held court in the middle of the piazza. He gloated that she would now have to submit to him, since he conquered her in battle. The villain had the dead bodies of Duke Rampaldo and her husband, Ruggiero, laid at her feet. She screamed like a mad woman and clawed at Beltramo's face.

"'Traitor!' she screamed as soldiers pulled her away. 'You will be damned to the deepest pit in Hell for the sin of patricide and fratricide. Your betrayal caused the deaths of thousands of people. Treachery of that magnitude is unforgivable. You are untrustworthy. You are without honor. My father will not reward a man like you. I would sooner couple with a rabid monkey than spend a night in your bed.'"

"I love her spirit," said Marfisa with tears streaming down her face.

"Now you know where yours comes from," said Ruggiero as he gave her hand a squeeze.

Atallah paused and his breathing became labored. He ran a hand over his face before speaking again. "Agolante and her brothers arrived during her speech, but her sole attention was on Beltramo and her husband's corpse. She knelt down to embrace Ruggiero one last time and then saw his wounds. A lance had been driven through his back. She responded in anger, 'Treachery! Whosoever killed this noble warrior is without honor. Warriors must be allowed to defend themselves. The coward who killed my husband by stabbing him in the back shall be reviled forever more.' She said this without knowing it was her brother, Almont, who had slain her husband."

"My Uncle Almont killed my father?" said Ruggiero with his fists clenched.

"Yes," said Atallah, his voice growing weaker. "Beltramo saw the gathered crowd sympathize with Galiziella. He knelt before Agolante and begged for his promised reward. Agolante demanded that he convert to Islam, but Beltramo refused. The traitor was then bound and thrown onto the bonfire."

Marfisa looked horrified. "What a terrible way to die."

Atallah nodded with a faraway look in his eyes. "His screams were inhuman and lasted for what seemed like hours. Galiziella stood before Amir Agolante. He was about to pass judgment on her. He accused her of betraying her family by marrying a Christian. She turned to Almont and reminded him of the advice he gave her on choosing a husband. 'Ruggiero was the only man who ever unhorsed me. He proved he was stronger than I was, so I married him.' She stood there looking defiant. Agolante stepped aside to confer with his sons. I did something bold and inserted myself into their inner circle. I told him if Galaziella's conversion to Christianity offended Allah, that He should be the one to decide her fate. I suggested she be placed in a small boat and set into the open sea without sails or oars. Agolante agreed and I was commanded to follow through on that order. I did, but I went in the boat with her. I used magic to guide us safely to the Libyan shores. Two months later, she gave birth. The happiest time of her life was when she held the two of you in her arms. Two days later, she died. She made me promise to raise you."

Atallah voice was thick with emotion. "I did my best to raise the two of you. I loved you as if you were my own children. My biggest failing is I did not keep up with my divination. Had I done so, I would have seen the dangers awaiting us at the market that day. My darling girl would not have been stolen from me."

"I forgive you," said Marfisa as she stroked his hair. "I know your heart. You did your best to raise me and my brother."

"I foresaw this day and willed myself to stay alive long enough so I could stop Ruggiero from killing you." Atallah smiled at Ruggiero. "I kept my word and did not cast a direct spell on you."

"Thank you, *Ustadh* Atallah, for all that you have done for me and for my sister," said Ruggiero.

Atallah joined Marfisa and Ruggiero's hands together. "Take care of each other."

"We will," said Marfisa.

Atallah looked at Bradamante and spoke in Frankish. "Give Ruggiero the love he needs."

"I promise," she said.

"Beyond this stand of trees there is a hole dug for my grave, along with water and cloths to perform *ghusl*. There is also the tunic I wore at the *Hajj* in Mecca many years ago. Use that as my burial shroud. *Inshallah,* we will all meet again in Heaven." He turned his eyes to the distance and whispered. "I see your parents smiling. They are proud of both of you. *Ma'a salama.*"

Atallah closed his eyes and took his final breath.

Aistulf turned his attention from Flordelis to five sailors surrounding them with swords drawn. There was no time for him to ask Flordelis who these men were or the ship's destination.

"Who are you?" one sailor asked in Arabic.

Aistulf dismounted and spoke Arabic in his most authoritative sounding voice. "*As-salaam-alaikum.* I am a messenger of Caliph Harun al-Rashid. He is the Commander of the Faithful, the leader of the *ummah,* and the rightful heir to Prophet Muhammad, peace be upon him."

"*Wa-alaikum-salaam,*" the men said as they knelt.

"I have a message for your commander, Amir Akramont."

"We will take you to him," said one man as he started barking orders to his men.

Flordelis grew alarmed as the sails were turned and the ship changed direction. No longer was it headed for the small island on the horizon. She spoke Arabic to them in an agitated manner with a fervent tone. Aistulf was uncertain as to what she said, but he made out the words "island," "prisoners," "Arles," and "morrow."

The captain turned to Aistulf and asked him a question in Arabic. He knew he had to continue to bluff his understanding of a foreign language. Aistulf knelt before Flordelis and kissed her hand. "First we must honor the lady."

The captain nodded, issued new orders for the men to change the sails to head once again in the direction of the island. Flordelis gave a sigh of relief as she took Aistulf's hand and then his arm. They walked to the prow of the ship, away from the sailors.

"Thank you," she whispered in Frankish. "These men are untrustworthy, although you may have instilled the fear of Allah into them. Brandimart and Oliver are being held prisoner on that island along with about two-dozen warriors. Earlier today, your cousin Bradamante defeated their leader and these men were ordered to release all of the prisoners."

Aistulf wanted to ask her about his fair cousin and the man she defeated, but he dared not divert attention from the task at hand.

"I overheard the sailors before you came," she said. "They are planning on only picking up the guards. That is after they take turns with me. On the morrow, they would leave me and the prisoners on the island to starve to death."

"I will make sure that does not happen. I have a plan," Aistulf whispered as he squeezed her hand.

Bradamante watched Ruggiero and Marfisa on their knees praying over Atallah's lifeless body. She had not understood much of what the old man had said about Ruggiero's past, but recognized it dealt with Marfisa. She felt like an intruder observing another's tragedy and was unsure of how she could help in this time of need.

Ruggiero finally stood, took Bradamante by the hand and beckoned Marfisa over to stand near them. "My love, I would like to introduce you to my twin sister, Marfisa. I did not know this truth until Atallah told us, but my heart has always known. I felt a kinship toward her as soon as we met."

Bradamante felt relieved at his proclamation. She nodded and smiled at the warrior queen. Ruggiero turned to Marfisa and spoke in Arabic introducing her to Bradamante. Marfisa's face broke into a grin.

"You love him?" Marfisa asked.

"Yes," said Bradamante. "I was jealous. I thought you were his lover."

"Why would you think that?" asked Ruggiero.

"Rumors from Arles made it to Montauban."

Marfisa scoffed. "Lies. I helped Ruggiero recover, but no man will ever have power over me."

Ruggiero squeezed Bradamante's hand. "My love, you are the only woman for me. I cannot love any other woman, because my heart belongs to you."

"And you are the only man I would ever consent to marry," said Bradamante.

He gave her a rueful smile. "I would enjoy nothing more than to spend my time with you, but I must leave your side so that I can bury Atallah. I ask that my bride and my sister set aside your differences and discover your many commonalities. I need both of you in my life."

He then repeated the request in Arabic to Marfisa. She nodded and motioned Bradamante to walk with her away from Atallah's corpse.

"Perhaps we could assist?" Bradamante said to Ruggiero. "It might take less time if you had help."

Ruggiero touched her cheek. "That is kind of you, but I must first prepare his body for burial by washing. It would not be proper for either you or Marfisa to see a man's body."

Bradamante felt the heat of a blush form on her cheeks. "Of course."

"I will return after he is buried."

Bradamante nodded. "I understand, but perhaps I can still be of help." She retrieved the shroud from Rabican's saddlebags and handed it to Ruggiero. "Please use this to bury Atallah. Last night, I made a vow it would be used today. However, I thought it would used for my burial after I confronted you." She averted her eyes and mumbled, "Or, possibly yours or Marfisa's."

Ruggiero placed the shroud on the ground and took her hands in his. "Did Hippalca deliver my letter to you?"

"Yes, I must have read it a thousand times. After a month of waiting, I worried that you had forgotten me. Then I heard that rumor. I did not want to go on living, but I could not take my own life. I wanted you to strike the killing blow. That or I wanted to kill you for breaking my heart."

Sorrow was etched on his face. "I feel shame that I caused you such anguish. If only I could have gotten another message to you, to explain my delay in fulfilling my vow to you."

"Now that I know the truth, I feel shame for having allowed jealousy and idle gossip to poison my heart. I will never again doubt your honor and your love for me."

Ruggiero took Bradamante into his arms and gave her a tender kiss. "We shall be together as husband and wife. That is my promise to you."

Bradamante resisted breaking down into tears as she broke their embrace. "I will make amends with your sister while you tend to Atallah."

She watched Ruggiero as he picked up Atallah's body and carried it behind a line of trees. Marfisa cleared her throat, causing Bradamante to turn and face her former adversary.

"I know some Frankish," said Marfisa in a kind voice.

"And I know some Arabic," said Bradamante.

The two women shared a smile and led their horses back to the marshy area where they had fought before Atallah caused the earthquake. The horses were allowed to drink and graze. Rabican began sniffing Marfisa's red mare. Bradamante chuckled to see the magical stallion show interest in the filly. There was an awkward silence between the two women warriors.

"What is your horse's name?" asked Bradamante.

"Gloriosa. Because she is a glorious mare."

"She is," agreed Bradamante. There was another long uncomfortable pause. "So, Ruggiero is your brother."

Marfisa nodded and then her composure crumbled as she gave a nervous laugh. "I have *a brother*. I have family," she choked up. "Ever since I can remember, I have always wanted a family." Tears welled in her eyes before she blinked a few times, sniffed and shook her head. "Tell me how you met him."

Bradamante closed her eyes and pictured the details of Ruggiero's face the first time she had seen him without his helmet. Love's arrows pierced her heart at that moment. She turned to Marfisa and began describing the battle of Toulouse while being mindful to speak slowly and use terms likely to be understood as well as any Arabic words she knew. Bradamante hoped that Marfisa's knowledge of Frankish exceeded her own comprehension of Arabic.

"I was dueling with Rodomont when Ruggiero came by."

"Rodomont," Marfisa spat. "He is a — "

The rest of her tirade was lost on Bradamante because Marfisa used a string of unfamiliar Arabic words. However, by the tone of Marfisa's voice Bradamante was certain they were epithets. This explosive reaction made Bradamante smile and feel a little envious of her companion. Being the niece of Charlemagne, she felt obligated to maintain a sense of decorum at all times because her behavior reflected on the reputation of her noble family. Marfisa had no such restrictions and was free to speak her mind.

"Charlemagne's troops had fled. The battle had ended for the day, but Rodomont and I were still fighting," Bradamante said. "Ruggiero came searching the battlefield for Atallah. He was worried that Atallah might be hurt or dead. When Ruggiero saw me and Rodomont fighting, he said that the Christian should leave and follow his king. Rodomont refused to let me leave the fight, so Ruggiero took my place."

"He did *what?*"

Bradamante smiled because Marfisa was astounded at Ruggiero's actions.

"Shortly after I rode away, I realized I made a mistake. I should not be the cause for a Muslim to fight a fellow Muslim."

"Rodomont is not a Muslim, he is godless," Marfisa said with contempt. "What happened in their duel?"

"I came back in time to see Ruggiero knock out Rodomont with a fierce two handed blow of his sword," she mimicked the stroke in the air with her arms. "Once Rodomont woke, he admitted his defeat and rode away."

Marfisa looked thoughtful. "*That* is why he hates my brother. Because Rodomont lost to Ruggiero." She then uttered another long string of Arabic profanities.

Once Marfisa finished, Bradamante continued. "After Rodomont left, Ruggiero and I talked. I told him my name and removed my helmet. He then realized I was a woman. We fell in love."

"Of course you did," said Marfisa. "How could you not fall in love with my handsome and courteous brother? And how could he not fall in love with you? My parents also met on the battlefield, except they fought each other. My father defeated my mother and once her helmet came off...love conquered him."

Marfisa then told the story about her mother. Bradamante was fascinated by the idea of only agreeing to marry a man who could defeat her.

"Ruggiero spoke of you the first day we met," said Marfisa. "He told me of your honor and skills as a fighter. He said he did not want the two of us to fight. Now I know why."

"I am grateful you helped rescue my kinsmen, Vivien and Maugis."

"It was my honor."

"And you met my twin, Richardet."

Marfisa laughed as she linked arms with Bradamante. They strolled near the water's edge. "We do have much in common. Had you met Atallah before? It seemed as if you knew one another."

"I met him twice before. After Ruggiero and I fell in love, we were set upon by soldiers patrolling the area. We became separated and later, Atallah took Ruggiero captive and held him in an enchanted castle. Atallah terrorized the Ariège by abducting lords and ladies to keep your brother company."

"Why did he do that?"

"He was trying to protect Ruggiero. I went on a mission and forced Atallah to release all of his captives. That was the first time I met him."

"I want to hear about this rescue," said Marfisa.

"There is much to tell. However, my reunion with Ruggiero was short-lived. He was tricked onto climbing the back of a magical beast that flew him far away." Bradamante's throat grew tight at the thought of him in the arms of the wicked Alcina. She could not bring herself to speak of that betrayal. "Later, Atallah tricked both Ruggiero and me and held us captive in a different magical castle. Unfortunately, we were under a spell that did not allow us to see each other even if we were in the same room. Once the curse was broken, I saw Atallah for the second time. Ruggiero forced his mentor to vow never to cast spells on either one of us again. Atallah then gave us his blessing and gave us gifts."

Marfisa smiled. "I am glad to hear of this. It brings me closer to you."

"Tell me how Ruggiero was wounded."

Bradamante listened as Marfisa told of Mandricardo, Khan of Tartary insulted Ruggiero's honor. She had a hard time following the tale, but recognized how dangerous that man was. Marfisa spoke of a duel that did not happen between Rodomont and Mandricardo and the chaos that ensued. Doralice of Granada was given the choice between the two men and she chose Mandricardo, which left Rodomont without a bride. Fiordespina was brought forth as a substitute bride, but was later murdered by Rodomont.

"I am glad I beat him earlier today," said Bradamante.

"Rodomont is around here?" asked Marfisa. "Where is that snake?"

"He built a bridge a few miles south, but he drowned in the Rhône River."

"I hope he suffered."

A kramont had a splitting headache. He sat in the cool of the palace garden with his head in his hands. The sun would be setting soon and he could finally get some food and drink. Having a full stomach would relieve some of his pain, but the losses of the day would still weigh heavily on his heart.

"Pardon me, brother. Where is Queen Marfisa?" asked Hala, her voice was tentative. "Now that I am no longer under quarantine, she promised to give me another sword fighting lesson. But, I have not seen her since early morning."

He raised his head and tried smiling, but faltered as he stared into his sister's big brown eyes. Worry lines were etched on her youthful face. She was still a child and he hated himself for bringing her along to this war and for his weakness in offering to marry her to a beast. All to secure victory against the Franks. A marriage to Rodomont would have condemned Hala to torture, thankfully she escaped that fate.

"I do not know where Marfisa is," he said.

"What was all the excitement about earlier? Was there a battle?"

"Yes."

"Were Marfisa and Ruggiero part of the battle?"

"Yes."

"And are they...dead?" she asked, her lower lip trembling.

"I do not know."

Sabri entered the courtyard. "My lord, the survey of the dead and wounded is complete. It did not reveal either Ruggiero or Queen Marfisa."

Hala brightened. "They are alive. I knew they would be."

"May I have a word?" asked Sabri.

Akramont grasped Hala's hand. "If I hear anything more, I will let you know. You should go and prepare for dinner."

She nodded and gave him a smile. "Ruggiero and Marfisa are alive and well, *inshallah*."

Sabri waited until Hala had left before he ushered in a middle-aged man who looked exhausted. "This is a messenger from Bizerta. He has been traveling for several days without rest."

"Tell me your news," said Akramont.

The man walked forward and bowed his head. "I bring a warning from Bucifer. An army has likely overtaken our city of Bizerta."

"Greeks?"

"No, my lord," the messenger said, hanging his head.

"Nubians?"

The man shook his head and slowly raised his eyes. "It was Caliph Harun al-Rashid's forces."

Akramont's throat went dry. "How large are the armies against us?"

"I cannot say for certain as I left as soon as we learned the Caliph was on his way. There were not many soldiers remaining in the city as we had just sent more reinforcements here."

Akramont waved his hand at the messenger. "Leave me, but do not go far. I may have more questions for you, but first I must consult with my wazir."

The messenger gave a bow and left. Sabri sat down next to Akramont.

"My lord, forgive me, but I am confused by his report and seek clarification."

"Ask," said Akramont.

"Was this mission to conquer the Frankish empire your idea and not done on the orders or even knowledge of the Caliph?"

Akramont kept his face impassive and did not answer.

"If that is true, all the governors who left their palaces to join your campaign were in essence committing treason against our own spiritual leader, but this treason was done in ignorance. Is that an accurate summary?" asked Sabri.

Akramont gave a curt nod.

Sabri's hands covered his face as he took a few deep breaths. After a few moments his calm demeanor was restored. "I left my palace in the hands of my son to guard the land, thinking that our only risks of invading forces would be from the Greeks, Nubians or Ethiopians. I did not worry that it would come from the brothers of my faith who would seek to remove me from office as punishment for my treachery."

"Yes, this was my doing," said Akramont with defiance. "Harun was happy to build his palace in Raqqa and surround himself with pleasures, while leaving expansion to others. Our forefathers were stopped seventy years ago by Charlemagne's grandfather in a field we marched through and burned on our way to Paris. I sought to conquer lands that were denied to our faith, but that are now in our grasp."

"African cities are once again being razed by Arabs and Persians," said Sabri. "None of our homes will be left standing. Or the doors will be barred to our re-entry and we will be executed should we risk returning. We must end this war before Charlemagne learns of our troubles at home."

Akramont gave a small humorless laugh. "Any suggestions as to how to accomplish that?"

Sabri nodded. "Charlemagne should have learned about the recent uprising of the Saxons by now. He will be eager to use his forces to put them down again. Beyond that, winter is coming and snows in the mountain passes make it dangerous to travel for months. The pressures for him to bring this war to a swift end will be to our advantage, until he discovers that Caliph Harun al-Rashid opposes us."

"Do you have a strategy in mind or did you simply want to torture me tonight with guilt?" asked Akramont.

"Issue a challenge of single combat to determine the outcome of the war."

"Single combat?"

"Yes. It is a long tradition with the Germanic tribes dating back to before Caesar. One man from either side in a duel to the death," said Sabri. "We must offer terms Charlemagne will accept. We control much of Provence including Narbonne and we recently retook Toulouse. It is not the entire Frankish Empire, but Charlemagne will want this war to have a quick end. If he believes his champion will win, then it will save the lives of thousands of his men in exchange for a small amount of territory. He can then use those men against the Saxons to protect his palace in Aachen."

"Who should we choose to champion our side?"

"Ideally it would be you. However, then the Frankish combatant should be Charlemagne and he is sixty years old. He would never agree to fight a strong young man such as yourself."

"And if he sent someone else to fight me in his place, it would be seen as a sign of weakness," said Akramont.

"Precisely, we cannot ask for single combat and offer you as the champion." Sabri looked off in the distance and began ticking off warriors on his fingers. "Rodomont is out. He would probably have accepted this chance for glory, but he defied you earlier today. It appears he was either defeated or killed after that because the Franks now control his bridge. Ruggiero and Marfisa are missing."

"Marfisa?" said Akramont. "I could not entrust my war effort on a girl. If she lost, my reputation and that of my ancestors would be put to shame for placing a girl in such prominence. I would sooner surrender to Charlemagne and take my chances as to the consequences."

Sabri nodded. "And then Grandonio and Feraguto are both injured."

"Grandonio might have been a good choice twenty years ago."

"Fair point," said Sabri. "It seems that we are left with Gradasso. I have thought long and hard about him insulting you this morning. I plan on taking him to task and shaming him into being your champion."

The familiar sound of the *muezzin* announcing sunset and the call to prayer was heard.

"Finally," said Akramont. "After we say our prayers and have our *iftar,* you will summon Gradasso."

Ruggiero finished burying his late guardian and used the last of the water to cleanse his hands. It was time to rejoin his bride and his sister. Leaving the gravesite, he walked over to where they were waiting for him. He was pleased to see the two women talking with one another as if they had been longtime friends.

"It is done," he said. "Atallah has been laid to rest."

Marfisa grabbed his hand and squeezed it. "Just this morning I was an orphan with no family. This evening I have a twin brother and know the history of our brave parents."

They began walking toward the gravesite while Bradamante gathered the reins of the horses and brought them forward, but stayed a respectful distance away. Marfisa bowed her head and said a few words to Atallah as she stood near the grave.

Marfisa turned to Ruggiero and said, "Atallah told us about how our parents were betrayed and murdered because of their brothers. Had Atallah not intervened on our mother's behalf, we would never have been born."

"That is true," agreed Ruggiero.

"Akramont's father conspired in our parents' murder. Akramont is therefore our enemy. We have no choice. We must join Charlemagne's army. It is our legacy since our father once served him. Come, let us go with Bradamante to the Frankish camp."

Ruggiero did not move. "Akramont was a small child when those crimes were committed by his father, his uncle, and his grandfather. He cannot be blamed for the sins of his elders. Do you see our cousin Hala as an enemy as well? Even if she was not even born at the time of our parents' deaths?"

Marfisa scowled. "Does that mean you intend on continuing to serve Akramont? After knowing the truth?"

"I swore an oath of fealty to him. Akramont has done nothing that would make me consider him to be an enemy. His personal physician tended my wounds. The night our camp was attacked, he made plans to evacuate me. I could have been left behind to die. Had he done that, his wives might still be alive."

"I never swore any oath to him. I cannot serve him a moment longer."

"I understand," said Ruggiero. "I must find an honorable way to sever my bonds of service to him. I doubt that he knows of our kinship. To desert him, without notice, especially after the risks he took on my behalf, would be dishonorable."

Bradamante walked toward them. "Is there something I should know?"

"Marfisa never swore an oath to serve Akramont and will leave with you to join Charlemagne's forces," said Ruggiero. "Bear in mind that I am still bound by an oath of fealty to Akramont. To leave with you now would be to desert him and would be dishonorable. Your father would never bless our union if my character was considered disloyal. I will speak to Akramont and tell him that his father was responsible for the deaths of my parents, and because of that I seek to leave his service. Until we are together again, know my heart belongs to you."

"You saved my brother's life. You saved my cousins' lives. Those feats alone should be enough to earn my father's blessing. Please do not leave me again," she pleaded.

Ruggiero pulled her into his arms and whispered in her ear, "I will be by your side soon. If I abandon Akramont now I would always be looked at with suspicion. You are the niece of Charlemagne. You cannot have a husband with a cloud hanging over his head. Earlier you said you would never again doubt my honor or love for you. Please remember your love is the most important aspect of my life, and I am striving to earn your hand in marriage."

Bradamante nodded and gave him a tearful kiss goodbye. "Until we meet again, know that you will be in my prayers hoping to protect you from harm."

Marfisa embraced him. "Godspeed, brother. We will await you at Charlemagne's camp, where you rightfully belong."

Akramont's spirits were lifted by the prospect of Sabri moving beyond the role of sage advisor and would expand to manipulating Gradasso.

The Khan of Sericana entered the courtyard with an irritated disposition. "Why was I sent to have dinner with foot soldiers?" complained Gradasso. "I am a khan and deserve better."

Akramont sat at the table, eating green olives, and enjoying Gradasso's discomfort.

"Have a seat," said Sabri. "Earlier today you insulted the amir's leadership. A change in eating companions is a small taste of your new treatment should you continue your disrespectful behavior."

"What are you threatening me with?"

"A change in accommodations."

Gradasso growled. "What is it you want?"

"Why did you come to the west? Was it not to seize the best warhorse and best sword? Is it because you want to be regarded as the greatest warrior the world has ever known?"

"That is why I came here," said Gradasso.

"It has been said that you invaded al-Andalus with one hundred thousand soldiers or was that number an exaggeration?"

Gradasso smirked and shrugged his shoulders.

"You were expecting the Franks would come to Amir Marsilio's aid," continued Sabri. "Then you would somehow capture or kill Orlando and Renaud. Was that your plan?"

"Yes."

"Yet your strategy did not go as planned. Orlando was in the east defending Angelica so you could not get his sword. Then your duel with Renaud was overshadowed with sorcery and you did not obtain his horse. Your army forced Amir Marsilio's surrender, but then the Franks fled back to their own lands and your forces pursued them all the way to Paris. You even captured Charlemagne himself and could have controlled all of the Frankish Empire and al-Andalus, but all you wanted was a certain horse and sword. True?"

"True."

"Charlemagne's release was to be made after the surrender of Renaud's horse, but for some inexplicable reason you agreed to a joust. A joust with the silliest of Charlemagne's twelve paladins. Mandricardo heard of your humiliation when he was still in Tartary. He laughed as he regaled of you losing in one pass to 'the court's jester.' It is likely word has spread to Sericana by now."

Gradasso's face twisted. "Why are you insulting me in this manner?"

Sabri took a slow drink of water. "You brought nothing of value to this war effort. After losing the joust to a fool, you took what was left of your forces and fled Paris. But you never made it back to Sericana. Somehow you became trapped in a magical realm, until Mandricardo earned your release. Both you and Mandricardo joined Amir Akramont's side, but brought nothing except for your titles and a sense of entitlement. You both expected to be exalted and given the best tents, the best food, and deference paid to you. Akramont praised you in front of his army at the old Roman arena outside Paris. The amir wanted to inspire his forces onto victory. How did you repay him? You disrupted a duel between Mandricardo and Rodomont, and demanded that a sword you coveted be handed over to you."

Sabri stood and began pacing. "You possess that sword now because Akramont gifted it to you after Mandricardo's death. By all rights, it should belong to Ruggiero since he was the one who bested Mandricardo. You now possess Renaud's horse, but there are rumors swirling around that magic was used to spirit the horse away. Perhaps that conquest was not honorable."

Gradasso opened his mouth, but Sabri silenced him with a wave of his hand.

"That leads us to this morning, when you refused to assist in Akramont's war effort other than serve as an advisor. Did you take part in the battle today?"

"No."

"As expected. You wish to stay behind these walls until the war is over and then return to Sericana with someone else's troops and expect your kingdom will welcome you back with open arms and open gates. Why should they? Why should they welcome someone who is thought to be a foolish, selfish monarch who squandered the lives of tens of thousands of men?"

"I am their king!" Gradasso bellowed as he pounded a fist on the table.

"You abandoned your kingdom in your quest for vanity items. Your reputation is in tatters, but it can be redeemed. Then perhaps you can reclaim your throne without difficulty."

"What do you propose?" asked Gradasso.

Sabri gave a smile and turned to Akramont.

"We have lost too many men in this war," said Akramont. "After today's battle, we will once again have to bury hundreds of men. I am sending a messenger to Charlemagne and issue a challenge to end this war by single armed combat. I want you to be my champion."

Gradasso's face was like stone. He had been driven into a corner. The only way out of the corner was to fight.

Akramont's seneschal appeared in the doorway. "I have news, my lord."

"What is it?"

"Ruggiero has returned."

Akramont sat up straight. "Is he unharmed?"

"He is, my lord."

Akramont gave a sigh of relief. "Bring him here at once." He then turned to Gradasso. "You are dismissed. Your accommodations will remain unchanged for now."

Bradamante had not wanted to part ways with Ruggiero, but realized it would be disrespectful to argue about his sense of honor, especially when he was in mourning. A somber mood hung in the air as she and Marfisa rode between the stone tombs in the cemetery. The women did not speak, and the only sounds were the muffled clip clop of hooves over a blanket of fallen yellow and orange leaves from the poplar trees lining the graveyard.

Atallah's death made her reflect on failing to carry out Melissa's orders to kill the wizard when she first met him outside of Foix. Bradamante had shown mercy to the old man when he spoke of his devotion to Ruggiero, but she later regretted sparing his life after Atallah sent her beloved to Alcina's island. However, she now felt vindicated. Her union with Ruggiero was delayed, but not rendered impossible due to Atallah's actions. Had she killed the old wizard as Melissa instructed, Ruggiero might have never forgiven her for committing violence against his mentor and he would never have known about the full history of his family.

As they emerged from the north end of the cemetery, Bradamante looked over her left shoulder at the walled city of Arles. The battle was over for the day and marked by the wounded being carried away on stretchers and the dead placed into wagons. She urged her horse to take an overland path far east of the walls, to avoid arrows being shot at them from guards. After traveling a mile northward, they returned to the Via Agrippa and enjoyed the peace of riding between rows of plane trees. Another mile further, the road bent to the east allowing for a large clearing of land on the banks of the river.

Marfisa broke the silence. "What is that?"

"Charlemagne's camp," said Bradamante with pride at sight of the imposing military encampment in the distance.

"I have never seen anything like it before."

"The emperor patterns his military camps after those of Julius Caesar."

A tall wooden fence built in the shape of a square created a barricade around the encampment built near the banks of the Rhone River. All four corners had a guard tower with parapets. Trenches were dug three feet deep and five feet wide surrounding the perimeter. There were four gates, one on each side of the square and guarded by ten sentries.

"Before we arrive in camp, I must tell you that no one there knows I love your brother," said Bradamante. "He is still technically an enemy, and it would destroy my reputation as a virtuous maiden if my relationship with him became known before he is baptized. You must guard my secret."

"You have my word," said Marfisa.

Upon arrival at the entrance a guard said, "State your name and purpose."

"My name is Bradamante from the House of Lyon. I am daughter to Aymon, Duke of the Dordogne, sister to Renaud, Count of Montauban, and niece to Emperor Charlemagne. I am bringing a powerful new ally and recruit to the Frankish army, the infamous Queen Marfisa. We wish to take our rightful place in Charlemagne's camp."

The young guard went slack-jawed at the pronouncement. An older guard blew a horn with three short blasts.

"The Maid is here! Lady Bradamante is here!" he shouted before turning to another guard. "Send word to Count Renaud, tell him that his sister is here." The man then turned his attentions to Bradamante and apologized. "Forgive us, we did not recognize your standard."

Marfisa frowned as she looked at Bradamante's shield. "Is that mud?"

"Yes. A sign of how upset I was with the rumors I heard," said Bradamante. "I will clean it and reveal a better design."

They entered the camp in the troop assembly area. The site had multiple stacks of wooden planks that would be used to build a barricade around the city of Arles. The men dropped their tools and ran over to cheer the warrior women. Marfisa beamed at the adulation showered on them. Bradamante smiled at her admirers as she led the way to the center of the camp where she knew she would find Charlemagne's tent.

About halfway through the camp, a familiar figure waited for them.

"This is a sight I never dared dream would happen," said Renaud with a large grin on his face. "My sister befriended Queen Marfisa. I thought if the two of you met, you would have fought each other to the death."

"We tried, but then discovered how much we had in common and set aside our differences along with our arms," said Bradamante. "She wants to join our side and be baptized."

Both women dismounted. Bradamante was swept up in a bear hug by her brother. After letting her down, Renaud greeted Marfisa with a bow and a kiss to her hand.

"Having fought both with and against you in Cathay, I can honestly say that I prefer you as an ally," he said. "Welcome to Charlemagne's camp."

Renaud then noticed Bradamante's horse. "Is that...Rabican? And Aistulf's saddle? How did you —"

"I saw Aistulf over a month ago. He asked me to care for Rabican while he set out on an adventure."

"Why did you not tell me this back in Montauban?"

"You would have insisted on taking Rabican rather than Nikephoros," she said. "I promised Aistulf to care for his horse, and I do not break my vows."

Renaud laughed. "Had I bothered to step foot into the stables and not simply depend on my squire to care for the horses, I might have known this amazing animal was there. Nonetheless, I am delighted to hear that our ne'er-do-well cousin is alive and well. Hopefully we will see him again soon and he will join in our victory."

"Can I take your horses?" asked a squire.

"I shall see to that, thank you," said Renaud. "Rabican was once my horse while I was in Cathay. That is before Aistulf returned Bayard to me, so I know how difficult Rabican can be to handle."

"Care needs to be taken to secure Aistulf's golden saddle and lance as well," said Bradamante.

"A golden lance," said Renaud, with a touch of surprise in his voice. "That looks like the lance Angelica's brother Argalia used. I had wondered what became of it. I shall place those prized possessions in my tent for safekeeping. Marfisa, I will store your saddle as well. No one would dare steal from me."

They continued walking through the camp until they came to the royal tent with Charlemagne's banners flapping in the breeze. The flags were divided down the center with a black eagle on a field of yellow on the left and six golden *fleur de lis* on a field of blue on the right. Guards flanked an imposing man in his fifties, who stood at the entrance wearing a coat of mail. He stood with ramrod posture, had a full mustache, a thinning head of hair, and held a wax tablet.

"Audulf, this is my sister, Bradamante, and Queen Marfisa, they wish to have an audience with the emperor," said Renaud.

The seneschal made a few notations on his tablet before looking up and giving the barest of smiles to Bradamante. "What is this regarding?"

"Queen Marfisa wishes to be baptized as a Christian and join Charlemagne's army," said Bradamante.

Audulf looked at Marfisa from head to toe. "Very well, I shall add you to the list. Since she is not sworn to serve Charlemagne yet, she must relinquish her arms before entering his tent."

Renaud nodded. "He is right. I shall safeguard your sword and dagger as well. We cannot risk having armed warriors in his tent who might wish the emperor harm."

Marfisa looked as if she was about to argue, but then shrugged and handed over her weapons.

Bradamante then remembered a solemn prayer to God she had made weeks before. She vowed that the next time she saw Charlemagne, she would confess to murdering Pinabel. "I also have a private matter I need to speak with the emperor about."

"Perhaps tomorrow," sniffed Audulf. "He does not have time for that today."

"Please see to their comfort while they wait to speak with the emperor," said Renaud. "They will also need a tent. There is a vacant one not too far from mine. See that it is prepared for their stay along with a meal waiting for them. I will return after taking care of their steeds and I will fetch Archbishop Turpin."

Audulf gave him a curt nod. "Manfred, show these ladies to the holding tent. And bring the messenger back here."

A balding man of slight build made his way toward them. His presence was welcoming as opposed to that of the seneschal. "Hello, I am the emperor's chamberlain. If you ladies would follow me."

Bradamante and Marfisa were led into a small tent. A table was in the center and covered with unleavened bread, smoked fish, fresh fruit, wine, and a bowl of water. At the sight of food, Bradamante's stomach grumbled. It seemed like an eternity since she last ate a meal.

"Help yourself to some refreshment while you wait," said Manfred.

"Come, let us eat," Bradamante said to Marfisa.

The two women washed their hands and sat down at the table.

Manfred spoke to a man wearing traveling clothes. "The emperor will see you now."

Bradamante and Marfisa were left alone in the tent. She spoke in a whisper so her voice would not carry. "Dear Lord, thank you for this day. You have renewed my faith in Ruggiero's love for me and we pledged our love to each other. You have brought my beloved the history of his parents, and the gift of knowing he has a twin sister. You turned my heart from jealousy to sisterly love toward Marfisa. Your love has brought her here, and to being baptized as a Christian. Bless the soul of Atallah and welcome him to your kingdom in Heaven. And bless this food set before us. Thank you. Amen."

"Amen," said Marfisa. "I will need your help in becoming a Christian."

Bradamante smiled. "Of course. Your faith in the one true god that we both worship is strong. The main difference is our customs and our holy days. You will learn those over time. Do not be nervous."

After a period of time, Audulf, the seneschal, returned and led the women to the royal tent. Before entering he said, "We shall wait in the back until the emperor signals that he is ready, and then I will announce you."

He lifted the flap and held it while the women walked inside. Charlemagne's tent was easily three times larger than those for ordinary soldiers. There were multiple poles holding up the center of the tent. Large rugs covered the ground, making it seem like a movable palace. Charlemagne was deep in thought as he studied maps spread out on a large table. He cut an imposing figure standing over six feet tall and being full-bodied. Even at sixty years of age, his vitality was evident and exceeded that of most men. He was also one of the few warriors to wear polished iron plate armor. Most warriors in the Frankish army wore either chain mail, scale mail, or thick gambesons.

Duke Namo of Bavaria and Ogier the Dane stood next to the emperor. They were engaged in pointing at the maps and speaking in hushed tones. The duke had rounded shoulders and white hair, signifying his advanced age whereas Ogier was a tall, handsome man in his forties.

The emperor appeared angry. His disposition changed as he looked up from the table, saw Bradamante, and smiled. "My beloved niece, I am happy you have returned to my service. I heard that you liberated the bridge earlier today and released several of our imprisoned warriors. Is that true?"

"Yes."

"Wonderful. Our forces now control that bridge and we shall soon control the Rhône River. And, who is this with you?"

"I present Queen Marfisa," announced Audulf. He bowed and left the tent.

"Queen Marfisa, I have heard stories of you. Step forward."

Marfisa gave a polite bow of her head. "Your grace, as a small child I was kidnapped and sold into slavery. As a young woman, I fought off my king who tried to steal my virtue, and instead, I stole his throne. He was the first of many kings that I overthrew. I came to the west, because I envied your fame. I wanted to challenge you. That changed today. I learned my father was Ruggiero of Reggio and served you. My mother was Galiziella, another famous warrior. They wanted me raised a Christian. I am here fulfilling their wishes. I want to be baptized and serve you as my father did."

"This is a remarkable day," said Charlemagne. "Renaud has spoken about you and your skills. I am honored to have you join my forces. We must have you baptized at once." He turned to a guard. "Have Audulf send for Archbishop Turpin."

Ruggiero was ushered to the inner courtyard of the palace. "Have you done your evening prayers?" asked Akramont. Ruggiero opened his mouth to respond, but the amir sensed the answer. "Of course, you did." He snapped his fingers at an attendant. "Bring a meal for Ruggiero."

The table was soon covered with breads, dates, olives, meats, and cheeses. As Ruggiero broke a piece of bread and dipped it in oil, Akramont huddled in a corner with Governor Sabri. The two spoke in hushed tones and both had serious looks on their faces. After Sabri left, the amir sat down next to Ruggiero. A servant filled their cups with tea.

Akramont warmed his hands on his cup. "I am grateful for your safe return. It has been a long, arduous day with more casualties. I had worried you might be among the fallen."

Ruggiero, unsure of how to respond, continued chewing.

"Do you know the fate of Queen Marfisa?" asked the amir.

"She is alive and well. However, she left to join Charlemagne's forces."

"Why would she —" Akramont looked perplexed at first, but then waved a hand. "I should have expected this day would come. King Sacripant warned me of her fickle nature and how she was notorious for changing sides. I suppose I should feel honored she lasted as an ally for long as she did."

"Do you wish to know why she left?"

"She is a girl," Akramont said with a wave of his hand. "That is all the explanation I need."

Ruggiero closed his eyes. The insult to his sister's integrity was upsetting, but he still needed to find a way to explain himself to the amir. "Do you wonder why it took me so long to return?"

"Yes. What happened?" Akramont set his cup down.

"I was drawn away from the fighting with the Franks and saw my guardian, Atallah. He finally told me the truth about my mother, my father...and my sister."

"Sister? What sister?"

"Marfisa is my twin sister. Our mother was the daughter of the Queen of Feminoro and of Amir Agolante."

Akramont looked surprised. "But, he was my grandfather."

"Our grandfather," corrected Ruggiero.

A broad smile came across Akramont's face. "That makes you my cousin."

He stood and motioned Ruggiero to likewise stand. The two men embraced. Tears welled in Akramont's eyes. "Allah brought you back to me for a purpose. This war has devastated my family. I lost my cousin, Daniso, his wife and son. I lost my wife, Anika, and my wife, Alia. But Allah has now expanded my family with acknowledging a new kinsman. You are the answer to my prayers."

Akramont embraced him again, but Ruggiero did not return the embrace. He waited until the amir took a step back before speaking.

"Marfisa is also your cousin. She changed her allegiance once she learned our parents had wanted us raised as Christians."

"Wait," said Akramont. "Your mother abandoned our faith?"

"She married a Christian and was baptized in his faith."

"Agolante would never have consented to that marriage. How did his daughter marry an infidel?"

The word stung Ruggiero. The slur was used by Muslims to insult Christians, and he was certain that the slur was used by Christians to insult Muslims. He chose to ignore the insult to the faith of his parents and instead respond to the broader question.

"My mother and father met on a battlefield. My mother was defeated. It was the first time anyone had beaten her on the field of glory. While she was conquered by my father's power, he was conquered by my mother's beauty."

"I do not understand," said Akramont.

"Think of Marfisa. Can you imagine her ever agreeing to marry a man who was weaker than she is? She would have no respect for him. No amount of protocol in finding an appropriate husband would work for either my sister or my mother."

Akramont shook his head, clearly disinterested in talking about women. "You are still an orphan. What happened to your parents?"

"My father, Ruggiero of Reggio, was murdered by our Uncle Almont. My mother was condemned to death by our Grandfather Agolante.

Thankfully, her fate was put into Allah's hands and she was set adrift in a small boat. She landed on the Libyan shores and a few months later died after giving birth. Atallah was there and served as guardian for me and Marfisa, until she was kidnapped as a small child."

"That is a tragic tale," said Akramont, without any note of sympathy in his voice.

"I came back here so that I could inform you and Hala of our kinship and to extend my gratitude for all that you have done on my behalf."

"I sense you have more to say," said Akramont as he traced a finger-tip on the rim of his teacup.

"I wish to join my sister in the Frankish camp and be baptized in the faith of our parents."

Akramont closed his eyes and gave a small chuckle. "You wish to be relieved of your oath of fealty to me."

"I do."

He sat back in his chair and sighed. "I will grant your request, but not until sundown tomorrow. Until then, you must remain as my loyal knight. You must fulfill any command I give you. Otherwise, I will have you slapped in chains and punished as a traitor."

"On my honor as a knight," agreed Ruggiero.

"You are not only a descendant of Hector of Troy on your father's side, but you are also a descendant of Alexander the Great on your mother's side. For one more day you will be in my service, after that you can abandon your newly discovered extended family. Otherwise, should you decide to stay in my service, you will be awarded a gover-norship in the Maghreb, for there are many vacancies. Or you could chose to rule over a city in these newly conquered lands. It will be your choice."

T he sun had set, but the sky was still light as the ship arrived at the small island. It was as if land sprang up in the middle of the Mediterranean Sea to serve as a haven for malevolent deeds. Had Aistulf set out to find the island with vague directions, it is unlikely he would have found it without magical aid by Melissa. Trees covered most of the isle with a well-worn path leading to a rock-strewn hilltop.

Guards were waiting along the sandy shoreline. Once the ship touched the beach, the sailors and the guards worked together to pull the ship onshore and the men spoke in hushed tones with one another.

Aistulf helped Flordelis onto the back of the hippogriff before he climbed into the saddle. He pulled on the reins and the winged beast took to flight before landing on the large hill overseeing the entire island. He could see a group of men shackled together and held in a pit surrounded by a wooden fence. The prisoners looked half-starved, were filthy, sunburned, and wore only breeches.

After dismounting, Aistulf brought out his book of magic spells from his satchel and read a few passages. He raised his right hand and uttered a few magic words. Fishing nets appeared and ensnared Rodomont's men. Howls of protest rang out.

"Translate for me," said Aistulf to Flordelis. "You were ordered to release all of your prisoners and return them to the Frankish Empire. Yet you were overheard plotting to violate that command and leave these men here to starve to death. What do you say to those charges?"

Flordelis remained on the back of the hippogriff and spoke in a loud, clear voice that caused the men to stop struggling with the netting that ensnared them and look up at her. After she finished speaking, the men began arguing with one another and no one voice responded to her query.

"Enough," said Aistulf. "They have proven themselves untrustworthy. Not even the Caliph could change their hearts."

He raised his right hand and said a few more words. The men collapsed in a heap.

"What did you do?" asked Flordelis.

"They are asleep. I will not sink to their level and cause their deaths. They will remain asleep until I lift the spell. I will deliver them to Charlemagne who may be able to fetch ransoms for them. Did I hear you say something earlier about the city of Arles?"

"Yes, the war has shifted to Arles. Akramont's forces are behind the city's walls while Charlemagne's forces are camped nearby. I will tell you everything, but first we must release the prisoners."

"Agreed," said Aistulf. "Let us get the key to unshackle the men."

They flew down to the shore and retrieved the key from a sleeping guard. Flordelis ran toward the men and wept tears of joy as she knelt before her husband. She fumbled with the key for the shackles on his wrists. As soon as his hands were free, he held her face and covered it with kisses.

Aistulf was moved to tears to see such a display of love and devotion between two people. He had never experienced such a bond with another person and doubted if he ever would. Cautiously, he stepped forward and picked up the key that had fallen from Flordelis' hands and unshackled Brandimart's feet. The lovers sensed the release from bondage and stood. Their hands and lips were occupied with each other and could not spare an instant for Aistulf. Instead, they left and sought a place to be alone together.

Oliver was sitting with a large smile on his face. "Can I be next? And did you bring my wife as well?"

Aistulf chuckled as he used the key to unlock his friend.

"Thank you, brother paladin," said Oliver. "I began to think I was going to die on this forsaken island. What did you do with the guards?"

"They are asleep and will remain that way for as long as I see fit. Let us release the others, then we shall put these shackles on those who imprisoned you."

"I will gladly help with that chore."

The two paladins made quick work of releasing the other prisoners. They then set about removing and untangling the netting from the captors and Aistulf placed it in lockers on the ship while Oliver put his former tormentors in shackles.

"Now that is done, we should secure food for our evening meal," said Oliver. "However, I am afraid we may be too late, as the others may have eaten what was left of the meager food stores."

"Do not worry about food," said Aistulf. "I will prepare a feast for you and the loving couple. Go cleanse yourself in the ocean. It will do you a world of good. Then meet me on top of the hill."

The hippogriff was fed first before Aistulf conjured a meal of warm bread and a variety of seafood including octopus, shrimp, oysters, and white fish. He had not eaten since breaking his fast in the morning with Isaac. As he watched the sunset, he reflected on the many events of the day and was grateful he would be breaking bread with trusted friends.

Oliver made his way up the hill, his hair wet. He gaped at the meal spread out before him. "I have been to royal banquets with less food. I will not question how you managed all this, I will simply enjoy."

Aistulf handed his friend a plate. "Help yourself. You look like you have not had a full belly in a long time."

As the two friends ate, Oliver told Aistulf how the war started in Provence, moved to Toulouse and then became a siege on Paris. Charlemagne had been so impressed by Brandimart's skills on the battlefield and close friendship with Orlando that he named the former Muslim to be his latest paladin. The mood turned somber when Oliver spoke of Orlando abandoning his duty and going off in search of Angelica.

"Orlando is the heart and soul of Charlemagne's army. Without his brave leadership, we suffered. Thankfully, Renaud came from Britannia with reinforcements and we fought a fierce battle in Paris causing severe losses in the Saracen camp. The next morning, Charlemagne sent Renaud and Guichard off in search of Orlando. They searched, but did not find him. Renaud returned to Paris with enough men and guile to destroy Akramont's camp in the middle of the night." Oliver took a swig of wine from the jug. "The Saracen army — or what was left of it — escaped with their lives and retreated to the fortified city of Arles. Charlemagne then granted Brandimart and me permission to go on our own mission to find Orlando."

"Did you find him?" asked Aistulf.

"We did, near Arles. My oldest and dearest friend from childhood has gone mad. The man I saw was a beast, not capable of rational thought." Oliver paused to clear his throat. "Orlando was fighting on a bridge over the Rhône River with Rodomont. They both fell into the water. I was worried that Orlando would drown, but thankfully he did not. I tried crossing the bridge to help him, but was ensnared in a scheme by Rodomont to imprison honorable knights."

Oliver related how the guards joked about how Rodomont offered lances to his opponents that were shorter than his and would ensure his victory. All so he could force men to serve him back in Sarza once the war was over.

Aistulf was disgusted. Then he remembered how he gave a golden lance to Bradamante for safekeeping. Perhaps that is why she vanquished that horrible man, he thought.

"It is fortunate that you brought Flordelis here tonight," said Oliver. "Without her, I am certain that Brandimart would still be in bondage worrying about her safety, even if his iron chains were removed. I have never seen two people more devoted to one another. Each is like half of a person when they are separated. I hope they grow old together, for I worry that should one die, the other would soon perish of a broken heart."

As the night wore on, Brandimart and Flordelis joined them on the hilltop. The lovers ate, but it seemed their sustenance came more from being in each other's arms than from food.

Once the conversation again turned to Orlando, Flordelis became agitated. "Orlando is frightening to behold. Our beloved friend has lost his mind."

Brandimart squeezed her hand. "Tomorrow, once we return to Arles, we will search for him once again. Somehow we will find and help him. He saved our lives many times over, we are indebted to him."

"I am determined to help you in this task," said Aistulf. "He is my kinsman and I may have the remedy for what ails him. If he is as mad as you say, we must subdue him first so that the elixir I have will not be broken."

"We will follow your lead," said Oliver.

"Flordelis, do you still have that feather?"

"Of course."

"On the morrow, I will follow the magical winds on my hippogriff," said Aistulf. "The ship will set sail after me. Together we shall find Orlando, restore his wits, and then we will all return to Charlemagne's service."

Bradamante anxiously awaited Marfisa's baptism. Renaud, Ogier the Dane, Namo, and Charlemagne stood nearby as Archbishop Turpin began the ceremony.

Archbishop Turpin was one of the few clean-shaven men in the Frankish army, as most wore mustaches. He wore white vestments and a miter on his head. A sense of calm surrounded the holy man who carried a small basin of water and an aspergillum, which looked like a wand with a ball at its end. He walked directly to Marfisa.

"You wish to be baptized as a Christian?"

"Yes, sir."

"Is there anyone here who will serve as her spiritual guide?" he asked.

"I will be her sponsor," said Bradamante.

"What will your Christian name be?" asked Turpin.

"My Christian mother named me Marfisa. No need to change."

The archbishop raised the wand and shook water droplets at Marfisa's face. "I baptize thee, Marfisa, *in nomine Patris et Filii et Spiritus Sancti.*" He then drew a cross on her forehead with the drops of water. A single tear fell down Marfisa's cheek.

Audulf appeared and made a gesture for Charlemagne to speak with him in a corner. The two men spoke in hushed tones. The emperor nodded and returned to the ceremony while the seneschal left the tent.

"Before we begin the oath of fealty," Archbishop Turpin said to Marfisa, "I must first know where you are from."

Marfisa looked confused. She turned to Bradamante. "What is he asking?"

"Tell him that you are Marfisa from the Duchy of Reggio Calabria."

A look of relief washed over the warrior queen's face and she answered the archbishop.

"Please kneel and repeat after me," he said. "I, Marfisa of the Duchy of Reggio Calabria..."

"I, Marfisa of the Duchy of Reggio Calabria..."

"Pledge my life, my honor, and my sword to protect and defend Charlemagne, his rightful heirs, and the laws and customs of the faith and the crown, so help me God."

"Pledge my life, my honor, and my sword to protect and defend Charlemagne, his rightful heirs, and the laws and customs of the faith and the crown, so help me God," Marfisa repeated.

"Rise and be recognized as a sworn warrior in my army," said Charlemagne.

Marfisa stood and looked up to the emperor.

"I have heard tales of your bravery on the battlefield and you will share command duties with Bradamante for now," he said. "Once this war is over, I will endeavor to find a suitable post as a reward for your talents. You and Bradamante are dismissed."

Manfred stepped forward. "I will show you ladies to your tent."

A small crowd had gathered outside. As soon as Bradamante walked out into the night air her twin brother Richardet hugged her.

"Sister! I am glad you returned. So much has happened to me since I last saw you. You should call me Richard from now on since I am a man," he paused. "I killed Neron."

There was a fierce look in his eyes she had never seen before. She almost mentioned avenging Fiordespina's death by defeating Rodomont, but she held back because she wanted him to savor this moment of glory.

"I am glad to hear that serpent is dead, Richard," she said.

Vivien and Maugis stepped forward.

"My savior has returned," said Vivien, as he kissed Marfisa's hand. "What a glorious day this is."

Bradamante remembered the remarks Vivien made about wanting to bed Marfisa, and decided to warn her new friend about her kinsman's intentions. Four more soldiers stepped forward. Bradamante recognized Oliver's sons, Aquilant and Grifon, but she did not know the other two men. Marfisa laughed and embraced each of them.

Aquilant grinned. "I am looking forward to once again fighting alongside the fierce Queen Marfisa."

Marfisa smiled. She took several more accolades from Grifon before she turned her attention to a young black-haired soldier. "Guidone, I see you have found your brothers."

"I did," he said, with a voice just above a whisper.

"You have a sister as well," said Marfisa. "Here, Bradamante, this is Guidone Selvaggio. He is a brother of yours."

Bradamante thought she misheard Marfisa and did not understand what was meant at first.

"I am pleased to meet you, Lady Bradamante," Guidone said in a loud voice, before he hushed Marfisa. "Keep your voice down. My mother's reputation is at risk. I told you my story in secret."

"Secret? You said nothing about it being a secret," said Marfisa, sounding upset.

"How was I to know you would join the Frankish army? I swore Aquilant, Grifon, and Sansonetto to secrecy, as well as my new found brothers."

Richard, Alard, and Guichard came forward and stood next to Guidone. It was then that Bradamante saw the familial resemblance across the four men's faces. She felt sick and wanted to leave. No one laughed at her, but she felt as if she was the object of a cruel joke.

"My mother is the Duchess of Reggio," Guidone said in an undertone. "The duke thinks she is a widow. My story must be kept quiet."

Marfisa's demeanor changed. She grabbed Bradamante by the hand as Marfisa brought her face inches from Guidone's. "Reggio? *She* is the Duchess of Reggio?" Guidone took a step back. "The woman you blamed for *your* mother's misfortune was *my* mother. You will never speak of my mother again," she hissed. "My parents were meant for each other. They married for love, not for a dowry or titles. If you want to blame anyone, blame my grandfather, Duke Rampaldo. He feared how his people would react to my father marrying a Muslim, so he betrayed your mother."

Marfisa then yanked Bradamante along as if she were a rag doll and walked away from them.

Bradamante called out to the chamberlain, "Sir Manfred, take us to our tent."

"Of course," he said. "Follow me."

Manfred led them down the row of tents and turned right. He walked down six more tents and then lifted the flap. "Here you are."

The tent was sparsely furnished with two sleeping rolls and two chairs at a small table covered with the same foods they had before. Manfred lit a small oil lamp casting a yellowish glow inside the tent.

Once the chamberlain left, Marfisa let loose a string of curses in Arabic. Bradamante felt certain she was fortunate to not understand what was being said. Marfisa was enraged, and it eclipsed Bradamante's own sense of betrayal by her father.

Bradamante began massaging the hand that had almost been crushed, when Marfisa turned and became apologetic.

"Forgive me," she said. "I needed your strength."

"How so?"

"I was afraid that my first act as a Christian would be to murder your brother Guidone for insulting my mother." Marfisa then gave a nervous laugh and looked at Bradamante's face. "I was happy to learn today that Ruggiero was my brother, but how are you feeling about Guidone?"

Tears of frustration began to well in Bradamante's eyes. "It is different. You learned of your parents and that an honorable man is your twin. You are no longer alone in the world; you have a family. Whereas, I learned that my father is a liar. He has long spoken about the sanctity of marriage, yet you showed me living proof that he violated his marital vows." She sat down, poured herself a goblet of wine, and took a long drink. "Richard tried telling me that a few weeks ago while we were arguing. I was angry with him because he bedded a maiden after deceiving her. He and Fiordespina were in love, but theirs was a forbidden love with no chance of marriage. It almost led to his death. Thankfully, Ruggiero saved Richard's life."

"What is this?" said Marfisa as she sat down.

"Ruggiero stopped Richard from being executed the day before you met them." Bradamante began picking at grapes on the table. "I confronted Richard about putting Fiordespina's life and reputation at risk, he tried distracting me from my anger at him by bringing up the rumors about our father. I refused to listen. Because I believed my father. I believed he lived up to the ideals he espoused. I was a fool."

"You were a dutiful daughter," said Marfisa. "You believed your father was a loyal husband."

"I would not allow any doubt to creep in, even after Richard told me how my parents' marriage was arranged. I should have allowed for the possibility of his infidelity. If I had, I would not feel as betrayed as I do."

"What did he tell you about your parents?" asked Marfisa.

Bradamante took another drink of wine. "Charlemagne never wanted my mother to marry. She was to enter a convent like his sister,

Gisele. My father was the fourth son of a nobleman and had little prospects for an advantageous marriage. Then he distinguished himself in battle and saved Charlemagne's life."

"Did Charlemagne offer his sister's hand in marriage then?"

"No, but there was a drunken celebration and Charlemagne asked my father what he wanted as a reward for his bravery. He expected a request for land, riches or a title. My father secured all of those for a lifetime when he asked to marry my mother. He was twenty-five, she was fourteen." Bradamante poured herself more wine. "My uncle felt as if he was tricked, but he agreed to the marriage. My parents had never met before their wedding day, so how could he have loved her? He could have grown to love her, but I do not feel that has happened."

She tore a piece of bread and began chewing. After swallowing Bradamante shook her head. "My father is not the honorable man I thought he was. My brother Renaud is weak when it comes to women. Charlemagne has had many wives and concubines. The only man I know who has shown honor toward women is Ruggiero. He has honor. Today I thought the worst of him, and the worst of you. I believed the rumor that you two were in love and to be married. I thought he had forsaken me, and I was filled with despair. I wanted to kill myself or..."

"Kill me?" asked Marfisa.

"Yes," Bradamante said with a nervous laugh.

"That means you love him."

Bradamante took one of Marfisa's hands in hers. "I want to thank you for being by his side and bringing him back to health. I am sorry for my actions towards you earlier. I was jealous and insecure, while you were kind and supportive to him. I wish he were here now. I want to be in his arms. Tonight. I do not want to wait any longer. I love him and want to take him as my husband. And yet, I cannot. You are the only one here who knows my heart. For my honor's sake I have to pretend that I barely know him and have only respect for him."

Bradamante stood and began pacing. "Men such as my father, my brother, and my king can be unfaithful to their wives and still be considered respectable noblemen, but I cannot be with an honorable man who loves me out of fear of ruining my reputation. It is unfair."

Marfisa stood and embraced Bradamante. This act of compassion allowed her to lower her guard.

"If I could bring this war to an end by killing Akramont, I would leave right now," Bradamante sobbed on Marfisa's shoulder. "All I want is to love Ruggiero, and love him openly."

After Bradamante had grown silent in the protective embrace her companion, Marfisa grabbed her by the shoulders and looked her straight in the eye. "Knowing your heart as I do now, had I killed you — I would have to take my own life. I wanted to kill anyone who dared challenge Ruggiero. I fought for his honor because I cared for him. I now know it was love behind your acts. I saw you and Ruggiero pledge your love to one another. In my eyes, and in God's eyes, you are married. I claim you as my kinswoman. From this day forth, you are my sister. There can be no other woman worthy of my brother's love, save you."

Renaud wondered what the seneschal said to Charlemagne and had to wait until Bradamante and Marfisa left the royal tent.

"Send in the messenger," Charlemagne commanded.

An elderly man entered the tent alone. He wore armor, but carried no weapons or shield. He carried himself with a dignified air and stopped a respectful distance away from the emperor.

"I present Governor Sabri of Algocco," said Audulf.

Sabri bowed his head. "I am here on behalf of my lord, Amir Akramont, commander of the Muslim Army from the Maghreb."

"It has been many years since I last saw you, Governor Sabri."

"Indeed it has."

"Are you here to discuss terms of surrender?"

A flicker of a smile crossed Sabri's face. "Not surrender. Instead, the amir wishes to offer our armies a way out of this impasse. We recognize that the winter snows are coming and that the return to your palace in Aachen will become more treacherous the longer you remain in Arles."

Charlemagne gave a small sniff. "Go on."

"Our men have harvested the crops in this area and we have adequate stockpiles to feed our men for months to come. However, we lost many men today, because we were lured outside the protective walls of Arles. Should you wish to continue this war, we can remain inside the city while your men starve."

"Are you proposing that we pick up and leave after today's victory?" scoffed Charlemagne.

"Akramont's forces control the cities of Arles, Narbonne, recently reclaimed Toulouse and the lands between them. That is but a small portion of your vast empire. Amir Akramont recognizes that the number of lives lost on both sides has been a tragedy. He feels that to continue sacrificing the lives of soldiers for a small expanse of land may lead to a Pyrrhic victory."

"What does he propose?"

"An end to this war by using the age-old custom of two champions in a duel to determine the outcome."

"A fight to the death?"

"A fight to the death," Sabri repeated. "The victory will determine who will control the area conquered by Muslim forces."

"And what would happen should your champion lose?" asked Charlemagne.

"Amir Akramont will withdraw all of his forces and return to the Maghreb."

"I would need assurances there will not be repeat attempts at aggression in the future. I would require hostages to ensure compliance. Preferably family members."

"That is a matter for negotiation once we settle on terms of engagement."

"I must confer with my advisors," said Charlemagne. "Please return to the small tent to await my decision."

Sabri bowed and left.

Charlemagne called over Archbishop Turpin, Duke Namo, Ogier, and Renaud. "What are your thoughts?"

"This is fortunate," said Namo. "If this war ends on the morrow, we can devote our attention and forces into crushing the Saxon rebellion."

"The proposed duel would save many lives," said Archbishop Turpin.

"It would be an honor to serve as your champion," said Ogier, bowing his head.

Charlemagne smiled and nodded. "What say you, Renaud?"

"We should take Akramont up on his offer, but I insist on being your champion. Ogier would be a fine choice, but he is not a kinsman of yours. This honor should go to one who shares your blood. No doubt that if Orlando were here, he would be your favorite. I ask in his absence, that you consider me as a worthy second choice."

"Four of my paladins agree on something," said Charlemagne. "It is likely a gathering of all twelve would be the same. We shall agree to this duel and the Count of Montauban will be our champion." He turned to Renaud. "Do you have any preferences?"

"I do. It is likely that I will be fighting Gradasso," said Renaud. "He had Orlando's sword, Durindana, and my horse, Bayard. No doubt that he is eager to prove that he is the most powerful warrior in the world. I wish to level the playing field on him. I insist we fight on foot, armed only with a battle axe, a shield, and a dagger."

"Let us decide on the rest of our demands before we begin negotiations with Governor Sabri," said Charlemagne.

After several goblets of wine and Marfisa's companionship, Bradamante calmed down. She was still hurt about learning her father had sired a bastard, but could do nothing to change that truth. Perhaps he regretted his infidelity, but regrets do not absolve past indiscretions.

Marfisa explained how she had met Guidone Selvaggio. Once Renaud and Orlando were called back to the Frankish Empire, she decided to follow. The promised war between Akramont and Charlemagne sounded more exciting to her than the one in Cathay. Marfisa traveled westward with Grifon and Aquilant and had many adventures on the journey. Along the way, Sansonetto and Guidone Selvaggio joined them. After arriving in Francia, she parted ways with the foursome as she sought out Akramont's army.

Bradamante discovered that she enjoyed being in Marfisa's company. It was the first time she had ever felt she had a peer. Even though Marfisa had been raised as a slave and Bradamante had been raised as a noble, their commonalities of being women warriors in a sea of men gave them a strong bond.

Marfisa took another drink of wine. "I had no idea when Guidone complained about how unfair life had been to his mother that he blamed my own mother. Fie! I will beat him senseless if he ever dares speak another word about my mother."

Bradamante found it ironic that her father had bedded the same woman who was to have been wedded to Ruggiero's father. She knew little about Guidone's mother, but did not care to learn more. Instead, she wanted to know about Marfisa and Ruggiero's mother.

"Tell me more of what Atallah said," said Bradamante. "Any tale of a woman warrior is something I wish to hear."

Marfisa gave a wide smile and hugged herself. "She was born on the island of Feminoro."

A group of rowdy soldiers began singing outside. Their sound grew louder as more voices joined.

"Is that normal?" asked Marfisa.

"There are some nights when a few soldiers get drunk, but this seems different."

Then the words "Renaud is our hero" rang out with clarity. It was repeated again and again. Bradamante stood up and walked out of the tent with Marfisa close behind. Revelers were everywhere. Men were dancing in the rows between the tents. Some were banging on drums. She looked desperately to find a familiar face when she finally spotted Ogier the Dane.

"Ogier! What is going on?" asked Bradamante.

"The war will be over tomorrow," he said raising a tankard and taking a celebratory drink. "Charlemagne agreed to settle the matter with a duel to the death. Renaud will serve as our champion. The war is as good as won. The fight is tomorrow morning in the old Circus Maximus."

"Who will be the champion for Akramont's forces?" she asked, fear growing in the pit of her stomach.

"Do not worry," he said, waving a hand dismissively. "Your brother will have no trouble. We were worried it might be Gradasso. Instead, Akramont chose a warrior I have never heard of before. Ruggiero Taz-eem of Mount Carena. By tomorrow night at this time, we shall be celebrating in the streets of Arles and the infidels will be on their way home."

Bradamante stumbled as she turned to make her way back into the tent. As soon as she stepped inside she began to hyperventilate.

"No. No. No. No," she said between gasps of air.

Marfisa shook her by the shoulders. "Control yourself."

"I should have begged him today," said Bradamante as tears welled up in her eyes. "It is my fault. He is going to die because I was not strong enough to make him see reason..."

"No," said Marfisa. "My brother will not die tomorrow."

"Then Renaud will die," wailed Bradamante.

"That will not happen either. I cannot allow you to lose a brother and I will not lose my brother," said Marfisa. "There must be a way to stop a tragedy befalling either of our families."

Bradamante finally caught her breath and met Marfisa's fierce gaze. "You are right. I gave into despair before. I cannot do that again. We must create our own destiny."

"How do we do that?"

"I know someone who can help us."

"Who?"

"Her name is Melissa. She is an enchantress who supports my marriage to Ruggiero. Melissa used her magical powers in the past to help him. She must come to his aid once again on the morrow."

Marfisa nodded. "How do we summon her?"

"I do not know," said Bradamante. "But my cousin, Maugis, will."

END OF VOLUME TWO

APPENDICES

Maps

Map of Europe, Africa and Asia

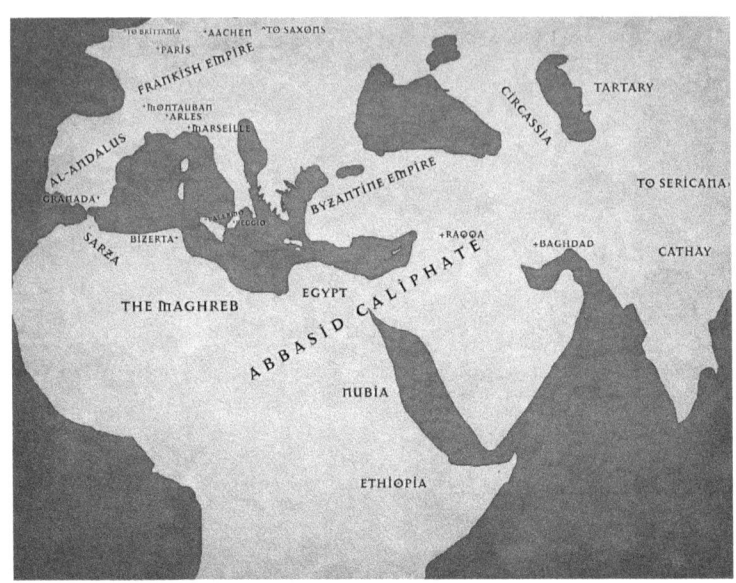

Map of the Frankish Empire

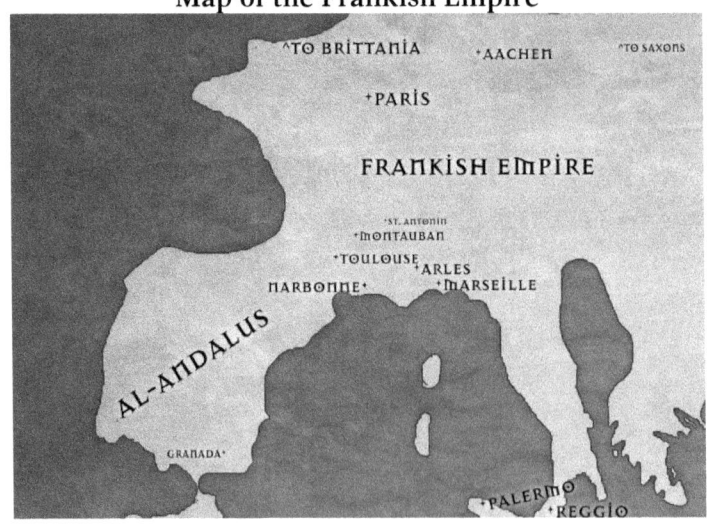

Map of Arles

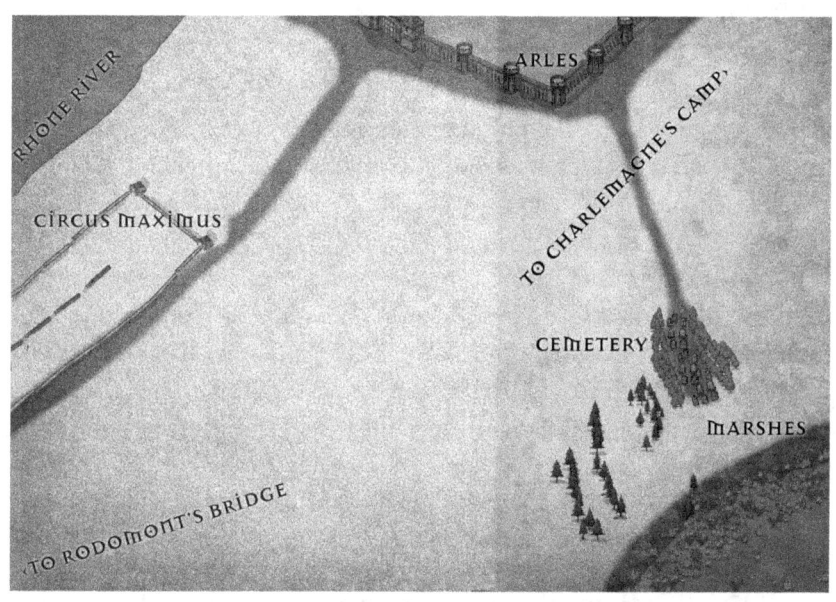

Map of Aistulf's Spiritual Journey Sites

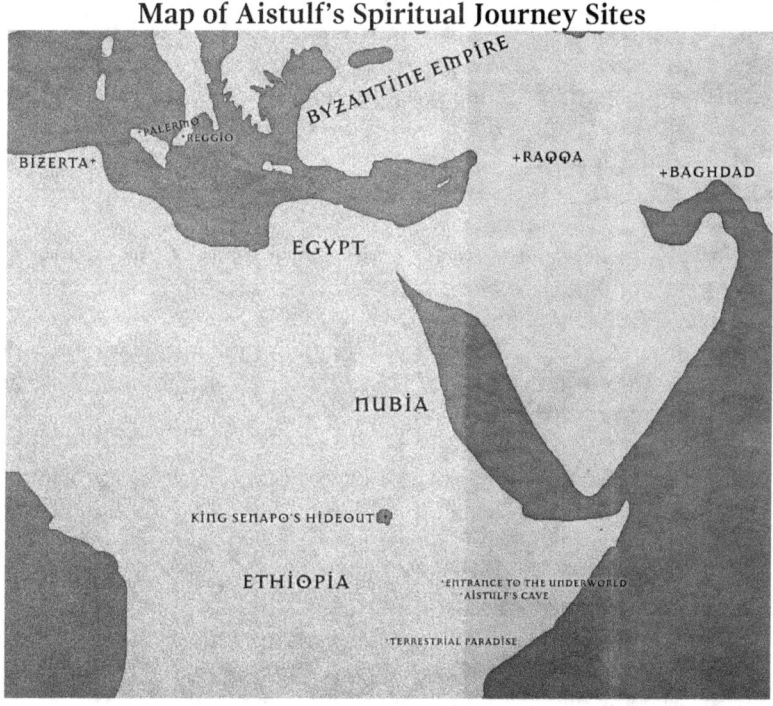

Alphabetical list of characters, locations, and story elements

Here are some aids to assist in remembering this large cast of characters, locations, and story elements. Included is also a pronunciation guide for character names. Like many words, there are variations and the reader should feel free to choose whichever pronunciation she or he prefers. The parentheses demonstrate the variety of names for these characters used by the poets Ariosto and Boiardo and some of the more popular versions used by various translators. There are also characters which are this author's invention to help assist in telling this grand adaptation and were not part of the original legends.

Aachen /AH ken/ Charlemagne's palace and cathedral were in this city. Also known as Aix la Chapelle in French.

Abbasid dynasty /ab BAH sid/ Ruling Islamic dynasty from the year 750 - 1258. Overthrew the previous Umayyad dynasty. Most famous ruler was Caliph Harun al-Rashid.

Abd al-Rahman /ahb dahl RAH mahn/ Historical figure. (731-788) Last remaining member of the Umayyad dynasty who escaped being executed along with his family. Sought refuge in Africa with Christians. Made his way to al-Andalus and founded a competing Muslim dynasty to the Abbasids.

Abdul /ahb DOOL/ Muslim soldier. Had been in Brunello's forces; became loyal to Rodomont.

Abu Nuwas /ah BOO NEW wahss/ Historical figure. (756 – 814) Poet and member of Caliph Harun al-Rashid's court. Mentioned in the tales of the Arabian Nights.

Agolant /ah go LAHNT/ (Agolante) Former Amir of the Maghreb. Father to Almont and Troiano. Grandfather to Akramont, Hala, and Daniso. Slain by Orlando.

Agrikhan /ah GRIH kahn/ (Agricane, Agrican) Asian warrior. King of Tartary, father of Mandricardo. Led siege in Cathay when Angelica refused to marry him. Killed by Orlando.

Agrismont /a griz MAHNT/ (Agrismonte) Castle owned by Duke Aymon's brother Beuve and guarded by his bastard son Aldigiero. Not far from the village of Saint Antonin.

Aistulf /AY stoolff/ (Astolfo) Christian warrior. One of twelve paladins of Charlemagne. Son of King Odo of Essex. Cousin to Orlando, Renaud, Alard, Guichard, Bradamante, Richardet, Vivien, Maugis, and

Aldigiero. Claimed the golden lance after Argalia's death. Jousted and beat Gradasso over ownership of Bayard. Had been lovers and then imprisoned by Alcina. Befriended Ruggiero after being liberated from Alcina's island. Freed Ruggiero and Bradamante from an enchanted castle. Gave Rabican to Bradamante to care for while he took the hippogriff to the skies.

Akramont /ah KRAH mahnt/ (Agramant, Agramante) Amir of the Maghreb (North Africa). His palace is in Bizerta, Tunisia. Commander of Muslim forces in the invasion of the Frankish Empire. Son of Amir Troiano. Grandson of Amir Agolant. Nephew to Almont. Descendant of Alexander the Great. Married to Alia and Anika. Brother to Hala. Cousin to Daniso.

al-Andalus /al ANDA loose/ Muslim name for the area that is now modern day Spain. The name in Latin was Hispania. Historical maps from that period also refer to it as the Umayyad Emirate or the Emirate of Córdoba.

Alard /ah LARD/ (Alardo) Christian warrior. Third son of Duke Aymon and Beatrice. Brother to Renaud, Guichard, Bradamante, and Richardet. Nephew to Charlemagne. Cousin to Orlando, Aistulf, Vivien, Maugis, and Aldigier.

Alcina /al CHEE nah/ Evil sorceress. Had an island east of India and took many lovers. The turned them into trees, rocks or statues when she was through with them. Had been lovers of both Aistulf and Ruggiero. Logistilla was her counterbalance on the island. Both died.

Alda /ALL duh/ (Aude) Sister to Oliver. Betrothed to Orlando. Aunt to Aquilant and Grifon.

Aldigier /al DEE jee ay/ (Aldigiero) Bastard son of Beuve, caretaker for Agrismont. Half-brother to Vivien and Maugis. Cousin to Aistulf, Orlando, Renaud, Guichard, Alard, Bradamante and Richardet. Wounded in Saint Antonin.

Alceste /ALL sest/ Warrior who was loved and rejected by Lydia.

Alexander the Great /al eks AND durr/ Historical figure. (356 – 323 BCE) Born and raised in Macedonia, conquered most of the known world including Egypt, Persia and India.

Alia /ah LEE ah/ - wife of Akramont, daughter of Sabri. Cousin to Anika.

Almont /al MAHNT/ (Almonte) Deceased Muslim warrior. Became Amir of the Maghreb at the death of his father. Older brother to Troiano. Father to Daniso. Uncle to Akramont. Killed both Bernard of Lyon and Milon. Later slain by a young Orlando. Previous owner of Durindana and Brigliodoro.

Altaripa /al tah REE pah/ Castle in the Midi-Pyrenees controlled by the House of Maganza. Enemies of the House of Lyon. Pinabel had compelled Aquilant, Grifon, Guidone Selvaggio, and Sansonetto into his service.

Ansel /an SELL/ (Anselmo) Elderly Christian Count of Altaripa. House
of Maganza. Father of Pinabel and Bertolai. Enemies of the House of
Lyon.
Angelica /an JELL ih kah/ Muslim princess of Cathay. Loved and pursued by many men. She owned a powerful magical ring that nullified
enchantments. Daughter of King Galafron, sister to Argalia.
Anika /ah NEE kah/ Wife of Akramont, daughter of the late governor
of Garamanta. Cousin to Alia.
Aquilant /ah qui LAHNT/ (Aquilante) Christian knight. Son of Oliver,
brother to Grifon.
Arden Woods /ar DEN woods/ Forest where Angelica and Renaud
drank waters of opposing magical powers.
Argalia /ar GAH lee ah/ Son of King Galafron of Cathay. Brother to Angelica. Owned an enchanted golden lance. Killed by Feraguto.
Arles /ARL/ A city in Southern France on the banks of the Rhône River.
Many ancient Roman monuments still remain standing.
Armenia /arr MEE nee uh/ Region east of the Byzantine Empire and
north of Baghdad.
Astolfo /ah STOLE foh/ Duke of Spoleto. Discovered his wife was un-
faithful and set out with Giacondo to seek revenge by seducing other
men's wives. (Astolfo is also the prevalent name for the character of
Aistulf in the legends of Charlemagne.)
Atallah /a TAHL ah/ (Atlas, Atlante, Atlantes) – Sufi mystic who raised
Ruggiero from infancy on Mount Carena. Fiercely protective of him.
Athena /ah THEE nah/ Greek goddess of wisdom and victory.
Audulf /OH dulf/ Historical figure. Seneschal for Charlemagne. He led
an army against Bretons in 786.
Aveyron River – River that passes by the village of Saint Antonin.
Aymon /AY mohn/ Christian warrior. Duke of Dordogne. Fourth son
of Bernard of Lyon. Brother to King Odo of Essex, Beuve of Agris-
mont, and Milon. Married to Beatrice, sister of Charlemagne. Father
of Renaud, Alard, Guichard, Bradamante, and Richardet. Uncle to
Orlando, Aistulf, Algidiero, Vivien, and Maugis.
Aymon /AY mohn/ Infant son to Renaud and Clarice. Named after his
Grandfather the Duke of Dordogne.
Baghdad - /BAG dad/ City founded in 762 by Caliph al-Mansur of the
Abbasid dynasty.
Balisarda /bah li SAR duh/ Ruggiero's sword given to him by Brunello.
Bardulasto /bar dew LAH stow/ Muslim warrior. Governor of Alcazar.
Ambushed and tried to kill Ruggiero at the tournament on Mount
Carena. Slain by Ruggiero.
Basheer /bah SHEER/ Follower of Caliph Harun al-Rashid that spoke to
the assembled crowd in Bizerta.

Bayard /bay ARD/ (Bayardo) Enchanted horse owned by Renaud. Powerful, swift with near-human intelligence. Coveted by Gradasso.

Beatrice /BEE ah triss/ (Aya) wife of Duke Aymon. Mother to Renaud, Guichard, Alard, Bradamante, and Richardet. Sister to Charlemagne. Aunt to Orlando, Aistulf, Vivien, Maugis, and Aldigier.

Belle /bell/ Deceased wife of Pinabel. She had coerced Aquilant, Grifon, Sansonetto, and Guidone Selvaggio into serving her husband and being her lover. Killed by Mandricardo.

Beltramo /bell TRAHM moe/ Uncle to Ruggiero. Betrayed his father and brother causing their deaths in Reggio Calabria.

Bernard of Lyon /burr NARD of LEE ohn/ (Clairmont in the poems) Late Christian warrior. Father to Odo, Beuve, Milon, and Aymon. Killed by Almont.

Bernard /burr NARD/ eldest son of Renaud and Clarice. Named after Duke Aymon's father.

Bertha /BURR thah/ (Bertrada) Sister of Charlemagne. Eloped with Milon. Mother of Orlando. Bertha was also the name of Charlemagne's mother, who was known as Bertha of the Big Foot or Goosefoot.

Bertolai /burr TOE lie/ member of the house of Maganza. Son of Count Ansel. Brother to Pinabel. Offered to pay the ransom of Vivien and Maugis from Lanfusa. Enemies to the house of Lyon.

Beuve /BWEV/ (Buovo) Christian soldier and lord of Agrismont. Second son of Bernard of Lyon. Brother to Odo, Milon, and Aymon. Father to Maugis, Vivien, and has a bastard son Aldiger.

Bizerta /bih ZURR tah/ Home of Akramont's palace. Site of where his war council decided to invade Francia. City in modern day Tunisia.

Bradamante /brah dah MAHNT/ or /brah dah MAHN tay/ (Bradamant) Christian warrior. Daughter of Duke Aymon and Beatrice. Sister of Renaud, Guichard, Alard, and twin to Richardet. Niece of Charlemagne. Cousin to Orlando, Aistulf, Vivien, Maugis, and Aldigiero. Loved by Ruggiero.

Brandimart /bran DEE mart/ (Brandimarte, Florismart) Noble warrior who became Orlando's close friend. Paladin of Charlemagne. He had been kidnapped as a child, raised as a Muslim in Rocca Silvana. Baptized as a Christian by Orlando. Married to Flordelis. Son of King Manodante.

Brigliodoro /bree lee yah DOOR oh/ Orlando's renowned horse that was claimed by Mandricardo. Once belonged to Ahlmadi.

Brittania /brit ANN ee ah/ Island comprised of numerous kingdoms.

Brunello /BREW nell oh/ African thief who stole Angelica's ring. Akramont rewarded the theft by making Brunello the governor of Tingitana. The ring allowed the enchanted castle on Mount Carena that hid Ruggiero to be revealed. Brunello gave Ruggiero his sword and Frontino.

Bruniquel /BREW nih kell/ Hilltop village on the Aveyron River where Richardet, Vivien, Maugis, Aldigier, and Hippalca spent the night after the rescue in Saint Antonin.

Bucephalus /BEW seff ah luss/ Alexander the Great's famed horse.

Bucifar /BOO siff far/ Muslim leader who was left in charge of Akramont's city of Bizerta while the amir was waging war in the Frankish Empire.

Calabria /kah lah BREE ah/ Region on the toe of the Italian peninsula.

Carloman /CAR lo man/ Historical figure. (751-771). Younger brother to Charlemagne, son of Pepin the Short. Inherited half of his father's kingdom along with his brother. Carloman's untimely death led Charlemagne to become king of all the Franks.

Carthage /KAR thij/

Cathay /CATH ay/ Kingdom in the east ruled by Angelica's father, King Galafron.

Caesar /SEE zer/ Historical figure. (100-44 BCE) Roman politician and military general.

Cerebus /SAIR uh buss/ Three headed dog guarding the gates of the Underworld in Greek mythology.

Charlemagne /SHAR le mane/ Historical figure, (742-814). King Charles the Great of the Frankish Empire, Emperor of the Western Roman Empire. Son of Pepin the Short and Bertha. Grandson to Charles Martel. Brother to Carloman and Gisela. As a character in this story he is also brother to the fictional characters Beatrice and Bertha; uncle to their children: Orlando, Renaud, Guichard, Alard, Bradamante, and Richardet.

Charles Martel /charlz mar TELL/ Historical figure, (686-741) Grandfather to King Charles the Great. Father to King Pepin. Mayor of the Palace. Repulsed invasion of Saracens at the Battle of Poitiers (Tours) in 732. Also known as Charles the Hammer.

Charon /KAIR on/ Ferryman on the River Styx bringing dead souls into the Underworld of Greek mythology.

Circassia /SER cahss ee ah/ Kingdom in Asia near the Black Sea, ruled by Sacripant.

Clarice /clah REESE/ Wife of Renaud. Mother to his sons, Bernard and Aymon.

Constantine /CON stan teen/ Historical figure. Son of Empress Irene and Leo IV. Emperor of the Byzantine Empire. Complicated ruling relationship with his mother.

Constantinople /CON stan tin oh pull/ Capital of the Byzantine Empire.

Costanza /COH stan zah/ (Gostanza) Mother of Guidone Selvaggio, later known as Valentina.

Coptic Christians /KOP tik KRISS chenz/ Christians in Africa developed a regional identity of Christianity separate from the Orthodox/Byzantine branch or the Catholic/Roman branch.

Cordes /cord/ A mountaintop village in the Midi-Pyrenees. The modern name is Cordes-sur-Ciel. It dates back to the 13th century, which is technically outside the time frame of this story, but it is situated in an area where a village is needed.

Daniforte /DAN ih fort/ Muslim warrior. Tried to stop Ruggiero from defending Bradamante. Killed.

Daniso /duh NEE so/ (Dardinello) – Deceased Muslim warrior. Governor of Zumara. Son of Almont. Nephew to Troiano. Grandson of Agolant. Cousin to Akramont and Hala.

Darius III/duh RIE uss/ Historical figure. (380-330 BCE) King of Persia defeated by Alexander the Great.

Deimos /DAY mohs/ Atallah's horse given to Ruggiero. Magical steed.

Devante /deh VAHNT/- Dwarf sent by Doralice to seek help by Rodomont.

Doralice /DOR ah leese/ or /door ah LEE chay/ Daughter of Governor Stordilano of Granada. Famed beauty betrothed to Rodomont. Abducted by and then married to Mandricardo.

Dordogne /DOR doh nya/ River and region in Southwest France. Duke Aymon is the Duke of Dordogne.

Durindana /dur in DAH nah/ Sword once owned by Hector of Troy. Thought to be the finest sword next to King Arthur's Excalibur. Owned by Orlando and coveted by Gradasso and Mandricardo. Orlando set aside the sword in *Quest of the Warrior Maiden* before his duel with Mandricardo. Orlando then went mad and Mandricardo claimed the abandoned sword.

Einhard /INE hard/ (775-840) Historical figure and member of Charlemagne's court. Wrote the biography *The Life of Charlemagne.*

Elijah /el EYE zhah/ Prophet from the Old Testament who was to have been taken to Heaven in a chariot of fire.

Emile /eh MEEL/ Squire for Renaud. Son of Guy, Duke of Burgundy.

Emirate of Córdoba (Hispania, al-Andalus) Area that is modern day Spain is shown on maps from Charlemagne's period refer as the Umayyad Emirate or the Emirate of Córdoba. The name in Latin was Hispania.

Eos /AY ohss/ Bradamante's pure white mare. Had been a gift from Charlemagne. Stolen by Pinabel after he tricked Bradamante into falling into a deep cave and left her for dead. Bradamante reclaimed the horse and killed Pinabel.

Erinyes /air RIHN eez/ Also known as the Avenging Furies. Three sisters who were avenging goddesses in Greek mythology. They tormented the living and the dead who had committed acts of evil.

Essex /ESS eks/ Kingdom in Brittania ruled by King Odo. Aistulf is the heir to the throne.

Ethiopia /ee thee OH pee ah/ Kingdom in Africa ruled by King Senapo.

Falerina /fa ler EE nah/ Evil fairy who was featured in adventures in the epic poem *Orlando innamorato*.

Fana / FAH nah/ Consort to King Senapo of Ethiopia. Died in childbirth.

Feraguto /fare uh GOO toh/ (Feragu, Ferraù) – Muslim soldier, son of Lanfusa, nephew to Amir Marsilio of al-Andalus. Killed Argalia.

Feminoro /FEM ih norr oh/ Magical island in the Mediterranean Sea populated with warrior women.

Ferrand /fair AHND/ Christian innkeeper near Arles.

Fidelia /fih DELL ee ah/ attendant to Doralice of Granada.

Fiordespina /fee OR de spee nah/ Daughter of Marsilio, the amir of al-Andalus. Sister to Matalista. Stepdaughter to Rosenda. Cousin to Feraguto. Lover of Richardet, friend to Bradamante.

Flamberge – (Floberge, Flamborge, Fusberta) Renaud's sword.

Flordelis /FLOR deh lee/ (Fiordigli, Fiordalisa) Wife of Brandimart. She was the daughter of the king and queen of Liza in Armernia and kidnapped as a small child. She was raised in the castle of Rocca Silvana.

Foix /FWA/ City near the Pyrenees Mountains. Atallah had created an enchanted castle that imprisoned Ruggiero along with knights and ladies. Bradamante liberated them.

Francia /FRAN see ah/ Name used for the lands ruled by Charlemagne.

Frankish Empire /FRANK ish/ Another name for Francia.

François /fran SWAH/ A son of the innkeeper near Arles.

Frontalatte /frahn tah LAH tay/ Sacripante's horse. Stolen from him in Cathay.

Frontino /frahn TEE noh/ Ruggiero's horse given to him by Brunello. Stolen by Rodomont near the village of Saint Antonin.

Galafron /GAL uh frahn/ King of Cathay. Father to Argalia and Angelica.

Galen /GAY len/ Monk from the abbey in Saint Antonin. Taught Greek to Bradamante.

Ganelon /GAN eh lon/ Count in the house of Maganza. Christian warrior, but enemy to the house of Lyon.

Galiziella /gal ee zee ELL ah/ (Galaciella, Galaziella) Wife of Ruggiero II, mother to Ruggiero III. Muslim warrior who converted to Christianity before marriage. Escaped the pillage of Reggio Calabria in small boat after her husband's murder. Landed on Libyan shores and died as she gave birth.

Gaston /GAA stohn/ Christian footsoldier from Bordeaux who was forced to work as a servant to the Muslim army in Arles.

Geoffroi /JEFF wah/ Christian knight. Count of Foix. Died in Marseille.

Giacondo /jih CON doh/ Roman man who discovered his wife was unfaithful. Sought revenge with another cuckholded husbank, Astolfo, Duke of Spoleto, by seducing a multitude of wives who were thought to be virtuous.

Gisela /jih ZELL uh/ Historical figure. (757-810) Gisela was the only sister to the historical Charlemagne. She never married and entered a convent, became Abbess of Chelles.

Gloriosa /glore ee OH sah/ Marfisa's mare.

Gradasso /grah DAH soh/ Asian warrior. King of Sericana. Obsessed with obtaining Bayard and Durindana. Invaded the Iberian Peninsula with one hundred and fifty thousand troops to obtain those items. Briefly held King Charles as prisoner, humiliated by Aistulf.

Grandonio /gran DOH nee oh/ North African Muslim. Governor of Morocco. Commander of the Muslim forces in Arles.

Grifon /GRIFF ohn/ (Grifone) Christian knight. Son of Oliver, brother to Aquilant.

Guichard /GWEE shard/ (Guicciardo) Christian knight. Second son of Duke Aymon and Beatrice. Brother to Renaud, Bradamante, and Richardet. Cousin to Orlando, Aistulf, Vivien, Maugis, and Aldigiero.

Guidone Selvaggio /GWEE dohn sel VAJJ ee oh/ Christian knight from the south of Italy. Travels with Aquilant, Grifon, and Sansonetto. Forced to serve Pinabel at Altaripa.

Guy /GHEE/ Christian Knight. Duke of Burgundy. Paladin of Charlemagne. Stationed in Marseille. Had been co-commander with Bradamante.

Hala /HAH lah/ Sister to Amir Akramont. Daughter of the late Amir Troiano. Granddaughter to the late Amir Agolant. Niece of the late Almont. Cousin of Daniso. Descended from Alexander the Great.

Hamad /HAH mahd/ North African soldier who serves Grandonio, the governor of Morocco. Becomes loyal to Rodomont.

Harpies /HAR peez/ Grotesque creatures from Greek mythology with the head and breasts of women and bodies of vultures.

Harun al-Rashid /ha ROON ahl RAH sheed/ Historical figure. (763-809) Fifth and most famous caliph of the Abbasid dynasty. Featured in the stories of 1001 Arabian Nights.

Heaven – The ultimate destination for devout Christians and Muslims.

Hector /heck TOR/ Acclaimed warrior of the legendary city of Troy. Noble ancestor to Ruggiero. Suit of armor worn by Mandricardo. Original owner of Durindana.

Hell – The destination for dead souls who are damned for their sins.

Hippalca /hip PALL kah/ Handmaid and confidante to Bradamante.

Hispania /hiss SPAHN ee ah/ The Latin name for Spain. The Muslim name for the area during the time of Charlemagne was al-Andalus. Historical maps from that period also refer to it as the Umayyad Emirate or the Emirate of Córdoba.

Iliad /ILL ee ed/ Epic poem written by Homer about the war between the Kingdom of Troy and the Greeks trying to reclaim Helen of Troy as being the queen of Sparta.

Irene /I reen/ Historical figure. (752 - 803) Empress of the Byzantine Empire. Married Leo IV. Mother to Constantine VI. Regent for her son after the death of her husband.

Isaac /I zick/ Historical figure. (? –after 802?) Jewish man sent on a mission with Lantfrid and Sigimund from Charlemagne to Caliph Harun al-Rashid.

Jacques /ZHAHQ/ A son of the innkeeper near Arles.

Jafar /JAH far/ Historical figure. (767-803) Close advisor and companion of Harun al-Rashid.

Jamar /jah MAR/ A young Muslim soldier with a baby-face who served Rodomont.

Kahina, Queen of the Berbers /kah HEE nah/ Historical figure. (??- 703) Queen of the Berbers and led the resistance to the Arab army that conquered Northern Africa.

Kamal /kah MAHL/ Name Ruggiero gave to the hippogriff.

Lanfusa /lan FOO sah/ Muslim noblewoman. Sister to Amir Marsilio. Mother of Feraguto. Held Vivien and Maugis hostage.

Lantfrid /LANT er frid/ Historical figure. (?-801?) Sent on a mission with Isaac and Sigimund from Charlemagne to Caliph Harun al-Rashid.

Lethe /LEETH/ Magical river of forgetfulness in Greek mythology. Alcina tricked Ruggiero into drinking of those magical waters and forgetting his life and sense of honor.

Liza /LEE zah/ Small kingdom in Armenia. Flordelis was the daughter of the king and queen and was kidnapped as a small child.

Logistilla /LOH ji still ah/ Good sorceress who opposed Alcina. They resided on opposite ends of the same island. Died at the same time Alcina did. Gave magical horn and book to Aistulf.

Lydia /LID ee ah/ Guide to Aistulf in the Underworld. Condemned to Hell for cruelly rejecting the love of Alceste.

Lyon house /LEE ohn/ The house of Bernard of Lyon, blood enemies to the house of Maganza. (Originally house of Clairmont.)

Maganza house /mah GAHN zah/ Wealthy Christian warriors. Longstanding blood feud with the Lyon house. A few of its members are Ansel, Bertolai, Ganelon, and Pinabel.

Maghreb /MAH greb/ Name used by Muslims to describe North Africa.

Malia /mah LEE ah/ Queen of Ethiopia, married to King Senapo. Had been princess of the kingdom of Nubia. Died of a broken heart.

Mambrino /mam BREE noh/ Famed Muslim warrior who was killed by Renaud in previous legends. He had owned a charmed golden helmet, which is now worn proudly by Renaud.

Mandricardo /man drih CAR doh/ Asian warrior. Khan of Tartary, son of Agrican. Wears arms once belonging to Hector of Troy. Dueled with Orlando and claimed the sword Durindana when Orlando abandoned the duel due to madness. Killed the armed escorts of Doralice of Granada, abducted her, then seduced and married her. Fought with Rodomont over Doralice. Fought with Ruggiero over the silver eagle standard which they both bear. Fought with Marfisa over insulting her dignity. Fragile truces formed with Rodomont, Ruggiero and Marfisa at end of *Quest of the Warrior Maid.*

Manfred /MAN fred/ (Meginfrid, Meginfred) Historical figure. Chamberlain for Charlemagne.

Manodante /man oh DAHN tay/ King of the Islands Far Away and father to Brandimart.

Marfisa /mar FEE sah/ Muslim warrior queen from the East. She besieged Angelica at Albraca.

Maria Antonia /mah REE ah an TOE nee ah/ Name that Costanza of Palermo was given when she was entered in a convent in Reggio.

Marseille /MAR say/ City on the Mediterranean coast. Bradamante led its defense alongside Guy, Duke of Burgundy.

Marsilio /mar SEE lee oh/ (Marsil, Marsilies, Marsilione) Amir of al-Andalus. Muslim. Ally of Akramont's invasion of Francia. Father of Matalista and Fiordespina. Married to Rosenda. Brother to Lanfusa. Uncle to Feraguto.

Masrur the eunuch /MAS roor/ One of Caliph Harun al-Rashid's loyal companions in the tales of the Arabian nights.

Massif Central /mah SEEF sen trahl/

Matalista /ma tah LEE stah/ Muslim warrior. Son of Amir Marsilio of al-Andalus. Brother to Fiordespina. Cousin to Feraguto.

Maugis /MOE zhee/ (Malagigi) Wizard. Christian warrior. Paladin of Charlemagne. Son of Beuve. Brother to Vivien. Half brother to Aldigiero. Cousin to Aistulf, Orlando, Renaud, Guichard, Alard, Bradamante, and Richardet. Had been held hostage with Vivien by Lanfusa. Rescued by Ruggiero, Marfisa, Richardet, and Aldigier.

Mecca /MEK ah/ Holiest city of Islam. Prayers are done facing the direction of Mecca.

Melissa /meh LISS uh/ Enchantress who uses her magic on behalf of Bradamante and Ruggiero.

Merlin's cave /MERR linn/ Cave near Foix where Bradamante was given the call to adventure by Melissa to rescue and marry Ruggiero.

Milon /mee LOHN/ (Melone, Milone) Christian warrior. Third son of Bernard of Lyon. Brother to Odo, Beuve and Aymon. Eloped with Bertha, the sister of King Charles. Lived in exile with Bertha in Sutri, Italy. Father of Orlando. Died in battle when Orlando was a small boy. Killed by Almont.

Mnemosyne /NEM oh seen/ Titaness from Greek Mythology. Goddess of memory. Mother to the Nine Muses who were fathered by Zeus sleeping with Mnemosyne nine nights in a row. A spring or river is named after her that restores or enhances memory. Melissa gave Ruggiero these waters to restore his memory.

Montauban /MOHN toh bohn/ (Montalbano) the ancestral home to Bradamante and her brothers. Renaud is now the Count of Montauban. The real city in France was founded in the twelfth century, but this location could not be changed for sake of historical accuracy because Renaud de Montauban is a strong part of the legends.

Morgana /more GAH nah/ Evil fairy featured in the epic poem *Orlando innamorato*.

Mount Carena /mount cah RAY nuh/ Mountain where Atallah raised Ruggiero. Somewhere in Tunisia

Muhammad, Prophet /mu HAH med/ Historical figure and founder of Islam. (570-632). His revelations were chronicled and later compiled into the Quran.

Namo /NAH moh/ Christian warrior. Duke of Bavaria, paladin and counselor to Charlemagne. Father of four sons.

Narbonne /NAR bun/ City in southern France near the Mediterranean Sea.

Neron /NAIR on/ Eunuch. Servant to Amir Marsilio.

Nikephoros /ni kee FORE ohss/ Bradamante's dappled gray gelding.

Nubia /NEW bee ah/ Kingdom in North Africa. South of Egypt and north of Ethiopia.

Odo /OH doh/ (Otto, Otone) Christian soldier. King of Essex. Married the maiden queen of Essex. Eldest son of Bernard of Lyon. Brother to Beuve, Milon, and Aymon. Father to Aistulf.

Odysseus /oh DISS ee us/ Greek hero of Homer's epic poems *The Iliad* and *The Odyssey*. He came up with the idea of the Trojan Horse which led to the sacking of Troy. King of Ithaca. His return to Greece after the end of the Trojan War took ten years. During that time he took both Circe and Calypso as lovers.

Ogier the Dane /OH zheer/ As a child he had been taken as a hostage when his father did not pay his tribute to Charlemagne. Grew up and became a paladin to Charlemagne.

Olibandro /oh li BAHN droh/ Asian warrior. Brother to King Sacripant of Circassia. Killed by Mandricardo.

Oliver /ah LIV er/ (Olivier, Oliviero) Christian warrior. Paladin of Charlemagne. Brother to Alda. Father to Aquilant and Grifon. Childhood friend of Orlando.

Orlando /or LAN doh/ (Roland) Christian soldier and paladin of Charlemagne. Son of Milon and Bertha. Nephew to Charlemagne. Count of Anglante. Cousin to Renaud, Guichard, Alard, Bradamante,

Richardet, Aistulf, Vivien, Maugis, and Aldigiero. Driven made by unrequited love from Angelica. Has enchanted skin that cannot be penetrated by any normal sword or weapon.

Palermo /pah LARE moh/ City in Sicily. Home of Roberto the painter, Costanza, and of puppet theatre celebrating the legends of Charlemagne.

Paris /PARE iss or PARE ee/ Large city in France. Gradasso conquered the city in his quest for Durindana and Bayard. Under siege by Akramont's army.

Pepin le Bref /PEP in leh BREFF/ Historical figure. (714-768) Father to Charlemagne, Carloman, and Gisela. Son of Charles Martel. Husband to Bertha. First king of the Carolingian dynasty starting in 751.

Persepolis /per SEPP oh liss/ Ancient capital city of Persia. Destroyed in 330 BCE by Alexander the Great.

Philip of Macedonia /FILL ipp/ Historical figure. (359 – 336 BCE) King of Macedonia and father to Alexander the Great.

Pinabel /PIN uh bell/ (Pinabello) Christian warrior. Knight in the house of Maganza. He is wealthy and treacherous. Tricked Bradamante into a cave and left her for dead. Coerced Aquilant, Grifon, Sansonetto, and Guidone Selvaggio of depriving knights and ladies of their wealth. Killed by Bradamante.

Placia /plah SEE ah/ Elderly female attendant to Fiordespina.

Pompey Magnus // Historical figure. (106 – 48 BCE) Renowned general and political leader of Rome. Allied with and later enemy to Julius Caesar.

Pont de bateaux /pahn deh bat OH/ Ancient bridge of boats used in Arles to span the Rhône River.

Purgatory /PURR gah tore ee/ A place where dead souls are sent to repent for their sins before they can be sent to Heaven.

Rabican /RAB ih can/ Magical horse capable of incredible speed and stamina. Won by Renaud after dueling with a giant. Given to Aistulf. Ruggiero rode this horse on Alcina's island. Aistulf gave this horse to Bradamante to care for while he set off for adventure on the back of the hippogriff.

Rampaldo /ram PAHL doh/ Duke of Reggio in Calabria. Father to Ruggiero II and Beltramo.

Raqqah /ROK ahh/ City in the Islamic Empire near the Byzantine Empire. Caliph Harun al-Rashid moved his court there from Baghdad to be nearer his enemy.

Reggio /rejj EE oh/ City on the toe of the Italian peninsula.

Renaud /reh NOH/ (Rinaldo, Ranaldo) Christian soldier. Paladin of Charlemagne. Count of Montauban. Eldest son of Duke Aymon and Beatrice. Esteemed warrior. Nephew to Charlemagne. Husband to Clarice. Brother to Guichard, Alard, Bradamante, and Richardet.

Father to Bernard and Aymon. Cousin to Orlando, Aistulf, Maugis, Vivien, and Aldigiero. Owns the coveted destrier Bayard.

Richardet/Richard /ree shar DAY/ /ree SHARD/ (Ricciardetto) Christian soldier. Fourth son of Duke Aymon and Beatrice. Nephew to Charlemagne. Brother to Renaud, Guichard, Alard, and twin to Bradamante. Loved Fiordespina.

Rhône River /RONE/ River outside of Arles that leads to the Mediterranean Sea.

Roana /roh AH nah/ Attendant to Doralice.

Roberto /roh BARE toe/ Painter hired to create a portrait of Bradamante.

Rocca Silvana /ROH kah seel VAH nah/ Castle where Brandimarte and Fiordigli were raised.

Rodomont /roh duh MAHNT/ (Rodamonte, Rodomonte) African soldier. Atheist. Governor of Sarza. Sworn to Akramont. Descendant of Nimrod. Owns enchanted dragon hide armor. Betrothed to Doralice of Granada. Hates Mandricardo and Ruggiero. Stole Frontino.

Rosenda /roh ZEN dah/ Second wife to Amir Marsilio. Stepmother to Fiordespina and Matalista. Mother to a small girl.

Ruggiero II /ruh JAIR oh/ Christian warrior. Son of Duke Rampaldo of Reggio. Brother to Beltramo. Husband to Galiziella. Father to Ruggiero III. Served King Charles as a knight. Betrayed by Beltramo and murdered during the North African army's attack on Reggio.

Ruggiero III /ruh JAIR oh/ Muslim warrior and descendant of Hector of Troy. Son of Ruggiero II and Galiziella. Raised on Mount Carena by wizard Atallah. Sworn to serve Amir Akramont. Loved by Bradamante.

Sabri /SAH bree/ (Sobrino) Devout Muslim. Elderly African Governor of Algocco. Serves as wazir to Amir Akramont, as he had done previously for Amir Troiano. He warned against invasion of Frankish Empire. Father to Alia.

Sacripant /sack rip PAHNT/ (Sacripante) Asian warrior. King of Circassia. In love with Angelica. Helped defend Cathay against Agrikhan's army. His brother Olibandro was killed by Mandricardo.

Saint Antonin /SAINT AN toh nin/ Climax of *Quest of the Warrior Maiden* took place here with numerous arguments between the warriors Mandricardo, Marfisa, Rodomont, and Ruggiero. Town on the Aveyron River in France. It dates back to the time of the Romans and had a monastery dedicated to the martyred Saint Antonin. Modern name is Saint-Antonin-Noble-Val.

Sansonetto /san soh NET oh/ Christian soldier coerced to fulfill harsh tributes of all knights and ladies to the castle Altaripa. Fought with Ruggiero. Companion of Aquilant, Grifon, and Guidone Selvaggio.

Seine River /SENN/ River in Paris.

Senapo /senn AH poh/ King of Ethiopia who was cursed for attempting to force his entry to Terrestrial Paradise.

Sericana /sair ih KAH nah/ Vast kingdom east of India ruled by Gradasso.

Sigimund /SIG ih mund/ Historical figure. (? – 801?) Sent on a mission with Isaac and Lantfrid from Charlemagne to Caliph Harun al-Rashid.

Sisyphus /siss UH fuss/ Clever man in Greek mythology who was punished for his crimes against the gods by having to push a large boulder to the top of a hill. It would slip before nearing the top and he would have to repeat this task indefinitely.

Stordilano /stor de LAH noh/ Muslim warrior. Governor of Granada who serves Marsilio, Amir of al-Andalus. Father to Doralice. Promised his daughter's hand in marriage to Rodomont.

Styx /stix/ Sacred river in the Underworld of Greek mythology.

Sword of Damocles /sord of dam oh CLEEZ/ A sword held aloft by a single horse's hair over the head of a ruler, denoting the ever present danger of being in power.

Tantalus /TAN tuh luss/ King in Greek mythology who was punished by being surrounded with succulent fruits and was standing in a river, but could not taste a drop of water or eat a bite of food.

Tartarus /TAR tar uss/ Deepest pit in Greek mythology's Underworld.

Tartary /TAR tar ee/ Kingdom in Asia north of India and east of Circassia. Ruled by Mandricardo.

Terrestrial Paradise /turr RESS tree ahl PARE uh diis/ A mythical place on earth that is close to Heaven.

Tingitana /tin ji TAHN ah/ Area of North Africa that Governor Brunello ruled.

Toulouse /TOO loos/ A city in southern France. Conquered by Akramont's army. Bradamante and Ruggiero met after the battle ended.

Troiano /troy AH noh/ Deceased African warrior. Son of Amir Agolant. Brother of Almont. Became amir at the death of his brother. Father of Akramont and Hala. Uncle to Daniso. Killed by Orlando.

Trojan War /TROH jun war/ War between the Kingdom of Troy and the Greeks over Helen of Sparta as described by Homer in the epic poem *The Iliad*.

Tunis /TOO niss/ City in North Africa south of Bizerta.

Tunisia /too NEE zha/ Amir Akramont was commander of this area as well as the Maghreb.

Turpin /TER pin/ Archbishop and paladin to Charlemagne.

Umayyad dynasty – First ruling Islamic dynasty (661-750). Overthrown by the Abbasid dynasty.

Underworld – In Greek mythology the place where dead souls go for eternity.

Valentina /val enn TEE nah/ Name that Costanza of Palermo used after the liberation of Reggio from Agolant's army.

Via Agrippa /VEE ah AH gripp ah/ Old Roman Road that connected Arles to Lyon.

Visigoths /VIZZ ih goths/ Nomadic tribes that conquered Hispania and sacked Rome. Their rule in Hispania was ended by the Muslim army in 711.

Visigothic eagle pendant /VIZZ ih goth ik/ A gift from Fiordespina to Bradamante.

Vivien /VIV ee ahn/ (Viviano) Christian warrior. Son of Beuve. Brother to Maugis, half brother to Aldigiero. Cousin to Aistulf, Orlando, Renaud, Guichard, Alard, Bradamante and Richardet. Had been held hostage with Maugis by Lanfusa. Rescued by Ruggiero, Marfisa, Richardet, and Aldigier.

Index of useful terms

aspergillum – Tool used to sprinkle holy water in religious ceremonies.

As-salaam-alaikum – greeting used by Muslims meaning "peace be with you."

Bible – sacred text for Christians.

bismillah /bis MILL ah/ – Term meaning "in the name of Allah." It is used to begin ceremonial cleansing ceremonies for Muslims.

caliph /KAH leef/ - Spiritual leader of the Islamic empire.

chamberlain – servant of a noble.

Commander of the Faithful – term used to denote the spiritual leadership of caliphs.

Contravallation – a series of defensive walls surrounding another set of fortifications.

crenellations – upright projections at the top of fortifications that resemble teeth.

cuirass /kwa RAHS/ Armor with a front and back plate.

destrier – a warhorse.

divination – an attempt to determine future events by using magic.

dolium – a large clay vessel used to transport liquid. (Plural is dolia).

enchantress – a woman using magic for benevolent reasons.

fenestral – style of window made with fabric rather than glass.

gambeson – heavy quilted garment worn under armor.

ghusl – /GOO suhl/ Ceremonial preparing of the dead for burial according to Islamic custom.

Hajj – Holy pilgrimage to Mecca.

halal – meat that has been slaughtered according to Islamic law.

hauberk /HAW berk/ mail armor, usually extending to the knees.

heartsease – a small flower that resembles violets and pansies. Used medicinally to treat heart ailments.

hippogriff – a mythological creature born of the mating of a mare with a griffin. The front half is an eagle, the back half is the hindlegs of a horse.

iftar- meal eaten after sunset by Muslims during the month of Ramadan

inshallah /in sha ALLAH/ –Islamic term that means "if Allah wills it" and is similar to the Christian "God willing" phrase.

jinn – malevolent spirit in Islamic tradition

kosher – food that is in accordance with Judaic law.

ma'a salama – "peace be with you" as a way of saying goodbye in Arabic.

muezzin – man who sings the call to prayer in the Islamic faith.

Muslim – a follower of the Prophet Muhammad and the Quran.

paladins – twelve knights of Charlemagne who were considered his "peers." They were regarded with great honor and distinction.

palfrey – a light riding horse, generally associated with women.

parapet – a walkway at the top of ramparts that are part of a fortification built to protect a city or castle

peristylium – enclosed garden in Roman villas.

prophecy – prediction of future events.

Quran – sacred book for Islam, collected revelations of the Prophet Muhammad. Believed to be the word of God delivered to him by the archangel Gabriel.

rakats – prescribed movements and recitations of words during prayers by Muslims

Ramadan – holiest month in the Islamic calendar. Fasting is performed by healthy adults from sunrise to sunset.

ramparts – part of fortifications built around a city, castle, or military camp.

Saracen – archaic term used to describe Arabic people who were not Jews. It dates back to Biblical times with Abraham's children of Hagar as being not "of Sara." In the medieval period it became a term used by Christians to describe Muslims.

scrying – a method of divination using water, crystal balls, or other reflective surfaces.

seneschal – servant of a noble family that oversees running the household, but is higher in rank to the chamberlain.

sorceress – a woman using magic for selfish or evil reasons.

Sufi mystic – Sufism is a mystical expression of Islam. A mystic is one with magical powers.

suhoor – morning feast prior to sunrise during Ramandan.

trenches

ummah – term for the collective Islamic faithful.

ustadh – a title of respect given to Muslim teachers.

Wa-alaikum-salaam– response to the greeting *As-salaam-alaikum*. "And unto you peace."

wazir – Islamic term for advisor.

wizard – a male practitioner of magic.

wudu – ceremonial cleansing by Muslims before prayers.

vallation –ramparts surrounding a military camp.

Author notes and acknowledgments

For my readers who take the time to read these notes, I want thank you for wanting insight into my writing process. However, I want to issue a warning that if you haven't finished reading the story, there might be spoilers.

This is the second installment in a trilogy. My intent in writing this book was to include enough detail that it could be considered a "stand alone" book for those who may not have read volume one. I would recommend for those who haven't read *Quest of the Warrior Maiden* to do so. You will gain a deeper appreciation of this grand tale. Reading a short narrative summary about how Bradamante and Ruggiero met and fell in love is not as satisfying as reading the actual scene.

That is how I felt when I was introduced to this genre by reading Ludovico Ariosto's masterpiece *Orlando furioso*. I was drawn to the love story of Bradamante and Ruggiero more than any other storyline in that epic poem. However, that poem did not include how they met each other. I had to read Matteo Maria Boiardo's *Orlando innamorato* for that satisfaction. It was out of sequence, but I finally got the answers to my questions as to how they met.

My dedication to Bradamante and Ruggiero's love story led me to become one in a long line of storytellers of the legends of Charlemagne. The Carolingian legend cycle was popularized in the south of France and in the north of Italy by troubadours, jongleurs, and poets. These tales entertained the masses and the nobles for several centuries. They began in the oral tradition and were later written down for posterity. These chivalric legends are still popular on the island of Sicily where they are kept alive through puppet theater.

I learned enough French to perform research trips in France. I found my way around museums, historical sites, and I asked questions. The hardest part for me was understanding replies if spoken in French and not in Franglais. I will readily admit that my grasp of the Italian language is less than that of my French.

I cannot read and understand any of the legends of Charlemagne written in French or Italian. Therefore I depend upon the scholarship of those who translate these stories into English. I am grateful to the following individuals who have done this work for me: Charles Stanley

Ross for translating *Orlando innamorato,* Barbara Reynolds and Guido Waldman for translating *Orlando furioso,* and Michael Newth's translation of *Chanson d'Aspremont.* I would like to mention my specific gratitude to Professor Gloria Allaire for generously sharing with me her notes translating Andrea da Barberino's *L'Aspramonte.* This helped me understand how Ruggiero's parents met, fell in love, and their tragic deaths. More than anything, I wanted to know that origin story and to include it in this volume. There was one tidbit included in her notes about Galiziella being given the name Gostanza (Costanza) as a Christian name. That rang bells with me because it was the name of Guidone Selvaggio's mother, but she was supposed to be from the Black Sea. I became inspired to overlay Costanza's story with Galiziella's to create another layer of conflict and irony.

Eleanora Stoppino's book *Genealogies of Fiction: Women Warriors and the Dynastic Imagination in the 'Orlando furioso'* was also helpful in adding layers of background texture to my narrative. Professor Diane Wright once mentioned the legend of the Amazon Queen Thalestris having a love affair with Alexander the Great. That came in handy in describing the relationship of Galiziella's mother and father.

One important thing to note is while this series is considered epic historic fantasy, it is clearly fiction and not depicting real events. The war between the North African Muslim army and the Frankish Empire did not happen. It was an exciting storyline written to entertain.

The majority of these characters are fictional and those who are historical characters are depicted in fictional events and situations. That being said, I grounded my storyline in a time and place with historically accurate details. Unless accuracy interfered with my dramatic narrative, in that case I chose drama every time.

Here are some examples of when I bent the historical rules:

The walls as described around Paris were not built during that time period. I discussed this at length in my author notes in *Quest of the Warrior Maiden.* Similarly, I previously mentioned that the city of Montauban was founded over three centuries after Charlemagne's death and why I continued to use that city in my story.

While I performed a lot of research, I could not find answers to all of my historical questions. I had unanswered questions relating to Charlemagne and his military campaigns. At a certain point, I gave myself the artistic freedom to tell my tale in the manner I wanted. I did not find any definitive explanation of how his military camps were constructed, so I used the example of Roman legion camps and mentioned he was a student of history.

It is difficult to know the state of any Roman ruin as it stood during the beginning of the ninth century. This uncertainty and doubt allows me the freedom to describe decaying monuments such as the Circus Maximus in Arles in ways that support my dramatic needs.

For simplicity's sake, I included the name of the Byzantine Empire even though that term was not coined until long after its fall. There are more historical anachronisms inherent with the inclusion of the Byzantines, and suffice it to say those were done to serve my dramatic needs. More about that in Book Three.

Similarly, King Charles may not have been called Charlemagne during his lifetime. He was followed by other kings named Charles who then were distinguished by descriptors. Charlemagne is French for "Charles the Great." Some of the other kings were called "Charles the Bald," "Charles the Fat," and "Charles the Simple." Charlemagne's grandfather had already been given the nickname "Charles the Hammer" or Charles Martel. Out of all of those choices, "the Great" seems the best. And given that all of the legends of Charlemagne I have read include using the name of Charlemagne, I am as well.

Fans of *Orlando innamorato* and *Orlando furioso* will notice that I have changed some plot points. I cut many subplots and characters if they didn't fit my through line for the Bradamante and Ruggiero story. The character of Isabella doesn't appear in my version, but the plot required her bridge. I rechristened it as Fiordespina's bridge.

Some aspects of the poems seemed thin, so I supplemented the story in order to satisfy my own dramatic needs. That can be distinctly noted in Aistulf's spiritual journey. I added the idea of placing Senapo's hideaway on an island in Lake Tana, and chose to include the spectacular Sof Omar Caves as one of the entrances to the Underworld.

Another notable addition is the character of Caliph Harun al-Rashid. My inclusion of this historical figure was influenced by Jeff Sypeck's book *Becoming Charlemagne: Europe, Baghdad, and the Empires of A.D. 800.* Sypeck detailed Charlemagne and Caliph Harun al-Rashid exchanging diplomatic gifts. This made me consider how the caliph would feel betrayed if a subordinate led a military attack undermining his own diplomatic maneuvers with a foreign leader. That was a layer of intrigue and conflict begging to be utilized in my fiction.

The scene where Aistulf met Caliph Harun al-Rashid was inspired by the meeting Joan of Arc (*Jeanne d'Arc*) had with the dauphin Charles VII. As a test, when she arrived at the castle in Chinon asking for an audience with Charles, she was led to an imposter. Somehow, she knew he was not the man she sought and found the real heir to the French throne amongst his courtiers.

Caliph Harun al-Rashid was also a literary figure in the *Arabian Nights* and was depicted as having three constant companions who I also included in my story. By changing the army who attacks Bizerta, I was able to change a part of Ariosto's story that just didn't work for me. Aistulf led King Senapo's army and pushed boulders down a hill, which magically turned into horses. He then placed handfuls of leaves into the Mediterranean Sea. Those leaves were transformed into tall ships to transport the warriors and horses. That magic was beyond what I thought was plausible and instead I chose real world warriors.

Sypeck included the names of three men sent by Charlemagne as emissaries to Caliph Harun al-Rashid. I included them as Easter eggs for history buffs. Similarly, while doing some research I came across the historical names of Charlemagne's chamberlain and seneschal. Their names were late additions to my tale. There serve no real plot function, but it is my attempt to help rescue them from historical obscurity.

I debated as to whether or not to create the name of Akramont's seneschal to have some parity, but decided against it for the same reason I didn't name Beatrice's secretary or Renaud's chamberlain. Those characters are the literary equivalent of "woman at counter" in a movie's credits. They fill a purpose, but unnamed characters do not require focused attention by the reader.

Speaking of names, I am fully aware that the names of my characters are strange. Some are downright hard to pronounce and there are so many! For that I give my heartfelt condolences and hope that my index of names helps. Please feel free to pronounce the names of the characters in whatever manner you choose. The characters are not alive to feel slighted by any mispronunciation.

The overwhelming majority of names come from the source material. Some were modified to reflect the origins of the characters. With that in mind, I chose to make Rinaldo di Montalbano into the French version of Renaud de Montauban. Orlando could have become Roland, except I included the legend of this titular hero being born in a cave in Sutri, Italy. Therefore, Orlando retains his Italian name, as does his childhood friend of Oliver.

I created some characters to flesh out my story and tried to find names reflecting their place of origin, have underlying symbolic meaning, and weren't quite as difficult to pronounce. Examples are: Abdul, Fidelia, Hala, Neron, and Rosenda.

I also recognize that the name Brandimart is too similar to Bradamante and may cause confusion. I looked, but couldn't find a good Arabic replacement name, and I didn't care for the other alternate name of Florismart. That name made me think of a warehouse for florists, rather than an heroic character. His wife's name was another dilemma. Her name is seen as Flordelis, Fiordelisa, and Fiordigli. I already had the character of Fiordespina and having two names starting with Fior was too confusing. I even wrote the wrong character's name in an early draft. I knew that if *I* was getting confused, my readers would have difficulty with those two women's names. Therefore, I chose to use Flordelis. Having the names of Flordelis and Florismart as a couple, didn't work for me. So, we are stuck with Brandimart.

Another niggling aspect of historical detail is found when my characters had to write something down. I purposefully did not have them use any commas. The timing of when it entered into popular use in the format we know today was far later than the ninth century of when this story takes place. This made those passages read more formal than they might have otherwise.

I am grateful to Jonathan Rome for reviewing my manuscript and making recommendations regarding Roman ruins in general and Arles in specific. The following people read passages or engaged in conversations with me and gave valuable feedback: Brenda Bickett, Antonia Bosanquet, Will Hatcher, Kamran Pasha, James Schian, Margaret Silvestri, Mike Wilson, Diane Wright. Doctors John Tomasin, R. Steven Vargas, and Edward Wang all gave advice as to how to wound, then treat, Ruggiero so he would be able to return to (almost) full strength after a duel.

I want to thank Karen Hart, Waights Taylor, Jr., Patrice Garrett, Gay Barner, Ann McCabe, and Don McCabe for serving as beta readers. Ana

Manwaring served as my content and copy editor. I am grateful for her attention to detail and for her enthusiasm toward this project.

I want to thank all of my readers who kept after me about the sequel. This is a massive story and the crafting of it takes time. I appreciated hearing from fans that they were anxiously waiting to get the next installment. Hopefully volume three will not take as long for me to write as this one did.

Reading Club Discussion Guide

Here are a few questions to help stimulate conversations for reading clubs. The author will make herself available by Zoom to answer your questions. Please visit her website at www.LindaCMcCabe.com to schedule a chat.

1. This story not only has war, but features many tragic romantic relationships. Think about how women had no control over marital partners and how dangerous it could have been. Consider the cases of Fiordespina and Doralice.
2. Infidelity is a recurrent theme in this story. We see examples of women being expected to ignore their husband's indiscretions, but men (such as Rodomont, Ferrand, Giacondo, and Astolfo) seek revenge against unfaithful wives. Discuss how constraining this double standard this would have been and if it still exists today.
3. Other examples of unfortunate love stories abounded in this novel such as Costanza of Palermo being betrayed and later abandoned, King Senapo's closed heart, Lydia's rejection of Alceste, Richardet and Fiordespina's clandestine relationship. Discuss how the differences and similarities of these unhappy love stories.
4. There are many examples of discord between famed warriors in Akramont's campaign. Is there one you feel is more important than the others and one so trivial the warriors should have "gotten over it" and not want to fight to the death?
5. Doralice was allowed to make a life changing decision. Did you expect what would happen? How would her life have been different had she made another choice?
6. Bradamante is filled with despair at the beginning of this story, thinking that all is lost. At the cliffhanger ending she has a different outlook. Discuss the difference in her attitude.
7. Ruggiero apparently did not realize he was the subject of a prophecy until Akramont announced it to the Muslim army outside of Paris. Try imagining how he felt about that revelation.

About the Author

Linda C. McCabe outside of the cathedral in Ferrara, Italy. Photo by Scott C. Nevin.

Linda C. McCabe lives in the Northern California Wine Country with her college sweetheart and son. She received a master's degree as an historian of science from Sonoma State University, and loves to travel. To aid in her novel's research, she traveled twice to France scouring museums in Paris and trekking through medieval hilltop villages in the Midi-Pyrenees. She has had opinion/editorials published in the *Santa Rosa Press Democrat*, the *Los Angeles Times* and essays published in several of the Redwood Writers' anthologies. Her first novel, *Quest of the Warrior Maiden,* was recognized as the Best Historic Fantasy by the Bay Area Independent Publishers Association (BAIPA) and given an Honorable Mention for Genre-Based Fiction by the Hollywood Book Festival. Visit her website at www.LindaCMcCabe.com

www.ingramcontent.com/pod-product-compliance
Lightning Source LLC
Chambersburg PA
CBHW071634260626
47170CB00001B/102